Henry Fielding's bawdy story of the lively and passionate adventures of that amorous young rogue, Tom Jones, has long been acclaimed as one of the greatest English novels of all time, although the great Dr. Johnson said of it. 'Shocking! I scarcely know of a more corrupt work.' This specially edited edition aims primarily at giving the modern reader the essential vigour of this memorable story.

Henry Fielding

The History of
Tom Jones

A Panther Book

A Panther Book

This abridgement first published in Panther Books 1962. Reprinted 1964 (twice), 1965 (twice) 1966, 1967, 1969. Copyright © Todd Publishing Group Ltd. 1961. The special arrangements of this edition of Henry Fielding's *Tom Jones* is copyright and may not be used without the copyright owner's written permission.

This book is published at a net price and is supplied subject to the Publishers Association Standard Conditions of Sale registered under the Restrictive Trade Practices Act, 1956. *Printed in England by Cox and Wyman Ltd, London, Reading and Fakenham, and published by Panther Books, 3 Upper James St., London, W.1*

THE
HISTORY
OF
TOM JONES,
A
FOUNDLING.

In SIX VOLUMES.

By HENRY FIELDING Esq;

——— *Mores hominum multorum vidit.* ———

LONDON:
Printed for A. MILLAR, over-against
Catharine-street in the *Strand.*
MDCCXLIX.

A reproduction of the title page of an
early edition of *Tom Jones*

CHAPTER ONE

A SHORT DESCRIPTION OF SQUIRE ALLWORTHY

IN that part of the western division of this kingdom which is commonly called Somersetshire, there lately lived, and perhaps lives still, a gentleman whose name was Allworthy, and who might well be called the favourite of both nature and fortune. From the former of these, he derived an agreeable person, a sound constitution, a solid understanding, and a benevolent heart; by the latter, he was decreed to the inheritance of one of the largest estates in the county.

This gentleman had in his youth married a very worthy and beautiful woman, of whom he had been extremely fond: by her he had three children, all of whom died in their infancy. He had likewise had the misfortune of burying this beloved wife herself, about five years before the time in which this history chooses to set out. He now lived, for the most part, retired in the country, with one sister, for whom he had a very tender affection. This lady was now somewhat past the age of thirty, and was of that species of women whom you commend rather for good qualities than beauty, and who are generally called, by their own sex, very good sort of women. Indeed, she was so far from regretting want of beauty, that she never mentioned that perfection, if it can be called one, without contempt; and would often thank God she was not as handsome as Miss Such-a-one, whom perhaps beauty had led into errors which she might have otherwise avoided. Miss Bridget Allworthy (for that was the name of this lady) very rightly conceived the charms of a person in a woman to be no better than snares for herself, as well as for others.

Mr Allworthy had been absent a full quarter of a year in London, on some very particular business, though I know not what it was; but judge of its importance by its having detained him so long from home, whence he had not been absent a month at a time during the space of many years. He came to his house very late in the evening, and after a short supper with his sister, retired much fatigued to his chamber. Here, having spent some minutes on his knees—a custom which he never broke through on any account—he was preparing to step into bed, when, upon opening the clothes, to his great surprize he beheld an infant, wrapt up in some coarse linen, in a sweet and profound sleep, between his sheets. He stood some time lost in astonishment at this sight; then rang his bell, and ordered an elderly woman-servant to rise immediately, and come to him; and in the meantime was so eager in contemplating the beauty of innocence, appearing in those lively colours with which infancy and sleep always display it, that his thoughts were too much engaged to reflect that he was in his shirt when the matron came in. She had indeed given her master sufficient time to dress himself; for out of respect to him, and regard to decency, she had spent many minutes in adjusting her hair at the looking-glass, notwithstanding all the hurry in which she had been summoned by the servant, and though her master, for aught she knew, lay expiring in an apoplexy, or in some other fit.

It will not be wondered at that a creature who had so strict a regard to decency in her own person, should be shocked at the least deviation from it in another. She therefore no sooner opened the door, and saw her master standing by the bedside in his shirt, with a candle in his hand, than she started back in a most terrible fright, and might perhaps have swooned away, had he not now recollected his being undrest, and put an end to her terrors by desiring her to stay without the door till he had thrown some clothes over his back, and was become incapable of shocking the pure eyes of Mrs Deborah Wilkins, who, though in the fifty-second year of her age, vowed she had never beheld a man without his coat.

When Mrs Deborah returned into the room, and was acquainted by her master with the finding the little infant, her consternation was rather greater than his had been; nor could she refrain from crying out, with great horror of accent as well as look, 'My good sir! what's to be done?' Mr Allworthy answered, she must take care of the child that evening, and in the morning he would give orders to provide it a nurse. 'Yes, sir,' says she; 'and I hope your worship will send out your warrant to take up the hussy its mother, for she must be one of the neighbourhood; and I should be glad to see her committed to Bridewell, and whipt at the cart's tail. I don't know what is worse, than for such wicked strumpets to lay their sins at honest men's doors; and though your worship knows your own innocence, yet the world is censorious; and it hath been many an honest man's hap to pass for the father of children he never begot; and if your worship should provide for the child, it may make the people the apter to believe.'

There were some strokes in this speech which perhaps would have offended Mr Allworthy, had he strictly attended to it; but he had now got one of his fingers into the infant's hand, which, by its gentle pressure, seeming to implore his assistance, had certainly out-pleaded the eloquence of Mrs Deborah, had it been ten

8

times greater than it was. He now gave Mrs Deborah positive orders to take the child to her own bed, and to call up a maid-servant to provide it pap, and other things, against it waked. He likewise ordered that proper clothes should be procured for it early in the morning, and that it should be brought to him as soon as he was stirring.

The Gothic stile of building could produce nothing nobler than Mr Allworthy's house. There was an air of grandeur in it that struck you with awe, and rivalled the beauties of the best Grecian architecture; and it was as commodious within as venerable without.

It stood on the south-east side of a hill, but nearer the bottom than the top of it, so as to be sheltered from the north-east by a grove of old oaks which rose above it in a gradual ascent of near half a mile, and yet high enough to enjoy a most charming prospect of the valley beneath.

In the midst of the grove was a fine lawn, sloping down towards the house, near the summit of which rose a plentiful spring, gushing out of a rock covered with firs, and forming a constant cascade of about thirty feet, till it fell into a lake at the foot of the hill, about a quarter of a mile below the house on the south side, and which was seen from every room in the front.

The scene presented the view of a very fine park, composed of very unequal ground, and agreeably varied with all the diversity that hills, lawns, wood, and water, laid out with admirable taste, but owing less to art than to nature, could give. Beyond this, the country gradually rose into a ridge of wild mountains, the tops of which were above the clouds.

It was now the middle of May, and the morning was remarkably serene, when Mr Allworthy walked forth on the terrace, where the dawn opened every minute that lovely prospect we have before described to his eye.

Miss Bridget rings her bell, and Mr Allworthy is summoned to breakfast. The usual compliments having past between them and the tea being poured out, he summoned Mrs Wilkins, and told his sister he had a present for her, for which she thanked him—imagining, I suppose, it had been a gown, or some ornament for her person.

But if such was her expectation, how was she disappointed when Mrs Wilkins, according to the order she had received from her master, produced the little infant? Great surprizes, as hath been observed, are apt to be silent; and so was Miss Bridget, till her brother began, and told her the whole story.

Miss Bridget had always exprest so great a regard for what the ladies are pleased to call virtue, and had herself maintained such a severity of character, that it was expected, especially by Wilkins,

9

that she would have vented much bitterness on this occasion, and would have voted for sending the child, as a kind of noxious animal, immediately out of the house; but, on the contrary, she rather took the good-natured side of the question, intimated some compassion for the helpless little creature, and commended her brother's charity in what he had done.

A consultation was now entered into how to proceed in order to discover the mother. A scrutiny was first made into the characters of the female servants of the house, who were all acquitted by Mrs Wilkins, and with apparent merit; for she had collected them herself, and perhaps it would be difficult to find such another set of scarecrows.

The next step was to examine among the inhabitants of the parish; and this was referred to Mrs Wilkins, who was to inquire with all imaginable diligence, and to make her report in the afternoon.

Miss Bridget, having looked some time earnestly at the child, as it lay asleep in the lap of Mrs Deborah, could not forbear giving it a hearty kiss, at the same time declaring herself wonderfully pleased with its beauty and innocence.

She now proceeded to execute the commission given her by her brother, and gave orders for providing all necessaries for the child, appointing a very good room in the house for his nursery. Her orders were indeed so liberal, that, had it been a child of her own, she could not have exceeded them.

CHAPTER TWO

A SHORT ACCOUNT OF JENNY JONES

MRS DEBORAH, having disposed of the child according to the will of her master, now prepared to visit those habitations which were supposed to conceal its mother.

It is the nature of such persons as Mrs Wilkins to insult and tyrannize over little people. Whenever Mrs Deborah had occasion to exert any extraordinary condescension to Miss Bridget, and by that means had a little soured her natural disposition, it was usual with her to walk forth among these people, in order to refine her temper, by venting, and, as it were, purging off all ill-humours;

on which account she was universally dreaded and hated by them all.

She went immediately to the habitation of an elderly matron; to whom, as this matron had the good fortune to resemble herself in the comeliness of her person, as well as in her age, she had generally been more favourable than to any of the rest. To this woman she imparted what had happened, and the design upon which she was come thither that morning. These two began presently to scrutinize the characters of the several young girls who lived in any of those houses, and at last fixed their strongest suspicion on one Jenny Jones, who, they both agreed, was the likeliest person to have committed this fact.

This Jenny Jones was no very comely girl, either in her face or person; but nature had given her a very uncommon share of understanding. This gift Jenny had a good deal improved by erudition. She had lived several years a servant with a schoolmaster, who, discovering a great quickness in the girl, and an extraordinary desire of learning had the good-nature, or folly to instruct her so far, that she obtained a competent skill in the Latin language, and was, perhaps, as good a scholar as most of the young men of quality of the age. This advantage, however, like most others of an extraordinary kind, was attended with some small inconveniences: for it is not to be wondered at, that this superiority in Jenny should produce among the rest some little envy and ill-will towards her.

Their envy did not, however, display itself openly, till poor Jenny, to the surprize of everybody, and to the vexation of all the young women in these parts, had publicly shone forth on a Sunday in a new silk gown, with a laced cap, and other proper appendages to these.

The flame, which had before lain in embryo, now burst forth. Jenny had, by her learning, increased her own pride, which none of her neighbours were kind enough to feed with the honour she seemed to demand; and now, instead of respect and adoration, she gained nothing but hatred and abuse by her finery. The whole parish declared she could not come honestly by such things; and parents, instead of wishing their daughters the same felicitated themselves that their children had them not.

Hence, perhaps, it was, that the good woman first mentioned the name of this poor girl to Mrs Wilkins; but there was another circumstance that confirmed the latter in her suspicion; for Jenny had lately been often at Mr Allworthy's house. She had officiated as nurse to Miss Bridget, in a violent fit of illness, and had sat up many nights with that lady; besides which, she had been seen there the very day before Mr Allworthy's return, by Mrs Wilkins herself, though that sagacious person had not at first conceived any suspicion of her on that account; for, as she herself said, 'She had always esteemed Jenny as a very sober girl, and had rather suspected some of those wanton trollops, who gave themselves airs, because, forsooth, they thought themselves handsome.'

Jenny was now summoned to appear in person before Mrs Deborah, which she immediately did. When Mrs Deborah, putting on the gravity of a judge, with somewhat more than his austerity, began an oration with the words, 'You audacious strumpet!' in which she proceeded rather to pass sentence on the prisoner than to accuse her.

Though Mrs Deborah was fully satisfied of the guilt of Jenny, from the reasons above shewn, it is possible Mr Allworthy might have required some stronger evidence to have convicted her; but she saved her accusers any such trouble, by freely confessing the whole fact with which she was charged.

Mrs Deborah having succeeded beyond her hopes in her inquiry, returned with much triumph, and, at the appointed hour, made a faithful report to Mr Allworthy, who was much surprized at the relation; for he had heard of the extraordinary parts and improvements of this girl, whom he intended to have given in marriage, together with a small living, to a neighbouring curate. His concern, therefore, on this occasion, was at least equal to the satisfaction which appeared in Mrs Deborah.

When Jenny appeared, Mr Allworthy took her into his study, and spoke to her as follows: 'You know, child, it is in my power as a magistrate, to punish you very rigorously for what you have done; and you will, perhaps, be the more apt to fear I should execute that power, because you have in a manner laid your sins at my door.

'But, perhaps, this is one reason which hath determined me to act in a milder manner with you: for, as no private resentment should ever influence a magistrate, I will be so far from considering your having deposited the infant in my house as an aggravation of your offence, that I will suppose, in your favour, this to have proceeded from a natural affection to your child, since you might have some hopes to see it thus better provided for than was in the power of yourself, or its wicked father, to provide for it. I should indeed have been highly offended with you had you exposed the little wretch in the manner of some inhuman mothers, who seem no less to have abandoned their humanity, than to have parted with their chastity.

'How base and mean must that woman be, how void of that dignity of mind, and decent pride, who can bear to level herself with the lowest animal, and to sacrifice all that is great and noble in her, all her heavenly part, to an appetite which she hath in common with the vilest branch of the creation! For no woman, sure, will plead the passion of love for an excuse. This would be to own herself the mere tool and bubble of the man. Now in what light, but that of an enemy, can a reasonable woman regard the man who would purchase to himself a short, trivial, contemptible pleasure, so greatly at her expense! For, by the laws of custom, the whole shame, with all its dreadful consequences, falls entirely upon her. I have talked thus to you, child, not to insult you for what is past and irrevocable, but to caution and strengthen you for the future.

'As to your child, let no thoughts concerning it molest you; I will provide for it in a better manner than you can ever hope. And now nothing remains but that you inform me who was the wicked man that seduced you; for my anger against him will be much greater than you have experienced on this occasion.'

Jenny now lifted her eyes from the ground, and with a modest look and decent voice thus began:

'To know you, sir, and not love your goodness, would be an argument of total want of sense or goodness in any one. In me it would amount to the highest ingratitude, not to feel the great degree of goodness you have been pleased to exert. But now, sir, I must on my knees entreat you not to persist in asking me to declare the father of my infant. I promise you faithfully you shall one day know; but I am under the most solemn ties and engagements of honour, as well as the most religious vows and protestations, to conceal his name at this time.'

Mr Allworthy hesitated a moment before he replied, and then told her, she had done wrong to enter into such engagements to a villain; but since she had, he could not insist on her breaking them. He said, it was not from a motive of vain curiosity he had inquired, but in order to punish the fellow.

Jenny satisfied him by the most solemn assurances, that the man was entirely out of his reach.

The ingenuity of his behaviour had gained Jenny so much credit with this worthy man, that he easily believed what she told him; for as she had disdained to excuse herself by a lie, and had hazarded his further displeasure in her present situation, rather than she would forfeit her honour or integrity by betraying another, he had but little apprehensions that she would be guilty of falsehood towards himself.

When Mr Allworthy had retired to his study with Jenny Jones, Miss Bridget, with the good housekeeper, had betaken themselves to a post next adjoining to the said study; whence, through the conveyance of a keyhole, they sucked in at their ears the instructive lecture delivered by Mr Allworthy, together with the answers of Jenny, and indeed every other particular which passed in the last chapter.

This hole in her brother's study door was indeed as well known to Miss Bridget, and had been as frequently applied to by her.

13

This served to many good purposes. For by such means Miss Bridget became often acquainted with her brother's inclinations, without giving him the trouble of repeating them to her.

Both the good women kept strict silence during the whole scene between Mr Allworthy and the girl; but as soon as it was ended, and that gentleman was out of hearing, Mrs Deborah could not help exclaiming against the clemency of her master, and especially against his suffering her to conceal the father of the child, which she swore she would have out of her before the sun set.

At these words Miss Bridget discomposed her features with a smile (a thing very unusual to her), and with a voice sweet as the evening breeze, Miss Bridget gently reproved the curiosity of Mrs Deborah; a vice with which it seems the latter was too much tainted, and which the former inveighed against with great bitterness, adding, 'That, among all her faults, she thanked Heaven her enemies could not accuse her of prying into the affairs of other people."

She then proceeded to commend the honour and spirit with which Jenny had acted. She said, she could not help agreeing with her brother, that there was some merit in the sincerity of her confession, and in her integrity to her lover: that she had always thought her a very good girl and doubted not but she had been seduced by some rascal, who had been infinitely more to blame than herself, and very probably had prevailed with her by a promise of marriage, or some other treacherous proceeding.

Mrs Deborah approved all these sentiments, and the dialogue concluded with a general and bitter invective against beauty, and with many compassionate considerations for all honest plain girls who are deluded by the wicked arts of deceitful men.

Jenny returned home well pleased with the reception she had met with from Mr Allworthy, whose indulgence to her she industriously made public; partly perhaps as a sacrifice to her own pride, and partly from the more prudent motive of reconciling her neighbours to her, but when it was known in what manner Mr Allworthy had behaved, the tide turned against her. Every person made some malicious comment or other on the occasion, and reflected on the partiality of the justice.

Jenny was, however, by the care and goodness of Mr Allworthy, soon removed out of the reach of reproach; when malice being no longer able to vent its rage on her, began to seek another object of its bitterness, and this was no less than Mr Allworthy himself; for a whisper soon went abroad, that he himself was the father of the foundling child.

This supposition so well reconciled his conduct to the general opinion, that it met with universal assent; and the outcry against his lenity soon began to take another turn, and was changed into an invective against his cruelty to the poor girl. Very grave and good women exclaimed against men who begot children, and then disowned them.

These calumnies might have probably produced ill consequences, at the least might have occasioned some trouble, to a person of a more doubtful and suspicious character than Mr Allworthy was blessed with; but in his case they had no such effect; and, being heartily despised by him, they served only to afford an innocent amusement to the good gossips of the neighbourhood.

CHAPTER THREE

THE HOSPITALITY OF ALLWORTHY

NEITHER Mr Allworthy's house, nor his heart, were shut against any part of mankind, but they were both more particularly open to men of merit. Mr Allworthy was not one of those generous persons who are ready most bountifully to bestow meat, drink, and lodging on men of wit and learning, for which they expect no other return but entertainment, instruction, flattery, and subserviency; on the contrary, every person in this house was perfect master of his own time: and as he might at his pleasure satisfy all his appetites within the restrictions only of law, virtue, and religion; so he might absent himself from any meals, or retire from them, whenever he was so disposed.

Among this kind was Dr Blifil, a gentleman who had the misfortune of losing the advantage of great talents by the obstinacy of a father, who would breed him to a profession he disliked. In obedience to this obstinacy the doctor had in his youth been obliged to study physic, and unfortunately for him, the doctor was master of almost every other science but that by which he was to get his bread; the consequence of which was, that the doctor at the age of forty had no bread to eat.

Such a person as this was certain to find a welcome at Mr Allworthy's table, to whom misfortunes were ever a recommendation, when they were derived from the folly or villany of others, and not of the unfortunate person himself. Besides this negative merit, the doctor had one positive recommendation—this was a great appearance of religion.

If this part of his character pleased Mr Allworthy, it delighted Miss Bridget. She engaged him in many religious controversies;

on which occasions she constantly expressed great satisfaction in the doctor's knowledge, and not much less in the compliments which he frequently bestowed on her own.

The doctor found himself so agreeable to Miss Bridget, that he now began to lament an unfortunate accident which had happened to him about ten years before; namely, his marriage with another woman, who was not only still alive, but, what was worse, known to be so by Mr Allworthy. This was a fatal bar to that happiness which he otherwise saw sufficient probability of obtaining with this young lady; for as to criminal indulgences, he certainly never thought of them. He had not long ruminated on these matters, before it occurred to his memory that he had a brother who was under no such unhappy incapacity. This brother he made no doubt would succeed; for he discerned, as he thought, an inclination to marriage in the lady.

This gentleman was about thirty-five years of age. He was of a middle size, and what is called well built. He had a scar on his forehead, which did not so much injure his beauty as it denoted his valour (for he was a half-pay officer). He had good teeth, and something affable, when he pleased, in his smile; though naturally his countenance, as well as his air and voice, had much of roughness in it: yet he could at any time deposit this, and appear all gentleness and good humour. He was not ungenteel, nor entirely devoid of wit, and in his youth had abounded in sprightliness, which, though he had lately put on a more serious character, he could, when he pleased, resume.

He had, as well as the doctor, an academic education; for his father had, with the same paternal authority we have mentioned before, decreed him for holy orders; but as the old gentleman died before he was ordained, he chose the church military, and preferred the king's commission to the bishop's.

He had purchased the post of lieutenant of dragoons, and afterwards came to be a captain; but having quarrelled with his colonel, was by his interest obliged to sell; from which time he had entirely rusticated himself, had betaken himself to studying the Scriptures.

So the doctor sent for his brother, and easily found means to introduce him at Allworthy's as a person who intended only a short visit to himself.

The captain had not been in the house a week before the doctor had reason to felicitate himself on his discernment. The captain was indeed a great master of the art of love. He had besides received proper hints from his brother, which he failed not to improve to the best advantage.

Miss Bridget had not been many times in the captain's company before she was seized with passion. Nor did she go pining and moping about the house, like a puny, foolish girl, ignorant of her distemper: she felt, she knew, and she enjoyed, the pleasing sensation, of which, as she was certain it was not only innocent but laudable, she was neither afraid nor ashamed.

The captain no sooner perceived the passion of Miss Bridget, in which discovery he was very quick-sighted, than he faithfully returned it. The lady, no more than her lover, was remarkable for beauty. The captain very wisely preferred the more solid enjoyments he expected with this lady, to the fleeting charms of person. He was one of those wise men who regard beauty in the other sex as a very worthless and superficial qualification. The captain, ever since his arrival, long before he had discovered any flattering symptoms in Miss Bridget, had been greatly enamoured; that is to say, of Mr Allworthy's house and gardens, and of his lands, tenements, and hereditaments; of all which the captain was so passionately fond, that he would most probably have contracted marriage with them, had he been obliged to have taken the witch of Endor into the bargain.

As Mr Allworthy, therefore, had declared to the doctor that he never intended to take a second wife, as his sister was his nearest relation, and as the doctor had fished out that his intentions were to make any child of hers his heir, the doctor and his brother thought it an act of benevolence to give being to a human creature, who would be so plentifully provided with the most essential means of happiness.

Not to tire the reader, by leading him through every scene of this courtship the captain made his advances in form, the citadel was defended in form, and at length, in proper form, surrendered at discretion.

In all bargains, whether to fight or to marry, or concerning any other such business, little previous ceremony is required to bring the matter to an issue when both parties are really in earnest. This was the case at present, and in less than a month Captain Blifil and his lady were man and wife.

CHAPTER FOUR

A GREAT DISCOVERY MADE BY MRS DEBORAH WILKINS

EIGHT months after the celebration of the nuptials between Captain Blifil and Miss Bridget Allworthy, a young lady of great beauty, merit, and fortune, was Miss Bridget, by reason of a fright, delivered of a fine boy. The child was indeed to all appearances perfect; but the midwife discovered it was born a month before its full time.

Though the birth of an heir by his beloved sister was a circumstance of great joy to Mr Allworthy, yet it did not alienate his affections from the little foundling, to whom he had been godfather, had given his own name of Thomas, and whom he had hitherto seldom failed of visiting, at least once a day, in his nursery.

He told his sister, if she pleased, the new-born infant should be bred up together with little Tommy; to which she consented, though with some little reluctance: for she had truly a great complacence for her brother; and hence she had always behaved towards the foundling with rather more kindness than ladies of rigid virtue can sometimes bring themselves to show to these children, who, however innocent, may be truly called the living monuments of incontinence.

The captain could not so easily bring himself to bear what he condemned as a fault in Mr Allworthy. He gave him frequent hints, that to adopt the fruits of sin, was to give countenance to it. He said, 'Though the law did not positively allow the destroying such base-born children, yet it held them to be the children of nobody; that the Church considered them as the children of nobody; and that at the best, they ought to be brought up to the lowest and vilest offices of the commonwealth.'

Mr Allworthy answered to all this, and much more, which the captain had urged on this subject, 'That, however guilty the parents might be, the children were certainly innocent.'

While the captain was taking all opportunities to press the removal of the little foundling from Mr Allworthy's, of whose fondness for him he began to be jealous, Mrs Deborah had made a discovery, which, in its event, threatened at least to prove more fatal to poor Tommy than all the reasonings of the captain.

Whether the insatiable curiosity of this good woman had carried her on to that business, or whether she did it to confirm herself in the good graces of Mrs Blifil, who, notwithstanding her outward behaviour to the foundling, frequently abused the infant in private, and her brother too, for his fondness to it, I will not determine; but she had now, as she conceived, fully detected the father of the foundling.

My reader may please to remember he hath been informed that Jenny Jones had lived some years with a certain schoolmaster, who had, at her earnest desire, instructed her in Latin, in which, to do justice to her genius, she had so improved herself, that she was become a better scholar than her master.

Indeed, though this poor man had undertaken a profession to

which learning must be allowed necessary, this was the least of his commendations. He was one of the best-natured fellows in the world, and was, at the same time, master of so much pleasantry and humour, that he was reputed the wit of the country; and all the neighbouring gentlemen were so desirous of his company, that as denying was not his talent, he spent much time at their houses, which he might, with more emolument, have spent in his school.

His scholars were divided into two classes: in the upper of which was a young gentleman, the son of a neighbouring squire, who, at the age of seventeen, was just entered into his Syntaxis; and in the lower was a second son of the same gentleman, who, together with seven parish boys, was learning to read and write.

The stipend arising hence would hardly have indulged the schoolmaster in the luxuries of life, had he not added to this office those of clerk and barber, and had not Mr Allworthy added to the whole an annuity of ten pounds, which the poor man received every Christmas, and with which he was enabled to cheer his heart during that sacred festival.

Among his other treasures, the pedagogue had a wife, whom he had married out of Mr Allworthy's kitchen for her fortune, viz. twenty pounds, which she had there amassed.

This woman was not very amiable in her person.

She was, perhaps, somewhat soured by a circumstance which generally poisons matrimonial felicity; for children are rightly called the pledges of love; and her husband, though they had been married nine years, had given her no such pledges; a default for which he had no excuse, either from age or health, being not yet thirty years old, and what they call a jolly brisk young man.

In order to guard herself against matrimonial injuries in her own house, as she kept one maid-servant, she always took care to choose her out of that order of females whose faces are taken as a kind of security for their virtue; of which number Jenny Jones was one.

As the face of this young woman might be called pretty good security of the before-mentioned kind, and as her behaviour had been always extremely modest, she had passed above four years at Mr Partridge's (for that was the schoolmaster's name) without creating the least suspicion in her mistress.

But it is with jealousy as with the gout: when such distempers are in the blood, there is never any security against their breaking out; and that often on the slightest occasions, and when least suspected.

Thus it happened to Mrs Partridge, who had submitted four years to her husband's teaching this young woman, and had suffered her often to neglect her work in order to pursue her learning. For, passing by one day, as the girl was reading, and her

19

master leaning over her, the girl, I know not for what reason, suddenly started up from her chair: and this was the first time that suspicion ever entered into the head of her mistress.

This did not, however, at that time discover itself, but lay lurking in her mind, like a concealed enemy, who waits for a reinforcement of additional strength before he openly declares himself and proceeds upon hostile operations: and such additional strength soon arrived to corroborate her suspicion; for not long after, the husband and wife being at dinner, the master said to his maid, *Da mihi aliquid potum*: upon which the poor girl smiled, perhaps at the badness of the Latin, and, when her mistress cast her eyes on her, blushed, possibly with a consciousness of having laughed at her master. Mrs Partridge, immediately fell into a fury, and ordered Jenny immediately to pack up her alls and begone, for that she was determined she should not sleep that night within her walls.

Mr Partridge had profited too much by experience to interpose in a matter of this nature. He therefore had recourse to his usual receipt of patience.

Jenny offered to make protestations of her innocence; but the tempest was too strong for her to be heard. She then betook herself to the business of packing, for which a small quantity of brown paper sufficed; and, having received her small pittance of wages, she returned home.

The schoolmaster and his consort passed their time unpleasantly enough that evening; but something or other happened before the next morning, which a little abated the fury of Mrs Partridge; and she at length admitted her husband to make his excuses: to which she gave the readier belief, as he had, instead of desiring her to recall Jenny, professed a satisfaction in her being dismissed, saying, she was grown of little use as a servant, spending all her time in reading, and was become, moreover, very pert and obstinate; for, indeed, she and her master had lately had frequent disputes in literature; in which she was become greatly his superior.

Mrs Partridge was pretty well satisfied that she had condemned her husband without cause, and endeavoured by acts of kindness to make him amends for her false suspicion.

Then one day she was asked by one of her neighbours, if she had heard no news lately of Jenny Jones? To which she answered in the negative. Upon this the other replied, with a smile, That the parish was very much obliged to her for having turned Jenny away as she did.

Mrs Partridge, whose jealousy was long since cured, and who had no other quarrel to her maid, answered boldly, She did not know any obligation the parish had to her on that account; for she believed Jenny had scarce left her equal behind her.

'No, truly,' said the gossip, 'I hope not, though I fancy we have sluts enow too. Then you have not heard, it seems, that she hath been brought to bed of two bastards? but as they are not born here, my husband and the other overseer says we shall not be obliged to keep them.'

'Two bastards!' answered Mrs Partridge hastily: 'you suprize me! I don't know whether we must keep them; but I am sure they must have been begotten here, for the wench hath not been nine months gone away.'

Nothing can be so quick and sudden as the operations of the mind, especially when hope, or fear, or jealousy, to which the two others are but journeymen, set it to work. It occurred instantly to her, that Jenny had scarce ever been out of her own house while she lived with her. The leaning over the chair, the sudden starting up, the Latin, the smile, and many other things, rushed upon her all at once. The satisfaction her husband expressed in the departure of Jenny, appeared now to be only dissembled; again, in the same instant, to be real; but yet to confirm her jealousy, proceeding from satiety, and a hundred other bad causes. In a word, she was convinced of her husband's guilt, and immediately flew on the poor pedagogue. Her tongue, teeth, and hands, fell all upon him at once. His wig was in an instant torn from his head, his shirt from his back, and from his face descended five streams of blood, denoting the number of claws with which nature had unhappily armed the enemy.

Mr Partridge acted for some time on the defensive only; but as he found that his antagonist abated nothing of her rage, he thought he might, at least, endeavour to disarm her, or rather to confine her arms; in doing which her cap fell off in the struggle, and her hair being too short to reach her shoulders, erected itself on her head; her stays likewise, which were laced through one single hole at the bottom, burst open; her face was marked with the blood of her husband: her teeth gnashed with rage; and fire, such as sparkles from a smith's forge, darted from her eyes.

He had, at length, the good fortune, by getting possession of her arms, to render those weapons which she wore at the ends of her fingers useless; which she no sooner perceived, than the softness of her sex prevailed over her rage, and she presently dissolved in tears, which soon after concluded in a fit.

That small share of sense which Mr Partridge had hitherto preserved through this scene of fury, of the cause of which he was hitherto ignorant, now utterly abandoned him. He ran instantly into the street, hallowing out that his wife was in the agonies of death, and beseeching the neighbours to fly with the utmost haste to her assistance. Several good women obeyed his summons, who entering his house, and applying the usual

21

remedies on such occasions, Mrs Partridge was at length, to the great joy of her husband, brought to herself.

As soon as she had a little recollected her spirits, and somewhat composed herself with a cordial, she began to inform the company of the manifold injuries she had received from her husband; who, she said, was not contented to injure her in her bed; but, upon her upbraiding him with it, had treated her in the cruelest manner imaginable; had tore her cap and hair from her head, and her stays from her body, giving her, at the same time, several blows, the marks of which she should carry to the grave.

The poor man, who bore on his face many more visible marks of the indignation of his wife, bore all this patiently; but when his wife appealed to the blood on her face, as an evidence of his barbarity, he could not help laying claim to his own blood, for so it really was.

To this the women made no other answer, than that it was a pity it had not come from his heart, instead of his face; all declaring, that, if their husbands should lift their hands against them, they would have their hearts' bloods out of their bodies.

After much admonition the company at length departed, and left the husband and wife to a personal conference together, in which Mr Partridge soon learned the cause of all his sufferings.

CHAPTER FIVE

CONTAINING MUCH TO EXERCISE THE JUDGMENT OF THE READER

I BELIEVE it is a true observation, that few secrets are divulged to one person only; but certainly, it would be next to a miracle that a fact of this kind should be known to a whole parish, and not transpire any farther.

And, indeed, a very few days had past, before the country rung of the schoolmaster of Little Baddington; who was said to have beaten his wife in the most cruel manner. Nay, in some places it was reported he had murdered her; in others, that he had broke her arms; in others, her legs.

The cause of this quarrel was likewise variously reported; for as some people said that Mrs Partridge had caught her husband in bed with his maid, so many other reasons, of a very different kind, went abroad.

Mrs Wilkins had long ago heard of this quarrel; but, as a different cause from the true one had reached her ears, she thought proper to conceal it.

But Mrs Wilkins, whose eyes could see objects at a distance, had perceived a strong likelihood of Captain Blifil's being hereafter her master; and as she plainly discerned that the captain bore no great goodwill to the little foundling, she fancied it would be rendering him an agreeable service, if she could make any discoveries that might lessen the affection which Mr Allworthy seemed to have contracted for this child.

Mrs Wilkins having therefore, by accident, gotten a true scent of the above story, failed not to satisfy herself thoroughly of all the particulars; and then acquainted the captain, that she had at last discovered the true father of the little bastard, which she was sorry, she said, to see her master lose his reputation in the country, by taking so much notice of.

The captain chid her for the conclusion of her speech, as an improper assurance in judging of her master's actions: for if his honour, or his understanding, would have suffered the captain to make an alliance with Mrs Wilkins, his pride by no means have admitted it. But though he declared no satisfaction to Mrs Wilkins at this discovery, he enjoyed not a little from it in his own mind, and resolved to make the best use of it he was able.

He was one day engaged with Mr Allworthy in a discourse on charity: in which the captain, with great learning, proved to Mr Allworthy, that the word charity in Scripture nowhere means beneficence or generosity.

'The Christian religion,' he said, 'was instituted for much nobler purposes, than to enforce a lesson which savoured but little of that sublime, Christian-like disposition, that vast elevation of thought, in purity approaching to angelic perfection, to be attained, expressed, and felt only by grace.

'But though,' continued he, 'there is, I am afraid, little merit in benefaction, there would, I must confess, be much pleasure in them to a good mind, if it was not abated by one consideration. I mean, that we are liable to be imposed upon, and to confer our choicest favours often on the undeserving, as you must own was your case in your bounty to that worthless fellow Partridge.'

Mr Allworthy answered by asking, 'who that Partridge was, whom he had called a worthless fellow?'

'I mean,' said the captain, 'Partridge the barber, the schoolmaster, what do you call him? Partridge, the father of the little child which you found in your bed.'

Mr Allworthy exprest great surprize at this account, and the captain as great at his ignorance of it; for he said he had known it above a month: and at length recollected with much difficulty that he was told it by Mrs Wilkins.

Mr Allworthy determined to send for the criminal, and examine him *vivâ voce*. Mr Partridge, there, was summoned to attend, in order to his defence (if he could make any) against this accusation.

And now Mr Allworthy being seated in the chair of justice, Mr Partridge was brought before him. Having heard his accusation from the mouth of Mrs Wilkins, he pleaded not guilty, making many vehement protestations of his innocence.

Mrs Partridge was then examined, who, after a modest apology for being obliged to speak the truth against her husband, related all the circumstances with which the reader hath already been acquainted; and at last concluded with her husband's confession of his guilt.

Partridge still persisted in asserting his innocence, though he admitted he had made the above-mentioned confession; which he however endeavoured to account for, by protesting that he was forced into it by the continued importunity she used: who vowed, that, as she was sure of his guilt, she would never leave tormenting him till he had owned it; and faithfully promised, that, in such case, she would never mention it to him more. Hence, he said, he had been induced falsely to confess himself guilty, though he was innocent; and that he believed he should have confest a murder from the same motive.

Mrs Partridge could not bear this imputation with patience; and having no other remedy in the present place but tears, she called forth a plentiful assistance from them, and then addressing herself to Mr Allworthy, she said (or rather cried), 'May it please your worship, there never was any poor woman so injured as I am by that base man; for this is not the only instance of his falsehood to me. No, may it please your worship, he hath injured my bed many's the good time and often. I could have put up with his drunkenness and neglect of his business, if he had not broke one of the sacred commandments. Besides, if it had been out of doors I had not mattered it so much; but with my own servant, in my own house, under my own roof, to defile my own chaste bed, which to be sure he hath, with his beastly stinking whores.'

Partridge stood awhile silent, till, being bid to speak, he said he had already spoken the truth, and appealed to Heaven for his innocence, and lastly to the girl herself, whom he desired his worship immediately to send for.

Mr Allworthy, whose natural love of justice, joined to his coolness of temper, made him always a most patient magistrate in hearing all the witnesses which an accused person could produce in his defence, agreed to defer his final determination of this matter till the arrival of Jenny, for whom he immediately dispatched a messenger; and then he appointed them to attend again the third day; for he had sent Jenny a whole day's journey from his own house.

At the appointed time the parties all assembled, when the messenger returning brought word, that Jenny was not to be found; for that she had left her habitation a few days before, in company with a recruiting officer.

Mr Allworthy then declared that the evidence of such a slut as she appeared to be would have deserved no credit; but he said he could not help thinking that, had she been present, and would have declared the truth, she must have confirmed what so many circumstances, together with his own confession, and the declaration of his wife that she had caught her husband in the fact, did sufficiently prove. He therefore deprived him of his annuity, and recommended repentance to him on account of another world, and industry to maintain himself and his wife in this.

Partridge and his wife were therefore both obliged to submit to their fate; which was indeed severe enough: for so far was he from doubling his industry on the account of his lessened income, that he did in a manner abandon himself to despair; and as he was by nature indolent, that vice now increased upon him, by which means he lost the little school he had; so that neither his wife nor himself would have had any bread to eat, had not the charity of some good Christian interposed, and provided them with what was just sufficient for their sustenance.

As this support was conveyed to them by an unknown hand, they imagined that Mr Allworthy himself was their secret benefactor. Fortune at length took pity on this miserable couple, and considerably lessened the wretched state of Partridge, by putting a final end to that of his wife, who soon after caught the smallpox, and died.

Partridge having now lost his wife, his school, and his annuity, and the unknown person having now discontinued the charity, resolved to change the scene, and left the country. Though the captain had effectually demolished poor Partridge, yet had he not reaped the harvest he hoped for, which was to turn the foundling out of Mr Allworthy's house.

On the contrary, that gentleman grew every day fonder of little Tommy, as if he intended to counterbalance his severity to the father with extraordinary fondness and affection towards the son.

This a good deal soured the captain's temper, as did all the other daily instances of Mr Allworthy's generosity; for he looked on all such largesses to be diminutions of his own wealth.

In this, we have said, he did not agree with his wife; nor, indeed, in anything else. The captain, like a well-bred man, had, before marriage, always given up his opinion to that of the lady; and she, who had not the least doubt of his sincerity, retired always from the dispute with an admiration of her own understanding and a love for his.

But he grew weary of this condescension, and began to treat the opinions of his wife with that haughtiness and insolence, which none but those who deserve some contempt themselves can bestow, and those only who deserve no contempt can bear.

When the first torrent of tenderness was over, and when, in the calm and long interval between the fits, reason began to open the eyes of the lady, and she saw this alteration of behaviour in the captain, who at length answered all her arguments only with pish and pshaw, she was far from enduring the indignity with a tame submission. Indeed, it at first so highly provoked her, that it might have produced some tragical event, had it not taken a more harmless turn, by filling her with the utmost contempt for her husband's understanding, which somewhat qualified her hatred towards him.

The captain's hatred to her was of a purer kind: for he looked on a woman as on an animal of domestic use, of somewhat higher consideration than a cat, since her offices were of rather more importance; but the difference between these two was, in his estimation, so small, that, in his marriage contracted with Mr Allworthy's lands and tenements, it would have been pretty equal which of them he had taken into the bargain.

It was always a sufficient reason to either of them to be obstinate in any opinion, that the other had previously asserted the contrary. And for this reason, as the captain looked with an evil eye on the little foundling, his wife began now to caress it almost equally with her own child.

The captain was made large amends for the unpleasant minutes which he passed in the conversation of his wife (and which were as few as he could contrive to make them), by the pleasant meditations he enjoyed when alone.

These meditations were entirely employed on Mr Allworthy's fortune; for, he pleased himself with intended alterations in the house and gardens, and in projecting many other schemes, as well for the improvement of the estate as of the grandeur of the place.

Nothing was wanting to enable him to enter upon the immediate execution of his plans, but the death of Mr Allworthy; he satisfied himself, that as he had every day a chance of this happening, so had he more than an even chance of its happening within a few years.

But while the captain was one day busied in deep contemplations of this kind, one of the most unlucky as well as unseasonable accidents happened to him. In short, just at the very instant when his heart was exulting in meditations on the happiness which

26

would accrue to him by Mr Allworthy's death, he himself—died of an apoplexy.

This unfortunately befel the captain as he was taking his evening walk by himself, so that nobody was present to lend him any assistance, if indeed, any assistance could have preserved him.

Mr Allworthy, and his sister, were assembled at the accustomed hour in the supper-room, where, having waited a considerable time longer than usual, Mr Allworthy first declared he began to grow uneasy at the captain's stay (for he was always most punctual at his meals); and gave orders that the bell should be rung without the doors, and especially towards those walks which the captain was wont to use.

All these summons proving ineffectual (for the captain had, by perverse accident, betaken himself to a new walk that evening), Mrs Blifil declared she was seriously frightened.

She began to bewail herself in very bitter terms, and floods of tears accompanied her lamentations.

At this moment a servant came running in, out of breath, and cried out, The captain was found; and, before he could proceed farther, he was followed by two more, bearing the dead body between them.

Here the curious reader may observe another diversity in the operations of grief: for as Mr Allworthy had been before silent, from the same cause which had made his sister vociferous; so did the present sight, which drew tears from the gentleman, put an entire stop to those of the lady; who first gave a violent scream, and presently after fell into a fit.

The room was soon full of servants, some of whom were employed in care of the wife; and others, with Mr Allworthy, assisted in carrying off the captain to a warm bed; where every method was tried, in order to restore him to life.

And glad should we be, could we inform the reader that both these bodies had been attended with equal success; for those who undertook the care of the lady succeeded so well, that, after the fit had continued a decent time, she again revived, to their great satisfaction: but as to the captain, all experiments proved ineffectual. Death, that inexorable judge, had passed sentence on him, and refused to grant him a reprieve, though two doctors who arrived, and were fee'd at one and the same instant, were his counsel.

Our doctors were about to take their leave, when Mr Allworthy, having given over the captain, began to inquire after his sister, whom he desired them to visit before their departure.

This lady was now recovered of her fit, and, to use the common phrase, as well as could be expected for one in her condition, but she continued a whole month with all the decorations of sickness. During this time she was visited by physicians, attended by nurses, and received constant messages from her acquaintance to inquire after her health.

At length the decent time for sickness and immoderate grief being expired, the doctors were discharged, and the lady began to see company; being altered only from what she was before, by that colour of sadness in which she had dressed her person and countenance.

CHAPTER SIX

THE HERO OF THIS HISTORY APPEARS WITH VERY BAD OMENS

As we determined, when we first sat down to write this history, to flatter no man, but to guide our pen throughout by the directions of truth, we are obliged to bring our hero at about fourteen years of age, in a much more disadvantageous manner than we could wish; and to declare honestly, even at his first appearance, that it was the universal opinion of all Mr Allworthy's family that he was certainly born to be hanged.

Indeed, I am sorry to say there was too much reason for this conjecture; the lad having from his earliest years discovered a propensity to many vices; he had been already convicted of three robberies, viz. of robbing an orchard, of stealing a duck out of a farmer's yard, and of picking Master Blifil's pocket of a ball.

The vices of this young man were, moreover, heightened by the disadvantageous light in which they appeared when opposed to the virtues of Master Blifil, his companion; a youth of so different a cast from little Jones, that not only the family but all the neighbourhood resounded his praises. He was, indeed, a lad of remarkable disposition: sober, discreet, and pious beyond his age; qualities which gained him the love of every one who knew him: while Tom Jones was universally disliked; and many expressed their wonder that Mr Allworthy would suffer such a lad to be educated with his nephew, lest the morals of the latter should be corrupted by his example.

An incident which happened about this time will set the characters of these two lads more fairly before the discerning reader than is in the power of the longest dissertation.

Tom Jones, who, bad as he is, must serve for the hero of this history, had only one friend among all the servants of the family; the gamekeeper, a fellow of a loose kind of disposition.

To say the truth, some of that atrocious wickedness in Jones, of which we have just mentioned three examples, might perhaps be derived from the encouragement he had received from this fellow, who, in two or three instances, had been what the law calls an accessary after the fact: for the whole duck, and great part of the apples, were converted to the use of the gamekeeper and his family; though, as Jones alone was discovered, the poor lad bore the whole blame.

Contiguous to Mr Allworthy's estate was the manor of one of those gentlemen who are called preservers of the game.

Little Jones went one day a shooting with the gamekeeper; when happening to spring a covey of partridges near the border of that manor the birds flew into it, and were marked (as it is called) by the two sportsmen, in some furze bushes, about two or three hundred paces beyond Mr Allworthy's dominions.

Mr Allworthy had given the fellow strict orders, on pain of forfeiting his place, never to trespass on any of his neighbours; no more on those who were less rigid in this matter than on the lord of this manor. With regard to others, indeed, these orders had not been always very scrupulously kept; but as the disposition of the gentleman with whom the partridges had taken sanctuary was well known, the gamekeeper had never yet attempted to invade his territories. Nor had he done it now, had not the younger sportsman, who was excessively eager to pursue the flying game, overpersuaded him; but Jones being very importunate, the other, who was himself keen enough after the sport, yielded to his persuasions, entered the manor, and shot one of the partridges.

The gentleman himself was at that time on horse-back, at a little distance from them; and hearing the gun go off, he immediately made towards the place, and discovered poor Tom; for the gamekeeper had leapt into the thickest part of the furze-brake, where he had happily concealed himself.

The gentleman having searched the lad, and found the partridge upon him, denounced great vengeance, swearing he would acquaint Mr Allworthy. He was as good as his word: for he rode immediately to his house, and complained of the trespass on his manor in as high terms and as bitter language as if his house had been broken open, and the most valuable furniture stole out of it. He added, that some other person was in his company, though he could not discover him; for that two guns had been discharged almost in the same instant. And, says he, 'We have found only this partridge, but the Lord knows what mischief they have done.'

At his return home, Tom was presently convened before Mr Allworthy. He owned the fact, and alledged no other excuse but what was really true, viz. that the covey was originally sprung in Mr Allworthy's own manor.

Tom was then interrogated who was with him, which Mr Allworthy declared he was resolved to know, but Tom stoutly persisted in asserting that he was alone.

The gamekeeper, being a suspected person, was now sent for, and the question put to him; but he, relying on the promise which Tom had made him, to take all upon himself, very resolutely denied being in company with the young gentleman, or indeed having seen him the whole afternoon.

Poor Jones spent a very melancholy night; and the more so, as he was without his usual companion; for Master Blifil was gone abroad on a visit with his mother. Fear of the punishment he was to suffer was on this occasion his least evil; his chief anxiety being, lest his constancy should fail him, and he should be brought to betray the gamekeeper, whose ruin he knew must now be the consequence.

Nor did the gamekeeper pass his time much better. He had the same apprehensions with the youth; for whose honour he had likewise a much tenderer regard than for his skin.

In the morning, when Tom attended the reverend Mr Thwackum, the person to whom Mr Allworthy had committed the instruction of the two boys, he had the same questions put to him by that gentleman which he had been asked the evening before, to which he returned the same answers. The consequence of this was, so severe a whipping, that it possibly fell little short of the torture with which confessions are in some countries extorted from criminals.

Tom bore his punishment with great resolution; and though his master asked him, between every stroke, whether he would not confess, he was contented to be flead rather than betray his friend, or break the promise he had made.

The gamekeeper was now relieved from his anxiety, and Mr Allworthy himself began to be concerned at Tom's sufferings: for besides Mr Thwackum, being highly enraged that he was not able to make the boy say what he himself pleased, had carried his severity much beyond the good man's intention. Now, as cruelty and injustice were two ideas of which Mr Allworthy could by no means support the consciousness a single moment, he sent for Tom, and after many kind and friendly exhortations, said, 'I am convinced, my dear child, that my suspicions have wronged you; I am sorry that you have been so severely punished on this account.' And at last gave him a little horse to make him amends; again repeating his sorrow for what had past.

Tom's guilt now flew in his face more than any severity could make it. He could more easily bear the lashes of Thwackum, than the generosity of Allworthy. The tears burst from his eyes, and he fell upon his knees, crying, 'Oh, sir, you are too good to me. Indeed you are. Indeed I don't deserve it.' And at that very instant, from the fulness of his heart, had almost betrayed the secret; but the good genius of the gamekeeper suggested to him what might be the consequence to the poor fellow, and this consideration sealed his lips.

Thwackum did all he could to persuade Allworthy from showing any compassion or kindness to the boy, saying, 'He had persisted in an untruth'; but Mr Allworthy said the boy had suffered enough already for concealing the truth, even if he was guilty, seeing that he could have no motive but a mistaken point of honour for so doing.

This discourse happened at table when dinner was just ended; and there were present Mr Allworthy, Mr Thwackum, and a third gentleman, who now entered into the debate.

The name of this gentleman, who had then resided some time at Mr Allworthy's house, was Mr Square. His natural parts were not of the first rate, but he had greatly improved them by a learned education. He was deeply read and a master of all the works of Plato and Aristotle. Upon which great models he had principally formed himself; sometimes according with the opinion of the one, and sometimes with that of the other.

This gentleman and Mr Thwackum scarce ever met without a disputation; for their tenets were indeed diametrically opposite to each other. Square held human nature to be the perfection of all virtue, and that vice was a deviation from our nature, in the same manner as deformity of body is. Thwackum, on the contrary, maintained that the human mind, since the fall, was nothing but a sink of iniquity, till purified and redeemed by grace. In one point only they agreed, which was, in all their discourses on morality never to mention the word goodness. The favourite phrase of the former, was the natural beauty of virtue; that of the latter, was the divine power of grace.

Upon the whole, it is not religion or virtue, but the want of them, which is exposed. Had not Thwackum too much neglected virtue, and Square, religion, in the composition of their several systems, and had not both utterly discarded all natural goodness of heart, they had never been represented as the objects of derision in this history; in which we will now proceed.

A matter then, which put an end to the debate at dinner, was no other than a quarrel between Master Blifil and Tom Jones, the consequence of which had been a bloody nose to the former; for though Master Blifil, notwithstanding he was the younger, was in size above the other's match, yet Tom was much his superior at the noble art of boxing.

Tom, however, cautiously avoided all engagements with that

youth; for besides that Tommy Jones was an inoffensive lad amidst all his roguery, and really loved Blifil, Mr Thwackum being always the second of the latter, would have been sufficient to deter him.

But no man is wise at all hours; it is therefore no wonder that a boy is not so. A difference arising at play between the two lads, Master Blifil called Tom a beggarly bastard. Upon which the latter, who was somewhat passionate in his disposition, immediately caused that phenomenon in the face of the former, which we have above remembered.

Master Blifil now, with his blood running from his nose, and the tears galloping after from his eyes, appeared before his uncle and the tremendous Thwackum. In which court an indictment of assault, battery, and wounding, was instantly preferred against Tom; who in his excuse only pleaded the provocation, which was indeed all the matter that Master Blifil had omitted.

Upon which Master Blifil said, 'It is no wonder. Those who will tell one fib, will hardly stick at another. If I had told my master such a wicked fib as you have done, I should be ashamed to show my face.'

'What fib, child?' cries Thwackum pretty eagerly.

'Why, he told you that nobody was with him a-shooting when he killed the partridge; but he knows'—here he burst into a flood of tears—'yes, he knows, for he confessed it to me, that Black George the gamekeeper was there. Nay, he said—yes you did—deny it if you can, that you would not have confest the truth, though master had cut you to pieces.'

At this the fire flashed from Thwackum's eyes, and he cried out in triumph—'Oh! ho! this is your mistaken notion of honour!' But Mr Allworthy, with a more gentle aspect, turned towards the lad, and said, 'Is this true, child? How came you to persist so obstinately in a falsehood?'

Tom said, 'He scorned a lie as much as any one: but he t ought his honour engaged him to act as he did; for he had promised the poor fellow to conceal him: which,' he said, 'he thought himself farther obliged to, as the gamekeeper had begged him not to go into the gentleman's manor, and had at last gone himself, in compliance with his persuasions.' He said, 'This was the whole truth of the matter, and he would take his oath of it'; and concluded with very passionately begging Mr Allworthy 'to have compassion on the poor fellow's family, especially as he himself only had been guilty, and the other had been very difficultly prevailed on to do what he did. Indeed, sir,' said he, 'it could hardly be called a lie that I told; for the poor fellow was entirely innocent of the whole matter. I should have gone alone after the birds; nay, I did go at first, and he only followed me to prevent more mischief. Do, pray, sir, let me be punished; take my little horse away again; but pray, sir, forgive poor George.'

Mr Allworthy hesitated a few moments, and then dismissed the boys, advising them to live more friendly and peaceably together.

CHAPTER SEVEN

THE OPINION OF THE DIVINE AND THE PHILOSOPHER CONCERNING THE TWO BOYS

IT is probable, that by disclosing this secret, which had been communicated in the utmost confidence to him, young Blifil preserved his companion from a good lashing; for the offence of the bloody nose would have been of itself sufficient cause for Thwackum to have proceeded to correction; but now this was totally absorbed in the consideration of the other matter; and with regard to this, Mr Allworthy declared privately, he thought the boy deserved reward rather than punishment, so that Thwackum's hand was withheld by a general pardon.

Thwackum, whose meditations were full of birch, exclaimed against this weak, and, as he said he would venture to call it, wicked lenity. To remit the punishment of such crimes was, he said, to encourage them.

Square said, he had been endeavouring to reconcile the behaviour of Tom with his idea of perfect virtue, but could not. He owned there was something which at first sight appeared like fortitude in the action; but as fortitude was a virtue, and falsehood a vice, they could by no means agree or unite together. As both these learned men concurred in censuring Jones, so were they no less unanimous in applauding Master Blifil. All this, however, weighed very little with Mr Allworthy. He could not be prevailed on to sign the warrant for the execution of Jones.

Towards the gamekeeper the good man behaved with more severity. He presently summoned that poor fellow before him, and after many bitter remonstrances, paid him his wages, and dismist him from his service; for Mr Allworthy rightly observed, that there was a great difference between being guilty of a falsehood to excuse yourself, and to excuse another. He likewise urged, as the principal motive to his inflexible severity against this man, that he had basely suffered Tom Jones to undergo so heavy a punishment for his sake, whereas he ought to have prevented it by making the discovery himself.

When this story became public, many people differed from Square and Thwackum, in judging the conduct of the two lads on the occasion. Master Blifil was generally called a sneaking rascal, a poor-spirited wretch, with other epithets of the like kind; whilst Tom was honoured with the appellations of, a brave lad, a jolly dog, and an honest fellow. Indeed, his behaviour to Black George much ingratiated him with all the servants; for though that fellow was before universally disliked; yet he was no sooner turned away than he was as universally pitied; and the friendship and gallantry of Tom Jones was celebrated by them all with the highest applause; and they condemned Master Blifil as openly as they durst, without incurring the danger of offending his mother. For all this, however, poor Tom smarted in the flesh; for though Thwackum had been inhibited to exercise his arm on the foregoing account, yet was it easy to find a rod; and, indeed, the not being able to find one was the only thing which could have kept Thwackum any long time from chastising poor Jones.

Had the bare delight in the sport been the only inducement to the pedagogue, it is probable Master Blifil would likewise have had his share; but though Mr Allworthy had given him frequent orders to make no difference between the lads, yet was Thwackum altogether as kind and gentle to this youth, as he was harsh, nay even barbarous, to the other. To say the truth, Blifil had greatly gained his master's affections; partly by the profound respect he always showed his person, but much more by the decent reverence with which he received his doctrine.

Tom Jones, on the other hand, was not only deficient in outward tokens of respect, often forgetting to pull off his hat, or to bow at his master's approach; but was altogether as unmindful both of his master's precepts and example.

Mr Square had the same reason for his preference of the former lad; for Tom Jones showed no more regard to the learned discourses which this gentleman would sometimes throw away upon him, than to those of Thwackum.

Master Blifil, on the contrary, had address enough at sixteen to recommend himself at one and the same time to both these opposites. With one he was all religion, with the other he was all virtue. And when both were present, he was profoundly silent, which both interpreted in his favour and in their own.

Furthermore those two learned personages had, from their first arrival at Mr Allworthy's house, taken so great an affection, the one to his virtue, the other to his religion, that they had meditated the closest alliance with him.

For this purpose they had cast their eyes on that fair widow, Mrs Blifil.

It may seem remarkable, that, of four persons whom we have commemorated at Mr Allworthy's house, three of them should fix their inclinations on a lady who was never greatly celebrated for her beauty, and who was, moreover, now a little descended into the vale of years; but in reality bosom friends, and intimate acquaintance, have a kind of natural propensity to particular females at the house of a friend—viz. to his grandmother, mother, sister, daughter, aunt, niece, or cousin, when they are rich; and to his wife, sister, daughter, niece, cousin, mistress, or servant-maid, if they should be handsome.

Now, as both of these gentlemen were industrious in taking every opportunity of recommending themselves to the widow, they apprehended one certain method was, by giving her son the constant preference to the other lad; and as they conceived the kindness and affection which Mr Allworthy showed the latter, must be highly disagreeable to her, they doubted not but the laying hold on all occasions to degrade and vilify him, would be highly pleasing to her; who, as she hated the boy, must love all those who did him any hurt.

Whether Mrs Blifil had been surfeited with the sweets of marriage, or disgusted by its bitters, or from what other cause it proceeded, I will not determine; but she could never be brought to listen to any second proposals. However, she at last conversed with Square with such a degree of intimacy that malicious tongues began to whisper things of her. The pedagogue, 'tis certain, whipped on, without getting a step nearer to his journey's end.

Indeed he had committed a great error, and that Square discovered much sooner than himself. Mrs Blifil was not over and above pleased with the behaviour of her husband; nay, to be honest, she absolutely hated him, till his death at last a little reconciled him to her affections. It will not be therefore greatly wondered at, if she had not the most violent regard to the offspring she had by him. And, in fact, she had so little of this regard that, in his infancy she seldom saw her son, or took any notice of him; and hence she acquiesced, after a little reluctance, in all the favours which Mr Allworthy showered on the foundling.

However, when Tom grew up, and gave tokens of that gallantry of temper which greatly recommends men to women, this disinclination which she had discovered to him when a child, by degrees abated, and at last she so evidently demonstrated her affection to him to be much stronger than what she bore her own son, that it was impossible to mistake her any longer. She was so desirous of often seeing him, and discovered such satisfaction and delight in his company, that before he was eighteen years old he was become a rival to both Square and Thwackum; and what is worse, the whole country began to talk as loudly of her inclination to Tom, as they had before done of that which she had shown to Square: on which account the philosopher conceived the most implacable hatred for our poor hero.

CHAPTER EIGHT

A CHILDISH INCIDENT

THE reader may remember that Mr Allworthy gave Tom Jones a little horse, as a kind of smart-money for the punishment which he imagined he had suffered innocently.

This horse Tom kept above half a year, and then rode him to a neighbouring fair, and sold him.

At his return, being questioned by Thwackum what he had done with the money for which the horse was sold, he frankly declared he would not tell him.

'Oho!' says Thwackum, 'you will not! then I will have it out of you.'

Tom was now mounted on the back of a footman, and everything prepared for execution, when Mr Allworthy, entering the room, gave the criminal a reprieve, and took him with him into another apartment; where, being alone with Tom, he put the same question to him which Thwackum had before asked him.

Tom answered, he could in duty refuse him nothing; but as for that tyrannical rascal, he would never make him any other answer than with a cudgel, with which he hoped soon to be able to pay him for all his barbarities.

'Indeed, my dear sir, I love and honour you more than all the world. Could the little horse you gave me speak, I am sure he could tell you how fond I was of your present; for I had more pleasure in feeding him than in riding him. Indeed, sir, it went to my heart to part with him; nor would I have sold him upon any other account in the world than what I did. Indeed, sir, there never was any misery like theirs.'

'Like whose, child?' says Allworthy. 'What do you mean?'

'Oh, sir!' answered Tom, 'your poor gamekeeper, with all his large family, ever since your discarding him, have been perishing with all the miseries of cold and hunger: It was to save them from absolute destruction I parted with your dear present; I sold the horse for them; and they have every farthing of the money.'

Mr Allworthy now stood silent for some moments, and before he spoke the tears started from his eyes. He at length dismissed Tom with a gentle rebuke, advising him for the future to apply to him in cases of distress, rather than to use extraordinary means of relieving them himself.

This affair was afterwards the subject of much debate between Thwackum and Square. Thwackum held, that this was flying in Mr Allworthy's face, who had intended to punish the fellow for his disobedience.

Square argued strongly on the other side, in opposition perhaps to Thwackum, who seemed very much to approve what Jones had done. As to poor Tom, he was no sooner pardoned for selling the horse, than he was discovered to have some time before sold a fine Bible which Mr Allworthy gave him, the money arising from which sale he had disposed of in the same manner. This Bible Master Blifil had purchased, though he had already such another of his own, partly out of respect for the book, and partly out of friendship to Tom, being unwilling that the Bible should be sold out of the family at half-price. He therefore deposited the said half-price himself; and from the time when Master Blifil was first possessed of this Bible, he never used any other. Nay, he was seen reading in it much oftener than he had before been in his own. Now, as he frequently asked Thwackum to explain difficult passages to him, that gentleman unfortunately took notice of Tom's name, which was written in many parts of the book. This brought on an inquiry, which obliged Master Blifil to discover the whole matter.

Thwackum was resolved a crime of this kind, which he called sacrilege, should not go unpunished. He therefore proceeded immediately to castigation: and not contented with that he acquainted Mr Allworthy, at their next meeting, with this monstrous crime, as it appeared to him: inveighing against Tom in the most bitter terms, and likening him to the buyers and sellers who were driven out of the temple.

Square saw this matter in a very different light. He said, he could not perceive any higher crime in selling one book than in selling another. Mrs Blifil, who was present at this debate, declared herself absolutely on Mr Square's side. She argued, indeed, very learnedly in support of his opinion; and concluded with saying, if Tom had been guilty of any fault, she must confess her own son appeared to be equally culpable; for that she could see no difference between the buyer and the seller; both of whom were alike to be driven out of the temple.

Soon after this, an action was brought against the gamekeeper by Squire Western (the gentleman in whose manor the partridge

37

was killed), for depredations of the like kind. This was a most unfortunate circumstance for the fellow, as it not only of itself threatened his ruin, but actually prevented Mr Allworthy from restoring him to his favour: for as that gentleman was walking out one evening with Master Blifil and young Jones, the latter slily drew him to the habitation of Black George; where the family of that poor wretch, namely, his wife and children, were found in all the misery with which cold, hunger, and nakedness, can affect human creatures: for as to the money they had received from Jones, former debts had consumed almost the whole.

Such a scene as this could not fail of affecting the heart of Mr Allworthy. He immediately gave the mother a couple of guineas, with which he bid her cloth her children. The poor woman burst into tears at this goodness, and while she was thanking him, could not refrain from expressing her gratitude to Tom; who had, she said, long preserved both her and hers from starving. 'We have not,' says she, 'had a morsel to eat, nor have these poor children had a rag to put on, but what his goodness hath bestowed on us.' For, indeed, besides the horse and the Bible, Tom had sacrificed a night-gown, and others things, to the use of this distressed family.

On their return home, Tom made use of all his eloquence to display the wretchedness of these people, and the penitence of Black George himself; and in this he succeeded so well, that Mr Allworthy said, he thought the man had suffered enough for what was past; that he would forgive him, and think of some means of providing for him and his family.

Master Blifil fell very short of his companion in the amiable quality of mercy; but he as greatly exceeded him in one of a much higher kind, namely, in justice.

Master Blifil then, though he had kept silence in the presence of Jones, yet, when he had better considered the matter, could by no means endure the thought of suffering his uncle to confer favours on the undeserving.

The gamekeeper, about a year after he was dismissed from Mr Allworthy's service, and before Tom's selling the horse, being in want of bread, either to fill his own mouth or those of his family, as he passed through a field belonging to Mr Western espied a hare sitting in her form. This hare he had basely and barbarously knocked on the head, against the laws of the land, and no less against the laws of sportsmen.

The higgler to whom the hare was sold, being unfortunately taken many months after with a quantity of game upon him, was obliged to make his peace with the squire, by becoming evidence against some poacher. And now Black George was pitched upon by him, as being a person already obnoxious to Mr Western, and one of no good fame in the country. He was, besides, the best sacrifice the higgler could make, as he had supplied him with no game since; and by this means the witness had an opportunity of screening his better customers: for the squire, being charmed with the power of punishing Black George, whom a single transgression was sufficient to ruin, made no further inquiry.

Had this fact been truly laid before Mr Allworthy, it might probably have done the gamekeeper very little mischief. But Master Blifil had forgot the distance of the time. He varied likewise in the manner of the fact: and by the hasty addition of the single letter S he considerably altered the story; for he said that George had wired hares. These alterations might probably have been set right, had not Master Blifil unluckily insisted on a promise of secrecy from Mr Allworthy before he revealed the matter to him; but by that means the poor gamekeeper was condemned without having an opportunity to defend himself.

Short-lived then was the joy of these poor people; for Mr Allworthy the next morning declared he had fresh reason, without assigning it, for his anger, and strictly forbad Tom to mention George any more: though as for his family, he said he would endeavour to keep them from starving; but as to the fellow himself, he would leave him to the laws, which nothing could keep him from breaking.

Tom could by no means divine what had incensed Mr Allworthy, for of Master Blifil he had not the least suspicion. However, as his friendship was to be tired out by no disappointments, he now determined to try another method of preserving the poor gamekeeper from ruin.

Jones was lately grown very intimate with Mr Western. He had so greatly recommended himself to that gentleman, by leaping over five-barred gates, and by other acts of sportsmanship, that the squire had declared Tom would certainly make a great man if he had but sufficient encouragement.

By such kind of talents he had so ingratiated himself with the squire, that he was a most welcome guest at his table, and a favourite companion in his sport: everything which the squire held most dear, to wit, his guns, dogs, and horses, were now as much at the command of Jones, as if they had been his own. He resolved therefore to make use of this favour on behalf of his friend Black George.

For this purpose, then, Tom applied to Mr Western's daughter, a young lady of about seventeen years of age, whom her father, next after those necessary implements of sport just before mentioned, loved and esteemed above all the world.

CHAPTER NINE

A SHORT HINT OF WHAT WE CAN DO IN THE SUBLIME

READER, perhaps thou hast seen the statue of the *Venus de Medicis*. Perhaps, too, thou hast seen the gallery of beauties at Hampton Court. Yet is it possible, my friend, that thou mayest have seen all these without being able to form an exact idea of Sophia; for she did not exactly resemble any of them.

Sophia, then, the only daughter of Mr Western, was a middle-sized woman; but rather inclining to tall. Her shape was not only exact, but extremely delicate. Her hair, which was black, was so luxuriant, that it reached her middle, before she cut it to comply with the modern fashion; and it was now curled so gracefully in her neck, that few could believe it to be her own. Her eyebrows were full, even, and arched beyond the power of art to imitate. Her black eyes had a lustre in them, which all her softness could not extinguish. Her nose was exactly regular. Her cheeks were of the oval kind; and in her right she had a dimple, which the least smile discovered. Her complexion had rather more of the lily than of the rose; but when exercise or modesty increased her natural colour, no vermilion could equal it.

Such was the outside of Sophia; nor was this beautiful frame disgraced by an inhabitant unworthy of it. Her mind was every way equal to her person; nay, the latter borrowed some charms from the former; for when she smiled, the sweetness of her temper diffused that glory over her countenance which no regularity of features can give. Whatever mental accomplishments she had derived from nature, they were somewhat improved and cultivated by art: for she had been educated under the care of an aunt, who was a lady of great discretion, and was thoroughly acquainted with the world, having lived in her youth about the court, whence she had retired some years since into the country.

Though the different tempers of Mr Allworthy and of Mr Western did not admit of a very intimate correspondence, yet they lived upon what is called a decent footing together; by which means the young people of both families had been acquainted from their infancy; and as they were all near of the same age, had been frequent playmates together.

The gaiety of Tom's temper suited better with Sophia, than the grave and sober disposition of Master Blifil. And the preference which she gave the former of these, would often appear so plainly, that a lad of a more passionate turn than Master Blifil was, might have shown some displeasure at it.

Tom Jones, when very young, had presented Sophia with a little bird, which he had taken from the nest, had nursed up, and taught to sing.

Of this bird, Sophia, then about thirteen years old, was so extremely fond that her chief business was to feed and tend it, and her chief pleasure to play with it. By these means little Tommy, for so the bird was called, was become so tame, that it would feed out of the hand of its mistress, would perch upon the finger, and lie contented in her bosom, where it seemed almost sensible of its own happiness; though she always kept a small string about its leg, nor would ever trust it with the liberty of flying away.

One day, when Mr Allworthy and his whole family dined at Mr Western's, Master Blifil, being in the garden with little Sophia, and observing the extreme fondness that she showed for her little bird, desired her to trust it for a moment in his hands. Sophia presently complied with the young gentleman's request, and after some previous caution, delivered him her bird; of which he was no sooner in possession, than he slipt the string from its leg and tossed it into the air.

The foolish animal no sooner perceived itself at liberty, than forgetting all the favours it had received from Sophia, it flew directly from her, and perched on a bough at some distance.

Sophia, seeing her bird gone, screamed out so loud, that Tom Jones, who was at a little distance, immediately ran to her assistance.

He was no sooner informed of what had happened, than he cursed Blifil for a pitiful malicious rascal; and then immediately stripping off his coat he applied himself to climbing the tree to which the bird escaped.

Tom had almost recovered his little namesake, when the branch on which he was perched, and that hung over a canal, broke, and the poor lad plumped over head and ears into the water.

Sophia's concern now changed its object. And as she apprehended the boy's life was in danger, she screamed ten times louder than before; and indeed Master Blifil himself now seconded her with all the vociferation in his power.

The company, who were sitting in a room next the garden, were instantly alarmed, and came all forth; but just as they reached the canal, Tom (for the water was luckily pretty shallow in that part) arrived safely on shore.

Thwackum fell violently on poor Tom, who stood dropping and shivering before him, when Mr Allworthy desired him to have patience; and turning to Master Blifil, said, 'Pray, child, what is the reason of all this disturbance?'

Master Blifil answered, 'Indeed, uncle, I am very sorry for what I have done; I have been unhappily the occasion of it all. I had Miss Sophia's bird in my hand, and thinking the poor creature

41

languished for liberty, I own I could not forbear giving it what it desired; but if I had imagined Miss Sophia would have been so much concerned at it, I am sure I never would have done it; nay, if I had known what would have happened to the bird itself: for when Master Jones, who climbed up that tree after it, fell into the water, the bird took a second flight, and presently a nasty hawk carried it away.'

Poor Sophia, who now first heard of her little Tommy's fate (for her concern for Jones had prevented her perceiving it when it happened), shed a shower of tears. These Mr Allworthy endeavoured to assuage, promising her a much finer bird: but she declared she would never have another. Her father chid her for crying so for a foolish bird; but could not help telling young Blifil, if he was a son of his, his backside should be well flayed.

Sophia now returned to her chamber, the two young gentlemen were sent home, and the rest of the company returned to their bottle.

Square had no sooner lighted his pipe, than, addressing himself to Allworthy, he thus began: 'Sir, I cannot help congratulating you on your nephew; who, at an age when few lads have any ideas but of sensible objects, is arrived at a capacity of distinguishing right from wrong. To confine anything, seems to me against the law of nature, by which everything hath a right to liberty.'

Here Thwackum hastily interrupted, and spilling some of his wine, and swallowing the rest with great eagerness, answered, 'From another expression he made use of, I hope he will resemble much better men. The law of nature is a jargon of words, which means nothing.'

'Drink about,' says Western. 'Pox of your laws of nature! I don't know what you mean, either of you, by right and wrong. To take away my girl's bird was wrong, in my opinion. Pox! you have neither of you mentioned a word of that poor lad who deserves to be commended: to venture breaking his neck to oblige my girl was a generous-spirited action: I have learning enough to see that. D—n me, here's Tom's health! I shall love the boy for it the longest day I have to live.'

'Small things affect light minds,' was the sentiment of a great master of the passion of love. And certain it is, that from this day Sophia began to have some little kindness for Tom Jones, and no little aversion for his companion.

To say the truth, Sophia, when very young, discerned that Tom, though an idle, thoughtless, rattling rascal, was nobody's enemy but his own; and that Master Blifil, though a prudent, discreet, sober young gentleman, was at the same time strongly attached to the interest only of one single person. She honoured Tom Jones, and scorned Master Blifil, almost as soon as she knew the meaning of those two words.

Sophia had been absent upwards of three years with her aunt; during all which time she had seldom seen either of these young gentlemen. This young lady was now returned to her father; who gave her the command of his house, and placed her at the upper end of his table, where Tom (who for his great love of hunting was become a great favourite of the squire) often dined.

Tom behaved to Sophia with no particularity, unless perhaps by showing her a higher respect than he paid to any other.

Sophia, with the highest degree of innocence and modesty, had a remarkable sprightliness in her temper. This was so greatly increased whenever she was in company with Tom, that had he not been very young and thoughtless, he must have observed it: or had not Mr Western's thoughts been generally either in the field, the stable, or the dog-kennel, it might have perhaps created some jealousy in him: but so far was the good gentleman from entertaining any such suspicions, that he gave Tom every opportunity with his daughter which any lover could have wished; and this Tom innocently improved to better advantage, by following only the dictates of his natural gallantry and good nature, than he might perhaps have done had he had the deepest designs on the young lady.

Matters were in this situation, when Tom, one afternoon, finding Sophia alone, began, after a short apology, with a very serious face, to acquaint her that he had a favour to ask of her, which he hoped her goodness would comply with.

Though neither the young man's behaviour, nor indeed his manner of opening this business, were such as could give her any just cause of suspecting he intended to make love to her; yet whether Nature whispered something into her ear, or from what cause it arose I will not determine; certain it is, some idea of that kind must have intruded itself; for her colour forsook her cheeks, her limbs trembled, and her tongue would have faltered, had Tom stopped for an answer; but he soon relieved her from her perplexity, by proceeding to inform her of his request; which was to solicit her interest on behalf of the gamekeeper, whose own ruin, and that of a large family, must be, he said, the consequence of Mr Western's pursuing his action against him.

Sophia presently recovered her confusion, and, with a smile full of sweetness, said, 'Is this the mighty favour you asked with so much gravity? I will do it with all my heart. I really pity the poor fellow, and no longer ago than yesterday sent a small matter to his wife.' This small matter was one of her gowns, some linen, and ten shillings in money, of which Tom had heard, and it had, in reality, put this solicitation into his head.

Our youth, now, emboldened with his success, resolved to push the matter further, and ventured even to beg her recommendation of him to her father's service; protesting that he thought him one of the honestest fellows in the country, and extremely well qualified for the place of a gamekeeper, which luckily then happened to be vacant.

Sophia answered, 'Well, I will undertake this too; but now, Mr Jones, I must ask you a favour.'

'A favour, madam!' cries Tom: 'if you knew the pleasure you have given me in the hopes of receiving a command from you, you would think by mentioning it you did confer the greatest favour on me; for by this dear hand I would sacrifice my life to oblige you.'

He then snatched her hand, and eagerly kissed it, which was the first time his lips had ever touched her. The blood now rushed all over her face and neck with such violence, that they became all of a scarlet colour.

Sophia, as soon as she could speak (which was not instantly), informed him that the favour she had to desire of him was, not to lead her father through so many dangers in hunting; for that, from what she had heard, she was terribly frightened every time they went out together, and expected some day or other to see her father brought home with broken limbs.

Tom promised faithfully to obey her commands; and after thanking her for her kind compliance with his request, took his leave, and departed highly charmed with his success.

It was Mr Western's custom every afternoon, as soon as he was drunk, to hear his daughter play on the harpsichord; for he was a great lover of music, and indeed his most favourite tunes were Old Sir Simon the King, St George he was for England, Bobbing Joan, and some others.

His daughter was so devoted to her father's pleasure, that she learnt all those tunes to oblige him.

This evening, when the gentleman was retired from his bottle, she played all his favourites three times over without any solicitation. This so pleased the good squire, that he started from his couch, gave his daughter a kiss, and swore her hand was greatly improved. She took this opportunity to execute her promise to Tom; in which she succeeded so well, that the squire declared, if she would give him t'other bout of Old Sir Simon, he would give the gamekeeper his deputation the next morning.

Tom's success in this affair soon began to ring over the country. Young Blifil was greatly enraged at it. He had long hated Black George in the same proportion as Jones delighted in him; not from any offence which he had ever received, but from his great love to religion and virtue;—for Black George had the reputation of a loose kind of a fellow.

Thwackum and Square likewise sung to the same tune. They

44

were now (especially the latter) become greatly jealous of young Jones with the widow; for he now approached the age of twenty, was really a fine young fellow, and that lady, by her encouragements to him, seemed daily more and more to think him so.

Allworthy was not, however, moved with their malice. He declared himself very well satisfied with what Jones had done. He said the perseverance and integrity of his friendship was highly commendable, and he wished he could see more frequent instances of that virtue.

CHAPTER TEN

THE INSENSIBILITY OF MR JONES TO ALL THE CHARMS OF THE LOVELY SOPHIA

Now, though Tom was not insensible of the charms of Sophia; though he greatly liked her beauty, and esteemed all her other qualifications, she had made, however, no deep impression on his heart; for his heart was in the possession of another woman.

We have often mentioned the family of George Seagrim (commonly called Black George, the gamekeeper), which consisted at present of a wife and five children. The second of these children was a daughter, whose name was Molly, and who was esteemed one of the handsomest girls in the whole country.

The beauty of this girl made no impression on Tom, till she grew towards the age of sixteen, when Tom, who was near three years older, began first to cast the eyes of affection upon her. And this affection he had fixed on the girl long before he could bring himself to attempt the possession of her person: for though his constitution urged him greatly to this, his principles no less forcibly restrained him. To debauch a young woman, however low her condition was, appeared to him a very heinous crime; and the goodwill he bore the father, with the compassion he had for his family, very strongly corroborated all such sober reflections; so that he once resolved to get the better of his inclinations, and he actually abstained three whole months without ever going to Seagrim's house, or seeing his daughter.

Now, though Molly was generally thought a very fine girl yet her beauty was not of the most amiable kind. It had, indeed, very little of feminine in it, for youth and florid health had a very considerable share in the composition.

Nor was her mind more effeminate than her person. As this was tall and robust, so was that bold and forward. So little had she of modesty, that Jones had more regard for her virtue than she herself. And as most probably she liked Tom as well as he liked her, so when she perceived his backwardness she herself grew proportionably forward; and when she saw he had entirely deserted the house, she found means of throwing herself in his way. In a word, she soon triumphed over all the virtuous resolutions of Jones.

In the conduct of this matter Molly so well played her part, that Jones attributed the conquest entirely to himself, and considered the young woman as one who had yielded to the violent attacks of his passion. He likewise imputed her yielding to the ungovernable force of her love towards him; indeed, he was one of the handsomest young fellows in the world. He considered this poor girl as one whose happiness or misery he had caused to be dependent on himself.

This, then, was the true reason of that insensibility which he had shown to the charms of Sophia; for as he could not think of abandoning his Molly, poor and destitute as she was, so no more could he entertain a motion of betraying such a creature as Sophia.

Her mother first perceived the alteration in the shape of Molly; and in order to hide it from her neighbours, she foolishly clothed her in that sack which Sophia had sent her.

Molly was charmed with the first opportunity she ever had of showing her beauty to advantage; for though she could very well bear to contemplate herself in the glass, even when dressed in rags, yet she thought the addition of finery would much improve her charms, and extend her conquests.

Molly, therefore, having dressed herself out in this sack, with a new laced cap, and some other ornaments which Tom had given her, repairs to church with her fan in her hand the very next Sunday. The great are deceived if they imagine they have appropriated ambition and vanity to themselves.

Molly had seated herself some time before she was known by her neighbours. And then a whisper ran through the whole congregation, 'Who is she?' but when she was discovered, such sneering, giggling, tittering, and laughing ensued among the women, that Mr Allworthy was obliged to exert his authority to preserve any decency among them.

Mr Western had an estate in this parish; and as his house stood at little greater distance from this church than from his own, he very often came to Divine Service here; and both he and the charming Sophia happened to be present at this time.

Sophia was much pleased with the beauty of the girl, whom she

46

pitied for her simplicity in having dressed herself in that manner, as she saw the envy which it had occasioned among her equals. She no sooner came home than she sent for the gamekeeper; and ordered him to bring his daughter to her; saying she would provide for her in the family, and might possibly place the girl about her own person, when her own maid, who was now going away, had left her.

Poor Seagrim was thunderstruck at this; for he was no stranger to the fault in the shape of his daughter. He answered, in a stammering voice, 'That he was afraid Molly would be too awkward to wait on her ladyship, as she had never been at service.'—'No matter for that,' says Sophia; 'she will soon improve. I am pleased with the girl, and am resolved to try her.'

Black George now repaired to his wife, on whose prudent counsel he depended to extricate him out of this dilemma; but when he came thither he found his house in some confusion. So great envy had this sack occasioned, that when Mr Allworthy and the other gentry were gone from church, the rage, which had hitherto been confined, burst into an uproar; and, having vented itself at first in opprobrious words, laughs, hisses, and gestures, betook itself at last to certain missile weapons.

Molly, having endeavoured in vain to make a handsome retreat, faced about; and laying hold of ragged Bess, who advanced in the front of the enemy, she at one blow felled her to the ground. The whole army of the enemy (though near a hundred in number), seeing the fate of their general, gave back many paces, and retired behind a new-dug grave. But Goody Brown stopt short, and, calling aloud to all who fled, spoke as follows: 'Ye Somersetshire men, or rather ye Somersetshire women, are ye not ashamed thus to fly from a single woman? But if not other will oppose her, I myself and Joan Top here will have the honour of the victory.' Having thus said, she flew at Molly Seagrim, clawing off her cap from her head. Then laying hold of the hair of Molly with her left hand, she attacked her so furiously in the face with the right, that the blood soon began to trickle from her nose. Molly was not idle this while. She soon removed the clout from the head of Goody Brown, and then fastening on her hair with one hand, with the other she caused another bloody stream to issue forth from the nostrils of the enemy.

When each of the combatants had borne off sufficient spoils of hair from the head of her antagonist, the next rage was against the garments. In this attack they exerted so much violence, that in a very few minutes they were both naked to the middle.

The lucky arrival of Tom Jones at this instant put an immediate end to the bloody scene.

Master Blifil, who rode first, seeing such a mob assembled, and two women in the posture in which we left the combatants, stopt

47

his horse to inquire what was the matter. A country fellow, scratching his head, answered him: 'I don't know, measter, un't I; an't please your honour, here hath been a vight, I think, between Goody Brown and Moll Seagrim.'

'Who, who?' cries Tom; but without waiting for an answer, having discovered the features of his Molly through all the discomposure in which they now were, he hastily alighted, turned his horse loose, and, leaping over the wall, ran to her. She now first bursting into tears, told him how barbarously she had been treated. Tom raved like a madman, beat his breast, tore his hair, stamped on the ground, and vowed the utmost vengeance on all who had been concerned. He then pulled off his coat, and buttoned it round her, put his hat upon her head, wiped the blood from her face as well as he could with his handkerchief, and called out to the servant to ride as fast as possible for a side-saddle, or a pillion, that he might carry her safe home.

Master Blifil objected to the sending away the servant, as they had only one with them; but as Square seconded the order of Jones, he was obliged to comply.

The servant returned in a very short time with the pillion, and Molly, having collected her rags as well as she could, was placed behind him. In which manner she was carried home. Square, Blifil, and Jones attending.

Here Jones having received his coat, given her a sly kiss, and whispered her, that he would return in the evening, quitted his Molly, and rode on after his companions.

Molly had no sooner apparelled herself in her accustomed rags, than her sisters began to fall violently upon her. 'You'd better have minded what the parson says,' cries the eldest, 'and not a harkened after men voke.'—'Indeed, child, and so she had,' says the mother, sobbing; 'she hath brought a disgrace upon us all. She's the vurst of the vamily that ever was a whore.'

'You need not upbraid me with that, mother,' cried Molly; 'you yourself was brought-to-bed of sister there, within a week after you was married.'

'Yes, hussy,' answered the enraged mother, 'so I was, and what was the mighty matter of that? I was made an honest woman then; and if you was to be made an honest woman, I should not be angry; but you must have to doing with a gentleman, you nasty slut; you will have a bastard, hussy, you will; and that I defy any one to say of me.'

In this situation Black George found his family, when he acquainted the company with what Sophia had said to him.

Goody Seagrim then began to revile her daughter afresh. 'Here,' says she, 'you have brought us into a fine quandary indeed. What will madam say to that big belly? Oh, that ever I should live to see this day!'

Molly answered with great spirit, 'And what is this mighty place which you have got for me, father? I suppose it is to be under the cook; but I shan't wash dishes for anybody. My gentleman will provide better for me. See what he hath given me this afternoon.' And so saying, she pulled out several guineas, and gave her mother one of them.

The good woman no sooner felt the gold within her palm, than her temper began to be mollified, and the whole family were soon reduced to a state of perfect quiet.

CHAPTER ELEVEN

THE NARROW ESCAPE OF MOLLY SEAGRIM

TOM JONES had ridden one of Mr Western's horses that morning in the chase; so that having no horse of his own in the squire's stable, he was obliged to go home on foot. Just as he arrived at Mr Allworthy's outward gate, he met the constable and company with Molly in their possession, whom they were conducting to that house of correction where the inferior sort of people may learn one good lesson, viz. respect and deference to their superiors.

Tom was no sooner informed by the constable whither they were proceeding than he caught Molly in his arms, and embracing her tenderly before them all, swore he would murder the first man who offered to lay hold of her. He bid her dry her eyes and be comforted; for, wherever she went, he would accompany her. Then turning to the constable, who stood trembling with his hat off, he desired him, in a very mild voice, to return with him for a moment only to his father (for so he now called Allworthy).

The constable, who, I make no doubt, would have surrendered his prisoner had Tom demanded her, very readily consented to this request. So back they all went into Mr Allworthy's hall, where Tom desired them to stay till his return, and then went himself in pursuit of the good man. As soon as he was found, Tom threw himself at his feet, and having begged a patient hearing, confessed himself to be the father of the child of which Molly was then big. He entreated him to have compassion on the poor girl, and to consider, if there was any guilt in the case, it lay principally at his door.

'If there is any guilt in the case!' answered Allworthy warmly.

'Are you then so profligate and abandoned a libertine to doubt whether the breaking the laws of God and man, the corrupting and ruining a poor girl be guilt?'

'Whatever may be my fate,' says Tom, 'let me succeed in my intercessions for the poor girl. I confess I have corrupted her! but whether she shall be ruined, depends on you. For Heaven's sake, sir, revoke your warrant, and do not send her to a place which must unavoidably prove her destruction.'

Allworthy hesitated some time, and at last said, 'Well, I will discharge my mittimus.—You may send the constable to me.' He was instantly called, discharged, and so was the girl.

It will be believed that Mr Allworthy failed not to read Tom a very severe lecture on this occasion; but it is unnecessary to insert it here, as we have faithfully transcribed what he said to Jenny Jones.

While he was angry with the incontinence of Jones, he was no less pleased with the honour and honesty of his self-accusation. He began now to form in his mind the same opinion of this young fellow, which, we hope, our reader may have conceived. And in balancing his faults with his perfections, the latter seemed rather to preponderate.

The reader will be pleased, I believe, to return with me to Sophia. She passed the night in no very agreeable manner. Sleep befriended her but little, and dreams less. In the morning, when Mrs Honour, her maid, attended her at the usual hour, she was found already up and drest.

Persons who live two or three miles' distance in the country are considered as next-door neighbours, and transactions at the one house fly with incredible celerity to the other. Mrs Honour, therefore, had heard the whole story of Molly's shame; which she, being of a very communicative temper, had no sooner entered the apartment of her mistress, than she began to relate in the following manner:

'La, ma'am, what doth your la'ship think? The girl that your la'ship saw at church on Sunday, whom you thought so handsome; though you would not have thought her so handsome neither, if you had seen her nearer, but to be sure she hath been carried before the justice for being big with child. She seemed to me to look like a confident slut: and to be sure she hath laid the child to young Mr Jones. And all the parish says Mr Allworthy is so angry with young Mr Jones, that he won't see him. To be sure, one can't help pitying the poor young man, and nobody can deny but that Mr Jones is one of the most handsomest young men that ever——'

She was running on thus, when Sophia, with a more peevish voice than she had ever spoken to her in before, cried, 'Prithee, why dost thou trouble me with all this stuff? What concern have

I in what Mr Jones doth? Stop thy torrent of impertinence, and see whether my father wants me at breakfast.'

Mrs Honour then flung out of the room, muttering much to herself, of which 'Marry come up, I assure you,' was all that could be plainly distinguished.

The reader will be pleased to recollect, that a secret affection of Mr Jones had insensibly stolen into the bosom of this young lady. That it had there grown to a pretty great height before she herself had discovered it. When she first began to perceive its symptoms, the sensations were so sweet and pleasing, that she had not resolution sufficient to check or repel them; and thus she went on cherishing a passion of which she never once considered the consequences.

This incident relating to Molly first opened her eyes. She now first perceived the weakness of which she had been guilty; and though it caused the utmost perturbation in her mind, yet it had the effect of other nauseous physic, and for the time expelled her distemper.

That passion which had formerly been so exquisitely delicious, became now a scorpion in her bosom. She resolved therefore to avoid Tom Jones as much as possible; for which purpose she began to conceive a design of visiting her aunt, to which she made no doubt of obtaining her father's consent.

Mr Western grew every day fonder and fonder of Sophia, insomuch that his beloved dogs themselves almost gave place to her in his affections; but as he could not prevail on himself to abandon these, he contrived very cunningly to enjoy their company, together with that of his daughter, by insisting on her riding a hunting with him.

Sophia, to whom her father's word was a law, readily complied with his desires, though she had not the least delight in a sport, which was of too rough and masculine a nature to suit with her disposition.

The strongest objection was that which would have formerly been an inducement to her, namely the frequent meeting with young Jones, whom she had determined to avoid; but as the end of the hunting season now approached, she hoped, by a short absence with her aunt, to reason herself entirely out of her unfortunate passion.

On the second day of her hunting, as she was returning from the chase, and was arrived within a little distance from Mr Western's house, her horse, whose mettlesome spirit required a better rider, fell suddenly to prancing and capering in such a manner that she was in the most imminent peril of falling. Tom Jones, who was at a little distance behind, saw this, and immediately galloped up to her assistance. The unruly beast presently reared himself on his hind legs, and threw his lovely burthen from his back, and Jones caught her in his arms.

She soon after recovered her spirits, assured him she was safe, and thanked him for the care he had taken of her. Jones answered, 'If I have preserved you, madam, I am sufficiently repaid; for I promise you, I would have secured you from the least harm at the expense of a much greater misfortune to myself than I have suffered on this occasion.'

'What misfortune?' replied Sophia eagerly. 'I hope you have come to no mischief?'

'Be not concerned, madam,' answered Jones. 'Heaven be praised you have escaped so well, considering the danger you was in. If I have broke my arm, I consider it as a trifle, in comparison of what I feared upon your account.'

Sophia then screamed out, 'Broke your arm! Heaven forbid.'

'I am afraid I have, madam,' says Jones, 'but I beg you will suffer me first to take care of you. I have a right hand yet at your service, to help you into the next field, whence we have but a very little walk to your father's house.'

Sophia seeing his left arm dangling by his side, while he was using the other to lead her, no longer doubted of the truth. She now grew much paler than her fears for herself had made her before.

When they arrived at Mr Western's hall, Sophia, who had tottered along with much difficulty, sunk down in her chair; but by the assistance of hartshorn and water, she was prevented from fainting away, and had pretty well recovered her spirits.

Jones was then ordered into a bed, which Mr Western compelled him to accept at his own house, and sentence of water-gruel was passed upon him.

Mrs Honour was summoned to her mistress and when asked by her how the young gentleman did, presently launched into extravagant praises on the magnanimity, as she called it, of his behaviour, which, she said, 'was so charming in so pretty a creature.' She then burst forth into much warmer encomiums on the beauty of his person.

Mrs Honour was so entirely wrapped up in the subject on which she exercised her tongue that she gave her mistress time to conquer her confusion; which having done, she smiled on her maid, and told her, 'she was certainly in love with this young fellow.'—'I in love, madam!' answers she; 'upon my word, ma'am, I assure you, ma'am, upon my soul, ma'am, I am not.'—'Why, if you was,' cries her mistress, 'I see no reason that you should be ashamed of it; for he is certainly a pretty fellow.'—'Yes, ma'am,' answered the other, 'that he is, the most handsomest man I ever saw in my life; and, says I, one of the sweetest temperedest, best naturedest men in the world he is; and, says I, all the servants and neighbours all round the country loves him. And, to be sure, I could tell your ladyship something, but that I am afraid it would offend you.'—'What could you tell me, Honour?' says Sophia. 'I will know it this instant.'—'Why, ma'am,' answered Mrs Honour, 'he came into the room one day last week when I was at work, and there lay your ladyship's muff on a chair, and to be sure he put his hands into it; that very muff your ladyship gave me but yesterday. La! says I, Mr Jones, you will stretch my lady's muff, and spoil it: but he still kept his hands in it: and then he kissed it—to be sure I hardly ever saw such a kiss in my life as he gave it.'

Till something of a more beautiful red than vermilion be found out, I shall say nothing of Sophia's colour on this occasion. 'Ho—nour,' says she, 'I—if you will not mention this any more to me—nor to anybody else, I will not betray you—I mean, I will not be angry; but I am afraid of your tongue. Why, my girl, will you give it such liberties?'—'Nay, ma'am,' answered she, 'to be sure, I would sooner cut out my tongue than offend your ladyship. I am sure I would live and die with your ladyship; for, as poor Mr Jones said, happy is the man——'

Here the dinner bell interrupted a conversation which wrought such an effect on Sophia, that I shall not attempt to describe it, from despair of success.

CHAPTER TWELVE

IN WHICH MR JONES RECEIVES MANY FRIENDLY VISITS DURING HIS CONFINEMENT

TOM JONES had many visitors during his confinement, though some, perhaps, were not very agreeable to him. Mr Allworthy saw him almost every day; but though he pitied Tom's sufferings, and greatly approved the gallant behaviour which had occasioned them, he took occasion to remind him of his former miscarriages, but in the mildest and tenderest manner.

Thwackum was likewise pretty assiduous in his visits; and he too considered a sick-bed to be a convenient scene for lectures. His style, however, was more severe than Mr Allworthy's: he told his pupil, 'That he ought to look on his broken limb as a judgment from heaven on his sins.'

Square talked in a very different strain; he said, 'Such accidents as a broken bone were below the consideration of a wise man. That it was abundantly sufficient to reconcile the mind of any of these mischances, to reflect that they are liable to befall the wisest of mankind, and are undoubtedly for the good of the whole.'

Mr Blifil visited his friend Jones but seldom, and never alone. This worthy young man, however, professed much regard for him, and as great concern at his misfortune; but cautiously avoided any intimacy, lest, as he frequently hinted, it might contaminate the sobriety of his own character.

As to Squire Western, he was seldom out of the sick-room, unless when he was engaged either in the field or over his bottle. Nay, he would sometimes retire hither to take his beer, and it was not without difficulty that he was prevented from forcing Jones to take his beer too: for no quack ever held his nostrum to be a more general panacea than he did this; which, he said, had more virtue in it than was in all the physic in an apothecary's shop. He was, however, by much entreaty, prevailed on to forbear the application of this medicine; but from serenading his patient every hunting morning with the horn under his window, it was impossible to withhold him; nor did he ever lay aside that hallow, with which he entered into all companies, which he visited Jones, without any regard to the sick person's being at that time either awake or asleep.

Among other visitants, who paid their compliments to the young gentleman in his confinement, Mrs Honour came into his room, and finding him alone, began in the following manner: 'La, sir, where do you think I have been? I warrants you, you would not guess in fifty years. Nay, I don't see why it should be kept a secret for my part; for to be sure she is the best lady in the world.' Upon this, Jones began to beg earnestly to be let into this secret, and faithfully promised not to divulge it. She then proceeded thus: 'Why, you must know, sir, my young lady sent me to inquire after Molly Seagrim, and to see whether the wench wanted anything; my lady bid me go and carry her some linen, and other things. She is too good. If such forward sluts were sent to Bridewell, it would be better for them. I told my lady, says I, madam, your la'ship is encouraging idleness.'—'And was my Sophia so good?' says Jones. 'My Sophia! I assure you, marry come up,' answered Honour. 'And yet if you knew all—indeed, if I was as Mr Jones, I should look a little higher than such trumpery as Molly Seagrim.'—'What do you mean by these words,' replied Jones,—'I mean what I mean,' says Honour. 'Don't you remember putting your hands in my lady's muff once? Then to be sure, my lady gave me that muff; and afterwards, upon hearing what you had done——'—'Then you told her what I had done?' interrupted Jones. 'If I did, sir,' answered she, 'you need not be angry with me. About a day or two after I had told her the story, she quarrels with her new muff, and to be sure it is the prettiest that ever was seen. Honour, says she, this is an odious muff; it is too big for me, I can't wear it: till I can get another, you must let me have my old one again, and you may have this in the room on 't—for she's a good lady, and scorns to give a thing and take a thing, I promise you that. So to be sure I fetched it her back again, and, I believe, she hath worn it upon her arm almost ever since, and I warrants hath given it many a kiss when nobody hath seen her.'

Here the conversation was interrupted by Mr Western himself, who came to summon Jones to the harpsichord; whither the poor young fellow went all pale and trembling.

Sophia looked this evening with more than usual beauty, and we may believe it was no small addition to her charms, in the eye of Mr Jones, that she now happened to have on her right arm this very muff.

She was playing one of her father's favourite tunes, and he was leaning on her chair, when the muff fell over her fingers, and put her out. This so disconcerted the squire, that he snatched the muff from her, and with a hearty curse threw it into the fire. Sophia instantly started up, and with the utmost eagerness recovered it from the flames.

The citadel of Jones was now taken by surprise. All those considerations of honour and prudence which our hero had lately with so much military wisdom placed as guards over the avenues of his heart, ran away from their posts, and the god of love marched in, in triumph.

But though this victorious deity easily expelled his avowed enemies from the heart of Jones, the concern for what must become of poor Molly greatly disturbed and perplexed the mind of the worthy youth. The superior merit of Sophia totally eclipsed, or rather extinguished, all the beauties of the poor girl; but compassion instead of contempt succeeded to love. He was convinced the girl had placed all her affections, and all her prospect of future happiness, in him only.

At length it occurred to him, that he might possibly be able to make Molly amends another way; namely, by giving her a sum of money.

One day, accordingly, when his arm was so well recovered that he could walk easily with it slung in a sash, he stole forth, at a season when the squire was engaged in his field exercises, and visited his fair one. Her mother and sisters, whom he found taking their tea, informed him first that Molly was not at home; but afterwards the eldest sister acquainted him, with a malicious smile, that she was above stairs a-bed. Tom had no objection to this situation of his mistress, and immediately ascended the ladder which led towards her bed-chamber; but when he came to the top, he, to his great surprise, found the door fast; nor could he for some time obtain any answer, from within; but after the first transports of their meeting were over, Molly, bursting into a flood of tears, began to unbraid him in the following words: 'And this is your love for me, to forsake me in this manner, now you have ruined me! All other men are nothing to me. If the greatest squire in all the country would come a suiting to me to-morrow, I would not give my company to him. No, I shall always hate and despise the whole sex for your sake——'

She was proceeding thus, when an accident put a stop to her tongue, before it had run out half its career. The room, or rather garret, in which Molly lay, being up one pair of stairs, was of a sloping figure; so it was impossible to stand upright anywhere but in the middle. Now, as this room wanted the conveniency of a closet, Molly had, to supply that defect, nailed up an old rug against the rafters of the house, which enclosed a little hole where her best apparel was hung up and secured from the dust.

Now, whether Molly, in the agonies of her rage, pushed this rug with her feet; or Jones might touch it; or whether the pin or nail gave way of its own accord, I am not certain; but as Molly pronounced those last words, the wicked rug got loose from its fastening, and discovered everything hid behind it; where among other female utensils appeared—with shame I write it, and with sorrow will it be read—the philosopher Square, in a posture (for the place would not near admit his standing upright) as ridiculous as can possibly be conceived.

He had a nightcap belonging to Molly on his head, and his two large eyes, the moment the rug fell, stared directly at Jones; so that when the idea of philosophy was added to the figure now discovered, it would have been very difficult for any spectator to have refrained from immoderate laughter.

Mr Square happened to be at church on that Sunday, when the appearance of Molly in her sack had caused all that disturbance. Here he first observed her, and was so pleased with her beauty, that he prevailed with the young gentlemen to change their intended ride that evening, that he might pass by the habitation of Molly, and by that means might obtain a second chance of seeing her.

Among other particulars which constituted the unfitness of things in Mr Square's opinion, danger and difficulty were two. The difficulty which he apprehended there might be in corrupting this young wench, and the danger which would accrue to his character on the discovery, were such strong dissuasives, that it is probable he at first intended to have contented himself with the pleasing ideas which the sight of beauty furnishes us with.

But when the philosopher heard, a day or two afterwards, that the fortress of virtue had already been subdued, he began to give a larger scope to his desires. His appetite was not of that squeamish kind which cannot feed on a dainty because another hath tasted it. In short, he liked the girl the better for the want of that chastity, which, if she had possessed it, must have been a bar to his pleasures; he pursued and obtained her.

The reader will be mistaken, if he thinks Molly gave Square the preference to her younger lover: on the contrary, had she been confined to the choice of one only, Tom Jones would undoubtedly have been, of the two, the victorious person. Nor was it solely the consideration that two are better than one (though this had its proper weight) to which Mr Square owed his success: the absence of Jones during his confinement was an unlucky circumstance; and in that interval some well-chosen presents from the philosopher so softened and unguarded the girl's heart, that a favourable opportunity became irresistible, and Square triumphed over the poor remains of virtue which subsisted in the bosom of Molly.

It was now about a fortnight since this conquest, when Jones paid the above-mentioned visit to his mistress, at a time when she and Square were in bed together. This was the true reason why the mother denied her as we have seen; for as the old woman shared in the profits arising from the iniquity of her daughter, she encouraged and protected her in it to the utmost of her power; but such was the envy and hatred which the elder sister bore towards Molly, that she had acquainted Jones with her being above-stairs in bed, in hopes that he might have caught her in Square's arms.

Square no sooner made his appearance than Molly flung herself back in her bed, cried out she was undone, and abandoned herself to despair. This poor girl, who was yet but a novice in her business, had not arrived to that perfection of assurance which helps off a town lady in any extremity. As to the gentleman behind the arras, he was not in much less consternation. He stood for a while motionless, and seemed equally at a loss what to say, or whither to direct his eyes. Jones, though perhaps the most astonished of the three, first found his tongue; and immediately burst into a loud laughter, and then saluting Mr Square, advanced to take him by the hand.

'Well,' cries Jones, 'it shall be your own fault, if you ever hear any more of this adventure. Behave kindly to the girl, and I will never open my lips concerning the matter to any one. And, Molly, do you be faithful to your friend, and I will not only forgive your infidelity to me, but will do you all the service I can.' So saying, he took a hasty leave, and, slipping down the ladder, retired with much expedition.

As for Molly, being recovered from her confusion, she began

at first to upbraid Square with having been the occasion of her loss of Jones; but that gentleman soon found the means of mitigating her anger, partly by caresses, and partly by a small nostrum from his purse, of wonderful and approved efficacy in purging off the ill humours of the mind, and in restoring it to a good temper.

She then poured forth a vast profusion of tenderness towards her new lover; turned all she had said to Jones, and Jones himself, into ridicule; and vowed, though he once had the possession of her person, that none but Square had ever been master of her heart.

CHAPTER THIRTEEN

MR ALLWORTHY ON A SICK BED

MR ALLWORTHY had been for some days indisposed with a cold, which had been attended with a little fever. This he had, however, neglected; as it was usual with him to do all manner of disorders which did not confine him to his bed, or prevent his several faculties from performing their ordinary functions.

Mr Allworthy's distemper, by means of this neglect, gained such ground, that, when the increase of his fever obliged him to send for assistance, the doctor at his first arrival shook his head, wished he had been sent for sooner, and intimated that he thought him in very imminent danger. Mr Allworthy, who had settled all his affairs in this world, and was as well prepared as it is possible for human nature to be for the other, received this information with the utmost calmness and unconcern.

The good man gave immediate orders for all his family to be summoned round him. None of these were then abroad, but Mrs Blifil, who had been some time in London, and Mr Jones.

The news of Mr Allworthy's danger (for the servant told him he was dying) drove all thoughts of love out of his head.

And now the whole family, namely, Mr Blifil, Mr Jones, Mr Thwackum, Mr Square, and some of the servants (for such were Mr Allworthy's orders), being all assembled round his bed, the good man sat up in it, and was beginning to speak, when Blifil fell to blubbering, and began to express very loud and bitter lamentations. Upon this Mr Allworthy shook him by the hand, and said, 'Do not sorrow thus, my dear nephew, at the most ordinary of all human occurrences. When misfortunes befall our friends we are justly grieved; for those are accidents which might often have been avoided, and which may seem to render the lot of one man more peculiarly unhappy than that of others; but death is certainly unavoidable, and is that common lot in which alone the fortunes of all men agree; nor is the time when this happens to us very material.

'My physician having acquainted me (which I take very kindly of him) that I am in danger of leaving you all very shortly, I have determined to say a few words to you at this our parting, before my distemper, which I find grows very fast upon me, puts it out of my power.

'But I shall waste my strength too much. I intended to speak concerning my will, which, though I have settled long ago, I think proper to mention such heads of it as concern any of you, that I may have the comfort of perceiving you are all satisfied with the provision I have there made for you.

'Nephew Blifil, I leave you the heir to my whole estate, except only £500 a-year, which is to revert to you after the death of your mother, and except one other estate of £500 a-year, which I have bestowed in the following manner:

'The estate of £500 a-year I have given to you, Mr Jones: and as I know the inconvenience which attends the want of ready money, I have added £1000 in specie.'

Jones flung himself at his benefactor's feet, and taking eagerly hold of his hand, assured him his goodness to him, both now and all other times, had so infinitely exceeded not only his merit but his hopes, that no words could express his sense of it.

Allworthy then gently squeezed his hand, and proceeded thus: 'I am convinced, my child, that you have much goodness, generosity, and honour, in your temper.

'I find myself growing faint, so I shall refer you to my will for my disposition of the residue. My servants will there find some tokens to remember me by; and there are a few charities which, I trust, my executors will see faithfully performed. Bless you all. I am setting out a little before you——'

Here a footman came hastily into the room, and said there was an attorney from Salisbury who had a particular message, which he said he must communicate to Mr Allworthy himself: that he seemed in a violent hurry, and protested he had so much business to do, that, if he could cut himself into four quarters, all would not be sufficient.

'Go, child,' said Allworthy to Blifil, 'see what the gentleman wants. I am not able to do any business now, nor can he have any with me, in which you are not at present more concerned than myself. Besides, I really am—I am incapable of seeing any one at present, or of any longer attention.' He then saluted them all, saying, perhaps he should be able to see them again, but he should be now glad to compose himself a little, finding that he had too much exhausted his spirits in discourse.

The physician now arrived, and began to inquire how we all did above-stairs? 'In a miserable way,' answered Thwackum. 'It is no more than I expected,' cries the doctor. 'But pray what symptoms have appeared since I left you?'—'No good ones, I am afraid,' replied Thwackum. Then Mr Blifil came to them with a most melancholy countenance, and acquainted them that he brought sad news, that his mother was dead at Salisbury; that she had been seized on the road home with the gout in her head and stomach, which had carried her off in a few hours. 'Good-lack-a-day!' says the doctor. 'One cannot answer for events; but I wish I had been at hand, to have been called in. The gout is a distemper which it is difficult to treat; yet I have been remarkably successful in it.' Thwackum and Square both condoled with Mr Blifil for the loss of his mother, which the one advised him to bear like a man, and the other like a Christian.

It was now debated whether Mr Allworthy should be informed of the death of his sister. This the doctor violently opposed; in which, I believe, the whole college would agree with him: but Mr Blifil said, he had received such positive and repeated orders from his uncle, never to keep any secret from him for fear of the disquietude which it might give him, that he durst not think of disobedience, whatever might be the consequence. He was therefore resolved to communicate it to him: for if his uncle recovered (as he heartily prayed he might) he knew he would never forgive an endeavour to keep a secret of this kind from him.

The physician was forced to submit to these resolutions, which the two other learned gentlemen very highly commended. So together moved Mr Blifil and the doctor toward the sickroom; where the physician first entered, and approached the bed, in order to feel his patient's pulse, which he had no sooner done, than he declared he was much better; that the last application had succeeded to a miracle, and had brought the fever to intermit: so that, he said, there appeared now to be as little danger as he had before apprehended there were hopes.

Mr Allworthy had no sooner lifted up his eyes, and thanked Heaven for these hopes of his recovery, than Mr Blifil drew near, with a very dejected aspect, and having applied his handkerchief to his eyes, he communicated to his uncle what the reader hath been just before acquainted with.

When he first heard Blifil tell his uncle this story, Jones could hardly contain the wrath which kindled in him at the other's indiscretion, especially as the doctor shook his head, and declared his unwillingness to have the matter mentioned to his patient. But as his passion did not so far deprive him of all use of his understanding, he suffered his anger to die in his own bosom, without ever mentioning it to Blifil.

The physician dined that day at Mr Allworthy's; and having after dinner visited his patient, he returned to the company, and told them, that he had now the satisfaction to say, with assurance, that his patient was out of all danger: that he had brought his fever to a perfect intermission, and doubted not to prevent its return.

This account so pleased Jones, and threw him into such immoderate excess of rapture, that he might be truly said to be drunk with joy.

It was now a pleasant evening in the latter end of June, when our hero was walking in a most delicious grove, where the gentle breezes fanning the leaves, together with the sweet trilling of a murmuring stream, and the melodious notes of nightingales, formed altogether the most enchanting harmony. In this scene, so sweetly accommodated to love, he meditated on his dear Sophia. While his wanton fancy roamed unbounded over all her beauties, he started up, and beheld—not his Sophia—no; without a gown, in a shift that was somewhat of the coarsest, and none of the cleanest, with a pitchfork in her hand, Molly Seagrim approached.

Here ensued a parley, which lasted a full quarter of an hour, at the conclusion of which they retired into the thickest part of the grove.

No sooner had our hero retired with his Dido, but Thwackum and the young squire, who were taking a serious walk, arrived at the stile which leads into the grove.

Blifil knew Jones very well, though he was at above a hundred yards' distance, and he was as positive to the sex of his companion, though not to the individual person. He started, blessed himself, and uttered a very solemn ejaculation.

Thwackum expressed some surprize at these sudden emotions, and asked the reason of them. To which Blifil answered, 'He was certain he had seen a fellow and wench retire together among the bushes, which he doubted not was with some wicked purpose.' As to the name of Jones, he thought proper to conceal it.

The parson, who was not only strictly chaste in his own person, but a great enemy to the opposite vice in all others, desired Mr Blifil to conduct him immediately to the place, which as he approached he breathed forth vengeance mixed with lamentations.

The way through which our hunters were to pass in pursuit of their game was so beset with briars, that it caused such a rustling, that Jones had sufficient warning of their arrival before they could surprize him. And now Thwackum, having first darted some livid lightning from his fiery eyes, began to thunder forth,

'Fie upon it! Fie upon it! Mr Jones. Is it possible you should be the person?'—'You see,' answered Jones, 'it is possible I should be here.'—'And who,' said Thwackum, 'is that wicked slut with you?'—'If I have any wicked slut with me,' cries Jones, 'it is possible I shall not let you know who she is.' 'Then I must tell you plainly,' said Thwackum, 'I am resolved to discover the wicked wretch.'—'And I must tell you plainly,' returned Jones, 'I am resolved you shall not.' Thwackum then offered to advance, and Jones laid hold of his arms; which Mr Blifil endeavoured to rescue, declaring, 'he would not see his old master insulted.'

Jones now finding himself engaged with two, thought it necessary to rid himself of one of his antagonists as soon as possible. He therefore applied to the weakest first; and, letting the parson go, he directed a blow at the young squire's breast, which luckily reduced him to measure his length on the ground.

Thwackum had been a champion in his youth, and collecting all his force, attacked Jones in the front.

Many lusty blows were given on both sides: at last a violent fall, in which Jones had thrown his knees into Thwackum's breast, so weakened the latter, that victory had been no longer dubious, had not Blifil, who had now recovered his strength, again renewed the fight.

The victory was like to be decided by numbers, when, on a sudden, a fourth pair of fists appeared in the battle, and immediately paid their compliments to the parson; and the owner of them at the same time crying out, 'Are not you ashamed, and be d—n'd to you, to fall two of you upon one?'

The battle, which was of the kind that for distinction's sake is called royal, now raged with the utmost violence during a few minutes; till Blifil being a second time laid sprawling by Jones, Thwackum condescended to apply for quarter to his new antagonist, who was now found to be Mr Western himself; for in the heat of the action none of the combatants had recognized him.

The rest of Mr Western's company were now come up, being Mrs Western, the aunt of Sophia and the lovely Sophia herself.

At this time, the following was the aspect of the bloody field. In one place lay on the ground, all pale, and almost breathless, the vanquished Blifil. Near him stood the conqueror Jones, almost covered with blood, part of which was naturally his own, and part had been lately the property of the Reverend Mr Thwackum. In a third place stood the said Thwackum, sullenly submitting to the conqueror. The last figure in the piece was Western the Great, most gloriously forbearing the vanquished foe.

Now a more melancholy and a more lovely object lay motionless. This was no other than the charming Sophia herself, who, from the sight of blood, or from fear for her father, or from some other reason, had fallen down in a swoon, before any one could get to her assistance.

Mrs Western first saw her and screamed. Immediately two or three voices cried out, 'Miss Western is dead.' Hartshorn, water, every remedy was called for, almost at one and the same instant.

Jones was rubbing Blifil's temples, for he began to fear he had given him a blow too much, when the words, Miss Western and Dead, rushed at once on his ear. He started up, left Blifil to his fate, and flew to Sophia, whom he caught up in his arms, and then ran away with her over the field to the rivulet where, plunging himself into the water, he contrived to be-sprinkle her face, head, and neck very plentifully.

The tragical scene was now converted into a sudden scene of joy. In this our hero was certainly the principal character; for as he probably felt more ecstatic delight in having saved Sophia than she herself received from being saved, so neither were the congratulations paid to her equal to what were conferred on Jones, especially by Mr Western himself, who, after having once or twice embraced his daughter, fell to hugging and kissing Jones. He called him the preserver of Sophia, and declared there was nothing, except her, or his estate, which he would not give him; but upon recollection, he afterwards excepted his fox-hounds, the Chevalier, and Miss Slouch (for so he called his favourite mare).

All fears for Sophia being now removed, Jones became the object of the squire's consideration.—'Come, my lad,' says Western, 'd'off thy quoat and wash thy feace; for att in a devilish pickle I promise thee. Come, come, wash thyself, and shat go huome with me; and we'l zee to vind thee another quoat.'

The company now moved backwards, and soon arrived where Thwackum had got Mr Blifil again on his legs.

Western began now to inquire into the original rise of this quarrel. To which neither Blifil nor Jones gave any answer; but Thwackum said surlily, 'I believe the cause is not far off; if you beat the bushes well you may find her.'—'Find her?' replied Western. 'What! have you been fighting for a wench?'—'Ask the gentleman in his waistcoat there,' said Thwackum; 'he best knows.'—'Nay then,' cries Western, 'it is a wench certainly. Ah, Tom, Tom, thou art a liquorish dog. But come, gentlemen, be all friends, and go home with me, and make final peace over a bottle.'

Sophia now desired her father to return home; saying she found herself very faint, and apprehended a relapse. The squire immediately complied with his daughter's request (for he was the fondest of parents). He earnestly endeavoured to prevail with the whole company to go and sup with him: but Blifil and Thwackum absolutely refused; the former saying, there were more reasons than he could then mention, why he must decline this honour; and the latter declaring (perhaps rightly) that it was not proper for a person of his function to be seen at any place in his present condition.

Jones was incapable of refusing the pleasure of being with his Sophia; so on he marched with Squire Western and his ladies.

CHAPTER FOURTEEN

THE CHARACTER OF MRS WESTERN. HER GREAT LEARNING AND
KNOWLEDGE OF THE WORLD

SOPHIA retained some gravity of countenance the next morning at breakfast; whence she retired likewise earlier than usual, leaving her father and aunt together. The squire took no notice of this change in his daughter's disposition.

Mrs Western had now, as she thought, made a discovery of something in the mind of Sophia. The first hint of this she took from the behaviour of the young lady in the field of battle; and the suspicion which she then conceived, was greatly corroborated by some observations which she had made that evening and the next morning.

Being at length, however, thoroughly satisfied of the truth of her observation, she took an opportunity, one morning, when she was alone with her brother, to interrupt one of his whistles in the following manner:

'Pray, brother, have you not observed something very extraordinary in my niece lately?'—'No, not I,' answered Western; 'is anything the matter with the girl?'—'I think there is,' replied she; 'and something of much consequence too.'—'Why, she doth not complain of anything,' cries Western; 'and she hath had the small-pox.'—'Brother,' returned she, 'you are convinced I know the world, and I promise you I was never more deceived in my life, if my niece be not most desperately in love.'—'How! in love!' cries Western, in a passion; 'in love, without acquainting me! I'll disinherit her; I'll turn her out of doors, stark naked, without a farthing. Is all my kindness vor 'ur, and vondness o'ur come to this, to fall in love without asking me leave?'—'But you will not,' answered Mrs Western, 'turn this daughter, whom you love better than your own soul, out of doors, before you know whether you shall approve her choice. Suppose she should have fixed on the very person whom you yourself would wish, I hope

64

you would not be angry then?'—'No, no,' cries Western, 'that would make a difference. If she marries the man I would ha' her, she may love whom she pleases, I shan't trouble my head about that.'—'That is spoken,' answered the sister, 'like a sensible man. And now, good sir, what think you of Mr Blifil? Did she not faint away on seeing him lie breathless on the ground? Did she not, after he was recovered, turn pale again the moment we came up to that part of the field where he stood? And pray what else should be the occasion of all her melancholy that night at supper, the next morning, and indeed ever since?'—"Fore George!' cries the squire, 'now you mind me on't, I remember it all. It is certainly so, and I am glad on't with all my heart. I knew Sophy was a good girl, and would not fall in love to make me angry. I was never more rejoiced in my life; for nothing can lie so handy together as our two estates. I had this matter in my head some time ago: for certainly the two estates are in a manner joined together in matrimony already, and it would be a thousand pities to part them. Well but, sister, what would you advise me to do; for I tell you women know these matters better than we do?'—'Oh, your humble servant, sir,' answered the lady, 'we are obliged to you for allowing us a capacity in anything. Since you are pleased to ask my advice, I think you may propose the match to Allworthy yourself.' 'Well,' said the squire, 'I will propose it; but I shall certainly lend un a flick, if he should refuse me.'—'Fear not,' cries Mrs Western; 'the match is too advantageous to be refused.'

The squire having settled matters with his sister was so greatly impatient to communicate the proposal to Allworthy, that Mrs Western had the utmost difficulty to prevent him from visiting that gentleman in his sickness, for this purpose.

Mr Allworthy had been engaged to dine with Mr Western at the time when he was taken ill. He was therefore no sooner discharged out of the custody of physic, but he thought (as was usual with him on all occasions, both the highest and the lowest) of fulfilling his engagement.

In the interval between the time of the dialogue just now reported, and this day of public entertainment, Sophia had, from certain obscure hints thrown out by her aunt, collected some apprehension that the sagacious lady suspected her passion for Jones. She now resolved to take this opportunity of wiping out all such suspicions, and for that purpose to put an entire constraint on her behaviour.

First, she endeavoured to conceal a throbbing melancholy heart with the utmost sprightliness in her countenance, and the highest gaiety in her manner. Secondly, she addressed her whole discourse to Mr Blifil, and took not the least notice of poor Jones the whole day.

The squire was so delighted with this conduct of his daughter, that he scarce ate any dinner, and spent almost his whole time in watching opportunities of conveying signs of his approbation by winks and nods to his sister; who was not at first altogether so pleased with what she saw as was her brother.

In short, Sophia so greatly overacted her part, that her aunt was at first staggered, and began to suspect some affection in her niece; but as she was herself a woman of great art, so she soon attributed this to extreme art in Sophia.

Dinner being ended, and the company retired into the garden, Mr Western, who was thoroughly convinced of the certainty of what his sister had told him, took Mr Allworthy aside, and very bluntly proposed a match between Sophia and young Mr Blifil.

Mr Allworthy was not one of those men whose hearts flutter at any unexpected and sudden tidings of worldly profit. He received, therefore, Mr Western's proposal without any visible emotion, or without any alteration of countenance. He said the alliance was such as he sincerely wished; then launched forth into a very just encomium on the young lady's merit; acknowledged the offer to be advantageous in point of fortune; and after thanking Mr Western for the good opinion he had professed of his nephew, concluded, that if the young people liked each other, he should be very desirous to complete the affair.

As soon as Mr Allworthy returned home, he took Mr Blifil apart, and communicated to him the proposal which had been made by Mr Western, and at the same time informed him how agreeable this match would be to himself.

The charms of Sophia had not made the least impression on Blifil; not that his heart was pre-engaged; neither was he totally insensible of beauty, or had any aversion to women; but his appetites were by nature so moderate, that he was able, by philosophy, or by study, or by some other method, easily to subdue them.

But though he was so entirely free from passion, of which the virtues and beauty of Sophia formed so notable an object; yet was he altogether as well furnished with some other passions, that promised themselves very full gratification in the young lady's fortune. Blifil, therefore, after a very short hesitation, answered Mr Allworthy, that matrimony was a subject on which he had not yet thought; but that he was so sensible of his friendly and fatherly care, that he should in all things submit himself to his pleasure.

Allworthy, with Mr Blifil's consent therefore, wrote the next morning to Mr Western, acquainting him that his nephew had very thankfully and gladly received the proposal, and would be ready to wait on the young lady, whenever she should be pleased to accept his visit.

CHAPTER FIFTEEN

WHAT PASSED BETWEEN SOPHIA AND HER AUNT

SOPHIA was in her chamber, reading, when her aunt came in. The moment she saw Mrs Western, she shut the book with so much eagerness, that the good lady could not forbear asking her, What book that was which she seemed so much afraid of showing? 'Well, but show me,' said the aunt, 'what was you reading when I came in; there was something very tender in that, I believe, and very loving too. You blush, my dear Sophia. Ah! child, did you think, because you have been able to impose upon your father, that you could impose upon me? Do you imagine I did not know the reason of your overacting all that friendship for Mr Blifil yesterday? I have seen a little too much of the world, to be so deceived. Nay, nay, do not blush again. I tell you it is a passion you need not be ashamed of. It is a passion I myself approve, and have already brought your father into the approbation of it. And this very afternoon your father hath appointed for you to receive your lover.' 'This afternoon!' cries Sophia. 'Dear aunt, you frighten me out of my senses.'—'O, my dear,' said the aunt, 'you will soon come to yourself again; for he is a charming young fellow, that's the truth on't.'—'Nay, I will own,' says Sophia, 'I know none with such perfections. So brave, and yet so gentle; so witty, yet so inoffensive; so humane, so civil, so genteel, so handsome! What signifies his being base born, when compared with such qualifications as these?'—'Base born? What do you mean?' said the aunt, 'Mr Blifil base born!' Sophia turned instantly pale at this name, and faintly repeated it. Upon which the aunt cried, 'Mr Blifil—ay, Mr Blifil, of whom else have we been talking?'—'Good heavens,' answered Sophia, ready to sink, 'of Mr Jones, I thought; I am sure I know no other who deserves——'—'I protest,' cries the aunt, 'you frighten me in your turn. Is it Mr Jones, and not Mr Blifil, who is the object of your affection?'—'Mr Blifil!' repeated Sophia. 'Sure it is impossible you can be in earnest; if you are, I am the most miserable woman alive.' Mrs Western now stood a few moments silent, while sparks of fiery rage flashed from her eyes. At length, collecting all her force of voice, she thundered forth in the following articulate sounds:

'And is it possible you can think of disgracing your family by allying yourself to a bastard? Can the blood of the Westerns submit to such contamination?'

'Madam,' answered Sophia, trembling, 'what I have said you

67

have extorted from me. I do not remember to have ever mentioned the name of Mr Jones with approbation to any one before; nor should I now had I not conceived he had your approbation. Whatever were my thoughts of that poor, unhappy young man, I intended to have carried them with me to my grave—to that grave where only now, I find, I am to seek repose.' Here she sunk down in her chair, drowned in her tears, and, in all the moving silence of unutterable grief, presented a spectacle which must have affected almost the hardest heart.

Mrs Western stood a moment looking at her, and then, having recollected herself, said, 'That on one consideration only she would keep the secret from her brother; and this was, that Sophia should promise to entertain Mr Blifil that very afternoon as her lover, and to regard him as the person who was to be her husband.'

Poor Sophia was too much in her aunt's power to deny her anything positively; she was obliged to promise that she would see Mr Blifil, and be as civil to him as possible; but begged her aunt that the match might not be hurried on. She said, 'Mr Blifil was by no means agreeable to her, and she hoped her father would be prevailed on not to make her the most wretched of women.'

Mrs Western having obtained that promise from her niece, withdrew; and presently after arrived Mrs Honour. She was at work in a neighbouring apartment, and had been summoned to the keyhole by some vociferation in the preceding dialogue, where she had continued during the remaining part of it. At her entry into the room, she found Sophia standing motionless, with the tears trickling from her eyes. Upon which she immediately ordered a proper quantity of tears into her own eyes, and then began, 'O Gemini, my dear lady, what is the matter?'—'My father,' cries Sophia, 'is going to marry me to a man I both despise and hate.'—'O dear, ma'am,' answered the other, 'who is this wicked man? for to be sure he is very bad, or your la'ship would not despise him.'—'His name is poison to my tongue,' replied Sophia: 'thou wilt know it too soon.' Indeed, to confess the truth, she knew it already, and therefore was not very inquisitive as to that point. She then proceeded thus: 'I don't pretend to give your la'ship advice, whereof your la'ship knows much better than I can pretend to, being but a servant; but, i-fackins! no father in England should marry me against my consent. And, to be sure, the 'squire is so good, that if he did but know your la'ship despises and hates the young man, to be sure he would not desire you to marry him. Poor gentleman! I wishes some misfortune hath not happened to him, for he hath been walking about with his arms across, and looking so melancholy, all this morning: I vow and protest it made me almost cry to see him.'—'To see whom?' says Sophia. 'Poor Mr Jones,' answered Honour. 'See him! why, where did you see him?' cries Sophia. 'By the canal, ma'am,' says Honour. 'There he hath been walking all this morning, and at last there he laid himself down: I believe he lies there still. To be sure, if it had not been for my modesty, being a maid, as I am, I should have gone and spoke to him. Do, ma'am, let me go and see, only for a fancy, whether he is there still.'—'Pugh!' says Sophia. 'There! no, no: what should he do there? He is gone before this time, to be sure. Besides, why—what—why should you go to see? Besides, I want you for something else. Go, fetch me my hat and gloves. I shall walk with my aunt in the grove before dinner.' Honour did immediately as she was bid, and Sophia put her hat on; when, looking in the glass, she fancied the ribbon with which her hat was tied did not become her, and so sent her maid back again for a ribbon of a different colour; and then giving Mrs Honour repeated charges not to leave her work on any account, as she said it was in violent haste, and must be finished that very day, she muttered something more about going to the grove, and then sallied out the contrary way, and walked, as fast as her tender trembling limbs could carry her, directly towards the canal.

Jones had been there as Mrs Honour had told her; he had indeed spent two hours there that morning in melancholy contemplation on his Sophia, and had gone out from the garden at one door the moment she entered it at another.

That afternoon Mr Western, for the first time, acquainted his daughter with his intention; telling her, he knew very well that she had heard it before from her aunt. Sophia looked very grave upon this, nor could she prevent a few pearls from stealing into her eyes. 'Come, come,' says Western, 'none of your maidenish airs; I know all; I assure you sister hath told me all.'

'Is it possible,' says Sophia, 'that my aunt can have betrayed me already?'—'Ay, ay,' says Western; 'betrayed you! ay. Why, you betrayed yourself yesterday at dinner. You showed your fancy very plainly, I think. But you young girls never know what you would be at. Mr Blifil is a brisk young man, and will soon put an end to your squeamishness. Come, cheer up, cheer up; I expect un every minute.'

Sophia was now convinced that her aunt had behaved honourably to her: and she determined to go through that disagreeable afternoon with as much resolution as possible, and without giving the least suspicion in the world to her father.

Mr Blifil soon arrived; and Mr Western soon after withdrawing, left the young couple together.

Here a long silence of near a quarter of an hour ensued; for the gentleman who was to begin the conversation had all the unbecoming modesty which consists in bashfulness. He often attempted to speak, and as often suppressed his words just at the very point of utterance.

He was indeed perfectly well satisfied with his prospect of success; for as to that entire and absolute possession of the heart of his mistress which romantic lovers require, the very idea of it never entered his head. Her fortune and her person were the sole objects of his wishes, of which he made no doubt soon to obtain the absolute property; as Mr Western's mind was so earnestly bent on the match; and as he well knew the strict obedience which Sophia was always ready to pay to her father's will, and the greater still which her father would exact, if there was occasion.

From these reasons, therefore, Mr Blifil saw no bar to his success with Sophia. He concluded her behaviour was like that of all other young ladies on a first visit from a lover, and it had indeed entirely answered his expectations.

Mr Western took care to waylay the lover at his exit from his mistress. He found him so elevated with his success, so enamoured with his daughter, and so satisfied with her reception of him, that the old gentleman began to caper and dance about his hall, and by many other antic actions to express the extravagance of his joy.

As soon as Blifil was departed, which was not till after many hearty kisses and embraces bestowed on him by Western, the good squire went instantly in quest of his daughter, whom he no sooner found than he poured forth the most extravagant raptures, bidding her choose what clothes and jewels she pleased.

Sophia perceiving her father in this fit of affection, thought she should never have a better opportunity of disclosing herself than at present, as far at least as regarded Mr Blifil; and she too well foresaw the necessity which she should soon be under of coming to a full explanation. After having thanked the squire, therefore, for all his professions of kindness, she added, with a look full of inexpressible softness, 'And is it possible my papa can be so good to place all his joy in his Sophy's happiness?' which Western having confirmed by a great oath, and a kiss; she then laid hold of his hand, and, falling on her knees, she begged him 'Oh! sir, not only your poor Sophy's happiness; her very life, her being, depends upon your granting her request. I cannot live with Mr Blifil. To force me into this marriage would be killing me.'— 'You can't live with Mr Blifil?' says Western. 'No, upon my soul I can't,' answered Sophia. 'Then die and be d—d,' cries he, spurning her from him. 'Oh! sir,' cries Sophia, catching hold of the skirt of his coat, 'take pity on me, I beseech you. Don't look and say such cruel—— Can you be unmoved while you see your Sophy in this dreadful condition? Can the best of fathers break my heart? Will he kill me by the most painful, cruel, lingering death?' —'Pooh! pooh!' cries the squire; 'all stuff and nonsense; all maidenish tricks. Kill you, indeed! Will marriage kill you?'— 'Oh! Sir,' answered Sophia, 'such a marriage is worse than death.

He is not even indifferent; I hate and detest him.'—'If you detest un never so much,' cries Western, 'you shall ha'un.' This he bound by an oath too shocking to repeat; and after many violent asseverations, concluded in these words: 'I am resolved upon the match, and unless you consent to it I will not give you a groat, not a single farthing; no, though I saw you expiring with famine in the street, I would not relieve you with a morsel of bread. This is my fixed resolution, and so I leave you to consider on it.' He then broke from her with such violence, that her face dashed against the floor; and he burst directly out of the room, leaving poor Sophia prostrate on the ground.

When Western came into the hall, he there found Jones; who seeing his friend looking wild, pale, and almost breathless, could not forbear inquiring the reason of all these melancholy appearances. Upon which the squire immediately acquainted him with the whole matter, concluding with bitter denunciations against Sophia, and very pathetic lamentations of the misery of all fathers who are so unfortunate to have daughters.

Jones departed instantly in quest of Sophia, whom he found just risen from the ground, where her father had left her, with the tears trickling from her eyes, and the blood running from her lips. He presently ran to her, and with a voice full at once of tenderness and terror, cried, 'O my Sophia, what means this dreadful sight?' She looked softly at him for a moment before she spoke, and then said, 'Mr Jones, for Heaven's sake how came you here? Leave me, I beseech you, this moment.'—'Do not,' says he, 'impose so harsh a command upon me—my heart bleeds faster than those lips. O Sophia, how easily could I drain my veins to preserve one drop of that dear blood.'—'I have too many obligations to you already,' answered she, 'for sure you meant them such.' Here she looked at him tenderly almost a minute, and then bursting into an agony, cried, 'Oh, Mr Jones, why did you save my life? My death would have been happier for us both.'—'Happier for us both!' cried he. 'Could racks or wheels kill me so painfully as Sophia's—I cannot bear the dreadful sound. Do I live but for her?' Both his voice and looks were full of inexpressible tenderness when he spoke these words; and at the same time he laid gently hold on her hand, which she did not withdraw from him; to say the truth, she hardly knew what she did or suffered. A few moments now passed in silence between these lovers, while his eyes were eagerly fixed on Sophia, and hers declining towards the ground: at last she recovered strength enough to desire him again to leave her, for that her certain ruin would be the consequence of their being found together; adding, 'Oh, Mr Jones, you know not, you know not what hath passed this cruel afternoon.'—'I know all, my Sophia,' answered he; 'your cruel father hath told me all, and he himself hath sent me hither to you.'—'My father sent you to me!' replied she; 'sure you dream.'—'Would to Heaven,' cries he, 'it was but a dream! Oh, Sophia, your father hath sent me to you, to be an advocate for my odious rival, to solicit you in his favour. Sure no one ever loved, ever doted like me.' She stood a moment silent, and covered with confusion; then lifting up her eyes gently towards him, she cried, 'What would Mr Jones have me say?'—'O do but promise,' cries he, 'that you never will give yourself to Blifil.'—'Name not,' answered she, 'the detested sound. Be assured I never will give him what is in my power to withhold from him.'—'I fear no destruction,' cries he, 'but the loss of Sophia. If you would save me from the most bitter agonies, recall that cruel sentence. Indeed, I can never part with you, indeed I cannot.'

The lovers now stood both silent and trembling, Sophia being unable to withdraw her hand from Jones, and he almost as unable to hold it; the scene was interrupted by one of a different nature.

Soon after Jones had left Mr Western, his sister came to him, and was presently informed of all that had passed between her brother and Sophia relating to Blifil.

This behaviour in her niece the good lady construed to be an absolute breach of the condition on which she had engaged to keep her love for Mr Jones a secret. She considered herself, therefore, at full liberty to reveal all she knew to the squire, which she immediately did in the most explicit terms.

The idea of a marriage between Jones and his daughter, had never once entered into the squire's head, either in the warmest minutes of his affection towards that young man, or from suspicion, or on any other occasion.

He became, therefore, like one thunderstruck at his sister's relation. He was, at first, incapable of making any answer, having been almost deprived of his breath by the violence of the surprize. This, however, soon returned with redoubled force and fury.

So poor Sophia turned pale at the noise of her father, who, in a voice most dreadful to hear, came on swearing, cursing, and vowing the destruction of Jones.

And now the squire, having burst open the door, beheld an object which instantly suspended all his fury against Jones; this was the ghastly appearance of Sophia, who had fainted away in her lover's arms. This tragical sight Mr Western no sooner beheld, than all his rage forsook him; he roared for help with his utmost violence; ran first to his daughter, then back to the door calling for water, and then back again to Sophia, never considering in whose arms she then was, nor perhaps once recollecting that there was such a person in the world as Jones.

Mrs Western and a great number of servants soon came to the assistance of Sophia with water, cordials, and everything necessary on those occasions. These were applied with such success, that Sophia in a very few minutes began to recover, and all the symptoms of life to return. Upon which she was presently led off by her own maid and Mrs Western.

The moment Sophia was departed, Jones advanced in a very suppliant manner to Mr Western, and begged him to be pacified.

'I wull have satisfaction o' thee,' answered the squire, 'so doff thy clothes. *At unt* half a man, and I'll lick thee as well as wast ever licked in thy life.' He then bespattered the youth with abundance of that language which passes between country gentlemen who embrace opposite sides of the question.

To all such wit, Jones very calmly answered, 'Sir, this usage may perhaps cancel every other obligation you have conferred on me; but there is one you can never cancel; nor will I be provoked by your abuse to lift my hand against the father of Sophia.'

Jones immediately departed, and no sooner had the squire swallowed a large draught than he declared a resolution of going the next morning early to acquaint Mr Allworthy.

CHAPTER SIXTEEN

IN WHICH MR WESTERN VISITS MR ALLWORTHY

MR ALLWORTHY was retired from breakfast with his nephew, well satisfied with the report of the young gentleman's successful visit to Sophia, when Mr Western broke abruptly in upon them, and without any ceremony began as follows:

'There, you have done a fine piece of work truly! You have brought up your bastard to a fine purpose; not that I believe you have had any hand in it neither, that is, as a man may say, designedly: but there is a fine kettle-of-fish made on't up at our house.'—'What can be the matter, Mr Western?' said Allworthy. 'O, matter enow of all conscience: my daughter hath fallen in love with your bastard, that's all; but I won't ge her a hapeny, not the twentieth part of a brass varden. I always thought what would come o' breeding up a bastard like a gentleman, and letting un come about to vok's houses. He shan't ever have a morsel of meat of mine, or a varden to buy it: if she will ha un, one smock shall be her portion.'—'I am in amazement,' cries Allworthy, 'at what you tell me, after what passed between my nephew and the young

73

lady no longer ago than yesterday.'—'Yes, sir,' answered Western, 'it was after what passed between your nephew and she that the whole matter came out. Mr Blifil there was no sooner gone than the son of a whore came lurching about the house. Little did I think when I used to love him for a sportsman that he was all the while a poaching after my daughter.' Allworthy then asked Western what he would have him do upon this occasion. To which the other answered, 'That he would have him keep the rascal away from his house, and that he would go and lock up the wench; for he was resolved to make her marry Mr Blifil.'

When Allworthy and Blifil were again left together, a long silence ensued between them; all which interval the young gentleman filled up with sighs, which proceeded partly from disappointment, but more from hatred; for the success of Jones was much more grievous to him than the loss of Sophia.

At length his uncle asked him what he was determined to do, and he answered in the following words: 'Alas! sir, can it be a question what step a lover will take, when reason and passion point different ways? The lady, I am sure, will be undone in every sense; for, besides the loss of most part of her own fortune, she will be not only married to a beggar, but the little fortune which her father cannot withhold from her will be squandered on that wench with whom I know he yet converses. Nay, that is a trifle; for I know him to be one of the worst men in the world.'—'How!' said Allworthy; 'hath he done anything worse than I already know?' —'You know, sir,' said Blifil, 'I never disobeyed you; but I am sorry I mentioned it, since it may now look like revenge, whereas, I thank Heaven, no such motive ever entered my heart. But one evening, as Mr Thwackum and myself were taking the air in the fields, we unluckily saw him engaged with a wench in a manner not fit to be mentioned. Mr Thwackum, with more boldness than prudence, advanced to rebuke him, when (I am sorry to say it) he fell upon the worthy man, and beat him so outrageously that I wish he may have yet recovered the bruises. Nor was I without my share of the effects of his malice, while I endeavoured to protect my tutor; but that I have long forgiven; nay, I prevailed with Mr Thwackum to forgive him too.'—'O child!' said Allworthy, 'I know not whether I should blame or applaud your goodness, in concealing such villany a moment: but where is Mr Thwackum? Not that I want any confirmation of what you say; but I will examine all the evidence of this matter, to justify to the world the example I am resolved to make of such a monster.'

Thwackum was now sent for, and presently appeared. He corroborated every circumstance which the other had deposed; nay, he produced the record upon his breast, where the hand-writing of Mr Jones remained very legible in black and blue.

It was Mr Allworthy's custom never to punish any one, not

even to turn away a servant, in a passion. He resolved therefore to delay passing sentence on Jones till the afternoon.

The poor young man attended at dinner, as usual; but his heart was too much loaded to suffer him to eat. His grief too was a good deal aggravated by the unkind looks of Mr Allworthy; whence he concluded that Western had discovered the whole affair between him and Sophia; but as to Mr Blifil's story, he had not the least apprehension, for of much the greater part he was entirely innocent; and for the residue, as he had forgiven and forgotten it himself, so he suspected no remembrance on the other side. When dinner was over, and the servants departed, Mr Allworthy began to harangue. He set forth, in a long speech, the many iniquities of which Jones had been guilty, particularly those which this day had brought to light; and concluded by telling him, 'That unless he could clear himself of the charge, he was resolved to banish him his sight for ever. I cannot avoid saying, there is no part of your conduct which I resent more than your illtreatment of that good young man (meaning Blifil) who hath behaved with so much tenderness and honour towards you.'

These last words were a dose almost too bitter to be swallowed. A flood of tears now gushed from the eyes of Jones, and every faculty of speech and motion seemed to have deserted him. It was some time before he was able to obey Allworthy's peremptory commands of departing; which he at length did, having first kissed his hands with a passion difficult to be affected, and as difficult to be described.

One thing must not be omitted, that, in their censures on this occasion, none ever mentioned the sum contained in the paper which Allworthy gave Jones, which was no less than five hundred pounds; but all agreed that he was sent away penniless, and some said naked, from the house of his inhuman father.

Jones was commanded to leave the house immediately, and told, that his clothes and everything else should be sent to him whithersoever he should order them.

He accordingly set out, and walked above a mile, not regarding, and indeed scarce knowing, whither he went. At length he began to come a little to himself. His grief now took another turn, and discharged itself in a gentler way, till he became at last cool enough to reason with his passion, and to consider what steps were proper to be taken in his deplorable condition.

He determined to write a farewell letter to Sophia; and accordingly proceeded to a house not far off, where, being furnished with proper materials, he wrote as follows:

'MADAM,

'When you reflect on the situation in which I write, I am sure your good nature will pardon any inconsistency or absurdity

75

which my letter contains; for everything here flows from a heart so full, that no language can express its dictates.

'I have resolved, madam, to obey your commands, in flying for ever from your dear, your lovely sight. Cruel indeed those commands are; but it is a cruelty which proceeds from fortune, not from my Sophia.

'O Sophia! it is hard to leave you; it is harder still to desire you to forget me; yet the sincerest love obliges me to both. Think I never loved you; or think truly how little I deserve you; and learn to scorn me for a presumption which can never be too severely punished.—I am unable to say more.—May guardian angels protect you for ever!'

He was now searching his pockets for his wax, but found none, nor indeed anything else, therein; for in truth he had, in his frantic disposition, tossed everything from him, and amongst the rest, his pocket-book, which he had received from Mr Allworthy, which he had never opened, and which now first occurred to his memory.

The house supplied him with a wafer for his present purpose, with which, having sealed his letter, he returned hastily towards the brook side, in order to search for the things which he had there lost. In his way he met his old friend Black George, who heartily condoled with him on his misfortune; for this had already reached his ears, and indeed those of all the neighbourhood.

Jones acquainted the gamekeeper with his loss, and he as readily went back with him to the brook, where they searched every tuft of grass in the meadow, as well where Jones had not been as where he had been; but all to no purpose, for they found nothing; for, indeed, though the things were then in the meadow, they omitted to search the only place where they were deposited; to wit, in the pockets of the said George; for he had just before found them, and being luckily apprized for their value, had very carefully put them up for his own use.

Jones now gave over all hopes of recovering his loss, and almost all thoughts concerning it, and turning to Black George, asked him earnestly if he would do him the greatest favour in the world by being desired to convey a letter to Sophia, which with great pleasure he promised to do. And indeed I believe there are few favours which he would not have gladly conferred on Mr Jones; for he bore as much gratitude towards him as he could, and was as honest as men who love money better than any other thing in the universe, generally are.

Mrs Honour was agreed by both to be the proper means by which this letter should pass to Sophia. They then separated; the gamekeeper returned home to Mr Western's, and Jones walked to an alehouse at half a mile's distance, to wait for his messenger's return.

George no sooner came home to his master's house than he met with Mrs Honour; to whom, having first sounded her with a few previous questions, he delivered the letter for her mistress, and received at the same time another from her, for Mr Jones; which Honour told him she had carried all that day in her bosom, and with it, a purse, which contained sixteen guineas, being, indeed, the whole stock of Sophia; for though her father was very liberal to her, she was much too generous to be rich.

The gamekeeper returned hastily and joyfully to Jones, who, having received Sophia's letter from him, instantly withdrew, and eagerly breaking it open, read as follows:

'SIR,
'It is impossible to express what I have felt since I saw you. Your submitting, on my account, to such cruel insults from my father, lays me under an obligation I shall ever own. As you know his temper, I beg you will, for my sake, avoid him. I wish I had any comfort to send you; but believe this, that nothing but the last violence shall ever give my hand or heart where you would be sorry to see them bestowed.'

Jones read this letter a hundred times over, and kissed it a hundred times as often. His passion now brought all tender desires back into his mind. However, when his cool reflections returned, he plainly perceived that his case was neither mended nor altered by Sophia's billet, unless to give him some little glimpse of hope, from her constancy, of some favourable accident hereafter. He therefore resumed his resolution, and taking leave of Black George, set forward to a town about five miles distant, whither he had desired Mr Allworthy, unless he pleased to revoke his sentence, to send his things after him.

CHAPTER SEVENTEEN

CONTAINING SEVERAL DIALOGUES

THE morning in which Mr Jones departed, Mrs Western summoned Sophia into her apartment; and proceeded to read her a long lecture on the subject of matrimony; which she treated not as a romantic scheme of happiness arising from love, as it hath been described by the poets; nor did she mention any of those purposes for which we are taught by divines to regard it as instituted by sacred authority; she considered it rather as a fund in which prudent women deposit their fortunes to the best advantage, in order to receive a larger interest for them than they could have elsewhere.

When Mrs Western had finished, Sophia answered, 'That she was very incapable of arguing with a lady of her aunt's superior knowledge and experience, especially on a subject which she had so very little considered, as this of matrimony.'

'Argue with me, child!' replied the other; 'I do not indeed expect it. I should have seen the world to very little purpose truly, if I am to argue with one of your years. I have taken this trouble, in order to instruct you. But however, if you have not hitherto considered of this matter, I promise you it is now high time, for my brother is resolved immediately to conclude the treaty with Mr Blifil; and indeed I am a sort of guarantee in the affair, and have promised your concurrence.'

'Indeed, madam,' cries Sophia, 'this is the only instance in which I must disobey both yourself and my father. For this is a match which requires very little consideration in me to refuse.'

'If I was not as great a philosopher as Socrates himself,' returned Mrs Western, 'you would overcome my patience. What objection can you have to the young gentleman?'

'A very solid objection, in my opinion,' says Sophia. 'I hate him.'

'Will you never learn a proper use of words?' answered the aunt. 'It is impossible you should hate a man from whom you have received no injury. By hatred, therefore, you mean no more than dislike, which is no sufficient objection against your marrying of him. I have known many couples, who have entirely disliked each other, lead very comfortable genteel lives. Believe me, child, I know these things better than you.'

Sophia then flung herself upon her knees, and tears began to trickle from her shining eyes. She entreated her aunt, 'to have mercy upon her, and not to resent so cruelly her unwillingness to make herself miserable'; often urging, 'that she alone was concerned, and that her happiness only was at stake.'

Not less blind to the tears, or less deaf to every entreaty of Sophia was the politic aunt, nor less determined was she to deliver over the trembling maid into the arms of the gaoler Blifil. She answered with great impetuosity, 'So far, madam, from your being concerned alone, your concern is the least, or surely the least important. It is the honour of your family which is concerned in this alliance; you are only the instrument.'

Western, who had been within hearing during the greater part of the preceding dialogue, had now exhausted all his patience; he therefore entered the room in a violent passion, crying, 'D—n me then if shatunt ha'un, d—n me if shatunt, that's all—that's all; d—n me if shatunt.'

Mrs Western had collected a sufficient quantity of wrath for the use of Sophia; but she now transferred it all to the squire. She flew into the most violent rage, uttered phrases improper to be here related, and instantly burst out of the house.

Mr Western having finished his holla, and taken a little breath, began to lament, in very pathetic terms, the unfortunate condition of men, who are, says he, 'always whipt in by the humours of some d—n'd b— or other. I think I was hard run enough by your mother for one man; but after giving her a dodge, here's another b— follows me upon the foil; but curse my jacket if I will be run down in this manner by any o' um.'

Sophia never had a single dispute with her father, till this unlucky affair of Blifil, on any account, except in defence of her mother, whom she had loved most tenderly, though she lost her in the eleventh year of her age. The squire, to whom that poor woman had been a faithful upper-servant all the time of their marriage, had returned that behaviour by making what the world calls a good husband. He very seldom swore at her (perhaps not above once a week) and never beat her: she had not the least occasion for jealousy, and was perfect mistress of her time; for she was never interrupted by her husband, who was engaged all the morning in his field exercises, and all the evening with bottle companions. She scarce indeed ever saw him but at meals; for when he repaired to her bed, he was generally so drunk that he could not see; and in the sporting season he always rose from her before it was light. Hence perhaps she had contracted a little gloominess of temper, for she was rather a good servant than a good wife; nor had she always the gratitude to return the extraordinary degree of roaring mirth, with which the squire received her, even with a good-humoured smile.

For this last, and many other good reasons, Western at length heartily hated his wife; and as he never concealed this hatred before her death, so he never forgot it afterwards; but when anything in the least soured him, as a bad scenting day, or a distemper among his hounds, or any other such misfortune, he constantly vented his spleen by invectives against the deceased, saying, 'If my wife was alive now, she would be glad of this.'

These invectives he was especially desirous of throwing forth before Sophia; for as he loved her more than he did any other, so he was really jealous that she had loved her mother better than him. And this jealousy Sophia seldom failed of heightening on these occasions; for he was not contented with violating her ears with the abuse of her mother, but endeavoured to force an explicit approbation of all this abuse; with which desire he never could prevail upon her by any promise or threats to comply.

Sophia kept silence during the foregoing speech of her father, nor did she once answer otherwise than with a sigh; but as he understood none of the language, or, as he called it, lingo of the eyes, so he was not satisfied without some further approbation of his sentiments, which he now demanded of his daughter; telling her, in the usual way, 'he expected she was ready to take the part of everybody against him, as she had always done that of the b— her mother.' Sophia remaining still silent, he cryed out, 'What, art dumb? why dost unt speak? Was not thy mother a d—d b— to me? answer me that. What, I suppose you despise your father too, and don't think him good enough to speak to?'

'For Heaven's sake, sir,' answered Sophia, 'do not give so cruel a turn to my silence. I am sure I would sooner die than be guilty of any disrespect towards you; but how can I venture to speak, when every word must either offend my dear papa, or convict me of the blackest ingratitude as well as impiety to the memory of the best of mothers; for such, I am certain, my mamma was always to me.'

'And your aunt, I suppose, is the best of sisters too!

'And a second wife to me so you will take her part too! You won't confess that she hath acted the part of the vilest sister in the world?'

'Upon my word, sir,' cries Sophia, 'I must belie my heart wickedly if I did. I know my aunt and you differ very much in your ways of thinking; but I have heard her a thousand times express the greatest affection for you; and I am convinced, so far from her being the worst sister in the world, there are very few who love a brother better.'

'The English of all which is,' answered the squire, 'that I am in the wrong. Ay, certainly. Ay, to be sure the woman is in the right, and the man in the wrong always.'

'Pardon me, sir,' cries Sophia. 'I do not say so.'

'What don't you say?' answered the father. 'You have the impudence to say she's in the right: doth it not follow then of course that I am in the wrong? I have not quarrelled with sister this many years but upon your account; and now you would throw the whole blame upon me. You have lost the hare, and I must draw every way to find her again? Indeed, if I was certain ——' Here he stopt, and Sophia throwing in more entreaties, at length prevailed upon him; so that after venting two or three bitter sarcastical expressions against his daughter, he departed as fast as he could to recover his sister, before her equipage could be gotten ready.

The squire overtook his sister just as she was stepping into the coach, and partly by force, and partly by solicitations, prevailed upon her to order her horses back into their quarters. He succeeded in this attempt without much difficulty; for the lady was, as we have already hinted, of a most placable disposition, and greatly loved her brother, though she despised his parts, or rather his little knowledge of the world.

Poor Sophia, who had first set on foot this reconciliation, was now made the sacrifice to it. They both concurred in their censures on her conduct; jointly declared war against her, and directly proceeded to counsel, how to carry it on in the most vigorous manner.

These matters were resolved on, when Mr Blifil came to pay a visit to his mistress. The squire no sooner heard of his arrival, than he stept aside, by his sister's advice, to give his daughter orders for the proper reception of her lover: which he did with the most bitter execrations and denunciations of judgment on her refusal.

In pursuance of her father's peremptory command, Sophia now admitted Mr Blifil's visit. It is possible the great art used by Blifil at this interview would have prevailed on Sophia to have made another man in his circumstances her confident, and to have revealed the whole secret of her heart to him; but she had contracted so ill an opinion of this young gentleman, that she was resolved to place no confidence in him; for simplicity, when set on its guard, is often a match for cunning. Her behaviour to him, therefore, was entirely forced, and indeed such as is generally prescribed to virgins upon the second formal visit from one who is appointed for their husband.

But though Blifil declared himself to the squire perfectly satisfied with his reception; yet that gentleman, who, in company with his sister, had overheard all, was not so well pleased. 'Follow her, boy, follow her; run in, run in; that's it, honeys. Dead, dead, dead. Never be bashful, nor stand shall I, shall I? Allworthy and I can finish all matters between us this afternoon, and let us ha' the wedding to-morrow.'

Blifil suffered himself to be overpowered by the forcible rhetoric of the squire; and it being agreed that Western should close with Allworthy that very afternoon, the lover departed home, having first earnestly begged that no violence might be offered to the lady by this haste, in the same manner as a popish inquisitor begs the lay power to do no violence to the heretic delivered over to it, and against whom the church hath passed sentence.

CHAPTER EIGHTEEN

A STRANGE RESOLUTION OF SOPHIA, AND ONE OF MR JONES

THOUGH Mrs Honour was principally attached to her own interest, she was not without some little attachment to Sophia. To say truth, it was very difficult for any one to know that young lady without loving her. She no sooner therefore heard a piece of news than she ran hastily to inform her.

The beginning of her discourse was as abrupt as her entrance into the room. 'O dear ma'am!' says she, 'what doth your la'ship think? To be sure I am frightened out of my wits; and yet I thought it my duty to tell your la'ship, though perhaps it may make our ladies angry; for, to be sure, I overheard my master talking to parson Supple about getting a licence this very afternoon; and to be sure I heard him say, your la'ship should be married to-morrow morning.' Sophia turned pale at these words, and repeated eagerly, 'To-morrow morning!'—'Yes, ma'am,' replied the trusty waiting-woman, 'I will take my oath I heard my master say so.'—'Honour,' says Sophia, 'you have both surprized and shocked me to such a degree that I have scarce any breath or spirits left. What is to be done in my dreadful situation?'—'Indeed, ma'am,' cries Honour, 'I wish your la'ship and I could change situations; that is, I mean without hurting your la'ship; for to be sure I don't wish you so bad as to be a servant; but because that if so be it was my case, I should find no manner of difficulty in it; for, in my poor opinion, young Squire Blifil is a charming, sweet, handsome man.'—'Don't mention such stuff,' cries Sophia. 'Such stuff!' repeated Honour; 'why, there. Well, to be sure, what's one man's meat is another man's poison, and the same is altogether as true of women. If your la'ship hath such a violent aversion, and hates the young gentleman so very bad, that you can't bear to think of going into bed to him; for to be sure there may be such antipathies in nature, and one had lieverer touch a toad than the flesh of some people——'

Sophia had been too much wrapt in contemplation to pay any great attention to the foregoing excellent discourse of her maid; interrupting her therefore, without making any answer to it, she said, 'Honour, I am come to a resolution. I am determined to leave my father's house this very night; and if you have the friendship for me which you have often professed, you will keep me company.'—'That I will, ma'am, to the world's end,' answered Honour; 'but I beg your la'ship to consider the consequence before you undertake any rash action. Where can your la'ship possibly go?'—'There is,' replied Sophia, 'a lady of quality in London, a relation of mine, who spent several months with my aunt in the country; during all which time she treated me with great kindness, and expressed so much pleasure in my company, that she earnestly desired my aunt to suffer me to go with her to London. As she is a woman of very great note, I shall easily find her out, and I make no doubt of being very well and kindly received by her.'

'Well, but, ma'am,' answered Honour, 'how doth your la'ship think of making your escape? Where will you get any horses or conveyance? For as for your own horse, as all the servants know a little how matters stand beween my master and your la'ship, Robin will be hanged before he will suffer it to go out of the stable without my master's express orders.'—'I intend to escape,' said Sophia, 'by walking out of the doors when they are open. I thank Heaven my legs are very able to carry me. I intend to take horses at the very first town we come to, and we shall hardly be attacked in our way thither. Look'ee, Honour, I am resolved to go; and if you will attend me, I promise you I will reward you to the very utmost of my power.'

This last argument had a stronger effect on Honour than all the preceding. And since she saw her mistress so determined, she desisted from any further dissuasions.

But before we proceed any farther with Sophia, we must now look back to Mr Jones.

Mr Jones was on his road to Bristol; being determined to seek his fortune at sea, or rather, indeed, to fly away from his fortune on shore.

Jones, on arrival at a village, inquired of the first fellow he saw, whether they were in the road to Bristol. 'Whence did you come?' cries the fellow. 'No matter,' says Jones, a little hastily; 'I want to know if this be the road to Bristol?'—'The road to Bristol!' cries the fellow, scratching his head; 'why, measter, I believe you will hardly get to Bristol this way to-night. It is almost dark, and the road is difficult to hit; besides, there have been several robberies committed lately between this and Bristol. Here is a very creditable good house just by, where thou may'st find good entertainment for thyself and thy cattle till morning.' Jones, after a little persuasion, agreed to stay in this place till the morning, and was conducted by his friend to the public-house.

The landlord, who was a very civil fellow, told Jones, 'He hoped he would excuse the badness of his accommodation; for that his wife was gone from home, and had locked up almost everything, and carried the keys along with her.' Indeed the fact was, that a favourite daughter of hers was just married, and gone that morning home with her husband; and that she and her mother together had almost stript the poor man of all his goods, as well as money.

Jones being assured that he could have no bed, very contentedly betook himself to a great chair made with rushes, when sleep, which had lately shunned his company in much better apartments, generously paid him a visit in his humble cell.

As for the landlord, he continued still waking in his chair, till a violent thundering at his outward gate called him from his seat, and obliged him to open it; which he had no sooner done, than his kitchen was immediately full of gentlemen in red coats, who all rushed upon him in as tumultuous a manner as if they intended to take his little castle by storm.

The landlord was now forced to furnish his numerous guests with beer, which they called for with great eagerness; and upon his second or third return from the cellar, he saw Mr Jones standing before the fire in the midst of the soldiers; for it may easily be believed, that the arrival of so much good company should put an end to any sleep.

The company having now pretty well satisfied their thirst, nothing remained but to pay the reckoning.

A violent dispute now arose, in which every word may be said to have been deposed upon oath; for the oaths were at least equal to all the other words spoken.

The dispute now grew so very warm that it seemed to draw towards a military decision, when Jones, stepping forward, silenced all their clamours at once, by declaring that he would pay the whole reckoning, which indeed amounted to no more than three shillings and fourpence.

This declaration procured Jones the thanks and applause of the whole company. The terms honourable, noble, and worthy gentleman, resounded through the room.

The serjeant informed Mr Jones that they were marching against the rebels, and expected to be commanded by the glorious Duke of Cumberland. By which the reader may perceive (a circumstance which we have not thought necessary to communicate before) that this was the very time when the Jacobite rebellion was at the highest; and indeed the banditti were now marched into England, intending, as it was thought, to fight the king's forces, and to attempt pushing forward to the metropolis.

Jones had some heroic ingredients in his composition, and was a hearty well-wisher to the glorious cause of liberty, and of the Protestant religion. It is no wonder, therefore, that in circumstances which would have warranted a much more romantic and wild undertaking, it should occur to him to serve as a volunteer in this expedition, so Jones contented, walked off with his new comrades.

All that day the serjeant and the young soldier marched together; and the former, who was an arch fellow, told the latter many entertaining stories of his campaigns, though in reality he had never made any; for he was but lately come into the service, and had, by his own dexterity, so well ingratiated himself with his officers, that he had promoted himself to a halberd; chiefly indeed by his merit in recruiting, in which he was most excellently well skilled.

Much mirth and festivity passed among the soldiers during their march. In which the many occurrences that had passed at their last quarters were remembered, and every one, with great freedom, made what jokes he pleased on his officers, some of which were of the coarser kind, and very near bordering on scandal.

Our little army, which consisted of two companies of foot, were now arrived at the place where they were to halt that evening. The serjeant then acquainted his lieutenant, who was the commanding officer, that they had picked up two fellows in that day's march, one of which, he said (meaning Jones) would do well enough for the rear rank.

The new soldiers were now produced before the officer, who came to survey Jones: at the first sight of whom, the lieutenant could not help showing some surprize; for besides that he was very well dressed, and was naturally genteel, he had a remarkable air of dignity in his look, which is rarely seen among the vulgar, and is indeed not inseparably annexed to the features of their superiors.

'Sir,' said the lieutenant, 'my serjeant informed me that you are desirous of enlisting in the company I have at present under my command; if so, sir, we shall very gladly receive a gentleman who promises to do much honour to the company by bearing arms in it.'

Jones answered, 'That he had not mentioned anything of enlisting himself; that he was most zealously attached to the glorious cause for which they were going to fight, and was very desirous of serving as a volunteer'; concluding with some compliments to the lieutenant, and expressing the great satisfaction he should have in being under his command.

The lieutenant returned his civility, commended his resolution, shook him by the hand, and invited him to dine with himself and the rest of the officers.

CHAPTER NINETEEN

THE ADVENTURE OF A COMPANY OF OFFICERS

THE lieutenant, who commanded this party, was now near sixty years of age. He had entered very young into the army, and had served in the capacity of an ensign at the battle of Tannieres; here he had received two wounds, and had so well distinguished himself, that he was by the Duke of Marlborough advanced to be a lieutenant, immediately after that battle.

This officer had many good qualities besides his merit in his profession; for he was a religious, honest, good-natured man; and had behaved so well in his command, that he was highly esteemed and beloved not only by the soldiers of his own company, but by the whole regiment.

As soon as dinner was ended, Jones informed the company of the merriment which had passed among the soldiers upon their march; 'and yet,' says he, 'notwithstanding all their vociferation, I dare swear they will behave more like Grecians than Trojans when they come to the enemy.'—'Grecians and Trojans!' says one of the ensigns, 'who the devil are they? I have heard of all the troops in Europe, but never of any such as these.'

'Don't pretend to more ignorance than you have, Mr Northerton,' said the worthy lieutenant. 'I suppose you have heard of the Greeks and Trojans, though perhaps you never read Pope's *Homer*.'

'D—n Homo with all my heart,' says Northerton; 'I have the marks of him on my a— yet. There's Thomas, of our regiment, always carries a Homo in his pocket; d—n me, if ever I come at it, if I don't burn it.'

Mr Adderly, which was the name of the other ensign, had sat hitherto kicking his heels and humming a tune, without seeming to listen to the discourse; he now answered, if *religion* was the no small motive to my becoming a volunteer in the cause.'

'I don't know, gentlemen,' said Jones, 'what may be your opinion; but for my own part, though I love my king and country, I hope, as well as any man in it, yet the Protestant interest is no small motive to my becoming a volunteer in the cause.'

Northerton now winked on Adderly, and whispered to him slily, 'Smoke the prig, Adderly, smoke him.' Then turning to Jones, said to him, 'I am very glad, sir, you have chosen our regiment to be a volunteer in; for if our parson should at any time take a cup too much, I find you can supply his place. I presume, sir, you have been at the university; may I crave the favour to know what college?'

'Sir,' answered Jones, 'so far from having been at the university, I have even had the advantage of yourself, for I was never at school.'

'I presumed,' cries the ensign, 'only upon the information of your great learning.'—'Oh! sir,' answered Jones, 'it is as possible for a man to know something without having been at school, as it is to have been at school and to know nothing.'

Northerton did not very well relish the sarcasm of Jones; but he thought the provocation was scarce sufficient to justify a blow, or a rascal, or scoundrel, which were the only repartees that suggested themselves. He was, therefore, silent at present; but resolved to take the first opportunity of returning the jest by abuse.

It now came to the turn of Mr Jones to give a toast, as it is called; who could not refrain from mentioning his dear Sophia. This he did the more readily, as he imagined it utterly impossible that any one present should guess the person he meant.

But the lieutenant, who was the toast-master, was not contented with Sophia only. He said, he must have her sir-name; upon which Jones hesitated a little, and presently after named Miss Sophia Western. Ensign Northerton declared he would not drink her health in the same round with his own toast, unless somebody would vouch for her. 'I knew one Sophy Western,' says he, 'that was lain with by half the young fellows at Bath; and perhaps this is the same woman.' Jones very solemnly assured him of the contrary; asserting that the young lady he named was one of great fashion and fortune. 'Ay, ay,' says the ensign, 'and so she is: d—n me, it is the same woman; and I'll hold half a dozen of Burgundy, Tom French of our regiment brings her into company with us at any tavern in Bridges-street.' He then proceeded to describe her person exactly (for he had seen her with her aunt), and concluded with saying, 'that her father had a great estate in Somersetshire.'

Jones, turning to the ensign with a stern aspect, he said, 'Pray, sir, choose some other subject for your wit; for I promise you I will bear no jesting with this lady's character.'—'Jesting!' cries the other, 'd—n me if ever I was more in earnest in my life. Tom French of our regiment had both her and her aunt at Bath.'— 'Then I must tell you in earnest,' cried Jones, 'that you are one of the most impudent rascals upon earth.'

He had no sooner spoken these words, than the ensign, together with a volley of curses, discharged a bottle full at the head of Jones, which hitting him a little above the right temple, brought him instantly to the ground.

The conqueror perceiving the enemy to lie motionless before him, and blood beginning to flow pretty plentifully from his wound, began now to think of quitting the field of battle, where no more honour was to be gotten; but the lieutenant interposed by stepping before the door, and thus cut off his retreat.

Northerton was very importunate with the lieutenant for his liberty; urging the ill-consequences of his stay, asking him, what he could have done less? 'Zounds!' says he, 'I was but in jest with the fellow. I never heard any harm of Miss Western in my life.' —'Have not you?' said the lieutenant; 'then you richly deserve to be hanged, as well for making such jests, as for using such a weapon: you are my prisoner, sir; nor shall you stir from hence till a proper guard comes to secure you.'

Soon afterwards arrived the surgeon, who having viewed the wound, having shaken his head, and blamed everything which was done, ordered his patient instantly to bed.

The lieutenant having collected from the surgeon that Mr Jones was in great danger, gave orders for keeping Mr Northerton under a very strict guard, designing in the morning to attend him to a justice of peace.

Very late that night Jones swallowed a large mess of chicken, or rather cock, broth, with a very good appetite, as indeed he would have done the cock it was made of, with a pound of bacon into the bargain; and now, finding in himself no deficiency of either health or spirit, he resolved to get up and seek his enemy.

Jones rose from his bed, and dressed himself entirely, putting on even his coat, which, as its colour was white, showed very visibly the streams of blood which had flowed down it; and now, he was going to issue forth, when the thought of what he was about to undertake laid suddenly hold of him, and he began to reflect that in a few minutes he might possibly deprive a human being of life, or might lose his own. 'Very well,' said he, 'and in what cause do I venture my life? Why, in that of my honour. And who is this human being? A rascal who hath injured and insulted me without provocation. But is not revenge forbidden by Heaven? Yes, but it is enjoined by the world. I'll think no more; I am resolved, and must fight him.'

The clock had now struck twelve, and every one in the house were in their beds, except the sentinel who stood to guard Northerton, when Jones softly opening his door, issued forth in pursuit of his enemy, of whose place of confinement he had received a perfect description from the drawer. It is not easy to conceive a much more tremendous figure than he now exhibited. He had on, as we have said, a light-coloured coat, covered with streams of blood. His face, which missed that very blood, was pallid. Round his head was a quantity of bandage, not unlike a turban. In the right hand he carried a sword, and in the left a candle.

When the sentinel first saw our hero approach, his hair began gently to lift up his grenadier cap; and in the same instant his knees fell to blows with each other. Presently his whole body was seized with worse than an ague fit. He then fired his piece, and fell flat on his face.

Whether fear or courage was the occasion of his firing, or whether he took aim at the object of his terror, I cannot say. If he did, however, he had the good fortune to miss his man.

Jones seeing the fellow fall, guessed the cause of his fright, at which he could not forbear smiling, not in the least reflecting on the danger from which he had just escaped. He then passed by the fellow, who still continued in the posture in which he fell, and entered the room where Northerton, as he had heard, was confined. Here, in a solitary situation, he found—an empty quart pot standing on the table, on which some beer being spilt, it looked as if the room had lately been inhabited; but at present it was entirely vacant.

Perceiving the bird was flown, at least despairing to find him, and rightly apprehending that the report of the firelock would alarm the whole house, our hero now blew out his candle, and gently stole back again to his chamber, and to his bed.

The soldier was now found lying in the same place and posture in which we just now left him. Several immediately applied themselves to raise him, and some concluded him dead; but they presently saw their mistake, for he not only struggled with those who laid their hands on him, but fell a roaring like a bull. In reality, he imagined so many spirits or devils were handling him; for his imagination being possessed with the horror of an apparition, converted every object he saw or felt into nothing but ghosts and spectres.

The soldier cried, 'You may punish me if you please; but I was as broad awake as I am now; and the devil carry me away if I did not see the man, as I tell you, with eyes as big and as fiery as two large flambeaux.'

The commander of the forces now arrived; for being awake at the time, and hearing the sentinel fire his piece, thought it his duty to rise immediately, though he had not great apprehensions of any mischief.

Our poor sentinel, to whom the sight of this officer was not much more welcome than the apparition, as he thought it, again related the dreadful story, and with many additions of blood and fire; but he had the misfortune to gain no credit with either of the last-mentioned persons: for the officer, though a very religious man, was free from all terrors of this kind.

But whether Northerton was carried away in thunder or fire, or in whatever other manner he was gone, it was now certain that his body was no longer in custody.

CHAPTER TWENTY

THE clock had struck five when Jones awaked from a nap of
seven hours, so much refreshed, and in such perfect health and
spirits, that he resolved to get up and dress himself; but first he
went down into the kitchen to bespeak something that might pacify
certain tumults he found rising within his stomach.

Meeting the landlady, he accosted her with great civility, and
asked, 'What he could have for dinner?'—'For dinner!' says she;
'it is an odd time a day to think about dinner. I believe there is a
piece of cold buttock and carrot, which will fit you.'—'Nothing
better,' answered Jones; 'but I should be obliged to you, if you
would let it be fried.' To which the landlady consented, and said,
smiling, 'she was glad to see him so well recovered'; for the sweetness of our hero's temper was almost irresistible; besides, she loved
money so much, that she hated everything which had the sem-
blance of poverty.

Jones now returned in order to dress himself, while his dinner
was preparing, and was, according to his orders, attended by the
barber.

This barber, who went by the name of Little Benjamin, was a
fellow of great oddity and humour, which had frequently let
him into small inconveniencies, such as slaps in the face, kicks in
the breech, broken bones, &c. For every one doth not understand a
jest; and those who do are often displeased with being themselves the subjects of it.

Jones being impatient to be drest, begged him to make haste;
to which the other answered with much gravity, 'I could never
discover more than two reasons for shaving; the one is to get a
beard, and the other to get rid of one. I conjecture, sir, it may
not be long since you shaved from the former of these motives.
Upon my word, you have had good success; for one may say of
your beard, that it is *tondenti gravior*.'—'I conjecture,' says Jones,
'that thou art a very comical fellow.'—'You mistake me widely,
sir,' said the barber. 'Too much learning hath been my ruin.'—

'Upon my word,' cries Jones, 'thou art a very odd fellow, and
I like thy humour extremely; I shall be very glad if thou wilt
come to me after dinner, and drink a glass with me; I long to be
better acquainted with thee.'

'O dear sir!' said the barber, 'I can do you twenty times as
great a favour, if you will accept of it.'—'What is that, my

friend?' cries Jones. 'Why, I will drink a bottle with you if you please; for I have no skill in physiognomy, if you are not one of the best-natured gentlemen in the universe.'

Jones was at dinner in the parlour. And Mr Benjamin, as we have said, attended him, and was very kindly desired to sit down. Jones then filling out a glass of wine, drank his health by the appellation of *doctissime tonsorum*. *'Ago tibi gratias, domine,'* said the barber; and then looking very steadfastly at Jones, he said, with great gravity, and with a seeming surprize, as if he had recollected a face he had seen before, 'Sir, may I crave the favour to know if your name is not Jones?' To which the other answered, 'That it was.' Says the barber; 'How strangely things come to pass! Mr Jones, I am your most obedient servant. I find you do not know me, which indeed is no wonder, since you never saw me but once, and then you was very young. Pray, sir, how doth the good Squire Allworthy? how doth *ille optimus omnium patronus?'*—'I find,' said Jones, 'you do indeed know me; but I have not the like happiness of recollecting you.'—'I do not wonder at that,' cries Benjamin; 'but I am surprized I did not know you sooner, for you are not in the least altered. I am sure I have a great respect for you, I do assure you I have, and have had ever since the good nature you showed to Black George, which was talked of all over the country, and I received more than one letter about it. Indeed, it made you beloved by everybody.'

Every profession of friendship easily gains credit with the miserable; it is no wonder therefore, if Jones, who, besides his being miserable, was extremely open-hearted, very readily believed all the professions of Benjamin, and received him into his bosom. Jones at length, after much entreaty, said, 'Since you have heard, my friend, so much of my affairs, and seem so desirous to know the truth, if you will have patience to hear it, I will inform you of the whole.'—'Patience!' cries Benjamin, 'that I will, if the chapter was never so long; and I am very much obliged to you for the honour you do me.'

Jones now began, and related the whole history, forgetting only a circumstance or two, namely, everything which passed on that day in which he had fought with Thwackum; and ended with his resolution to go to sea; till the rebellion in the North had made him change his purpose, and had brought him to the place where he then was.

Little Benjamin, who had been all attention, never once interrupted the narrative; but when it was ended he could not help observing, that there must be surely something more invented by his enemies, and told Mr Allworthy against him, or so good a man would never have dismissed one he had loved so tenderly, in such a manner. There was a circumstance behind which his curiosity, cold as it was, most eagerly longed for. Jones had mentioned the fact of his amour, and of his being the rival of Blifil, but had cautiously concealed the name of the young lady. The barber, therefore, after some hesitation, and many hums and hahs, at last begged leave to crave the name of the lady, who appeared to be the principal cause of all this mischief. Jones paused a moment, and then said, 'Since I have trusted you with so much, and since, I am afraid, her name is become too public already on this occasion, I will not conceal it from you. Her name is Sophia Western.'

'Squire Western hath a daughter grown a woman!'—'Ay, and such a woman,' cries Jones, 'that the world cannot match. No eye ever saw anything so beautiful; but that is her least excellence. Such sense! such goodness! Oh, I could praise her for ever, and yet should omit half her virtues!'—'Mr Western a daughter grown up!' cries the barber. 'I remember the father a boy; well, *Tempus edax rerum.*'

'Well,' continued Jones, 'you certainly are one of the oddest, most comical fellows I ever met with, and must have something very surprizing in your story, which you must confess I have a right to hear.'—'I do confess it,' answered Benjamin, 'and I must begin by telling you, sir, that you yourself have been the greatest enemy I ever had.' Jones was a little startled at this sudden declaration. 'I your enemy, sir!' says he, with much amazement, and some sternness in his look. 'Nay, be not angry,' said Benjamin, 'for I promise you I am not. You are perfectly innocent of having intended me any wrong; for you was then an infant: but I shall, I believe, unriddle all this the moment I mention my name. Did you never hear, sir, of one Partridge, who had the honour of being reputed your father, and the misfortune of being ruined by that honour?'—'I have, indeed, heard of that Partridge,' says Jones, 'and have always believed myself to be his son.'—'Well, sir,' answered Benjamin, 'I am that Partridge; but I here absolve you from all filial duty, for I do assure you, you are no son of mine.'—'How!' replied Jones, 'and is it possible that a false suspicion should have drawn all the ill consequences upon you, with which I am too well acquainted?'—'It is possible,' cries Benjamin, 'for it is so: but though it is natural enough for men to hate even the innocent causes of their sufferings, yet I am of a different temper. I have loved you ever since I heard of your behaviour to Black George, as I told you; and I am convinced, from this extraordinary meeting, that you are born to make me amends for all I have suffered on that account.'

'I should be very glad, Mr Partridge,' answered Jones, 'to have it in my power to make you amends for your sufferings on my account, though at present I see no likelihood of it; however, I assure you I will deny you nothing which is in my power to grant.'

'It is in your power sure enough,' replied Benjamin; 'for I

desire nothing more than leave to attend you in this expedition.'

Jones, who was as much pleased with Partridge as Partridge could be with him, at last gave his consent; but then recollecting himself, he said, 'Perhaps, Mr Partridge, you think I shall be able to support you, but I really am not'; and then taking out his purse, he told out nine guineas, which he declared were his whole fortune.

Partridge answered, 'That his dependence was only on his future favour; for he was thoroughly convinced he would shortly have enough in his power. At present, sir,' said he, 'I believe I am rather the richer man of the two; but all I have is at your service, and at your disposal. I insist upon your taking the whole, and I beg only to attend you in the quality of your servant.' But to this generous proposal concerning the money, Jones would by no means submit.

It was resolved to set out the next morning, and then the barber departed, in order to prepare everything for his intended expedition.

CHAPTER TWENTY-ONE

CONTAINING A VERY SURPRIZING ADVENTURE INDEED, WHICH MR JONES MET WITH IN HIS WALK

AURORA now first opened her casement, when Jones walked forth in company with the barber, and mounted Mazard Hill; of which they had no sooner gained the summit than one of the most noble prospects in the world presented itself to their view.

Here they heard at a distance the most violent screams of a woman, proceeding from the wood below them. Jones listened a moment, and then, without saying a word to his companion ran, or rather slid, down the hill, and, without the least apprehension or concern for his own safety, made directly to the thicket, whence the sound had issued.

He had not entered far into the wood before he beheld a most shocking sight indeed, a woman stript half naked, under the hands of a ruffian, who had put his garter round her neck, and was endeavouring to draw her up to a tree. Jones asked no questions at this interval, but fell instantly upon the villain, and made such good use of his trusty oaken stick that he laid him sprawling on the ground before he could defend himself, indeed almost before he knew he was attacked; nor did he cease the prosecution of his blows till the woman herself begged him to forbear.

The poor wretch then fell upon her knees to Jones, and gave him a thousand thanks for her deliverance. He presently lifted her up, and told her he was highly pleased with the extraordinary accident which had sent him thither for her relief. 'Nay,' answered she, 'I could almost conceive you to be some good angel; and, to say the truth, you look more like an angel than a man in my eyes.' Indeed he was a charming figure; and if a very fine person, and a most comely set of features, adorned with youth, health, strength, freshness, spirit, and good nature, can make a man resemble an angel, he certainly had that resemblance.

The redeemed captive seemed to be at least of the middle age, nor had her face much appearance of beauty; but her clothes being torn from all the upper part of her body, her breasts, which were well formed and extremely white, attracted the eyes of her deliverer, and for a few moments they stood silent, and gazing at each other; till the ruffian on the ground beginning to move, Jones took the garter which had been intended for another purpose, and bound both his hands behind him. And now, on contemplating his face, he discovered, greatly to his surprize, and perhaps not a little to his satisfaction, this very person to be no other than ensign Northerton. Nor had the ensign forgotten his former antagonist, whom he knew the moment he came to himself. His surprize was equal to that of Jones; but I conceive his pleasure was rather less on this occasion.

Jones helped Northerton upon his legs, and then looking him steadfastly in the face, 'I fancy, sir,' said he, 'you did not expect to meet me any more in this world, and I confess I had as little expectation to find you here. However, fortune, I see, hath brought us once more together, and hath given me satisfaction for the injury I have received, even without my own knowledge.'

Then turning to the woman, he asked her if she was near her home. She answered she was an entire stranger in that part of the world. Jones then recollecting himself, said he would carry the woman to Upton, which, he said, was the nearest town, and there he would be sure of furnishing her with all manner of conveniences.

Our hero had considered, that as the ruffian's hands were tied behind him, he was incapable of executing any wicked purposes. But Jones unluckily forgot, that though the hands of Northerton were tied, his legs were at liberty; nor did he lay the least injunction on the prisoner that he should not make what use of these he pleased. Northerton therefore, took up his legs, which were at liberty, and walked off through the wood, which favoured his retreat; nor did the woman, whose eyes were perhaps rather turned toward her deliverer, once think of his escape.

Jones would have spent some time in searching for Northerton, but she would not permit him; earnestly entreating that he would accompany her to the town 'As to the fellow's escape,' said she, 'it gives me no uneasiness; but for you, sir, I am concerned at the trouble I give you; nay, indeed, my nakedness may well make me ashamed to look you in the face; and if it was not for the sake of your protection, I should wish to go alone.'

Jones offered her his coat; but, I know not for what reason, she absolutely refused the most earnest solicitations to accept it. He then begged her to forget both the causes of her confusion. 'With regard to the former,' says he, 'I have done no more than my duty in protecting you; and as for the latter, I will entirely remove it, by walking before you all the way; for I would not have my eyes offend you, and I could not answer for my power of resisting the attractive charms of so much beauty.'

Thus our hero and the redeemed lady walked safe into the famous town of Upton.

Mr Jones and his fair companion no sooner entered the town, than they went directly to that inn which in their eyes presented the fairest appearance to the street. Here Jones, having ordered a servant to show a room above stairs, was ascending, when the dishevelled fair, hastily following, was laid hold on by the master of the house, who cried, 'Heyday, where is that beggar wench going? Stay below stairs, I desire you.' But Jones at that instant thundered from above, 'Let the lady come up,' in so authoritative a voice, that the good man instantly withdrew his hands.

Here Jones wished her joy of her safe arrival, and then departed, in order to send the landlady with some clothes. The poor woman thanked him heartily for all his kindness, and said, she hoped to thank him a thousand times more. During this short conversation, she covered her white bosom as well as she could possibly with her arms; for Jones could not avoid stealing a sly peep or two, though he took all imaginable care to avoid giving any offence.

Our travellers had happened to take up their residence at a house of exceeding good repute, whither Irish ladies of strict virtue, and many northern lasses of the same predicament, were accustomed to resort in their way to Bath. The landlady therefore would by no means have admitted any conversation of a disreputable kind to pass under her roof. Indeed, so foul and contagious are all such proceedings, that they contaminate the very innocent scenes where they are committed, and give the name of a bad house, or of a house of ill repute, to all those where they are suffered to be carried on.

Not that I would intimate that strict chastity can possibly be maintained at a public inn. My good landlady did not hope for such a blessing, nor would any of the ladies I have spoken of, or indeed any others of the most rigid note, have expected or insisted on any such thing. But to exclude all vulgar concubinage, and to drive all whores in rags from within the walls, is within the power of every one. This my landlady very strictly adhered to, and said so.

A serjeant and a file of musqueteers, with a deserter in their custody, arrived about this time. The serjeant presently inquired for the principal magistrate of the town, and was informed by my landlord, that he himself was vested in that office. He then demanded his billets, together with a mug of beer, and complaining it was cold, spread himself before the kitchen fire.

Mr Jones was at this time comforting the poor distressed lady, who sat down at a table in the kitchen, and leaning her head upon her arm, was bemoaning her misfortunes; but lest my fair readers should be in pain concerning a particular circumstance, I think proper here to acquaint them, that she had so well covered herself that her regard to decency was not in the least violated by the presence of so many men as were now in the room.

One of the soldiers now went up to the serjeant, and whispered something in his ear; upon which he steadfastly fixed his eyes on the lady, and having looked at her for near a minute, he came up to her, saying, 'I ask pardon, madam; but I am certain I am not deceived; you can be no other person than Captain Waters's lady?'

The poor woman, who in her present distress had very little regarded the face of any person present, no sooner looked at the serjeant than she presently recollected him, and calling him by his name, answered, 'That she was indeed the unhappy person he imagined her to be'; but added, 'I wonder any one should know me in this disguise.' To which the serjeant replied, 'He was very much surprized to see her ladyship in such a dress, and was afraid some accident had happened to her.'—'An accident hath happened to me, indeed,' says she, 'and I am highly obliged to this gentleman' (pointing to Jones) 'that it was not a fatal one, or that I am now living to mention it.'—'Whatever the gentleman hath done,' cries the serjeant, 'I am sure the captain will make him amends for it; and if I can be of any service, your ladyship may command me, and I shall think myself very happy to have it in my power to serve your ladyship; and so indeed may any one, for I know the captain will well reward them for it.'

The landlady, who heard from the stairs all that past between the serjeant and Mrs Waters, came hastily down, and running directly up to her, 'Lud! madam,' says she, 'how should I have imagined that a lady of your fashion would appear in such dress? I hope your ladyship will accept of a gown, till you can get your own clothes.'

'Prithee, woman,' says Mrs Waters, 'cease your impertinence: how can you imagine I should concern myself about anything which comes from the lips of such low creatures as yourself?'

Here Jones begged Mrs Waters to accept her gown: 'for I must confess,' cries he, 'our appearance was a little suspicious when first we came in.'

Whether cold, shame, or the persuasions of Mr Jones prevailed most on Mrs Waters, I will not determine, but she suffered herself to be pacified by my landlady, and retired with that good woman, in order to apparel herself in a decent manner.

Partridge, who had been all this time washing at the pump, returned into the kitchen at the instant when matters were thus restored to a perfect calm; at which the serjeant, though it may seem so contrary to the principles of his profession, testified his approbation. 'Why now, that's friendly,' said he; 'd—n me, I hate to see people bear ill-will to one another.'

He then proposed a libation as a necessary part of the ceremony at all treaties of this kind. The good people now ranged themselves round the kitchen fire, where good humour seemed to maintain an absolute dominion; and Partridge converted hunger into thirst, and soon became extremely facetious. We must, however, quit this agreeable assembly for a while, and attend Mr Jones to Mrs Waters's apartment, where the dinner which he had bespoke was now on the table.

CHAPTER TWENTY-TWO

A DESCRIPTION OF A BATTLE OF THE AMOROUS KIND

MR JONES was, in reality, one of the handsomest young fellows in the world. His face, besides being the picture of health, had in it the most apparent marks of sweetness and good nature. He was besides active, genteel, gay, and good-humoured; and had a flow of animal spirits which enlivened every conversation where he was present.

When the reader hath duly reflected on these many charms which all centred in our hero, and considers at the same time the fresh obligations which Mrs Waters had to him, it will be a mark more of prudery than candour to entertain a bad opinion of her because she conceived a very good opinion of him.

Mrs Waters had, in truth, not only a good opinion of our hero, but a very great affection for him. To speak out boldly at once, she was in love. So she endeavoured to engage him by all the coquetry practised with good success in the drawing-room on the much more sensible as well as tender hearts of the fine gentlemen there.

We are no sooner in love than it becomes our principal care to engage the affection of the object beloved. For what other purpose indeed are our youth instructed in all the arts of rendering themselves agreeable? In short, all the graces which young ladies and young gentlemen too learn from others, and the many improvements which, by the help of a looking-glass, they add of their own, are in reality, the whole artillery of love.

Now Mrs Waters and our hero had no sooner sat down together than the former began to play this artillery upon the latter.

First, from two lovely blue eyes, whose bright orbs flashed lightning at their discharge, flew forth two pointed ogles; but happily for our hero, hit only a vast piece of beef which he was then conveying to his plate, and harmless spent their force. The fair warrior perceived their miscarriage, and immediately from her fair bosom drew forth a deadly sigh. A sigh which none could have heard unmoved, and which was sufficient at once to have swept off a dozen beaus; so soft, so sweet, so tender, that the insinuating air must have found its subtle way to the heart of our hero, had it not luckily been driven from his ears by the coarse bubbling of some bottled ale, which at that time he was pouring forth.

No sooner then was the cloth removed than she again began her operations. First, having planted her right eye sidewise against Mr Jones, she shot from its corner a most penetrating glance; though by this means she designed only to draw him from his guard, and indeed to open his eyes, through which she intended to surprise his heart. And now, she discharged a volley of small charms at once from her whole countenance in a smile. Not a smile of mirth, nor of joy; but a smile of affection, which most ladies have always ready at their command, and which serves them to show at once their good humour, their pretty dimples, and their white teeth.

This smile our hero received full in his eyes, and was immediately staggered with its force. He then began to see the designs of the enemy, and indeed to feel their success. A parley now was set on foot between the parties; during which the artful fair so slily and imperceptibly carried on her attack, that she had almost subdued the heart of our hero. To confess the truth, I am afraid Mr Jones maintained a kind of Dutch defence, and treacherously delivered up the garrison, without duly weighing his allegiance to the fair Sophia. In short, no sooner had the more amorous parley ended and the lady had unmasked the royal battery, by carelessly letting her handkerchief drop from her neck, than the heart of

Mr Jones was entirely taken, and the fair conqueror enjoyed the usual fruits of her victory.

While our lovers were entertaining themselves they were likewise furnishing out an entertainment for their good friends in the kitchen. And this in a double sense, by affording them matter for their conversation, and, at the same time, drink to enliven their spirits.

There were now assembled round the kitchen fire, besides my landlord and landlady, who occasionally went backward and forward, Mr Partridge, the serjeant, and the coachman who drove a young lady and her maid.

Partridge having acquainted the company with the situation in which Mrs Waters had been found by Jones, the serjeant proceeded to that part of her history which was known to him. He said she was the wife of Mr Waters, who was a captain in their regiment, and had often been with him at quarters. 'Some folks,' says he, 'used indeed to doubt whether they were lawfully married in a church or no. And the lady, to give the devil his due, is a very good sort of lady, and loves the cloth, and is always desirous to do strict justice to it; for she hath begged off many a poor soldier, and, by her goodwill, would never have any of them punished. But yet, to be sure, Ensign Northerton and she were very well acquainted together at our last quarters; that is the very right and truth of the matter. But the captain he knows nothing about it; and as long as there is enough for him too, what does it signify?' 'All a parcel of scandalous stuff,' answered the mistress of the house. 'I am sure, now she is drest, she looks like a very good sort of lady, and she behaves herself like one; for she gave me a guinea for the use of my clothes.'

The serjeant asked Partridge whither he and his master were travelling? 'None of your magisters,' answered Partridge; 'I am no man's servant, I assure you; for, though I have had misfortunes in the world, I write gentleman after my name; and, as poor and simple as I may appear now, I have taught grammar-school in my time. And I promise you my friend is one of the greatest gentlemen in the kingdom' (at which words both landlord and landlady pricked up their ears). 'He is the heir of Squire All-worthy.'—'What, the squire who doth so much good all over the country?' cries my landlady. 'Even he,' answered Partridge. 'Then I warrant,' says she, 'he'll have a swinging great estate hereafter.' —'Most certainly,' answered Partridge. 'Well,' replied the landlady, 'I thought the first moment I saw him he looked like a good sort of gentleman.'

The young lady was now desirous to depart, and had given orders for her coach to be prepared: but all in vain, for the coachman was disabled from performing his office for that evening. An ancient heathen would perhaps have imputed this disability to the god of drink. To speak plainly, serjeant and coachman were both dead drunk, nor was Partridge in a much better situation. As for my landlord, drinking was his trade; and the liquor had no more effect on him than it had on any other vessel in his house.

The mistress of the inn, now being summoned to attend Mr Jones and his companion, gave a full relation of the latter part of the foregoing scene; and at the same time expressed great concern for the young lady, 'who,' she said, 'was under the utmost uneasiness at being prevented from pursuing her journey. She is a sweet pretty creature,' added she, 'and I am certain I have seen her face before. I fancy she is in love, and running away from her friends. Who knows but some young gentleman or other may be expecting her, with a heart as heavy as her own?'

Jones fetched a heavy sigh at those words; of which, though Mrs Waters observed it, she took no notice while the landlady continued in the room; but, after the departure of that good woman, she could not forbear giving our hero certain hints on her suspecting some very dangerous rival in his affections. The awkward behaviour of Mr Jones on this occasion convinced her of the truth, without his giving her a direct answer to any of her questions; but she was not nice enough in her amours to be greatly concerned at the discovery. The beauty of Jones highly charmed her eye; but as she could not see his heart, she gave herself no concern about it.

CHAPTER TWENTY-THREE

CONTAINING THE ARRIVAL OF AN IRISH GENTLEMAN

It was now midnight; and the company at the inn, as well those who have been already mentioned in this history, as some others who arrived in the evening, were all in bed. Only Susan Chambermaid was now stirring, she being obliged to wash the kitchen before she retired to the arms of a fond expecting hostler.

In this posture were affairs at the inn when a gentleman arrived there post. He immediately alighted from his horse, and, coming up to Susan, inquired of her, in a very abrupt and confused manner, being almost out of breath with eagerness Whether there was any lady in the house? The hour of night, and the behaviour of the man, who stared very wildly all the time, a little surprized Susan, so that she hesitated before she made any answer; upon which the gentleman, with redoubled eagerness, begged her to give him a true information, saying, he had lost his wife, and was come in pursuit of her. 'Upon my shoul,' cries he, 'I have been near catching her already in two or three places, if I had not found her gone just as I came up with her. If she be in the house, do carry me up in the dark and show her to me.' He then pulled out a handful of guineas, a sight which would have bribed persons of much greater consequence than this poor wench to much worse purposes.

Susan, from the account she had received of Mrs Waters, made not the least doubt but that she was the very identical stray whom the right owner pursued. As she concluded, therefore, with great appearance of reason, that she never could get money in an honester way than by restoring a wife to her husband, she made no scruple of assuring the gentleman that the lady he wanted was then in the house; and was presently afterwards prevailed upon to conduct him to the bedchamber of Mrs Waters.

It hath been a custom long established in the polite world, and that upon very solid and substantial reasons, that a husband shall never enter his wife's apartment without first knocking at the door. Knock, indeed, he did at the door, but not with one of those gentle raps which is usual on such occasions. On the contrary, when he found the door locked, he flew at it with such violence, that the lock immediately gave way, the door burst open, and he fell headlong into the room.

He had no sooner recovered his legs than forth from the bed, upon his legs likewise, appeared—with shame and sorrow are we obliged to proceed—our hero himself, who, with a menacing voice, demanded of the gentleman who he was, and what he meant by daring to burst open his chamber in that outrageous manner.

The gentleman at first thought he had committed a mistake, and was going to ask pardon and retreat, when, on a sudden, as the moon shone very bright, he cast his eyes on stays, gowns, petticoats, caps, ribbons, stockings, garters, shoes, clogs, all which lay in a disordered manner on the floor. All these, operating on the natural jealousy of his temper, so enraged him, that he lost all power of speech; and, without returning any answer to Jones, he endeavoured to approach the bed.

Jones immediately interposing, a fierce contention arose, which soon proceeded to blows on both sides. And now Mrs Waters (for we must confess she was in the same bed), being, I suppose, awakened from her sleep, and seeing two men fighting in her bedchamber, began to scream in the most violent manner, crying out murder! robbery! and more frequently rape! which last, some, perhaps, may wonder she should mention.

Next to the lady's chamber was deposited the body of an Irish gentleman who arrived too late at the inn to have been mentioned before. This gentleman was one of those whom the Irish call a cavalier. He was a younger brother of a good family, and, having no fortune at home, was obliged to look abroad in order to get one; for which purpose he was proceeding to the Bath, to try his luck with cards and the women.

This young fellow lay in bed reading. He no sooner heard the violent uproar in the next room, than he leapt from his bolster, and, taking his sword in one hand, and the candle which burnt by him in the other, he went directly to Mrs Waters's chamber.

If the sight of another man in his shirt at first added some shock to the decency of the lady, it made her presently amends by considerably abating her fears; for no sooner had the calabalaro entered the room than he cried out, 'Mr Fitzpatrick, what the devil is the maning of this?' Upon which the other immediately answered, 'O, Mr Maclachlan! I am rejoiced you are here. This villain hath debauched my wife, and is got into bed with her.' —'What wife?' cries Maclachlan; 'do not I know Mrs Fitzpatrick very well, and don't I see that the lady whom the gentleman who stands here in his shirt, is lying in bed with, is none of her?'

Fitzpatrick, now perceiving by the glimpse he had of the lady that he had made a very unfortunate mistake, began to ask many pardons of the lady; and then, turning to Jones, he said, 'I would have you take notice I do not ask your pardon, for I am resolved to have your blood in the morning.'

Jones treated this menace with much contempt; and Mr Maclachlan answered, 'Indeed, Mr Fitzpatrick, you may be ashamed of your own self, to disturb people at this time of night; if all the people in the inn were not asleep, you would have awakened them as you have me. The gentleman has served you very rightly. Upon my conscience, though I have no wife, if you had treated her so, I would have cut your throat.'

Jones was so confounded with his fears for his lady's reputation, that he knew neither what to say or do; but the invention of women is much readier than that of men. She recollected that there was a communication between her chamber and that of Mr Jones; relying, therefore, on his honour and her own assurance, she answered, 'I know not what you mean, villains! I am wife to none of you. Help! Rape! Murder! Rape!' And now, the landlady coming into the room, Mrs Waters fell upon her with the utmost virulence, saying, 'She thought herself in a sober inn, and not in a bawdyhouse; but that a set of villains had broke into her room, with an intent upon her honour, if not upon her life; and both were equally dear to her.'

The landlady now began to roar as loudly as the poor woman in

102

bed had done before. She cried, 'What, in the devil's name, is the reason of all this disturbance in the lady's room?' Fitzpatrick, hanging down his head, repeated, 'That he had committed a mistake, for which he heartily asked pardon,' and then retired with his countryman. Jones, who was too ingenious to have missed the hint given him by his fair one, boldly asserted, 'That he had run to her assistance upon hearing the door broke open, with what design he could not conceive, unless of robbing the lady; which, if they intended, he said, he had the good fortune to prevent.'

When the men were all departed, Mrs Waters, recovering from her anger, spoke in much gentler accents to the landlady, who did so readily quit her concern for the reputation of the house, in favour of which she began to number the many great persons who had slept under her roof; but the lady stopt her short, and having absolutely acquitted her of having had any share in the past disturbance, begged to be left to her repose, which, she said, she hoped to enjoy unmolested during the remainder of the night. Upon which the landlady, after much civility and many courtsies, took her leave.

CHAPTER TWENTY-FOUR

Now arrived a post-boy at the gate; upon which Susan, being ordered out, returned, introducing two young women in riding habits, one of which was so very richly laced, that Partridge instantly started from his chair, and my landlady fell to her courtsies, and her ladyships, with great eagerness.

The lady in the rich habit said, with a smile of great condescension, 'If you will give me leave, madam, I will warm myself a few minutes at your kitchen fire, for it is really very cold; but I must insist on disturbing no one from his seat.' This was spoken on account of Partridge, who had retreated to the other end of the room, struck with the utmost awe and astonishment at the splendour of the lady's dress. Indeed, she had a much better title to respect than this; for she was one of the most beautiful creatures in the world.

The lady earnestly desired Partridge to return to his seat; but could not prevail. She then pulled off her gloves, and displayed to the fire two hands, which had every property of snow in them, except that of melting. Her companion, who was indeed her maid, likewise pulled off her gloves, and discovered what bore an exact resemblance, in cold and colour, to a piece of frozen beef.

'I wish, madam,' quoth the latter, 'your ladyship would not think of going any farther to-night. I am terribly afraid your ladyship will not be able to bear the fatigue.'

'Why sure,' cries the landlady, 'her ladyship's honour can never intend it. O, bless me! farther to-night, indeed! let me beseech your ladyship not to think on't—I am sorry, madam, all my best rooms are full. Several people of the first quality are now in bed. Here's a great young squire, and many other great gentlefolks of quality.—If they be gentlemen, I am certain, when they know it is for her ladyship, they will get up again.'

'Not upon my account,' says the lady; 'I will have no person disturbed for me. If you have a room that is commonly decent, it will serve me very well, though it be never so plain.'—'O, madam!' cries the other, 'I have several very good rooms for that matter, but none good enough for your honour's ladyship. However, as you are so condescending to take up with the best I have, do, Susan, get a fire in the Rose this minute. Will your ladyship be pleased to go up now, or stay till the fire is lighted?'—'I think I have sufficiently warmed myself,' answered the lady; 'so, if you please, I will go now; I am afraid I have kept people, and particularly that gentleman' (meaning Partridge), 'too long in the cold already. Indeed, I cannot bear to think of keeping any person from the fire this dreadful weather.' She then departed with her maid, the landlady marching with two lighted candles before her.

The lady had no sooner laid herself on her pillow than the waiting-woman returned to the kitchen.

The company, at her entrance, shewed her the same respect which they had before paid to her mistress, by rising; but she forgot to imitate her, by desiring them to sit down again. Indeed, it was scarce possible they should have done so, for she placed her chair in such a posture as to occupy almost the whole fire. She then ordered a chicken to be broiled that instant, declaring, if it was not ready in a quarter of an hour, she would not stay for it. My landlady was obliged to confess that she had none in the house; 'but, madam,' said she, 'I can get any kind of mutton in an instant from the butcher's.'

'Do you think, then,' answered the waiting-gentlewoman, 'that I have the stomach of a horse, to eat mutton at this time of night? Sure you people that keep inns imagine your betters are like yourselves. Indeed, I expected to get nothing at this wretched place. I wonder my lady would stop at it. I suppose none but tradesmen and grasiers ever call here.' The landlady fired at this indignity offered to her house; however, she suppressed her temper, and contented herself with saying, 'Very good quality frequented it, she thanked heaven!'—'Don't tell me,' cries the other, 'of quality! And so, madam, you tell me your house 's frequented by people of great quality?'

The landlady answered in the affirmative, saying, 'There were a great many very good quality and gentlefolks in it now. There's young Squire Allworthy, as that gentleman there knows.'

'And pray who is this young gentleman of quality, this young Squire Allworthy?' said Abigail.

'Who should he be,' answered Partridge, 'but the son and heir of the great squire Allworthy, of Somersetshire!'

'Upon my word,' said she, 'you tell me strange news; for I know Mr Allworthy of Somersetshire very well, and I know he hath no son alive.'

The landlady pricked up her ears at this, and Partridge looked a little confounded. However, after a short hesitation, he answered, 'Indeed, madam, it is true, everybody doth not know him to be Squire Allworthy's son; for he was never married to his mother; but his son he certainly is, and will be his heir too, as certainly as his name is Jones.' At that word, Abigail cried out, 'You surprize me, sir! Is it possible Mr Jones should be now in the house?' '*Quare non?*' answered Partridge, 'it is possible, and it is certain.'

Abigail now made haste and repaired back to her mistress. As in the month of April, the gentle, constant dove, perched on some fair boughs, sits meditating on her mate, so, looking a hundred charms and breathing as many sweets, her thoughts being fixed on her Tommy, with a heart as good and innocent as her face was beautiful, Sophia (for it was she herself) lay reclining her lovely head on her hand, when her maid entered the room, and, running directly to the bed, cried, 'Madam—madam—who doth your ladyship think is in the house?' Sophia starting up, cried, 'I hope my father hath not overtaken us.'—'No, madam, it is one worth a hundred fathers; Mr Jones himself is here at this very instant.'—'Mr Jones!' says Sophia. 'It is impossible! I cannot be so fortunate.' Her maid averred the fact, and was presently detached by her mistress to order him to be called; for she said she was resolved to see him immediately.

Mrs Honour discharged her commission, by bidding the landlady immediately wake Mr. Jones, and tell him a lady wanted to speak with him. The landlady referred her to Partridge, saying, 'he was the squire's friend: but, for her part, she never called men-folks, especially gentlemen,' and then walked sullenly out of the kitchen. Honour applied herself to Partridge; but he refused, 'for my friend,' cries he, 'went to bed very late, and he would be very angry to be disturbed so soon.' Mrs Honour insisted still to have him called, saying, 'she was sure, instead of being angry, that he would be to the highest degree delighted when he knew the occasion.'—'Another time, perhaps he might,' cries Partridge; 'but one woman is enough at once for a reasonable man.'—'What do you mean by one woman, fellow?' cries Honour. 'None of your fellow,' answered Partridge. He then proceeded to inform her plainly that Jones was in bed with a wench, and made use of an expression too indelicate to be here inserted; which so enraged Mrs Honour, that she called him jackanapes, and returned in a violent hurry to her mistress, whom she acquainted with the success of her errand, and with the account she had received; which, if possible, she exaggerated, being as angry with Jones as if he had pronounced all the words that came from the mouth of Partridge. She discharged a torrent of abuse on the master, and advised her mistress to quit all thoughts of a man who had never shown himself deserving of her. She then ripped up the story of Molly Seagrim, and gave the most malicious turn to his formerly quitting Sophia herself.

The spirits of Sophia were too much dissipated by concern to enable her to stop the torrent of her maid. At last, however, she interrupted her, saying, 'I never can believe this; some villain hath belied him. You say you had it from his friend; but surely it is not the office of a friend to betray such secrets.'—'I suppose,' cries Honour, 'the fellow is his pimp; for I never saw so ill-looked a villain. Besides, such profligate rakes as Mr Jones are never ashamed of these matters.'

While Sophia, tormented with anxiety, knew not what to believe, nor what resolution to take, Susan arrived with the supper. Mrs Honour immediately advised her mistress, in a whisper, to pump this wench, who probably could inform her of the truth. Sophia approved it, and began as follows: 'Come hither, child; now answer me truly what I am going to ask you, and I promise you I will very well reward you. Is there a young gentleman in this house, a handsome young gentleman, that ——' Here Sophia blushed and was confounded. 'A young gentleman,' cries Honour, 'that came hither in company with that saucy rascal who is now in the kitchen?' Susan answered, 'There was.'—'Do you know anything of any lady?' continues Sophia, 'any lady? I don't ask you whether she is handsome or no; perhaps she is not; that's nothing to the purpose; but do you know of any lady?'—'La, madam,' cries Honour, 'you will make a very bad examiner. Hark'ee, child,' says she, 'is not that very young gentleman now in bed with some nasty trull or other?' Here Susan smiled, and was silent. 'Answer the question, child,' says Sophia, 'and here's a guinea for you.' —'A guinea! madam,' cries Susan; 'la, what's a guinea? If my mistress should know it I shall certainly lose my place that very instant.'—'Here's another for you,' says Sophia, 'and I promise you faithfully your mistress shall never know it.' Susan, after a very short hesitation, took the money, and told the whole story, concluding with saying, 'If you have any great curiosity, madam, I can steal softly into his room, and see whether he be in his own bed or no.' She accordingly did this by Sophia's desire, and returned with an answer in the negative.

Sophia now trembled and turned pale. Mrs Honour begged her to be comforted, and not to think any more of so worthless a fellow. 'Why there,' says Susan, 'I hope, madam, your ladyship won't be offended.'

Sophia gave her a third guinea, and, telling her she would certainly be her friend if she mentioned nothing of what had passed, dismissed the girl, with orders to the post-boy to get the horses ready immediately.

Being now left alone with her maid, she told her trusty waiting-woman, 'That she never was more easy than at present. I am now convinced,' said she, 'he is not only a villain, but a low despicable wretch. Yes, Honour, I am now easy; I am indeed; I am very easy'; and then she burst into a violent flood of tears.

After a short interval spent by Sophia, chiefly in crying, and assuring her maid that she was perfectly easy, Susan arrived with an account that the horses were ready, when a very extraordinary thought suggested itself to our young heroine, by which Mr Jones would be acquainted with her having been at the inn, in a way which, if any sparks of affection for her remained in him, would be at least some punishment for his faults.

The reader will be pleased to remember a little muff, which hath had the honour of being more than once remembered already in this history. This muff, ever since the departure of Mr Jones, had been the constant companion of Sophia by day, and her bedfellow by night; and this muff she had at this very instant upon her arm; whence she took it off with great indignation, and, having writ her name with her pencil upon a piece of paper which she pinned to it, she bribed the maid to convey it into the empty bed of Mr Jones, in which, if he did not find it, she charged her to take some method of conveying it before his eyes in the morning.

Then, having paid for what Mrs Honour had eaten, in which bill was included an account for what she herself might have eaten, she mounted her horse, and, once more assuring her companion that she was perfectly easy, continued her journey.

CHAPTER TWENTY-FIVE

MORE ADVENTURES AT THE INN AT UPTON

IT was now past five in the morning, and other company began to rise and come to the kitchen, among who were the serjeant and the coachman, who drank a hearty cup together.

In this drinking nothing more remarkable happened than the behaviour of Partridge, who, when the serjeant drank a health to King George, repeated only the word King; nor could he be brought to utter more; for though he was going to fight against his own cause, yet he could not be prevailed upon to drink against it.

Mr Jones, being now returned to his own bed (but from whence he returned we must beg to be excused from relating), summoned Partridge from this agreeable company, who delivered himself as follows:

Saying he believed they were then in a bawdy house, and that he had with much ado prevented two wenches from disturbing his honour in the middle of the night. 'Heyday!' says he, 'I believe they got into your chamber whether I would or no; for here lies the muff of one of them on the ground.' Indeed, as Jones returned to his bed in the dark, he had never perceived the muff on the quilt, and, in leaping into his bed, he had tumbled it on the floor. This Partridge now took up, and was going to put into his pocket, when Jones desired to see it. The muff was so very remarkable, that our hero might possibly have recollected it without the information annexed. But his memory was not put to that hard office; for at the same instant he saw and read the words Sophia Western upon the paper which was pinned to it. His look now grew frantic in a moment, and he eagerly cried out, 'Oh Heavens! how came this muff here?'—'I know no more than your honour,' cried Partridge; 'but I saw it upon the arm of one of the women who would have disturbed you, if I would have suffered them.'—'Where are they?' cries Jones, jumping out of bed, and laying hold of his clothes. 'Many miles off, I believe, by this time,' said Partridge. And now Jones, upon further inquiry, was sufficiently assured that the bearer of this muff was no other than the lovely Sophia herself.

The behaviour of Jones on this occasion, his thoughts, his looks, his words, his actions, were such as beggar all description. After many bitter execrations on Partridge, and not fewer on himself, he ordered the poor fellow, who was frightened out of his wits, to run down and hire him horses at any rate; and a very few minutes afterwards, having shuffled on his clothes, he hastened downstairs to execute the orders himself, which he had just before given.

But before we proceed to what passed on his arrival in the kitchen, it will be necessary to recur to what had there happened since Partridge had first left it on his master's summons.

The serjeant was just marched off with his party, when the two Irish gentlemen arose, and came downstairs; both complaining that they had been so often waked by the noises in the inn, that they had never once been able to close their eyes all night.

The coach which had brought the young lady and her maid, was, indeed, a returned coach belonging to Mr King, of Bath, one of the worthiest and honestest men that ever dealt in horse-flesh, and whose coaches we heartily recommend to all our readers who travel that road.

The coachman, having but two passengers, and hearing Mr Maclachlan was going to Bath, offered to carry him thither at a very moderate price. Mr Maclachlan immediately closed with the proposal of the coachman, and, at the same time, persuaded his friend Fitzpatrick to accept of the fourth place in the coach. This conveyance the soreness of his bones made more agreeable to him than a horse; and, being well assured of meeting with his wife at Bath, he thought a little delay would be of no consequence.

Maclachlan, who was much the sharper man of the two, no sooner heard that this lady came from Chester, with the other circumstances which he learned from the hostler, than it came into his head that she might possibly be his friend's wife; and presently acquainted him with this suspicion. In the same manner, Mr Fitzpatrick instantly concurred, and flew directly upstairs, to surprize his wife, before he knew where she was; and unluckily ran his head against several doors and posts to no purpose. After a long fruitless search, Mr Fitzpatrick returned to the kitchen, where entered a gentleman hallowing as hunters do when the hounds are at a fault. He was just alighted from his horse, and had many attendants at his heels.

This gentleman just arrived was no other person than Squire Western himself, who was come hither in pursuit of his daughter; and, had he fortunately been two hours earlier, he had not only found her, but his niece into the bargain; for such was the wife of Mr Fitzpatrick, who had run away with her five years before, out of the custody of that sage lady, Madam Western.

Now this lady had departed from the inn much about the same time with Sophia; for, having been waked by the voice of her husband, she had sent up for the landlady, and being by her apprized of the matter, had bribed the good woman, at an extravagant price, to furnish her with horses for her escape.

Mr Western and his nephew were not known to one another;

nor indeed would the former have taken any notice of the latter if he had known him; for, this being a stolen match, and consequently an unnatural one in the opinion of the good squire, he had, from the time of her committing it, abandoned the poor young creature, who was then no more than eighteen, as a monster, and had never since suffered her to be named in his presence.

The kitchen was now a scene of universal confusion. Western inquiring after his daughter, and Fitzpatrick as eagerly after his wife, when Jones entered the room, unfortunately having Sophia's muff in his hand.

As soon as Western saw Jones, he set up the same holla as is used by sportsmen when their game is in view. He then immediately run up and laid hold of Jones, crying, 'We have got the dog fox, I warrant the bitch is not far off.'

Jones having, at length, shaken Mr Western off, and some of the company having interfered between them, our hero protested his innocence as to knowing anything of the lady. 'My daughter's muff!' cries the squire in a rage. 'Hath he not got my daughter's muff? Bear witness the goods are found upon him. I'll have him before a justice of peace this instant. Where is my daughter, villain?'—'Sir,' said Jones, 'I beg you would be pacified. The muff, I acknowledge, is the young lady's; but, upon my honour, I have never seen her.' At these words Western lost all patience, and grew inarticulate with rage.

Some of the servants had acquainted Fitzpatrick who Mr Western was. The good Irishman, therefore, thinking he had now an opportunity to do an act of service to his uncle, and by that means might possibly obtain his favour, stept up to Jones, and cried out, 'Upon my conscience, sir, you may be ashamed of denying your having seen the gentleman's daughter before my face, when you know I found you there upon the bed together. Then, turning to Western, he offered to conduct him immediately to the room where his daughter was; which offer being accepted, he, the squire, and some others, ascended directly to Mrs Waters's chamber, which they entered with no less violence than Mr Fitzpatrick had done before.

The poor lady started from her sleep with as much amazement as terror, and beheld at her bedside a figure which might very well be supposed to have escaped out of Bedlam. Such wildness and confusion were in the looks of Mr Western; who no sooner saw the lady than he started back, shewing sufficiently by his manner, before he spoke, that this was not the person sought after.

So much more tenderly do women value their reputation than their persons, that, though the latter seemed now in more danger than before, yet, as the former was secure, the lady screamed not with such violence as she had done on the other occasion. However, she no sooner found herself alone than she abandoned all thoughts of further repose; and, as she had sufficient reason to be dissatisfied with her present lodging, she dressed herself with all possible expedition.

Mr Western now proceeded to search the whole house, but to as little purpose as he had disturbed poor Mrs Waters. He then returned disconsolate into the kitchen, where he found Jones in the custody of his servants.

This violent uproar had raised all the people in the house, though it was as yet scarcely daylight. Among these was a grave gentleman, who had the honour to be in the commission of the peace for the county of Worcester. Of which Mr Western was no sooner informed than he offered to lay his complaint before him.

Here Mr Fitzpatrick offered to lend him his assistance, informing the company that he had been himself bred to the law. (And indeed he had served three years as clerk to an attorney in the north of Ireland, when he quitted his master, came over to England, and set up that business which requires no apprenticeship, namely, that of a gentleman, in which he had succeeded).

Mr Fitzpatrick declared that the law concerning daughters was out of the present case; that stealing a muff was undoubtedly felony, and the goods being found upon the person, were sufficient evidence of the fact.

Jones now desired to be heard, which was at last, with difficulty, granted him. He then produced the evidence of Mr Partridge, as to the finding it; but, what was still more, Susan deposed that Sophia herself had delivered the muff to her, and had ordered her to convey it into the chamber where Mr Jones had found it.

Whether a natural love of justice, or the extraordinary comeliness of Jones had wrought on Susan to make the discovery, I will not determine; but such were the effects of her evidence, that the magistrate, throwing himself back in his chair, declared that the matter was now altogether as clear on the side of the prisoner as it had before been against him. The justice then arose, acquitted the prisoner, and broke up the court.

Mr Western now gave every one present a hearty curse, and, immediately ordering his horses, departed in pursuit of his daughter, without taking the least notice of his nephew, Fitzpatrick, or returning any answer to his claim of kindred, notwithstanding all the obligations he had just received from that gentleman. In the violence, moreover, of his hurry, and of his passion, he luckily forgot to demand the muff of Jones: I say luckily; for he would have died on the spot rather than have parted with it.

Jones likewise, with his friend Partridge, set forward the moment he had paid his reckoning, in quest of his lovely Sophia, whom he now resolved never more to abandon the pursuit of. Nor could he bring himself even to take leave of Mrs Waters; of whom he detested the very thoughts, as she had been, though not

111

designedly, the occasion of his missing the happiest interview with Sophia, to whom he now vowed eternal constancy.

As for Mrs Waters, she took the opportunity of the coach which was going to Bath! for which place she set out in company with the two Irish gentlemen, the landlady kindly lending her her clothes; in return for which she was contented only to receive about double their value, as a recompence for the loan. Upon the road she was perfectly reconciled to Mr Fitzpatrick, who was a very handsome fellow, and indeed did all she could to console him in the absence of his wife.

CHAPTER TWENTY-SIX

THE ADVENTURES WHICH SOPHIA MET WITH AFTER HER LEAVING UPTON

OUR history mentioned the departure of Sophia and her maid from the inn; we shall now therefore pursue the steps of that lovely creature, and leave her unworthy lover a little longer to bemoan his ill luck, or rather his ill conduct.

Sophia having directed her guide to travel through bye-roads, across the country, they now passed the Severn, and had scarce got a mile from the inn, when the young lady, looking behind her, saw several horses coming after on full speed. This greatly alarmed her fears, and away they rode at full gallop. But the faster they went, the faster were they followed; and as the horses behind were somewhat swifter than those before, so the former were at length overtaken. A happy circumstance for poor Sophia; whose fears, joined to her fatigue, had almost overpowered her spirits; but she was now instantly relieved by a female voice, that greeted her in the softest manner, and with the utmost civility. This greeting Sophia, as soon as she could recover her breath, with like civility, and with the highest satisfaction to herself, returned.

The two parties proceeded three full miles together before any one offered again to open their mouths; when our heroine, having pretty well got the better of her fear (but yet being somewhat surprized that the other still continued to attend her, as she pursued no great road, and had already passed through several turnings), accosted the strange lady in a most obliging tone, and said, 'She was very happy to find they were both travelling the same way.' The other, who, like a ghost, only wanted to be spoke to, readily answered, 'That the happiness was entirely hers; that she was a perfect stranger in that country, and was so overjoyed at meeting a companion of her own sex, that she had perhaps been guilty of an impertinence, in keeping pace with her. More civilities passed between these two ladies; for Mrs Honour had now given place to the fine habit of the stranger, and had fallen into the rear.

Daylight at length appeared in its full lustre; and now the two ladies, who were riding over a common side by side, looking steadfastly at each other, at the same moment both their eyes became fixed; both their horses stopt, and, both speaking together, with equal joy pronounced, the one the name of Sophia, the other that of Harriet.

This unexpected encounter surprized the ladies much more than I believe it will the sagacious reader, who must have imagined that the strange lady could be no other than Mrs Fitzpatrick, the cousin of Miss Western, whom we before mentioned to have sallied from the inn a few minutes after her.

So great was the surprize and joy which these two cousins conceived at this meeting (for they had formerly been most intimate acquaintance and friends, and had long lived together with their aunt Western), that it is impossible to recount half the congratulations which passed between them, before either asked a very natural question of the other, namely, whither she was going?

This at last, however, came first from Mrs Fitzpatrick; but easy and natural as the question may seem, Sophia found it difficult to give it a very ready and certain answer. She begged her cousin therefore to suspend all curiosity till they arrived at some inn.

In this way they travelled many hours, till they came into a wide and well-beaten road, which, as they turned to the right, soon brought them to a very fair promising inn, where they all alighted: but so fatigued was Sophia, that she had sat her horse during the last five or six miles with great difficulty.

This violent fatigue which both her mind and body had undergone, almost overcame the excellent constitution of Sophia, and she had scarce strength sufficient to totter into the inn, leaning on the arm of her maid. Here she was no sooner seated than she called for a glass of water; but Mrs Honour, very judiciously, in my opinion, changed it into a glass of wine.

Mrs Fitzpatrick, hearing from Mrs Honour that Sophia had not been in bed during the two last nights, and observing her to look very pale and wan with her fatigue, earnestly entreated her to refresh herself with some sleep. Sophia was easily prevailed on to follow the counsel of her friend, which was heartily seconded by her maid. Mrs Fitzpatrick likewise offered to bear her cousin company, which Sophia, with more complacence, accepted.

The sun (for he keeps very good hours at this time of the year) had been some time retired to rest, when Sophia arose greatly refreshed by her sleep which, short as it was, nothing but her extreme fatigue could have occasioned; for, though she had told her maid, and perhaps herself too, that she was perfectly easy when she left Upton, yet it is certain her mind was a little affected with that malady which is attended with all the restless symptoms of a fever, and is perhaps the very distemper which physicians mean (if they mean anything) by the fever on the spirits.

Mrs Fitzpatrick likewise left her bed at the same time; and, having summoned her maid, immediately dressed herself. She was really a very pretty woman, and, had she been in any other company but that of Sophia, might have been thought beautiful. Perhaps Sophia never looked more beautiful than she did at this instant. We ought not, therefore, to condemn the maid of the inn for her hyperbole, who, when she descended, after having lighted the fire, declared, and ratified it with an oath, that if ever there was an angel upon earth, she was now above-stairs.

Sophia had acquainted her cousin with her design to go to London; and Mrs Fitzpatrick had agreed to accompany her; for the arrival of her husband at Upton had put an end to her design of going to Bath, or to her aunt Western.

The two cousins began now to impart to each other their reciprocal curiosity; to know what extraordinary accidents on both sides occasioned this so strange and unexpected meeting. At last Mrs Fitzpatrick, having obtained of Sophia a promise of communicating likewise in her turn, thus began: 'You, my Sophia, was always my superior, in everything, and I heartily hope you will be so in your fortune.

'Though you must have heard much of my marriage; yet, as matters may probably have been misrepresented, I will set out from the very commencement of my unfortunate acquaintance with my present husband; which was at Bath, soon after you left my aunt, and returned to your father.

'Among the gay young fellows who were at this season at Bath, Mr Fitzpatrick was one. He was handsome, *dégagé*, extremely gallant, and in his dress exceeded most others. In short, my dear, if you was unluckily to see him now, I could describe him no better than by telling you he was the very reverse of everything which he is: for he hath rusticated himself so long, that he is become an absolute wild Irishman. But to proceed in my story: the qualifications which he then possessed so well recommended him, that, though the people of quality at that time lived separate from the rest of the company, and excluded them from all their parties, Mr Fitzpatrick found means to gain admittance.

My aunt, though no person of quality herself, had always lived about the court, and so was enrolled in that party; Mr Fitzpatrick soon grew so very particular in his behaviour to her, that the scandal club first began to take notice of it, and the better disposed persons made a match between them. For my own part, I confess I made no doubt that his designs were strictly honourable, as the phrase is; that is, to rob a lady of her fortune by way of marriage. My aunt was, I conceived, neither young enough nor handsome enough to attract much wicked inclination; but she had matrimonial charms in great abundance. I could not be violently the enemy of a man with whose behaviour to me I was greatly pleased; and the more so, as I was the only object of such respect; for he behaved at the same time to many women of quality without any respect at all.

'Agreeable as this was to me, he soon changed it into another kind of behaviour, which was perhaps more so. He now put on much softness and tenderness, and languished and sighed abundantly. At times, indeed, whether from art or nature I will not determine, he gave his usual loose to gaiety and mirth; but this was always in general company, and with other women; for even in a country-dance, when he was not my partner, he became grave, and put on the softest look imaginable the moment he approached me. Indeed he was in all things so very particular towards me, that I must have been blind not to have discovered it. And, and, and——'—'And you was more pleased still, my dear Harriet,' cries Sophia; 'you need not be ashamed,' added she, sighing, 'for sure there are irresistible charms in tenderness, which too many men are able to affect.'—'True,' answered her cousin; 'men, who in all other instances want common sense, are very Machiavels in the art of loving. I was pleased with my man. I was pleased with my conquest. To rival my aunt delighted me; to rival so many other women charmed me. In short, I am afraid I did not behave as I should do, even upon the very first declaration—I wish I did not almost give him positive encouragement before we parted.

'The Bath now talked loudly—I might almost say, roared against me. Several young women affected to shun my acquaintance, not so much, perhaps, from any real suspicion, as from a desire of banishing me from a company in which I too much engrossed their favourite man.

'But I am afraid, my dear, I shall tire you with a detail of so many minute circumstances. To be concise, therefore, imagine me married; imagine me with my husband, at the feet of my aunt; and then imagine the maddest woman in Bedlam, in a raving fit, and your imagination will suggest to you no more than what really happened.

'We remained at Bath no longer than a fortnight after our wedding; for as to any reconciliation with my aunt, there were no hopes; and of my fortune, not one farthing could be touched till I was of age, of which I now wanted more than two years. My husband, therefore, was resolved to set out for Ireland; against

115

which I remonstrated very earnestly, and insisted on a promise which he had made me before our marriage, that I should never take this journey against my consent; and indeed I never intended to consent to it; but however, petitioned only for the reprieve of a month; but he had fixed the day, and to that day he obstinately adhered.

'I now made no farther objections to our setting out, which we did the next morning, and in a little more than a week arrived at the seat of Mr Fitzpatrick.

'This seat, then, is an ancient mansion-house: if I was in one of those merry humours in which you have so often seen me, I could describe it to you ridiculously enough. It looked as if it had been formerly inhabited by a gentleman. Here was room enough, and not the less room on account of the furniture; for indeed there was very little in it. In short, the whole scene was so gloomy and melancholy, that it threw my spirits into the lowest dejection; which my husband discerning, instead of relieving, increased by two or three malicious observations. "There are good houses, madam," says he, "as you find, in other places besides England; but perhaps you had rather be in a dirty lodgings at Bath."

'My companion, far from clearing up the gloom of solitude, soon convinced me that I must have been wretched with him in any place, and in any condition. In a word, he was a surly fellow. How shall I describe his barbarity? To my fondness he was cold and insensible. My little comical ways, which you, my Sophy, and which others, have called so agreeable, he treated with contempt. In my most serious moments he sung and whistled; and whenever I was thoroughly dejected and miserable, he was angry, and abused me; for, though he was never pleased with my good humour, yet my low spirits always offended him, and those he imputed to my repentance of having (as he said) married an Irishman.

'So we continued above two years. During this interval I wrote three very supplicating, and, I thought, moving letters to my aunt; but, as I received no answer to any of them, my disdain would not suffer me to continue my application.' Here she stopt, and, looking earnestly at Sophia, said, 'Methinks, my dear, I read something in your eyes which reproaches me of a neglect in another place, where I should have met with a kinder return.'—'Indeed, dear Harriet,' answered Sophia, 'your story is an apology for any neglect; but, indeed, I feel that I have been guilty of a remissness, without so good an excuse.—Yet pray proceed; for I long though I tremble, to hear the end.'

Thus, then, Mrs Fitzpatrick resumed her narrative: 'My husband now took a second journey to England, where he continued upwards of three months; during the greater part of this time I led a life which nothing but having led a worse could make me think tolerable; for perfect solitude can never be reconciled to a social mind, like mine, but when it relieves you from the company of those you hate. What added to my wretchedness was the loss of my little infant: not that I pretend to have had for it that extravagant tenderness of which I believe I might have been capable under other circumstances; but I resolved, in every instance, to discharge the duty of the tenderest mother; and this care prevented me from feeling the weight of that heaviest of all things, when it can be at all said to lie heavy on our hands.

'I had spent full ten weeks almost entirely by myself, having seen nobody all that time, except my servants and a very few visitors, when a young lady, a relation to my husband, came from a distant part of Ireland to visit me.

'A few days after her arrival, perceiving me in very low spirits, the young lady fell to compassionating my case. She said, "Though politeness had prevented me from complaining to my husband's relations of his behaviour, yet they all were very sensible of it, and felt great concern upon that account; but none more than herself." And after some more general discourse on this head, which I own I could not forbear countenancing, at last, after much previous precaution and enjoined concealment, she communicated to me, as a profound secret—that my husband kept a mistress. Contempt had not so kept down my anger to my husband, but that hatred rose again on this occasion.

'Well,' continued Mrs Fitzpatrick, 'my husband at last returned; and, if I am thoroughly acquainted with my own thoughts, I hated him now more than ever; but I despised him rather less: for certainly nothing so much weakens our contempt, as an injury done to our pride or our vanity.

'He now assumed a carriage to me so very different from what he had lately worn, and so nearly resembling his behaviour the first week of our marriage, that, had I now had any spark of love remaining, he might, possibly, have rekindled my fondness for him. His behaviour, at first, greatly surprized me; but he soon acquainted me with the motive. He had spent and lost all the ready money of my fortune.

'I told him, and I told him truly, that, had I been possessed of the Indies at our first marriage, he might have commanded it all; I was resolved to retain what little remained.

'I will not describe to you the passion into which these words, and the resolute air in which they were spoken, threw him: nor will I trouble you with the whole scene which succeeded between us. Out came, you may be well assured, the story of the mistress; and out it did come, with all the embellishments which anger and disdain could bestow upon it.

'Perhaps you will conclude he beat me; but this, though he hath approached very near to it, he never actually did. He confined me to my room, without suffering me to have either pen, ink, paper, or book: and a servant every day made my bed, and brought me my food.

'Here I remained a fortnight longer; and, to say the truth, my constancy was almost subdued, and I began to think of submission; when, one day, in the absence of my husband, who was gone abroad for some short time, by the greatest good fortune in the world, an accident happened. I—at a time when I began to give way to the utmost despair——everything would be excusable at such a time—at that very time I received——But it would take up an hour to tell you all particulars.—In one word, then, gold, the common key to all padlocks, opened my door, and set me at liberty.

'I now made haste to Dublin, where I immediately procured a passage to England; and was proceeding to Bath, in order to throw myself into the protection of my aunt, or of your father, or of any relation who would afford it me. My husband overtook me last night at the inn where I lay, and which you left a few minutes before me; but I had the good luck to escape him, and to follow you.

'And thus, my dear, ends my history: a tragical one, I am sure, it is to myself; but, perhaps, I ought to apologize to you for its dullness.'

Sophia heaved a deep sigh, and answered, 'Indeed, Harriet, I pity you from my soul!——But what could you expect? Why, why, would you marry an Irishman?'

'Upon my word,' replied her cousin, 'your censure is unjust. There are, among the Irish, men of as much worth and honour as any among the English: nay, to speak the truth, generosity of spirit is rather more common among them. I have known some examples there, too, of good husbands; and I believe these are not very plenty in England. Ask me, rather, what I could expect when I married a fool; and I will tell you a solemn truth; I did not know him to be so.'—'Can no man,' said Sophia, in a very low and altered voice, 'do you think, make a bad husband, who is not a fool?'—'That,' answered the other, 'is too general a negative; but none, I believe, is so likely as a fool to prove so. Among my acquaintance, the silliest fellows are the worst husbands; and I will venture to assert, as a fact, that a man of sense rarely behaves very ill to a wife who deserves very well.'

Sophia, now at the desire of her cousin, related—not what follows, but what hath gone before in this history: for which reason the reader will, I suppose, excuse me for not repeating it over again.

One remark, however, I cannot forbear making on her narrative, namely, that she made no more mention of Jones, from the beginning to the end, than if there had been no such person alive.

Just as Sophia arrived at the conclusion of her story, there arrived in the room where the two ladies were sitting a noise, not unlike, in loudness, to that of a pack of hounds just let out from their kennel.

To ease the reader's curiosity, therefore, rather than his apprehensions, we proceed to inform him that an Irish peer had arrived very late that evening at the inn, in his way to London. This nobleman had seen the attendant of Mrs Fitzpatrick, and upon a short inquiry, was informed that the lady, with whom he was very particularly acquainted, was above.

To say the truth, it was by his assistance that she had been enabled to escape from her husband; for this nobleman had the same gallant disposition with those renowned knights of whom we read in heroic story, and had delivered many an imprisoned nymph from durance. He was indeed as bitter an enemy to the savage authority too often exercised by husbands and fathers, over the young and lovely of the other sex, as ever knight-errant was to the barbarous power of enchanters.

This nobleman had an estate in the neighbourhood of Fitzpatrick, and had been for some time acquainted with the lady. No sooner, therefore, did he hear of her confinement, than he earnestly applied himself to procure her liberty; which he presently effected.

The peer, after a short conversation, could not forbear expressing some surprize at meeting the lady in that place; nor could he refrain from telling her he imagined she had been gone to Bath. Mrs. Fitzpatrick very freely answered, 'I was overtaken by my husband. I had the good fortune to escape in a most surprizing manner, and am now going to London with this young lady, who is a near relation of mine, and who hath escaped from as great a tyrant as my own.'

His lordship, concluding that this tyrant was likewise a husband, made a speech full of compliments to both the ladies, and ended his oration with an offer of his protection, and of his coach and six, which was instantly accepted by Mrs Fitzpatrick, and at last, upon her persuasions, by Sophia.

Our company, being arrived at London, were set down at his lordship's house, where, while they refreshed themselves after the fatigue of their journey, servants were dispatched to provide a lodging for the two ladies; for, as her ladyship was not then in town, Mrs Fitzpatrick would by no means consent to accept a bed in the mansion of the peer.

A lodging being prepared, Sophia accompanied her cousin for that evening; but resolved early in the morning to inquire after the lady into whose protection, as we have formerly mentioned, she had determined to throw herself when she quitted her father's house.

Sophia very easily found out the lady she sought; for indeed there was not a chairman in town to whom her house was not perfectly well known; and, as she received, in return of her first message, a most pressing invitation, she immediately accepted it.

The young lady, when she came to take leave of her cousin, could not avoid giving her a short hint of advice. She begged her, for heaven's sake, to take care of herself, and to consider in how dangerous a situation she stood; adding, she hoped some method would be found of reconciling her to her husband. 'You must remember, my dear,' says she, 'the maxim which my aunt Western hath so often repeated to us both; that whenever the matrimonial alliance is broken, and war declared between husband and wife, she can hardly make a disadvantageous peace for herself on any conditions. These are my aunt's very words, and she hath had a great deal of experience in the world.' Mrs. Fitzpatrick answered, with a contemptuous smile, 'Never fear me, child, take care of yourself; for you are younger than I. I will come and visit you in a few days.'

Thus the two cousins parted, and Sophia repaired directly to Lady Bellaston, where she found a most hearty, as well as a most polite, welcome. The lady had taken a great fancy to her when she had seen her formerly with her aunt Western. She was indeed extremely glad to see her, and was no sooner acquainted with the reasons which induced her to leave the squire and to fly to London, than she highly applauded her sense and resolution; and after expressing the highest satisfaction in the opinion which Sophia had declared she entertained of her ladyship, promised her all the protection which it was in her power to give.

CHAPTER TWENTY-SEVEN

WHAT BEFEL MR JONES ON ARRIVAL IN LONDON

WE must first trace the footsteps of Squire Western; for as he will soon arrive at the end of his journey, we shall then have full leisure to attend our hero.

The said squire departed from the inn in great fury. But at the next inn, his dinner was followed by a hearty bout of drinking, which ended in as hearty a nap. He had no sooner shaken this off, than he was persuaded by one Parson Supple among his attendants, that his daughter would soon be fatigued of her journey and would return to him and to Mr Blifil. He was therefore prevailed upon to return home, but not before he had first dispatched part of his retinue in quest of Sophia, after whom he sent a volley of the most bitter execrations he could invent.

Mr Jones meanwhile with his friend Partridge had proceeded to an inn at Gloucester, where the landlord was an intimate acquaintance of the landlord at Upton. The history of the extraordinary events at Upton had preceded him, and, upon arrival, he was soon made acquainted with the post-boy who had attended Mrs Fitzpatrick, by which means he quickly learned the destination of that lady, and the identity of the peer who had contrived her escape and that of the other young lady, of angelic beauty, whom he believed must be Miss Western.

Jones, as well as Partridge, was an entire stranger in London; and as he happened to arrive first in a quarter of the town, the inhabitants of which have very little intercourse with the householders of Hanover or Grosvenor-square (for he entered through Gray's-inn-lane), so he rambled about some time, before he at last yielded to the advice of Partridge, and retreated to the Bull and Gate in Holborn, where he retired to enjoy that kind of repose which usually attends persons in his circumstances.

Early in the morning he again set forth in pursuit of Sophia; and many a weary step he took to no better purpose than before. At last, he came into the very street which was honoured by his lordship's residence; and, being directed to the house, he gave one gentle rap at the door.

The porter, who, from the modesty of the knock, had conceived no high idea of the person approaching, conceived but little better from the appearance of Mr Jones. When Jones, therefore, inquired after the young lady who had come to town with his lordship, this fellow answered surlily, 'That there were no ladies there.' Jones then desired to see the master of the house; but was informed that his lordship would see nobody that morning. And upon growing more pressing the porter said, 'he had positive orders to let no person in; but if you think proper,' said he, 'to leave your name, I will acquaint his lordship; and if you call another time you shall know when he will see you.'

Jones now declared, 'that he had very particular business with the young lady, and could depart not without seeing her.' Upon which the porter, with no very agreeable voice or aspect, affirmed, 'that there was no young lady in that house, and consequently none could he see'; adding, 'Sure you are the strangest man I ever met with, for you will not take an answer.'

Jones now began to offer a bribe to the human Cerberus, which a footman overhearing, instantly advanced, and declared, 'if Mr Jones would give him the sum proposed, he would conduct him to the lady.' Jones instantly agreed, and was forthwith conducted to the lodging of Mrs Fitzpatrick, by the very fellow who had attended the ladies thither the day before.

Jones, who more than once already had experienced the insults of Fortune, was now again doomed to be tantalized; for he arrived at the door of Mrs Fitzpatrick about ten minutes after the departure of Sophia. He now addressed himself to the waiting-woman belonging to Mrs Fitzpatrick, who told him the disagreeable news that the lady was gone, but could not tell him whither; and the same answer he afterwards received from Mrs Fitzpatrick herself. For as that lady made no doubt but that Mr Jones was a person detached from her uncle Western, in pursuit of his daughter, so she was too generous to betray her.

Though Jones had never seen Mrs Fitzpatrick, yet he had heard that a cousin of Sophia was married to a gentleman of that name. This, however, in the present tumult of his mind, never once recurred to his memory; but when the footman, who had conducted him from his lordship's, acquainted him with the great intimacy between the ladies, and with their calling each other cousin, he then recollected the story of the marriage which he had formerly heard; and as he was presently convinced that this was the same woman, he became more surprized at the answer which he had received, and very earnestly desired leave to wait on the lady herself; but she as positively refused him that honour.

Jones, who, though he had never seen a court, was better bred than most who frequent it, was incapable of any rude or abrupt behaviour to a lady. When he had received, therefore, a peremptory denial, he retired for the present, saying to the waiting-woman, 'That if this was an improper hour to wait on her lady, he would return in the afternoon; and that he then hoped to have the honour of seeing her.' The civility with which he uttered this, added to the great comeliness of his person, made an impression on the waiting-woman, and she could not help answering, 'Perhaps, sir, you may'; and, indeed, she afterwards said everything to her mistress, which she thought most likely to prevail on her to admit a visit from the handsome young gentleman; for so she called him.

Jones very shrewdly suspected that Sophia herself was now with her cousin, and was denied to him; which he imputed to her resentment of what had happened at Upton. Having, therefore, dispatched Partridge to procure him lodgings, he remained all day in the street, watching the door where he thought his angel lay concealed; but no person did he see issue forth, except a servant of the house, and in the evening he returned to pay his visit to Mrs Fitzpatrick, which that good lady at last condescended to admit.

There is a certain air of natural gentility, which it is neither in the power of dress to give, nor to conceal. Mr Jones, as hath been before hinted, was possessed of this in a very eminent degree. He met, therefore, with a reception from the lady, somewhat different from what his apparel seemed to demand; and after he had paid her his proper respects, was desired to sit down.

The reader will not, I believe, be desirous of knowing all the particulars of this conversation, which ended very little to the satisfaction of poor Jones. For though Mrs Fitzpatrick soon discovered the lover (as all women have the eyes of hawks in those matters), yet she still thought it was such a lover, as a generous friend of the lady should not betray her to. In short, she suspected this was the very Mr Blifil, from whom Sophia had flown; and all the answers which she artfully drew from Jones, concerning Mr Allworthy's family, confirmed her in this opinion. She therefore strictly denied any knowledge concerning the place whither Sophia was gone; nor could Jones obtain more than a permission to wait on her again the next evening.

When Jones was departed, Mrs Fitzpatrick communicated her suspicion concerning Mr Blifil to her maid; who answered, 'Sure, madam, he is too pretty a man, in my opinion, for any woman in the world to run away from. I had rather fancy it is Mr Jones.'— 'Mr Jones!' said the lady, 'what Jones?' For Sophia had not given the least hint of any such person in all their conversation; but Mrs Honour had been much more communicative, and had acquainted her sister Abigail with the whole history of Jones, which this now again related to her mistress.

Mrs Fitzpatrick no sooner received this information, than she immediately agreed with the opinion of her maid; and, what is very unaccountable, saw charms in the gallant, happy lover, which she had overlooked in the slighted squire. 'Betty,' says she, 'you are certainly in the right: he is a very pretty fellow, and I don't wonder that my cousin's maid should tell you so many women are fond of him. I am sorry now I did not inform him where my cousin was; and yet, if he be so terrible a rake as you tell me, it is a pity she should ever see him any more; for what but her ruin can happen from marrying a rake and a beggar against her father's consent? I protest, if he be such a man as the wench described him to you, it is but an office of charity to keep her from him; and I am sure it would be unpardonable in me to do otherwise, who have tasted so bitterly of the misfortunes attending such marriages.'

When Mrs Fitzpatrick retired to rest, her thoughts were entirely taken up by her cousin Sophia and Mr Jones. She was, indeed, a little offended with the former, for the disingenuity which she now discovered. In which meditation she had not long exercised her imagination, before the following conceit suggested itself; that could she possibly become the means of preserving Sophia from this man, and of restoring her to her father, she should, in all human probability, by so great a service to the family, reconcile to herself both her uncle and her aunt Western.

The hope of success seemed so reasonable, that nothing remained but to consider of proper methods to accomplish her scheme.

The acquaintance which Sophia had with Lady Bellaston was contracted at the house of Mrs Western, and must have grown at the very time when Mrs Fitzpatrick lived with this latter lady, so that Mrs Fitzpatrick must have been acquainted with her likewise. They were, besides, both equally her distant relations.

After much consideration, therefore, she resolved to go early in the morning to that lady, and endeavour to see her, unknown to Sophia, and to acquaint her with the whole affair. For she did not in the least doubt, but that the prudent lady, who had often ridiculed romantic love, and indiscreet marriages, in her conversation, would very readily concur in her sentiments concerning this match, and would lend her utmost assistance to prevent it.

The next morning before the sun, at a very unfashionable, unseasonable, unvisitable hour, she went to Lady Bellaston, to whom she got access, without the least knowledge or suspicion of Sophia.

Mrs Fitzpatrick, with many apologies for an early abrupt visit, then opened the whole affair, told all she had heard from Betty; and did not forget the visit which Jones had paid to herself the preceding evening.

Lady Bellaston answered with a smile, 'Then you have seen this terrible man, madam; pray, is he so very fine a figure?'

'Indeed, madam, this is a matter of great consequence. Nothing can certainly be more commendable than the part you act; and I shall be very glad to have my share in the preservation of a young lady of so much merit, and for whom I have so much esteem.'

'Doth not your ladyship think,' says Mrs Fitzpatrick eagerly, 'that it would be the best way to write immediately to my uncle, and acquaint him where my cousin is?'

The lady pondered a little upon this, and thus answered: 'Why, no madam, I think not. Di Western hath described her brother to me to be such a brute, that I cannot consent to put any woman under his power who hath escaped from it. I have heard he behaved like a monster to his own wife, for he is one of those wretches who think they have a right to tyrannize over my sex. The business, dear cousin, will be only to keep Miss Western from seeing this young fellow, till the good company, which she will have an opportunity of meeting here, give her a properer turn.'

'If he should find out her, madam,' answered the other, 'your ladyship may be assured he will leave nothing unattempted to come at her.'

'But, madam,' replied the lady, 'it is impossible he should come here—though indeed it is possible he may get some intelligence where she is, and then may lurk about the house—I wish therefore I knew his person. Is there no way, madam, by which I could have a sight of him? for otherwise, you know cousin, you know, she may contrive to see him here without my knowledge.'

Mrs Fitzpatrick answered, 'That he had threatened her with another visit that afternoon, and that, if her ladyship pleased to do her the honour of calling upon her then, she would hardly fail of seeing him between six and seven: and if he came earlier she would, by some means or other, detain him till her ladyship's arrival.' Lady Bellaston replied, 'She would come the moment she could get from dinner, which she supposed would be by seven at farthest; for that it was absolutely necessary she should be acquainted with his person. Upon my word, madam,' says she, 'it was very good to take this care of Miss Western; but common humanity, as well as regard to our family, requires it of us both; for it would be a dreadful match indeed.'

Mrs Fitzpatrick failed not to make a proper return to the compliment which Lady Bellaston had bestowed on her cousin, and, after some little immaterial conversation, withdrew; and, getting as fast as she could into her chair, unseen by Sophia or Honour, returned home.

Mr Jones had walked within sight of a certain door during the whole day, which appeared to him to be one of the longest in the whole year. At length, the clock having struck five, he returned to Mrs Fitzpatrick, who, though it was a full hour earlier than the decent time of visiting, received him very civilly; but still persisted in her ignorance concerning Sophia.

Jones, in asking for his angel, had dropped the word cousin, upon which Mrs Fitzpatrick said, 'Then, sir, you know we are related: and, as we are, you will permit me the right of inquiring into the particulars of your business with my cousin.' Here Jones hesitated a good while, and at last a footman knocked, or rather thundered, at the door. Jones was a little surprized at the sound, having never heard it before; but Mrs Fitzpatrick very calmly said, that, if he pleased to stay, she had something to say to him.

The door of the room now flew open, and, after pushing in her hoop sideways before her, entered Lady Bellaston, who having first made a very low courtesy to Mrs Fitzpatrick, and as low a one to Mr Jones, was ushered to the upper end of the room.

The company were hardly well settled, before the arrival of the peer lately mentioned, caused a fresh disturbance, and a repetition of ceremonials.

These being over, the conversation began to be (as the phrase is) extremely brilliant. However, as nothing past in it which can be thought material to this history, or, indeed, very material in itself, I shall omit the relation.

Poor Jones was rather a spectator of this elegant scene, than an actor in it; for though, in the short interval before the peer's arrival, Lady Bellaston first, and afterwards Mrs Fitzpatrick, had addressed some of their discourse to him; yet no sooner was the noble lord entered, than he engrossed the whole attention of the two ladies to himself; and as he took no more notice of Jones than if no such person had been present, unless by now and then staring at him, the ladies followed his example.

The company had now staid so long, that Mrs Fitzpatrick plainly perceived they all designed to stay out each other. She therefore resolved to rid herself of Jones, he being the visitant to whom she thought the least ceremony was due. Taking therefore an opportunity of a cessation of chat, she addressed herself gravely to him, and said, 'Sir, if you please to leave word where I may send to you to-morrow——'

Jones had natural, but not artificial good-breeding. Instead, therefore, of communicating the secret of his lodging to a servant, he acquainted the lady herself with it particularly, and soon after very ceremoniously withdrew.

CHAPTER TWENTY-EIGHT

ADVENTURES WHICH HAPPENED TO MR JONES AT HIS LODGINGS, AND AT A MASQUERADE

THE next morning, as early as it was decent, Jones attended at Mrs Fitzpatrick's door, where he was answered that the lady was not at home; an answer which surprized him the more, as he had walked backwards and forwards in the street from break of day; and if she had gone out, he must have seen her. This answer, however, he was obliged to receive, and not only now, but to five several visits which he made her that day.

To be plain with the reader, the noble peer had from some reason or other, perhaps from a regard for the lady's honour, insisted that she should not see Mr Jones, whom he looked on as a scrub, any more; and the lady had complied in making that promise to which we now see her so strictly adhere.

But as our gentle reader may possibly have a better opinion of the young gentleman than her ladyship, we shall now give an account of his lodging, which was indeed in a very reputable house, and in a very good part of the town.

Mr Jones, then, had often heard Mr Allworthy mention the gentlewoman at whose house he used to lodge when he was in town. This person lived in Bond-street, was the widow of a clergyman, and was left by him, at his decease, in possession of two daughters.

Of these two daughters, Nancy, the elder, was now arrived at the age of seventeen, and Betty, the younger, at that of ten.

Hither Jones had dispatched Partridge, and in this house he was provided with a room for himself in the second floor, and with one for Partridge in the fourth.

The first floor was inhabited by one of those young gentlemen, who, in the last age, were called men of wit and pleasure about town, and properly enough. Play-houses, coffee-houses, and taverns were the scenes of their rendezvous. Wit and humour were the entertainment of their looser hours, and love was the business of their more serious moments.

When Jones had spent the whole day in vain inquiries after Mrs Fitzpatrick, he returned at last disconsolate to his apartment. Here, while he was venting his grief in private, he heard a violent uproar below-stairs; and soon after a female voice begged him for heaven's sake to come and prevent murder. Jones, who was never backward on any occasion to help the distressed, immediately ran downstairs; when stepping into the dining-room, whence all the noise issued, he beheld the young gentleman of wisdom just before mentioned, pinned close to the wall by his footman, and a young woman standing by, wringing her hands, and crying out, 'He will be murdered! he will be murdered!' and, indeed, the poor gentleman seemed in some danger of being choked, when Jones flew hastily to his assistance, and rescued him, just as he was breathing his last, from the unmerciful clutches of the enemy.

The former victor lay breathless on the ground, and the vanquished gentleman had recovered breath enough to thank Mr Jones for his seasonable assistance; he received likewise the hearty thanks of the young woman present, who was indeed no other than Miss Nancy, the eldest daughter of the house.

And now the young gentleman, whose name was Nightingale, very strenuously insisted that his deliverer should take part of a bottle of wine with him; to which Jones, after much entreaty, consented, though more out of complacence than inclination; for the uneasiness of his mind fitted him very little for conversation at this time. Miss Nancy likewise, who was the only female then in the house, her mamma and sister being both gone to the play, condescended to favour them with her company.

When the bottle and glasses were on the table, the gentleman began to relate the occasion of the preceding disturbance.

'I hope, sir,' said he to Jones, 'you will not from this accident conclude, that I make a custom of striking my servants, for I assure you this is the first time I have been guilty of it in my remembrance, and I have passed by many provoking faults in this very fellow, before he could provoke me to it; but in short, he cast a reflection——He mentioned the name of a young lady, in a manner—in such a manner that incensed me beyond all patience, and, in my passion, I struck him.'

Jones answered, 'That he believed no person living would blame him; for my part,' said he, 'I confess I should have done the same thing.'

Our company had not sat long before they were joined by the mother and daughter, at their return from the play. And now they all spent a very cheerful evening together; for all but Jones were heartily merry, and even he put on as much constrained mirth as possible.

As for Miss Nancy, though a very little creature, she was extremely pretty, and the widow had all the charms which can adorn a woman near fifty. She never thought, nor spoke, nor wished any ill, and had constantly that desire of pleasing, which may be called the happiest of all desires in this, that it scarce ever fails of attaining its ends, when not disgraced by affectation. In short, though her power was very small she was in her heart one of the warmest friends. She had been a most affectionate wife, and was a most fond and tender mother.

Nor was Jones a little pleased with the young gentleman himself, whose wine he had been drinking. He thought he discerned in him much good sense, though a little too much tainted with town-foppery; but what recommended him most to Jones were some sentiments of great generosity and humanity, which occasionally dropt from him; and particularly many expressions of the highest disinterestedness in the affair of love.

Our company brought together in the morning the same good inclinations towards each other, with which they had separated the evening before; but poor Jones was extremely disconsolate; for he had just received information from Partridge, that Mrs Fitzpatrick had left her lodgings, and that he could not learn whither she was gone. This news highly afflicted him, and his countenance, as well as his behaviour betrayed indications of a disordered mind.

The discourse turned at present, as before, on love; and Mr Nightingale again expressed many of those warm, generous, and disinterested sentiments upon this subject, which wise and sober men call romantic, but which wise and sober women generally regard in a better light. Mrs Miller (for so the mistress of the house was called) greatly approved these sentiments; but when the young gentleman appealed to Miss Nancy, she answered only, 'That she believed the gentleman who had spoke the least was capable of feeling most.'

'I am glad, Nancy,' says Mrs Miller, 'the gentleman hath made the observation; I protest I am almost of his opinion. What can be the matter with you, child? I never saw such an alteration. What is become of all your gaiety? Would you think, sir, I used to call her my little prattler? She hath not spoke twenty words this week.'

Here their conversation was interrrupted by the entrance of a maidservant, who brought a bundle in her hand, which, she said, 'was delivered by a porter for Mr Jones.' She added, 'That the man immediately went away, saying, it required no answer.'

Jones expressed some surprize on this occasion, and declared it must be some mistake; but the maid persisting that she was certain of the name, all the women were desirous of having the bundle immediately opened; which operation was at length performed by little Betsy, with the consent of Mr Jones: and the contents were found to be a domino, a mask, and a masquerade ticket.

Jones was now more positive than ever in asserting, that these things must have been delivered by mistake; but when Mr Nightingale was asked, he delivered a very different opinion. 'All I can conclude from it, sir,' said he, 'is, that you are a very happy man; for I make no doubt but these were sent you by some lady whom you will have the happiness of meeting at the masquerade.'

Mr Jones now determined to go to the masquerade that evening, and Mr Nightingale offered to conduct him thither. The young gentleman, at the same time, offered tickets to Miss Nancy and her mother; but the good woman would not accept them.

Mr Nightingale, who grew every minute fonder of Jones, was very desirous of his company that day to dinner at the tavern, where he offered to introduce him to some of his acquaintance; but Jones begged to be excused, 'as his clothes,' he said, 'were not yet come to town.'

To confess the truth, Mr Jones was now in a situation, which sometimes happens to be the case of young gentlemen of much better figure than himself. In short, he had not one penny in his pocket.

Partridge discovered this by intuition, and took the occasion to give some oblique hints concerning a return to Mr Allworthy.

'Partridge,' cries Jones, 'you cannot see my fortune in a more desperate light than I see it myself; and I begin heartily to repent that I suffered you to leave a place where you was settled, and to follow me. However, I insist now on your returning home.'

He spoke these words with so pathetic an accent, that Partridge, among whose vices ill nature or hardness of heart were not numbered, burst into tears; and after swearing he would not quit him in his distress, he began with the most earnest entreaties to urge his return home. 'For heaven's sake, sir,' says he, 'do but consider; what can your honour do?—how is it possible you can live in this town without money? Do what you will, sir, or go wherever you please, I am resolved not to desert you. But pray, sir, consider—do pray, sir, for your own sake, take into your consideration; and I'm sure,' says he, 'that your own good sense will bid you return home.'

'How often shall I tell thee,' answered Jones, 'that I have no home to return to? Had I any hopes that Mr Allworthy's doors would be open to receive me, I want no distress to urge me—nay, there is no other cause upon earth, which could detain me a moment from flying to his presence; but, alas! that I am for ever banished.'

Here passion stopt the mouth of Jones, as surprize for a moment did that of Partridge; on which he proceeded to comment, when he was interrupted by a message from Mr Nightingale, who desired his master's company in his apartment.

When the two gentlemen were both attired for the masquerade, Mr Nightingale gave orders for chairs to be sent for.

Our cavaliers now arrived at that temple. Mr Nightingale, having taken a turn or two with his companion, soon left him, and walked off with a female, saying, 'Now you are here, sir, you must beat about for your own game.'

Jones began to entertain strong hopes that his Sophia was present; and these hopes gave him more spirits than the lights, the music, and the company; though these are pretty strong antidotes against the spleen. He now accosted every woman he saw, whose stature, shape, or air, bore any resemblance to his angel.

Whilst he was talking with one of these last (who was in the habit of a shepherdess) a lady in a domino came up to him, and slapping him on the shoulder, whispered him, at the same time, in the ear, 'If you talk any longer with that trollop, I will acquaint Miss Western.'

Jones no sooner heard that name, than, immediately quitting his former companion, he applied to the domino, begging and entreating her to show him the lady she had mentioned, if she was then in the room.

The mask walked hastily to the upper end of the innermost apartment before she spoke; and then, instead of answering him, sat down, and declared she was tired. Jones sat down by her, and still persisted in his entreaties: at last the lady coldly answered, 'I imagined Mr Jones had been a more discerning lover, than to suffer any disguise to conceal his mistress from him.'—'Is she here, then, madam?' replied Jones, with some vehemence. Upon which the lady cries: 'Hush, sir, you will be observed. I promise you, upon my honour, Miss Western is not here.'

Jones, now taking the mask by the hand, fell to entreating her in the most earnest manner, to acquaint him where he might find Sophia: and when he could obtain no direct answer, he began to upbraid her gently for having disappointed him the day before; and concluded, saying, 'Indeed, my good fairy queen, I know your majesty very well, notwithstanding the affected disguise in your voice. Indeed, Mrs Fitzpatrick, it is a little cruel to divert yourself at the expense of my torments.'

The mask answered, 'Though you have so ingeniously discovered me, I must still speak in the same voice, lest I should be known by others. And do you think, good sir, that I have no greater regard for my cousin, than to assist in carrying on an affair between you two, which must end in her ruin, as well as your own? Besides, I promise you, my cousin is not mad enough to consent to her own destruction, if you are so much her enemy as to tempt her to it.'

'Alas, madam!' said Jones, 'you little know my heart, when you call me an enemy of Sophia.'

'And yet to ruin any one,' cries the other, 'you will allow, is the act of an enemy; and when by the same act you must knowingly and certainly bring ruin on yourself, is it not folly or madness, as well as guilt? Now, sir, my cousin hath very little more than her father will please to give her; very little for one of her fashion—you know him, and you know your own situation.'

Jones vowed he had no such design on Sophia, 'I would rather suffer the most violent of deaths than sacrifice her interest. I know how unworthy I am of her, every way. No, madam,' concluded he, 'my love is not of that base kind which seeks its own satisfaction at the expense of what is most dear to its object. I would sacrifice everything to the possession of my Sophia, but Sophia herself.'

To which the mask answered, 'And are you so little versed in the sex, to imagine you can well affront a lady more than be entertaining her with your passion for another woman? If the fairy queen had conceived no better opinion of your gallantry, she would scarce have appointed you to meet her at the masquerade.'

Jones had never less inclination to an amour than at present; but gallantry to the ladies was among his principles of honour; and he held it as much incumbent on him to accept a challenge to love, as if it had been a challenge to fight. Nay, his very love to Sophia made it necessary for him to keep well with the lady, as he made no doubt but she was capable of bringing him into the presence of the other.

He began therefore to make a very warm answer to her last speech, when a mask, in the character of an old woman, joined them. This mask was one of those ladies who go to a masquerade only to vent ill nature, by telling people rude truths, and by endeavouring, as the phrase is, to spoil as much sport as they are able. This good lady, therefore, having observed Jones, and his friend, whom she well knew, in close consultation together in a corner of the room, concluded she could nowhere satisfy her spleen better than by interrupting them. She attacked them, therefore, and soon drove them from their retirement; nor was she contented with this, but pursued them to every place which they shifted to avoid her; till Mr Nightingale, seeing the distress of his friend, at last relieved him, and engaged the old woman in another pursuit.

While Jones and his mask were walking together about the room, to rid themselves of the teazer, he observed his lady speak to several masks, with the same freedom of acquaintance as if they had been barefaced. He could not help expressing his surprize at this; saying, 'Sure, madam, you must have infinite discernment, to know people in all disguises.' To which the lady answered, 'You cannot conceive anything more insipid and childish than a masquerade to the people of fashion, who in general know one another as well here, as when they meet in an assembly or a drawing-room; the generality of persons whom you see here, may more properly be said to kill time in this place than in any other; and I begin to be in that situation myself. I protest it would be almost charity in me to go home for your sake.'—'I know but one charity equal to it,' cries Jones, 'and that is to suffer me to wait on you home.'—'Sure,' answered the lady, 'you have a strange opinion of me, to imagine, that upon such an acquaintance, I would let you into my doors at this time of night. Confess honestly; don't you consider this contrived interview as little better than a downright assignation? Are you used, Mr Jones, to make these sudden conquests?'—'I am not used, madam,' said Jones, 'to submit to such sudden conquests; but as you have taken my heart by surprize, the rest of my body hath a right to follow; so you must pardon me if I resolve to attend you wherever you go.' He accompanied these words with some proper actions; upon which the lady, after a gentle rebuke, and saying their familiarity would be observed, told him, 'She was going to sup with an acquaintance, whither she hoped he would not follow her; for if you should,' said she, 'I shall be thought an unaccountable creature, though my friend indeed is not censorious.'

The lady presently after quitted the masquerade, and Jones walked boldly on after the chair in which his lady rode.

The lady was set down in a street not far from Hanover-square, where the door being presently opened, she was carried in, and the gentleman, without any ceremony, walked in after her.

Jones and his companion were now together in a very well-furnished and well-warmed room; when the female, still speaking in her masquerade voice, said she was surprized at her friend, who must absolutely have forgot her appointment; at which, after venting much resentment, she suddenly exprest some apprehension from Jones, and asked him what the world would think of their having been alone together in a house at that time of night? But instead of a direct answer to so important a question, Jones began to be very importunate with the lady to unmask; and at length having prevailed, there appeared, not Mrs Fitzpatrick, but the Lady Bellaston herself.

It would be tedious to give the particular conversation, which consisted of very common and ordinary occurrences, and which lasted from two till six o'clock in the morning. It is sufficient to mention all of it that is anywise material to this history. And this was a promise that the lady would endeavour to find our Sophia, and in a few days bring him to an interview with her, on condition that he would then take his leave of her. When this was thoroughly settled, and a second meeting in the evening appointed at the same place, they separated; the lady returned to her house, and Jones to his lodgings.

CHAPTER TWENTY-NINE

IN WHICH THE READER WILL BE SURPRIZED

JONES having refreshed himself with a few hours' sleep, summoned Partridge to his presence; and delivering him a banknote of fifty pounds, ordered him to go and change it. Partridge received this with sparkling eyes, though, when he came to reflect farther, it raised in him some suspicions not very advantageous to the honour of his master: to these the dreadful idea he had of the masquerade, the disguise in which his master had gone out and returned, and his having been abroad all night, contributed. In plain language, the only way he could possibly find to account for the possession of this note, was by robbery: and, to confess the truth, the reader, unless he should suspect it was owing to the generosity of Lady Bellaston, can hardly imagine any other.

To clear, therefore, the honour of Mr Jones, and to do justice to the liberality of the lady, he had really received this present from her, who, though she did not give much into the hackney charities of the age, such as building hospitals, &c., was not, however, entirely void of that Christian virtue; and conceived (very rightly, I think) that a young fellow of merit, without a shilling in the world, was no improper object of this virtue.

In the evening Jones met his lady again, and a long conversation again ensued between them: but as it consisted only of the same ordinary occurrences as before, we shall avoid mentioning particulars.

Jones grew still more and more impatient to see Sophia; and finding, after repeated interviews with Lady Bellaston, no likelihood of obtaining this by her means (for, on the contrary, the lady began to treat even the mention of the name of Sophia with resentment), he resolved to try some other method. He made no doubt but that Lady Bellaston knew where his angel was, so he thought it most likely that some of her servants should be acquainted with the same secret. Partridge therefore was employed to get acquainted with those servants, in order to fish this secret out of them.

Few situations can be imagined more uneasy than that to which his poor master was at present reduced; for besides the difficulties he met with in discovering Sophia, besides the fears he had of having disobliged her, he had still a difficulty to combat, which was the exposing of her to be disinherited of all her father's estate, the almost inevitable consequence of their coming together without a consent, which he had no hopes of ever obtaining.

Add to all these the many obligations which Lady Bellaston, whose violent fondness we can no longer conceal, had heaped upon him; so that by her means he was now become one of the best-dressed men about town; and was actually raised to a state of affluence beyond what he had ever known.

Now, though there are many gentlemen who very well reconcile it to their consciences to possess themselves of the whole fortune of a woman, without making her any kind of return; yet to a mind, the proprietor of which doth not deserved to be hanged, nothing is, I believe, more irksome than to support love with gratitude only; especially where inclination pulls the heart a contrary way. Such was the unhappy case of Jones; for though the virtuous love he bore to Sophia, and which left very little affection for any other woman, had been entirely out of the question, he could never have been able to have made any adequate return to the generous passion of this lady, who was now entered at least into the autumn of life, though she wore all the gaiety of youth, both in her dress and manner; nay, she contrived still to maintain the roses in her cheeks; but these, like flowers forced out of season by art, had none of that lively blooming freshness with which Nature, at the proper time, bedecks her own productions.

Though Jones saw all these discouragements on the one side, he felt his obligations full as strongly on the other; nor did he less plainly discern the ardent passion whence those obligations proceeded, the extreme violence of which if he failed to equal, he well knew the lady would think him ungrateful; and, what is worse, he would have thought himself so. He knew the tacit consideration upon which all her favours were conferred; and as his necessity obliged him to accept them, so his honour, he concluded, forced him to pay the price. This therefore he resolved to do, whatever misery it cost him, and to devote himself to her, from that great principle of justice, by which the laws of some countries oblige a debtor, who is no otherwise capable of discharging his debt, to become the slave of his creditor.

While he was meditating on these matters, he received the following note from the lady:

'A very foolish, but a very perverse accident hath happened since our last meeting, which makes it improper I should see you any more at the usual place. I will, if possible, contrive some other place by to-morrow. In the meantime, adieu.'

This disappointment, perhaps, the reader may conclude was not very great; but if it was, he was quickly relieved; for in less than an hour afterwards another note was brought him from the same hand, which contained as follows:

'I have altered my mind since I wrote; a change which, if you are no stranger to the tenderest of all passions, you will not wonder at. I am now resolved to see you this evening at my own house, whatever may be the consequence. Come to me exactly at seven; I dine abroad, but will be at home by that time. A day, I find, to those that sincerely love, seems longer than I imagined.

'If you should accidentally be a few moments before me, bid them show you into the drawing-room.'

To confess the truth, Jones was less pleased with this last epistle than he had been with the former, as he was prevented by it from complying with the earnest entreaties of Mr Nightingale, with whom he had now contracted much intimacy and friendship. These entreaties were to go with that young gentleman and his company to a new play, which was to be acted that evening, and which a very large party had agreed to damn, from some dislike they had taken to the author, who was a friend to one of Mr Nightingale's acquaintance. And this sort of fun, our hero, we are ashamed to confess, would willingly have preferred to the above kind of appointment; but his honour got the better of his inclination.

Before we attend him to this intended interview with the lady, we think proper to account for both the preceding notes, as the reader may possibly be not a little surprized at the imprudence of Lady Bellaston, in bringing her lover to the very house where her rival was lodged.

First, then, the mistress of the house where these lovers had hitherto met, and who had been for some years a pensioner to that lady, was now become a methodist, and had that very morning waited upon her ladyship, and after rebuking her very severely for her past life, had positively declared that she would, on no account, be instrumental in carrying on any of her affairs for the future.

The hurry of spirits into which this accident threw the lady, made her despair of possibly finding any other convenience to meet Jones that evening; but as she began a little to recover from her uneasiness at the disappointment, she set her thoughts to work, when luckily it came into her head to propose to Sophia to go to the play, which was immediately consented to, and a proper lady provided for her companion. Mrs Honour was likewise dispatched on the same errand of pleasure; and thus her house was left free for the safe reception of Mr Jones, with whom she promised herself two or three hours of uninterrupted conversation, after her return from the place where she dined.

Mr Jones was rather earlier than the time appointed, and earlier than the lady; whose arrival was hindered by the distance of the place where she dined. He was accordingly shown into the drawing-room, where he had not been many minutes before the door opened, and in came——no other than Sophia herself, who had left the play before the end of the first act; for this, as we have already said, being a new play, at which two large parties met, the one to damn, and the other to applaud, a violent uproar, and an engagement between the two parties, had so terrified our heroine, that she was glad to put herself under the protection of a young gentleman, who safely conveyed her to her chair.

As Lady Bellaston had acquainted her that she should not be at home till late, Sophia, expecting to find no one in the room, came hastily in, and went directly to a glass which almost fronted her, without once looking towards the upper end of the room, where the statue of Jones now stood motionless. In this glass it was, after contemplating her own lovely face, that she first discovered the said statue; when, instantly turning about, she perceived the reality of the vision: upon which she gave a violent scream, and scarce preserved herself from fainting, till Jones was able to move to her, and support her in his arms.

To paint the looks or thoughts of either of these lovers, is beyond my power. As their sensations, from their mutual silence, may be judged to have been too big for their own utterance, it cannot be supposed that I should be able to express them: and the misfortune is, that few of my readers have been enough in love to feel by their own hearts what past at this time in theirs.

After a short pause, Jones, with faltering accents, said: 'I see, madam, you are surprized.'—'Surprized!' answered she. 'Oh heavens! Indeed, I am surprized. I almost doubt whether you are the person you seem.'—'Indeed,' cries he, 'my Sophia, pardon me, madam, for this once calling you so, I am that very wretched Jones, whom fortune, after so many disappointments, hath, at last, kindly conducted to you. Oh! my Sophia, did you know the thousand torments I have suffered in this long, fruitless pursuit.'— 'Pursuit of whom?' said Sophia, a little recollecting herself, and assuming a reserved air. 'Can you be so cruel to ask that question?' cries Jones. 'Need I say, of you?'—'Of me!' answered Sophia. 'Hath Mr Jones, then, any such important business with me?'—'Let us not, I beseech you,' cries Jones, 'lose one of these precious moments which fortune hath so kindly sent us. O, my Sophia! Thus, on my knees, let me ask your pardon.'—'My pardon!' cries she. 'Sure, sir, after what is past, you cannot expect, after what I have heard.'—'I scarce know what I say,' answered Jones. 'By heavens! I scarce wish you should pardon me. O my Sophia! henceforth never cast away a thought on such a wretch as I am. If any remembrance of me should ever intrude to give a moment's uneasiness to that tender bosom, think of my unworthiness; and let the remembrance of what passed at Upton blot me for ever from your mind.'

Sophia stood trembling all this while. Her face was whiter than snow, and her heart was throbbing through her stays. But at the mention of Upton, a blush arose in her cheeks, and her eyes, which before she had scarce lifted up, were turned upon Jones with a glance of disdain. He understood this silent reproach, and replied to it thus: 'O my Sophia! my only love! you cannot hate or despise me more for what happened there, than I do myself; but yet do me the justice to think, that my heart was never unfaithful to you. That had no share in the folly I was guilty of; it was even then unalterably yours. But if my heart had not been engaged, she, into whose company I accidently fell at that cursed place, was not an object of serious love. Believe me, my angel, I never have seen her from that day to this; and never intend or desire to see her again.' Sophia, in her heart, was very glad to hear this; but forcing into her face an air of more coldness than she had yet assumed, 'Why,' said she, 'Mr Jones, do you take the trouble to make a defence where you are not accused? If I thought it worth while to accuse you, I have a charge of an unpardonable nature indeed.'—'What is it, for heaven's sake?' answered Jones, trembling and pale, expecting to hear of his amour with Lady Bellaston. 'Oh,' said she, 'how is it possible! Can everything noble, and everything base, be lodged together in the same bosom?' Lady Bellaston, and the ignominious circumstance of having been kept, rose again in his mind, and stopt his mouth from any reply. 'Could I have expected,' proceeded Sophia, 'such treatment from you? Nay, from any gentleman, from any man of honour? To have my name traduced in public; in inns, among the meanest vulgar!'

Nothing could equal Jones's surprize at these words of Sophia; but yet, not being guilty, he was much less embarrassed how to defend himself, than if she had touched that tender string at which his conscience had been alarmed. By some examination he presently found, that her supposing him guilty of so shocking an outrage against his love, and her reputation, was entirely owing to Partridge's talk at the inn before landlords and servants; for Sophia confessed to him it was from them that she received her intelligence. He had no very great difficulty to make her believe that he was entirely innocent of an offence so foreign to his character; but she had a great deal to hinder him from going instantly home, and putting Partridge to death, which he more than once swore he would do. This point being cleared up, they soon found themselves so well pleased with each other, that Jones quite forgot he had begun the conversation with conjuring her to give up all thoughts of him; and she was in a temper to have given ear to a petition of a very different nature; for before they were aware they had both gone so far, that he let fall some words that sounded like a proposal of marriage. To which she replied, 'That, did not her duty to her father forbid her to follow her own inclinations, ruin with him would be more welcome to her than the most affluent fortune with another man.' At the mention of the word ruin, he started, let drop her hand, which he had held for some time, and striking his breast with his own, cried out, 'Oh, Sophia! can I then ruin thee? No; by heavens, no! I never will act to so base a part. Dearest Sophia, whatever it costs me, I will renounce you; I will give you up; I will tear all such hopes from my heart as are inconsistent with your real good. My love I will ever retain, but it shall be in silence; it shall be at a distance from you; it shall be in some foreign land; from whence no voice, no sigh of my despair, shall ever reach and disturb your ears. And when I am dead——' He would have gone on, but was stopt by a flood of tears which Sophia let fall in his bosom, upon which she leaned, without being able to speak one word. He kissed them off, which, for some moments, she allowed him to do without any resistance; but then recollecting herself, gently withdrew out of his arms; and, to turn the discourse from a subject too tender, and which she found she could not support, bethought herself to ask him a question she never had time to put to him before, 'How he came into that room?' He began to stammer, and would, in all probability, have raised her suspicions by the answer he was going to give, when, at once, the door opened, and in came Lady Bellaston.

Having advanced a few steps, and seeing Jones and Sophia together, she suddenly stopt; when, after a pause of a few moments, recollecting herself with admirable presence of mind, she said—though with sufficient indications of surprize both in voice and countenance—'I thought, Miss Western, you had been at the play?'

Though Sophia had no opportunity of learning of Jones by what means he had discovered her, yet, as she had not the least suspicion of the real truth, or that Jones and Lady Bellaston were acquainted, so she was very little confounded; and the less, as the lady had, in all their conversations on the subject, entirely taken her side against her father. With very little hesitation, therefore, she went through the whole story of what had happened at the playhouse, and the cause of her hasty return.

The length of this narrative gave Lady Bellaston an opportunity of rallying her spirits, and of considering in what manner to act. And as the behaviour of Sophia gave her hopes that Jones had not betrayed her, she put on an air of good humour, and said, 'I should not have broke in so abruptly upon you, Miss Western, if I had known you had company.'

Jones, ever since the arrival of Lady Bellaston, had been ready to sink with fear. He sat kicking his heels, playing with his fingers, and looking more like a fool, if it be possible, than a young booby squire, when he is first introduced into a polite assembly. He began, however, now to recover himself; and taking a hint from the behaviour of Lady Bellaston, who he saw did not intend to claim any acquaintance with him, he resolved as entirely to affect the stranger on his part.

But he saw the agitation of Sophia's mind, and resolved to take the only method of relieving her, which was by retiring; but, before he did this, he said, 'I must insist, madam, on the honour of being permitted to pay another visit here.'

'Sir,' replied the lady, 'I make no doubt that you are a gentleman, and my doors are never shut to people of fashion.'

Jones then, after proper ceremonials, departed, highly to his own satisfaction, and no less to that of Sophia; who was terribly alarmed lest Lady Bellaston should discover what she knew already but too well.

Upon the stairs Jones met his old acquaintance, Mrs Honour, who, notwithstanding all she had said against him, was now so well bred to behave with great civility. This meeting proved indeed a lucky circumstance, as he communicated to her the house where he lodged, with which Sophia was unacquainted.

Our heroine was perfectly satisfied that Lady Bellaston was ignorant of the person of Jones, so she determined to keep her in that ignorance, though at the expense of a little fibbing.

Jones had not been long gone, before Lady Bellaston cryed, 'Upon my word, a good pretty young fellow; I wonder who he is; for I don't remember ever to have seen his face before.'

'Nor I neither, madam,' cries Sophia.

'Yes; and he is a very handsome fellow,' said the lady; 'don't you think so?'

'I did not take much notice of him,' answered Sophia, 'but I thought he seemed rather awkward, and ungenteel than otherwise.'

'You are extremely right,' cries Lady Bellaston; 'you may see, by his manner, that he hath not kept good company. Nay, I almost question whether he is a gentleman.—I have always observed there is a something in persons well born, which others can never acquire.——I think I will give orders not to be at home to him. And indeed, Sophia, you must forgive me, indeed you must.'

'I forgive your ladyship!' said Sophia.

'Yes, indeed you must,' answered she, laughing; 'for I had a horrible suspicion when I first came into the room—— I vow you must forgive it; but I suspected it was Mr Jones himself.'

'Did your ladyship, indeed?' cries Sophia, blushing, and affecting a laugh.

'Yes, I vow I did,' answered she. 'I can't imagine what put it into my head: for, give the fellow his due, he was genteelly drest; which, I think, dear Sophy, is not commonly the case with your friend.'

'This raillery,' cries Sophia, 'is a little cruel, Lady Bellaston, after my promise to your ladyship.'

'Not at all, child,' said the lady;——'It would have been cruel before; but after you have promised me never to marry without your father's consent, in which you know is implied your giving up Jones, sure you can bear a little raillery on a passion which was pardonable enough in a young girl in the country, and of which you tell me you have so entirely got the better. What must I think, my dear Sophy, if you cannot bear a little ridicule even on his dress? I shall begin to fear you are very far gone indeed; and almost question whether you have dealt ingenuously with me.'

'Indeed, madam,' cries Sophia, 'your ladyship mistakes me, if you imagine I had any concern on his account.'

'On his account!' answered the lady. 'You must have mistaken me; I went no farther than his dress;——for I would not injure your taste by any other comparison—I don't imagine, my dear Sophy, if your Mr Jones had been such a fellow as this——'

'I thought,' says Sophia, 'your ladyship had allowed him to be handsome——'

'Whom, pray?' cried the lady hastily.

'Mr Jones,' answered Sophia;—and immediately recollecting herself, 'Mr Jones!—no, no; I ask your pardon;—I mean the gentleman who was just now here.'

'O Sophy! Sophy!' cries the lady; 'this Mr Jones, I am afraid, still runs in your head.'

'Then, upon my honour, madam,' said Sophia, 'Mr Jones is as entirely indfferent to me, as the gentleman who just now left us.'

'Upon my honour,' said Lady Bellaston, 'I believe it. Forgive me, therefore, a little innocent raillery; but I promise you I will never mention his name any more.'

And now the two ladies separated, infinitely more to the delight of Sophia than of Lady Bellaston, who would willingly have tormented her rival a little longer, had not business of more importance called her away. As for Sophia, her mind was not perfectly easy under this first practice of deceit; upon which, when she retired to her chamber, she reflected with the highest uneasiness and conscious shame. Nor could the peculiar hardship of her situation, and the necessity of the case, at all reconcile her mind to her conduct; for the frame of her mind was too delicate to bear the thought of having been guilty of a falsehood, however qualified by circumstances. Nor did this thought once suffer her to close her eyes during the whole succeeding night.

CHAPTER THIRTY

CONTAINING LETTERS AND OTHER MATTERS WHICH ATTEND AMOURS

JONES had not been long at home, before he received the following letter:

'I was never more surprized than when I found you was gone. When you left the room, I little imagined you intended to have left the house without seeing me again. Your behaviour is all of a piece, and convinces me how much I ought to despise a heart which can doat upon an idiot; though I know not whether I should not admire her cunning more than her simplicity: wonderful both! For she had the skill, the assurance, the——what shall I call it? to deny to my face that she knows you, or ever saw you before.——Was this a scheme laid between you, and have you been base enough to betray me?——O how I despise her, you, and all the world, but chiefly myself! for——I dare not write what I should afterwards run mad to read; but remember, I can detest as violently as I have loved.'

Jones had but little time given him to reflect on this letter, before a second was brought to him from the same hand; and this, likewise, we shall set down in the precise words.

'When you consider the hurry of spirits in which I must have writ, you cannot be surprized at any expressions in my former note.—Yet, perhaps, on reflection, they were rather too warm.—— How easy is it to think well of those we love!——Perhaps you desire I should think so. I have resolved to see you to-night; so come to me immediately.

'*PS*.—I have ordered to be at home to none but yourself.

'*PS*.—Mr Jones will imagine I shall assist him in his defence; for I believe he cannot desire to impose on me more than I desire to impose on myself.

'*PS*.—Come immediately.'

To the men of intrigue I refer the determination, whether the angry or the tender letter gave the greatest uneasiness to Jones. Certain it is, he had no violent inclination to pay any more visits that evening, unless to one single person. However, he thought his honour engaged, and had not this been motive sufficient, he would not have ventured to blow the temper of Lady Bellaston into that flame of which he had reason to think it susceptible, and of which he feared the consequence might be a discovery to Sophia, which he dreaded. After some discontented walks, therefore, about the room, he was preparing to depart, when the lady kindly prevented him, not by another letter, but by her own presence. She entered the room very disordered in her dress, and very discomposed in her looks, and threw herself into a chair, where, having recovered her breath, she said: 'You see, sir, when women have gone one length too far, they will stop at none. If any person would have sworn this to me a week ago, I would not have believed it of myself.'—'I hope, madam,' said Jones, 'my charming Lady Bellaston will be as difficult to believe anything against one who is so sensible of the many obligations she hath conferred upon him.'—'Indeed!' says she, 'sensible of obligations! Did I expect to hear such cold language from Mr Jones?'—'Pardon me, my dear angel,' said he, 'if, after the letters I have received, the terrors of your anger, though I know not how I have deserved it'——'And have I then,' says she, with a smile, 'so angry a countenance?—Have I really brought a chiding face with me?'—'If there be honour in man,' said he, 'I have done nothing to merit your anger.—You remember the appointment you sent me; I went in pursuance'—'I beseech you,' cried she, 'do not run through the odious recital.—Answer me but one question, and I shall be easy. Have you not betrayed my honour to her?' Jones fell upon his knees, and began to utter the most violent protestations, when Partridge came dancing and capering into the room, like one drunk with joy, crying out, 'She's found! she's found!—Here, sir, here, she's here—Mrs Honour is upon the stairs.'—'Stop her a moment,' cries Jones. 'Here, madam, step behind the bed, I have no other room nor closet, nor place on earth to hide you in; sure never was so damned an accident.'—'D—n'd indeed!' said the lady, as she went to her place of concealment: and presently afterwards in came Mrs Honour. 'Hey-day!' says she, 'Mr Jones, what's the matter?—That impudent rascal your servant would scarce let me come upstairs. I hope he hath not the same reason to keep me from you as he had at Upton.—I suppose you hardly expected to see me; but you have certainly bewitched my lady. Poor dear young lady! To be sure, I loves her as tenderly as if she was my own sister. Lord have mercy upon you, if you don't make her a good husband! and to be sure, if you do not, nothing can be bad enough for you.' Jones begged her only to whisper, for that there was a lady dying in the next room. 'A lady!' cries she; 'ay, I suppose one of your ladies.—O Mr Jones, there are too many of them in the world; I believe we are got into the house of one, for my Lady Bellaston, I darst to say, is no better than she should be.'—'Hush! hush!' cries Jones, 'every word is overheard in the next room.'—'I don't care a farthing,' cries Honour, 'I speaks no scandal of any one; but to be sure the servants make no scruple of saying as how her ladyship meets men at another place—where the house goes under the name of a poor gentlewoman; but her ladyship pays the rent, and many's the good thing besides, they say, she hath of her.' Here Jones, after expressing the utmost uneasiness, offered to stop her mouth. 'Hey-day! why sure, Mr Jones, you will let me speak; I speaks no scandal, for I only says what I heard from others—and thinks I to myself, much good may it do the gentlewoman with her riches, if she comes by it in such a wicked manner. To be sure it is better to be poor and honest.'

'I protest,' cries Jones, 'I can't hear this of a lady of such honour, and a relation of Sophia; besides, you will distract the poor lady in the next room.—Let me entreat you to walk with me downstairs.'—'Nay, sir, if you won't let me speak, I have done.—Here, sir, is a letter from my young lady—what would some men give to have this? But, Mr Jones, I think you are not over and above generous, and yet I have heard some servants say—— But I am sure you will do me the justice to own I never saw the colour of your money.' Here Jones hastily took the letter, and presently after slipped five pieces into her hand. He then returned a thousand thanks to his dear Sophia in a whisper, and begged her to leave him to read her letter: she presently departed, not without expressing much grateful sense of his generosity.

Lady Bellaston now came from behind the curtain. How shall I describe her rage? Her tongue was at first incapable of utterance; but streams of fire darted from her eyes, and well indeed they might, for her heart was all in a flame. And now, as soon as her voice found way, instead of expressing any indignation against Honour, she began to attack poor Jones. 'You see,' said she, 'what I have sacrificed to you; my reputation, my honour —gone for ever! And what return have I found? Neglected, slighted for a country girl, for an idiot.'—'What neglect, madam, or what slight,' cries Jones, 'have I been guilty of?'—'Mr Jones,' said she, 'it is in vain to dissemble; if you will make me easy, you must entirely give her up; and as a proof of your intention, show me the letter.'—'What letter, madam?' said Jones. 'Nay, surely,' said she, 'you cannot have the confidence to deny your having received a letter by the hands of that trollop.'—'And can your ladyship,' cries he, 'ask of me what I must part with my honour before I grant? Have I acted in such a manner by your ladyship? Could I be guilty of betraying this poor innocent girl to you, what security could you have that I should not act the same part by yourself? A moment's reflection will, I am sure, convince you, that a man with whom the secrets of a lady are not safe must be the most contemptible of wretches.'—'Very well,' said she. 'I need not insist on your becoming this contemptible wretch in your own opinion; for the inside of the letter could inform me of nothing more than I know already. I see the footing you are upon.' Here ensued a long conversation, which the reader will thank me for not inserting at length. It shall suffice, therefore, to inform him, that Lady Bellaston grew more and more pacified, and at length believed, or affected to believe, his protestations, that his meeting with Sophia that evening was merely accidental.

She was not, however, in her heart perfectly satisfied with his refusal to show her the letter; so deaf are we to the clearest reason, when it argues against our prevailing passions. She was, indeed, well convinced that Sophia possessed the first place in Jones's affections, and yet haughty and amorous as this lady was, she submitted at last to bear the second place.

It was at length agreed that Jones should visit at the house: for that Sophia, her maid, and all the servants, would place these visits to the account of Sophia, and that she herself would be considered as the person imposed upon.

This scheme was contrived by the lady, and highly relished by Jones, who was indeed glad to have a prospect of seeing his Sophia at any rate; and the lady herself was not a little pleased with the imposition on Sophia, which Jones, she thought, could not possibly discover to her for his own sake.

The next day was appointed for the visit, and then, after proper ceremonials, the Lady Bellaston returned home.

Jones was no sooner alone, than he eagerly broke open his letter, and read as follows:

'Sir, it is impossible to express what I have suffered since you left this house; and as I have reason to think you intend coming here again, I have sent Honour, though so late at night, as she tells me she knows your lodgings, to prevent you. I charge you, by all the regard you have for me, not to think of visiting here; for it will certainly be discovered; nay, I almost doubt, from some things which have dropt from her ladyship, that she is not already without some suspicion. Something favourable, perhaps, may happen; we must wait with patience; but I once more entreat you, if you have any concern for my ease, do not think of returning hither.'

This letter administered the same kind of consolation to poor Jones, which Job formerly received from his friends. Besides disappointing all the hopes which he promised to himself from seeing Sophia, he was reduced to an unhappy dilemma, with regard to Lady Bellaston; for there are some certain engagements, which, as he well knew, do very difficultly admit of any excuse for the failure; and to go, after the strict prohibition from Sophia, he was not to be forced by any human power. At length, after much deliberation, which during that night supplied the place of sleep, he determined to feign himself sick: for this suggested itself as the only means of failing the appointed visit, without incensing Lady Bellaston, which he had more than one reason of desiring to avoid.

The first thing, however, which he did in the morning, was, to write an answer to Sophia, which he enclosed in one to Honour. He then dispatched another to Lady Bellaston, containing the above-mentioned excuse; and to this he soon received the following answer:

'I am vexed that I cannot see you here this afternoon, but more concerned for the occasion; take great care of yourself, and have the best advice, and I hope there will be no danger.—I am so tormented all this morning with fools, that I have scarce a moment's time to write to you. Adieu.

'P.S.—I will endeavour to call on you this evening, at nine.—Be sure to be alone.'

Mr Jones now received a visit from Mrs Miller, who, after some formal introduction, began the following speech: 'I am very sorry, sir, to wait upon you on such an occasion; but I hope you will consider the ill consequence which it must be to the reputation of my poor girls, if my house should once be talked of as a house of ill fame. I hope you won't think me, therefore, guilty of impertinence, if I beg you not to bring any more ladies in at that time of night. The clock had struck two before one of them went away.'—'I do assure you, madam,' said Jones, 'the lady who was here last night, and who stayed the latest (for the other only brought me a letter), is a woman of very great fashion, and my near relation.'—'I don't know what fashion she is of,' answered Mrs Miller; 'but I am sure no woman of virtue, unless a very near relation indeed, would visit a young gentleman at ten at night, and stay four hours in his room with him alone; besides, sir, the behaviour of her chairmen shows what she was; for they did nothing but make jests all the evening in the entry, and asked Mr Partridge, in the hearing of my own maid, if madam intended to stay with his master all night; with a great deal of stuff not proper to be repeated.' Jones started and changed colour. 'Indeed, Mrs Miller,' answered he, a little warmly, 'I do not take this at all kind. I will never bring any slander on your house; but I must insist on seeing what company I please in my own room; and if that gives you any offence, I shall, as soon as I am able, look for another lodging.'—'I am sorry we must part then, sir,' said she; 'but I am convinced Mr Allworthy himself would never come within my doors, if he had the least suspicion of my keeping an ill house.'—'Very well, madam,' said Jones. 'I hope, sir,' said she, 'you are not angry; for I would not for the world offend any of Mr Allworthy's family. I have not slept a wink all night about this matter.'—'I am sorry I have disturbed your rest, madam,' said Jones, 'but I beg you will send Partridge up to me immediately'; which she promised to do, and then with a very low courtesy retired.

As soon as Partridge arrived, Jones fell upon him in the most outrageous manner. 'How often,' said he, 'am I to suffer for your folly, or rather for my own in keeping you? How durst you, after all the precautions I gave you, mention the name of Mr Allworthy in this house?' Partridge denied that he ever had, with many oaths. 'How else,' said Jones, 'should Mrs Miller be acquainted that there was any connexion between him and me?' 'O Lord, sir,' said Partridge, 'I desire only to be heard out; and to be sure, never was anything so unfortunate. When Mrs Honour came downstairs last night, she met me in the entry, and asked me when my master had heard from Mr Allworthy; and to be sure Mrs Miller heard the very words; and the moment Madam Honour was gone, she called me into the parlour to her. "Mr Partridge," says she, "what Mr Allworthy is it that the gentlewoman mentioned? is it the great Mr Allworthy of Somersetshire?"—"Upon my word, madam," says I, "I know nothing of the matter."—"Sure," says she, "your master is not the Mr Jones I have heard Mr Allworthy talk of?"—"Upon my word, madam," says I, "I know nothing of the matter."—"Then," says she, turning to her daughter Nancy, says she, "as sure as tenpence this is the very young gentleman, and he agrees exactly with the squire's description.' The Lord above knows who it was told her: for I am the arrantest villain that ever walked upon two legs if ever it came out of my mouth. I promise you, sir, I can keep a secret when I am desired.'

The simplicity of Partridge set Jones a laughing, and put a final end to his anger, which had indeed seldom any long duration in his mind; and he told him he intended presently to leave these lodgings, and ordered him to go and get him others.

Partridge had no sooner left Mr Jones, than Mr Nightingale, with whom he had now contracted a great intimacy, came to him, and, after a short salutation, said, 'So, Tom, I hear you had company very late last night. Upon my soul you are a happy fellow, who have not been in town above a fortnight, and can keep chairs waiting at your door till two in the morning.' He then ran on with much commonplace raillery of the same kind, till Jones at last interrupted him, saying, 'I suppose you have received all this information from Mrs Miller, who hath been up here a little while ago to give me warning. The good woman is afraid, it seems, of the reputation of her daughters.'—'Oh! she is wonderfully nice,' says Nightingale, 'upon that account if you will, we may, I believe, be again together; for, to tell you a secret, which I desire you won't mention in the family, I intend to quit the house to-day.'—'What, hath Mrs Miller given you warning too, my friend!' cries Jones. 'No,' answered the other; 'but the rooms are not convenient enough. Besides, I am grown weary of this part of the town. I want to be nearer the places of diversion; so I am going to Pall-mall.'—'And do you intend to make a secret of your going away?' said Jones. 'I promise you,' answered Nightingale, 'I don't intend to bilk my lodgings; but I have a private reason for not taking a formal leave.'—'Not so private,' answered Jones; 'I promise you, I have seen it ever since the second day of my coming to the house. Here will be some wet eyes on your departure. Poor Nancy, I pity her, faith! Indeed, Jack, you have played the fool with that girl. You have given her a longing, which I am afraid nothing will ever cure her of.' Nightingale answered, 'What the devil would you have me do? would you have me marry her to cure her?'—'No,' answered Jones, 'I would not have had you make love to her, as you have often done in my presence. The poor girl cannot conceal it a moment; her eyes are never off from you, and she always colours every time you come into the room.'—'What, do you suppose,' says Nightingale, 'that we have been a-bed together?'—'No, upon my honour,' answered Jones, very seriously, 'I do not suppose so ill of you; for I am sure thou art a very good-natured fellow, and such a one can never be guilty of a cruelty of that kind; but at the same time you have pleased your own vanity, without considering that this poor girl was made a sacrifice to it; and while you have had no design but of amusing an idle hour, you have actually given her reason to flatter herself that you had the most serious designs in her favour.'

'Well, well,' said Nightingale, 'I believe you, and I am convinced you acquit me of any such thing.'

'I do, from my heart,' answered Jones, 'of having debauched the girl, but not from having gained her affections.'

'If I have,' said Nightingale, 'I am sorry for it; for, to confess the truth to you—I never liked any girl half so much in my whole life; but I must let you into the whole secret, Tom. My father hath provided a match for me with a woman I never saw; and she is now coming to town, in order for me to make my addresses to her.'

At these words Jones burst into a loud fit of laughter; when Nightingale cried, 'Nay, prithee, don't turn me into ridicule. The devil take me if I am not half mad about this matter! my poor Nancy! Oh! Jones, Jones, I wish I had a fortune in my own possession.'

'I heartily wish you had,' cries Jones; 'for, if this be the case, I sincerely pity you both; but surely you don't intend to go away without taking your leave of her?'

'I would not,' answered Nightingale, 'undergo the pain of taking leave, for ten thousand pounds; besides, I am convinced, instead of answering any good purpose, if would only serve to inflame my poor Nancy the more. I beg, therefore, you would not mention a word of it to-day, and in the evening, or to-morrow morning, I intend to depart.'

Jones promised he would not; and said, upon reflection, he thought, as he had determined and was obliged to leave her, he took the most prudent method. He then told Nightingale he should be very glad to lodge in the same house with him; and it was accordingly agreed between them, that Nightingale should procure him either the ground floor, or the two pair of stairs; for the young gentleman himself was to occupy that which was between them.

CHAPTER THIRTY-ONE

A SHORT ACCOUNT OF THE HISTORY OF MRS MILLER

JONES this day eat a pretty good dinner for a sick man, that is to say, the larger half of a shoulder of mutton. In the afternoon, he received an invitation from Mrs Miller to drink tea; for that good woman, having learnt, either by means of Partridge, or by some other means natural or supernatural, that he had a connexion with Mr Allworthy, could not endure the thoughts of parting with him in an angry manner.

Jones accepted the invitation; and no sooner was the tea-kettle removed, and the girls sent out of the room, than the widow, without much preface, began as follows: 'Well, there are very surprizing things happen in this world; but certainly it is a wonderful business that I should have a relation of Mr Allworthy in my house, and never know anything of the matter. Alas! sir, you little imagine what a friend that best of gentlemen hath been to me and mine. Yes, sir, I am not ashamed to own it; it is owing to his goodness that I did not long since perish for want, and leave my poor little wretches, two destitute, helpless, friendless orphans, to the care, or rather to the cruelty, of the world.

'You must know, sir, though I am now reduced to get my living by letting lodgings, I was born and bred a gentlewoman. My father was an officer of the army, and died in a considerable rank: but he lived up to his pay; and, as that expired with him, his family, at his death, became beggars. Within a month from his decease I was married to a clergyman. Five years did I live in a state of perfect happiness with that best of men, till at last—Oh! cruel! cruel fortune, that deprived me of the kindest of husbands and my poor girls of the tenderest parent.—O my poor girls! you never know the blessing which ye lost. I had now two children to provide for; and was, if possible, more pennyless than ever; when that great, that good, that glorious man, Mr Allworthy, who had some little acquaintance with my husband, accidentally heard of my distress, and within a fortnight afterwards, Mr Allworthy—the blessed Mr Allworthy—came to pay me a visit, when he placed me in the house where you now see me, gave me a large sum of money to furnish it, and settled an annuity of £50 a-year upon me, which I have constantly received ever since. Judge, then, Mr Jones, in what regard I must hold a benefactor, to whom I owe the preservation of my life, and of those dear children, for whose sake alone my life is valuable. Do not, therefore, think me im-

149

pertinent, Mr Jones (since I must esteem one for whom I know Mr Allworthy has so much value), if I beg you not to converse with these wicked women. You are a young gentleman, and do not know half their artful wiles.'

'Upon my word, madam,' said Jones, 'you need make no farther apology; nor do I in the least take anything ill you have said; but give me leave, as no one can have more value than myself for Mr Allworthy, to deliver you from one mistake, which, perhaps, would not be altogether for his honour; I do assure you, I am no relation of his.'

'Alas! sir,' answered she, 'I know you are not, I know very well who you are; for Mr Allworthy hath told me all; but I do assure you, had you been twenty times his son, he could not have expressed more regard for you than he hath often expressed in my presence.'

Here Jones heaved a deep sigh, and then said, 'Since I perceive, madam, you really do know me, and Mr Allworthy hath thought proper to mention my name to you; and since you have been so explicit with me as to your own affairs, I will acquaint you with some more circumstances concerning myself.' And these Mrs Miller having expressed great desire and curiosity to hear, he began and related to her his whole history, without once mentioning the name of Sophia.

Mrs Miller believed all which Jones told her to be true, and exprest much pity and concern for him. She was beginning to comment on the story, but Jones interrupted her; for, as the hour of assignation now drew nigh, he began to stipulate for a second interview with the lady that evening, which he promised should be the last at her house; swearing, at the same time, that she was one of great distinction, and that nothing but what was entirely innocent was to pass between them; and I do firmly believe he intended to keep his word.

Mrs Miller was at length prevailed on, and Jones departed to his chamber, where he sat alone till twelve o'clock, but no Lady Bellaston appeared.

Mr Jones closed not his eyes during all the former part of the night; not owing to any uneasiness which he conceived at being disappointed by Lady Bellaston; nor was Sophia herself, though most of his waking hours were justly to be charged to her account, the present cause of dispelling his slumbers. In fact, poor Jones was one of the best natured fellows alive. He could not help, therefore, compassionating the situation of poor Nancy, whose love for Mr Nightingale seemed to him so apparent, that he was astonished at the blindness of her mother, who had more than once, the preceding evening, remarked to him the great change in the temper of her daughter, 'who from being,' she said, 'one of the liveliest, merriest girls in the world, was on a sudden, become all gloom and melancholy.'

Sleep, however, at length got the better of all resistance; and Mr Jones slept till eleven the next morning, and would, perhaps, have continued in the same quiet situation much longer, had not a violent uproar awakened him.

Partridge was now summoned, who, being asked what was the matter, answered, 'That there was a dreadful hurricane below-stairs; that Miss Nancy was in fits; and that the other sister, and the mother, were both crying and lamenting over her.' Jones expressed much concern at this news; which Partridge endeavoured to relieve, by saying, with a smile, 'He fancied the young lady was in no danger of death; for that Susan' (which was the name of the maid) 'had given him to understand, it was nothing more than a common affair. In short,' said he, 'Miss Nancy hath had a mind to be as wise as her mother; that's all; she was a little hungry, it seems, and so sat down to dinner before grace was said; and so there is a child coming for the Foundling Hospital.'
——'Prithee, leave thy stupid jesting,' cries Jones. 'Is the misery of these poor wretches a subject of mirth? Go immediately to Mrs Miller, and tell her I beg leave—stay, you will make some blunder; I will go myself; for she desired me to breakfast with her.' Jones was no sooner dressed than he walked downstairs, and knocking at the door, was presently admitted by the maid. Jones desired the maid to tell her mistress that he was heartily sorry for the occasion; and that if he could be of any service to her, she might command him.'

He had scarce spoke these words, when Mrs Miller, who heard them all, suddenly threw open the door, and coming out to him, in a flood of tears, said, 'O Mr Jones! you are certainly one of the best young men alive. I give you a thousand thanks for your kind offer of your service; but, alas! sir, it is out of your power to preserve my poor girl.—O my child! my child! she is undone, she is ruined for ever!'—'I hope, madam,' said Jones, 'no villain——'—'O Mr Jones!' said she, 'that villain who yesterday left my lodgings, hath betrayed my poor girl; hath destroyed her. That Nightingale, that barbarous villain, hath undone my daughter. She is—she is—oh! Mr Jones, my girl is with child by him; and in that condition he hath deserted her.'

They both stood silent during a minute, looking at each other; at last he began thus: 'I cannot express, madam, how much I am shocked, yet let me beg you to consider the reputation of your daughter.'——'It is gone, it is lost. Mr Jones,' cryed she, 'as well as her innocence. She received a letter in a room full of company, and immediately swooning away upon opening it, the contents were known to every one present. But the loss of her reputation, bad as it is, is not the worst;

I shall lose my child; she hath attempted twice to destroy herself already, and though she hath been hitherto prevented, vows she will not outlive it. O my poor Nancy, the darling of my soul! the delight of my eyes! the pride of my heart! too much, indeed, my pride; for to those foolish, ambitious hopes, arising from her beauty, I owe her ruin. Alas! I saw with pleasure the liking which this young man had for her. I thought it an honourable affection; and flattered my foolish vanity with the thoughts of seeing her married to one so much her superior.'

'I hope, madam,' said Jones, 'I can do some service to this little family of love. But whatever success may attend my endeavours, I am resolved to attempt it. I am very much deceived in Mr Nightingale, if, notwithstanding what hath happened, he hath not much goodness of heart at the bottom, as well as a very violent affection for your daughter. I will go instantly in quest of Mr Nightingale; and I hope to bring you good news.'

Mrs Miller fell upon her knees and invoked all the blessings of heaven upon Mr Jones; to which she afterwards added the most passionate expressions of gratitude. He then departed to find Mr Nightingale, and the good woman returned to comfort her daughter, who was somewhat cheered at what her mother told her; and both joined in resounding the praises of Mr Jones.

Jones found Mr Nightingale in his new lodgings, sitting melancholy by the fire, and silently lamenting the unhappy situation in which he had placed poor Nancy. He no sooner saw his friend appear, than he arose hastily to meet him; and said, 'Nothing could be more opportune than this kind visit; for I was never more in the spleen in my life.'

'I am sorry,' answered Jones, 'that I bring news very unlikely to relieve you: I come to you, Mr Nightingale, from a worthy family, which you have involved in misery and ruin.' Mr Nightingale changed colour at these words; but Jones, without regarding it, proceeded, in the liveliest manner, to paint the tragical story with which the reader was acquainted in the last chapter.

Nightingale never once interrupted the narration, though he discovered violent emotions at many parts of it. But when it was concluded, after fetching a deep sigh, he said, 'What you tell me, my friend, affects me in the tenderest manner. Sure there never was so cursed an accident as the poor girl's betraying my letter. Her reputation might otherwise have been safe, and the affair might have remained a profound secret; I promise you she hath my affections so absolutely, that my wife, whoever she is to be, will have very little share in them.'—'And is it possible, then,' said Jones, 'you can think of deserting her?'—'Why, what can I do?' answered the other. 'Ask Miss Nancy,' replied Jones warmly. 'In the condition to which you have reduced her, I sincerely think she ought to determine what reparation you shall make her. But if you ask me what you shall do, what can you do less than fulfil the expectations of her family, and her own? Nay, I sincerely tell you, they were mine too, ever since I first saw you together. Can you with honour be guilty of having under false pretences deceived a young woman and her family, and of having by these means treacherously robbed her of her innocence? Can you, with honour, be the knowing, the wilful occasion, nay, the artful contriver of the ruin of a human being? Can honour support such contemplations as these a moment?'

'Common sense, indeed,' said Nightingale, 'warrants all you say; but yet you well know the opinion of the world is so contrary to it, that, was I to marry a whore, though my own, I should be ashamed of ever showing my face again.'

'Fie upon it, Mr Nightingale!' said Jones, 'do not call her by so ungenerous a name: when you promised to marry her, she became your wife; and she hath sinned more against prudence than virtue. And what is this world, which you would be ashamed to face, but the vile, the foolish, and the profligate?'

'O, my dear friend!' cries Nightingale, 'I wanted not your eloquence to rouse me. I pity poor Nancy from my soul, and would willingly give anything in my power that no familiarities had ever passed between us. If I had no inclinations to consult but my own, I would marry her to-morrow morning: I would, by heaven! but you will easily imagine how impossible it would be to prevail on my father to consent to such a match; besides, he hath provided another for me; and to-morrow, by his express command, I am to wait on the lady.'

'I have not the honour to know thy father,' said Jones; 'but, suppose he could be persuaded, would you yourself consent to the only means of preserving these poor people?'—'As eagerly as I would pursue my happiness,' answered Nightingale; 'for I never shall find it in any other woman; could my father be induced to comply with my desires, nothing would be wanting to compleat my own happiness, or that of my Nancy.'

'Then I am resolved to undertake it,' said Jones. 'If you will therefore tell me where I may find the old gentleman, I will not lose a moment in the business; which, while I pursue, you cannot do a more generous action than by paying a visit to the poor girl.'

Nightingale immediately consented to the proposal; and now, having acquainted Jones with his father's lodging, and the coffee-house where he would most probably find him, he hesitated a moment, and then said, 'My dear Tom, you are going to undertake an impossibility. If you knew my father, you would never think of obtaining his consent.——Stay, there is one way—suppose you told him I was already married, it might be easier to reconcile him to the fact after it was done; and, upon my honour, I am so affected with what you have said, and I love my Nancy so passionately, I almost wish it was done, whatever might be the consequence.'

Jones greatly approved the hint, and promised to pursue it. They then separated, Nightingale to visit his Nancy, and Jones in quest of the old gentleman.

Jones found Mr Nightingale the elder in so critical a minute, that Fortune could not have contrived such another. In short, the old gentleman, and the father of the young lady whom he intended for his son, had been hard at it for many hours; and the latter was just now gone, and had left the former delighted with the thoughts that he had succeeded in a long contention, which had been between the two fathers of the future bride and bridegroom; in which both endeavoured to overreach the other, and, as it not rarely happens in such cases, both had retreated full satisfied of having obtained the victory.

This gentleman, who Mr Jones now visited, was what they call a man of the world; that is to say, a man who directs his conduct in this world as one who, being fully persuaded there is no other, is resolved to make the most of this. He had indeed conversed so entirely with money, that it may be almost doubted whether he imagined there was any other thing really existing in the world; this at least may be certainly averred, that he firmly believed nothing else to have any real value.

As money then was always uppermost in this gentleman's thoughts, so the moment he saw a stranger within his doors, it immediately occurred to his imagination, that such stranger was either come to bring him money, or to fetch it from him.

Unluckily for Jones, a young gentleman had visited him the day before, with a bill from his son for a play debt, so he apprehended, at the first sight of Jones, that he was come on such another errand. Jones therefore had no sooner told him that he was come on his son's account, than the old gentleman, being confirmed in his suspicion, burst forth into an exclamation, 'That he would lose his labour.'—'Is it then possible, sir,' answered Jones, 'that you can guess my business?'—'If I do guess it,' replied the other, 'I repeat again to you, you will lose your labour. What, I suppose you are one of those sparks who lead my son into all those scenes of riot and debauchery, which will be his destruction? but I shall pay no more of his bills, I promise you. I expect he will quit all such company for the future. If I had imagined otherwise, I should not have provided a wife for him; for I would be instrumental in the ruin of nobody.'

'How, sir,' said Jones, 'and was this lady of your providing?' 'Pray, sir,' answered the old gentleman, 'how comes it to be any concern of yours?'—'Nay, dear sir,' replied Jones, 'be not offended that I interest myself in what regards your son's happiness, for whom I have so great an honour and value. It was upon that very account I came to wait upon you. I can't express the esteem I have for you; who could be so generous, so good, so kind, so indulgent to provide such a match for your son; a woman, who, I dare swear, will make him one of the happiest men upon earth.'

Nightingale no sooner found that Jones had no demand on him, than he began to be pleased with his presence. 'Pray, good sir,' said he, 'be pleased to sit down. I do not remember to have ever had the pleasure of seeing you before; but if you are a friend of my son, and have anything to say concerning this young lady, I shall be glad to hear you. As to her making him happy, it will be his own fault if she doth not. I have discharged my duty, in taking care of the main article. She will bring him a fortune capable of making any reasonable, prudent, sober man happy.'— 'Undoubtedly,' cries Jones, 'for she is in herself a fortune; so beautiful, so genteel, so sweet-tempered, and so well educated; she is indeed a most accomplished young lady; sings admirably well, and hath a most delicate hand at the harpsichord.'—'I did not know any of these matters,' answered the old gentleman, 'for I never saw the lady: but I do not like her the worse for what you tell me; and I am the better pleased with her father for not laying any stress on these qualifications in our bargain. I shall always think it a proof of his understanding.'—'I do assure you, sir,' cries Jones, 'she hath them all in the most eminent degree, for sure it is little less than madness to consider money as the sole foundation of happiness. 'Such a woman as this with her little, her nothing of a fortune.'—'I find,' cries the old gentleman, 'you have a pretty just opinion of money, my friend, or else you are better acquainted with the person of the lady than with her circumstances. Why, pray, what fortune do you imagine this lady to have?'—'What fortune?' cries Jones, 'how much? Why, at the utmost, perhaps £200.'—'Do you mean to banter me, young gentleman?' said the father, a little angry. 'No, upon my soul,' answered Jones, 'I am in earnest: nay, I believe I have gone to the utmost farthing. If I do the lady an injury, I ask her pardon.'—'Indeed you do,' cries the father; 'I am certain she hath fifty times that sum, and she shall produce fifty to that before I consent that she shall marry my son.'—'Nay,' said Jones, 'it is too late to talk of consent now; if she had not fifty farthings, your son is married.'—'My son married!' answered the old gentleman, with surprize. 'Nay,' said Jones, 'I thought you was unacquainted with it.'—'My son married to Miss Harris!' answered he again. 'To Miss Harris!' said Jones; 'no, sir; to Miss Nancy Miller, the daughter of Mrs Miller, at whose house he lodged; a young lady, who, though her mother is reduced to let lodgings——'

While the father stood like one struck suddenly dumb at this news, a gentleman came into the room, and saluted him by the name of brother.

But though these two were in consanguinity so nearly related, they were in their dispositions almost the opposites to each other. The brother who now arrived had likewise been bred to trade, in which he no sooner saw himself worth £6,000 than he purchased a small estate with the greatest part of it, and retired into the country.

The young lady whom Mr Nightingale had intended for his son was a near neighbour of his brother, and in reality it was upon the account of his projected match, that he was now come to town; not, indeed, to forward, but to dissuade his brother from a purpose which he conceived would inevitably ruin his nephew; for he foresaw no other event from a union with Miss Harris, notwithstanding the largeness of her fortune, as neither her person nor mind seemed to promise any kind of matrimonial felicity: for she was very tall, very thin, very ugly, very affected, very silly, and very ill-natured.

His brother, therefore, no sooner mentioned the marriage of his nephew with Miss Miller, than he exprest the utmost satisfaction; and when the father had very bitterly reviled his son, and pronounced sentence of beggary upon him, the uncle began in the following manner:

'If you was a little cooler, brother, I would ask you whether you love your son for his sake or for your own.

'Now, brother, to prescribe rules of happiness to others hath always appeared to me very absurd, and to insist on doing this, very tyrannical. My nephew, I own, in marrying, without asking your advice, hath been guilty of a fault. And if he hath failed in his duty here, did you not as much exceed authority, when you absolutely bargained with him for a woman, without his knowledge, whom you yourself never saw, and whom, if you had seen and known as well as I, it must have been madness in you to have ever thought of bringing her into your family?'

Mr Nightingale, the father, instead of attempting to answer his brother, contented himself with only observing, that they had always differed in their sentiments concerning their children. 'I wish,' said he, 'brother, you would never have troubled yourself with my son, who hath, I believe, as little profited by your precepts, as by your example.' For young Nightingale was his uncle's godson, and had lived more with him than with his father. So that the uncle had often declared, he loved his nephew almost equally with his own child.

Jones fell into raptures with this good gentleman; and when,

156

after much persuasion, they found the father grew still more and more irritated, instead of appeased, Jones conducted the uncle to his nephew at the house of Mrs Miller.

At his return to his lodgings, Jones found the situation of affairs greatly altered from what they had been in at his departure. The mother, the two daughters, and young Mr Nightingale, were now sat down to supper together, when the uncle was, at his own desire, introduced without any ceremony into the company, to all of whom he was well known; for he had several times visited his nephew at that house.

The old gentleman immediately walked up to Miss Nancy, saluted and wished her joy, as he did afterwards the mother and the other sister; and lastly, he paid the proper compliments to his nephew, with the same good humour and courtesy, as if his nephew had married his equal or superior in fortune, with all the previous requisites first performed.

Miss Nancy and her supposed husband both turned pale, and looked rather foolish than otherwise upon this occasion; but Mrs Miller took the first opportunity of withdrawing; and having sent for Jones into the dining-room, she threw herself at his feet, and in a most passionate flood of tears, called him her good angel, the preserver of her poor little family.

After the first gust of her passion was a little over, she proceeded to inform Mr Jones that all matters were settled between Mr Nightingale and her daughter, and that they were to be married the next morning; at which Mr Jones having expressed much pleasure, the poor woman fell again into a fit of joy and thanksgiving, which he at length with difficulty silenced, and prevailed on her to return with him back to the company, whom they found in the same good humour in which they had left them.

Our company in about half an hour broke up, and the uncle carried off his nephew; but not before the latter had assured Miss Nancy, in a whisper, that he would attend her early in the morning, and fulfil all his engagements.

Jones was in his room, when the maid of the house informed him that a gentlewoman desired to speak with him.——He went immediately out, and, taking the candle from the maid, ushered his visitant upstairs, who, in the person of Mrs Honour, acquainted him with such dreadful news concerning his Sophia, that he immediately lost all consideration for every other person; and his whole stock of compassion was entirely swallowed up in reflections on his own misery, and on that of his unfortunate angel.

CHAPTER THIRTY-TWO

A VERY BLACK DESIGN AGAINST SOPHIA

I REMEMBER a wise old gentleman who used to say, 'When children are doing nothing, they are doing mischief.' When the effects of female jealousy do not appear openly in their proper colours of rage and fury, we may suspect that mischievous passion to be at work privately, and attempting to undermine, what it doth not attack above-ground.

This was exemplified in the conduct of Lady Bellaston, who, under all the smiles which she wore in her countenance, concealed much indignation against Sophia; and as she plainly saw that this young lady stood between her and the full indulgence of her desires, she resolved to get rid of her by some means or other; nor was it long before a very favourable opportunity of accomplishing this presented itself to her.

The reader may be pleased to remember, that when Sophia was thrown into that consternation at the playhouse, she had put herself under the protection of a young nobleman, who had very safely conducted her to her chair.

This nobleman, who frequently visited Lady Bellaston, had more than once seen Sophia there, since her arrival in town, and had conceived a very great liking to her; which liking had so encreased, that he might now, without any great impropriety, be said to be actually in love with her.

It may easily be believed, that he would not suffer so handsome an occasion of improving his acquaintance with the beloved object as now offered itself to elapse, when even good breeding alone might have prompted him to pay her a visit.

The next morning therefore, after this accident, he waited on Sophia, with the usual compliments, and hopes that she had received no harm from her last night's adventure.

Lady Bellaston had been apprized of his lordship's visit at his first arrival; and the length of it very well satisfied her, that things went as she wished, and as indeed she had suspected the second time she saw this young couple together. She therefore ordered her servants, that when my lord was going, they should tell him she desired to speak with him; and employed the intermediate time in meditating how best to accomplish a scheme, which she made no doubt but his lordship would very readily embrace the execution of.

Lord Fellamar (for that was the title of this young nobleman) was no sooner introduced to her ladyship than she attacked him in the following strain: 'Bless me, my lord, are you here yet? I thought my servants had made a mistake, and let you go away; and I wanted to see you about an affair of some importance.'——'Indeed, Lady Bellaston,' said he, 'I don't wonder you are astonished at the length of my visit; for I have staid above two hours, and I did not think I had staid above half-a-one.'—— 'What am I to conclude from thence, my lord?' said she. 'The company must be very agreeable which can make time slide away so very deceitfully.'—'Upon my honour,' said he, 'the most agreeable I ever saw. Pray tell me, Lady Bellaston, who is this blazing star which you have produced among us all of a sudden?'—— 'What blazing star, my lord?' said she, affecting a surprize. 'I mean,' said he, 'the lady I saw here the other day, whom I had last night in my arms at the playhouse, and to whom I have been making that unreasonable visit.'——'O, my cousin Western!' said she; 'why, that blazing star, my lord, is the daughter of a country booby squire, and hath been in town about a fortnight, for the first time.'——'Upon my soul,' said he, 'I should swear she had been bred up in a court; for besides her beauty, I never saw anything so genteel, so sensible, so polite.'——'O brave!' cries the lady, 'my cousin hath you, I find.'——'Upon my honour,' answered he, 'I wish she had; for I am in love with her to distraction.'——'Nay, my lord,' said she, 'it is not wishing yourself very ill neither, for she is a very great fortune: I assure you she is an only child, and her father's estate is a good £3,000 a-year.'—'Then I can assure you, madam,' answered the lord, 'I think her the best match in England.' 'As she is a relation of yours, will you do me the honour to propose it to her father?'—'Indeed, then,' said the lady, 'I will most readily propose your lordship to her father; and I can, I believe, assure you of his joyful acceptance of the proposal; but there is a bar, which I am almost ashamed to mention; and yet it is one you will never be able to conquer.—You have a rival, my lord, and a rival who, though I blush to name him, neither you, nor all the world, will ever be able to conquer.'— 'Upon my word, Lady Bellaston,' cries he, 'you have struck a damp to my heart, which hath almost deprived me of being.'—'Fie, my lord,' said she, 'I should rather hope I had struck fire into you. A lover, and talk of damps in your heart! I rather imagined you would have asked your rival's name, that you might have immediately entered the lists with him.'—'I promise you, madam,' answered he, 'there are very few things I would not undertake for your charming cousin; but pray, who is this happy man?' —'Why, he is,' said she, 'what I am sorry to say most happy men with us are, one of the lowest fellows in the world. He is a beggar, a bastard, a foundling, a fellow in meaner circumstances than one of your lordship's footmen. The family have already done all in their power; but the girl is, I think, intoxicated, and nothing less than ruin will content her. And to deal more openly with you, I expect every day to hear she is run away with him.' —'What is to be done?' cries my lord; 'what methods are to be taken?—Oh! Lady Bellaston! there is nothing which I would not undertake for such a reward'——'I really know not,' answered the lady, after a pause; and then pausing again, she cried out: 'Upon my soul, I am at my wit's end on this girl's account.— If she can be preserved, something must be done immediately; and, as I say, nothing but violent methods will do.——If your lordship hath really this attachment to my cousin, I think there may be one way, indeed it is a very disagreeable one, and what I am most afraid to think of.—My lord—I—I vow, I can't bear the apprehension of it.—No, it must not be.——At least every other method shall be tried. Can you get rid of your engagements, and dine here to-day? Your lordship will have an opportunity of seeing a little more of Miss Western.—I promise you we have no time to lose. Here will be nobody but Lady Betty, and Miss Eagle, and Colonel Hampsted, and Tom Edwards; they will all go soon—— and I shall be at home to nobody. Then your lordship may be a little more explicit. Nay, I will contrive some method to convince you of her attachment to this fellow.' My lord made proper compliments, accepted the invitation, and then they parted to dress.

Lady Bellaston was in reality a very considerable member of the little world; by which appellation was distinguished a very worthy and honourable society which not long since flourished in this kingdom.

Among other good principles upon which this society was founded, there was one very remarkable; for, it was a rule that every member should, within the twenty-four hours, tell at least one merry fib, which was to be propagated by all the brethren and sisterhood.

Edwards was likewise a member of this comical society. To him therefore Lady Bellaston applied as a proper instrument for her purpose, and furnished him with a fib, which he was to vent whenever the lady gave him her cue; and this was not to be till the evening, when all the company but Lord Fellamar and himself were gone, and while they were engaged in a rubbers at whist.

To this time then, which was between seven and eight in the evening, we will convey our reader; when Lady Bellaston, Lord Fellamar, Miss Western, and Tom, being engaged at whist, and in the last game of their rubbers, Tom received his cue from Lady Bellaston, which was, 'I protest, Tom, you are grown intolerable lately; you used to tell us all the news of the town, and now you know no more of the world than if you lived out of it.'

Mr Edwards then began as follows: 'The fault is not mine, madam: it lies in the dullness of the age, that doth nothing worth talking of.——O la! though now I think on't, there hath a terrible accident befallen poor Colonel Wilcox.——Poor Ned.—— You know him, my lord, everybody knows him; faith! I am very much concerned for him.'

'What is it, pray?' says Lady Bellaston.

'Why, he hath killed a man this morning in a duel, that's all.'

His lordship, who was not in the secret, asked gravely, whom he had killed? To which Edwards answered, 'A young fellow we none of us know; a Somersetshire lad just came to town one Jones his name is: a near relation of one Mr Allworthy, of whom your lordship I believe hath heard. I saw the lad lie dead in a coffee-house.—Upon my soul, he is one of the finest corpses I ever saw in my life!'

Sophia, who had just began to deal as Tom had mentioned that a man was killed, stopt her hand, and listened with attention, but no sooner had he arrived at the latter part of the story than she began to deal again; and having dealt three cards to one, and seven to another, and ten to a third, at last dropt the rest from her hand, and fell back in her chair.

The company behaved as usually on these occasions. The usual disturbance ensued, the usual assistance was summoned, and Sophia at last, as it is usual, returned again to life, and was soon after, at her earnest desire, led to her own apartment; where, at my lord's request, Lady Bellaston acquainted her with the truth, attempted to carry it off as a jest of her own, and comforted her with repeated assurances, that neither his lordship nor Tom, though she had taught him the story, were in the true secret of the affair.

There was no farther evidence necessary to convince Lord Fellamar how justly the case had been presented to him by Lady Bellaston; and now, at her return into the room, a scheme was laid between these two noble persons, which, though it appeared in no very heinous light to his lordship (as he faithfully promised, and faithfully resolved too, to make the lady all the subsequent amends in his power by marriage), yet many of our readers, we doubt not, will see with just detestation.

The next evening at seven was appointed for the fatal purpose, when Lady Bellaston undertook that Sophia should be alone, and his lordship should be introduced to her. The whole family were to be regulated for the purpose, most of the servants dispatched out of the house; and for Mrs Honour, who, to prevent suspicion, was to be left with her mistress till his lordship's arrival, Lady Bellaston herself was to engage her in an apartment as distant as possible from the scene of the intended mischief, and out of the hearing of Sophia.

CHAPTER THIRTY-THREE

CONTAINING SOME MATTERS WHICH MAY SURPRIZE THE READER

THE clock had now struck seven, and poor Sophia, alone and melancholy, sat reading a tragedy. It was the *Fatal Marriage*; and she was now come to that part where the poor distrest Isabella disposes of her wedding-ring.

Here the book dropt from her hand, and a shower of tears ran down into her bosom. In this situation she had continued a minute, when the door opened, and in came Lord Fellamar. Sophia started from her chair at his entrance; and his lordship advancing forwards, and making a low bow, said, 'I am afraid, Miss Western, I break in upon you abruptly.'—'Indeed, my lord,' says she, 'I must own myself a little surprized at this unexpected visit.'—'If this visit be unexpected, madam,' answered Lord Fellamar, 'my eyes must have been very faithless interpreters of my heart, when last I had the honour of seeing you; for surely you could not otherwise have hoped to detain my heart in your possession, without receiving a visit from its owner.' Sophia, confused as she was, answered this bombast (and very properly, I think) with a look of inconceivable disdain. My lord then made another and a longer speech of the same sort. Upon which Sophia, trembling, said, 'Am I really to conceive your lordship to be out of your senses? Sure, my lord, there is no other excuse for such behaviour.'— 'I am, indeed, madam, in the situation you suppose,' cries his lordship; 'and sure you will pardon the effects of a frenzy which you yourself have occasioned; for love hath so totally deprived me of reason, that I am scarce accountable for any of my actions.'— 'Upon my word, my lord,' said Sophia, 'I neither understand your words nor your behaviour.'—'Suffer me then, madam,' cries he, 'at your feet to explain both, by laying open my soul to you, and declaring that I doat on you to the highest degree of distraction. O most adorable, most divine creature! what language can express the sentiments of my heart?'—'I do assure you, my lord,' said Sophia, 'I shall not stay to hear any more of this.'—'Do not,' cries he, 'think of leaving me thus cruelly; could you know half the torments which I feel, that tender bosom must pity what those eyes have caused.' Then fetching a deep sigh, and laying hold of her hand, he ran on for some minutes in a strain which would be little more pleasing to the reader than it was to the lady; and at last concluded with a declaration,

'That if he was master of the world, he would lay it at her feet. I cannot lose you.—By heaven, I will sooner part with my soul!—You are, you must, you shall be only mine.'—'My lord,' says she, 'I intreat you to desist from a vain pursuit; for, upon my honour, I will never hear you on this subject. Let go my hand, my lord; for I am resolved to go from you this moment; nor will I ever see you more.'—'Then, madam,' cries his lordship, 'I must make the best use of this moment; for I cannot live, nor will I live without you.' He then caught her in his arms: upon which she screamed so loud, that she must have alarmed some one to her assistance, had not Lady Bellaston taken care to remove all ears.

But a more lucky circumstance happened for poor Sophia; another noise now broke forth, which almost drowned her cries; for now the whole house rang with, 'Where is she? D—n me, I'll unkennel her this instant. Show me her chamber, I say. Where is my daughter? I know she's in the house, and I'll see her if she's above-ground. Show me where she is.' At which last words the door flew open, and in came Squire Western, with a set of myrmidons at his heels.

Sophia, notwithstanding her fright, presently knew her father's voice; and his lordship, notwithstanding his passion, knew the voice of reason, which peremptorily assured him, it was not now a time for the perpetration of his villany. Hearing, therefore, the voice approach, he thought proper to relinquish his prey, having only disordered her handkerchief, and with his rude lips committed violence on her lovely neck.

Sophia tottered into a chair, where she sat disordered, pale, breathless, bursting with indignation at Lord Fellamar; affrighted, and yet more rejoiced, at the arrival of her father.

His lordship sat down near her, with the bag of his wig hanging over one of his shoulders, the rest of his dress being somewhat disordered, and rather a greater proportion of linen than is usual appearing at his bosom.

As to Squire Western, he happened at this time to be overtaken by an enemy, which very frequently pursues, and seldom fails to overtake, most of the country gentlemen in this kingdom. He was, literally speaking, drunk; which circumstance, together with his natural impetuosity, could produce no other effect than his running immediately up to his daughter, upon whom he fell foul with his tongue in the most inveterate manner.

My Lady Bellaston now entered the room, and came up to the squire, who no sooner saw her, than, resolving to follow the instructions of his sister, he made her a very civil bow, in the rural manner, and paid her some of his best compliments. He then immediately proceeded to his complaints, and said, 'There, my lady cousin; there stands the most undutiful child in the world; she hankers after a beggarly rascal, and won't marry one of the greatest matches in all England, that we have provided for her.'

'Indeed, cousin Western,' answered the lady, 'I am persuaded you wrong my cousin. I am sure she hath a better understanding. I am convinced she will not refuse what she must be sensible is so much to her advantage.'

This was a wilful mistake in Lady Bellaston, for she well knew whom Mr Western meant; though perhaps she thought he would easily be reconciled to his lordship's proposals.

'Do you hear there,' quoth the squire, 'what her ladyship says? All your family are for the match. Come, Sophy, be a good girl, and be dutiful, and make your father happy.'

'If my death will make you happy, sir,' answered Sohpia, 'you will shortly be so.'

'Indeed, Miss Western,' said Lady Bellaston, 'you injure your father; he hath nothing in view but your interest in this match; and I and all your friends must acknowledge the highest honour done to your family in the proposal.'

'Ay, all of us,' quoth the squire; 'nay, it was no proposal of mine. She knows it was her aunt proposed it to me first.—Come, Sophy, once more let me beg you to be a good girl, and gee me your consent before your cousin.'

'Let me give him your hand, cousin,' said the lady. 'It is the fashion nowadays to dispense with time and long courtships.'

'Pugh!' said the squire, 'what signifies time; won't they have time enough to court afterwards? People may court very well after they have been a-bed together.'

As Lord Fellamar was very well assured that he was meant by Lady Bellaston, so, never having heard nor suspected a word of Blifil, he made no doubt of his being meant by the father. Coming up, therefore, to the squire, he said, 'though I have not the honour, sir, of being personally known to you, yet, as I find I have the happiness to have my proposals accepted, let me intercede, sir, in behalf of the young lady, that she may not be more solicited at this time.'

'You intercede, sir!' said the squire; 'why, who the devil are you?'

'Sir, I am Lord Fellamar,' answered he, 'and am the happy man whom I hope you have done the honour of accepting for a son-in-law.'

'You are a son of a b——,' replied the squire, 'for all your laced coat. You my son-in-law, and be d—n'd to you!'

'I shall take more from you, sir, than from any man,' answered the lord; 'but I must inform you that I am not used to hear such language without resentment.'

'Resent my a——,' quoth the squire. 'Don't think I am afraid of

164

such a fellow as thee art! because hast got a spit there dangling at thy side. Lay by your spit, and I'll give thee enough of meddling with what doth not belong to thee. I'll teach you to father-in-law me. I'll lick thy jacket.'

'It's very well, sir,' said my lord, 'I shall make no disturbance before the ladies. I am very well satisfied. Your humble servant, sir; Lady Bellaston, your most obedient.'

His lordship was no sooner gone, that Lady Bellaston, coming up to Mr Western, said, 'Bless me, sir, what have you done? You know not whom you have affronted; he is a nobleman of the first rank and fortune, and yesterday made proposals to your daughter; and such as I am sure you must accept with the highest pleasure.'

'Answer for yourself, lady cousin,' said the squire, 'I will have nothing to do with any of your lords. My daughter shall have an honest country gentleman; I have pitched upon one for her— and she shall ha'un.—I am sorry for the trouble she hath given your ladyship with all my heart.' Lady Bellaston made a civil speech upon the word trouble; to which the squire answered: 'Why, that's kind—and I would do as much for your ladyship. To be sure relations should do for one another. So I wish your ladyship a good night.—Come, madam, you must go along with me by fair means, or I'll have you carried down to the coach.'

Sophia said she would attend him without force; but begged to go in a chair, for she said she should not be able to ride any other way.

'Prithee,' cries the squire, 'wout unt persuade me canst not ride in a coach, wouldst? That's a pretty thing surely! No, no, I'll never let thee out of my sight any more till art married, that I promise thee.'

Mrs Honour appeared below-stairs, and with a low curtsy to the squire offered to attend her mistress; but he pushed her away, saying, 'Hold, madam, hold, you come no more near my house.' —'And will you take my maid away from me?' said Sophia. 'Yes, indeed, madam, will I,' cries the squire; 'you need not fear being without a servant; I will get you another maid, and better maid than this, who, I'd lay five pounds to a crown, is no more a maid than my grannum. No, no, Sophy, she shall contrive no more escapes, I promise you.' He then packed up his daughter into the hackney coach, after which he mounted himself, and ordered it to drive to his lodgings.

Though the reader, in many histories, is obliged to digest much more unaccountable appearances than this of Mr Western, without and satisfaction at all; yet we shall now proceed to shew by what method the squire discovered where his daughter was.

We gave a hint (for it is not our custom to unfold at any time more than is necessary for the occasion) that Mrs Fitzpatrick, who was very desirous of reconciling her uncle and aunt Western, thought she had a probable opportunity, by the service of preserving Sophia from committing the same crime which had drawn on herself the anger of her family. After much deliberation, therefore, she resolved to inform her aunt Western where her cousin was.

Mrs Western was now at her brother's house, where she had resided ever since the flight of Sophia, in order to administer comfort to the poor squire in his affliction. Of this comfort, which she doled out to him in daily portions, we have formerly given a specimen.

She was now standing with her back to the fire, and, with a pinch of snuff in her hand, was dealing forth this daily allowance of comfort to the squire, while he smoked his afternoon pipe, when she received a letter from Harriet Fitzpatrick; which she had no sooner read than she delivered it to him, saying, 'There, sir, there is an account of your lost sheep. Fortune hath again restored her to you, and if you will be governed by my advice, it is possible you may yet preserve her.'

The squire had no sooner read the letter than he leaped from his chair, threw his pipe into the fire, and gave a loud huzza for joy. He then summoned his servants, called for his boots, and ordered the Chevalier and several other horses to be saddled. Having done this, he turned to his sister, caught her in his arms, and gave her a close embrace, saying, 'Zounds! you don't seem pleased; one would imagine you was sorry I have found the girl.'

'Brother,' answered she, 'it is true, indeed, things do look rather less desperate than they did formerly; but there is a delicacy required in this matter, which you will pardon me, brother, if I suspect you want. There is a decorum to be used with a woman of figure, such as Lady Bellaston, brother, which requires a knowledge of the world, superior, I am afraid, to yours. I will inform you how to proceed. As soon as you arrive in town, and have got yourself into a decent dress (for indeed, brother, you have none at present fit to appear in), you must send your compliments to Lady Bellaston, and desire leave to wait on her. When you are admitted to her presence, as you certainly will be, and have told her your story, and have made proper use of my name (for I think you just know one another only by sight, though you are relations), I am confident she will withdraw her protection from my niece, who has certainly imposed upon her. As my cousin, with that odious Irish name, justly says, I have that regard for the honour and true interest of my family, and that concern for my niece, who is a part of it, that I have resolved to go to town myself upon this occasion; for indeed, indeed, brother, you are not a fit minister to be employed at a polite court.'

'I thank Heaven,' cries the squire, 'I don't understand you now. However, I'll shew you I scorn to be behindhand in civility with you; and I take it very kind of you to go up to London; for I never was there but twice in my life, and then I did not stay above a fortnight at a time, and to be sure I can't be expected to know much of the streets and the folks in that time. I never denied that you know'd all these matters better than I. For me to dispute that would be all as one as for you to dispute the management of a pack of dogs, or the finding a hare sitting, with me.'—'Which I promise you,' says she, 'I never will.'—'Well, and I promise you,' returned he, 'that I never will dispute the t'other.'

Here then a league was struck between the parties; and now the horses being ready, the squire departed, having promised his sister to follow her advice, and she prepared to follow him the next day.

CHAPTER THIRTY-FOUR

IN WHICH VARIOUS MISFORTUNES BEFEL POOR JONES

AFFAIRS were in the aforesaid situation, when Mrs Honour arrived at Mrs Miller's, and called on Jones. She began as follows:

'O, my dear sir! how shall I get spirits to tell you; you are undone, sir, and my poor lady's undone, and I am undone.'—'Hath anything happened to Sophia?' cries Jones, staring like a madman. 'All that is bad,' cries Honour. 'Oh, I shall never get such another lady! Oh, that I should ever live to see this day!' At these words Jones turned pale as ashes, trembled, and stammered; but Honour went on: 'O! Mr Jones, I have lost my lady for ever.'—'How? what! for Heaven's sake, tell me. O, my dear Sophia!'—'You may well call her so,' said Honour; 'she was the dearest lady to me. I shall never have such another place.'——'D—n your place!' cries Jones; 'where is—what—what is become of my Sophia?'—'Ay, to be sure,' cries she, 'servants may be d—n'd. It signifies nothing what becomes of them, though they are turned away, and ruined ever so much. To be sure they are not flesh and blood like other people.' 'What hath happened?' cries Jones, in almost a raving fit. 'What?—What?' said Honour. 'Why, the worst that could have happened both for you and for me.—Her father is come to town, and hath carried her away from us both.' Here Jones fell on his knees in thanksgiving that it was no worse. 'No worse!' repeated Honour; 'what could be worse for either of us? He carried her off, swearing she should marry Mr Blifil; that's for your comfort; and, for poor me, I am turned out of doors.'—'Indeed, Mrs Honour,' answered Jones, 'you frightened me out of my wits. I imagined some most dreadful sudden accident had happened to Sophia; something, compared to which, even seeing her married to Blifil would be a trifle; but while there is life there are hopes, my dear Honour. Women, in this land of liberty, cannot be married by actual brutal force.'—'To be sure, sir,' said she, 'that's true. There may be some hopes for you; but alack-a-day! what hopes are there for poor me? And to be sure, sir, you must be sensible I suffer all this upon your account. All the quarrel the squire hath to me is for taking your part, as I have done, against Mr Blifil. The squire is set against me: and yet, if you should ever have my lady, as to be sure I now hopes heartily you will; for you are a generous, good-natured gentleman; and I am sure you loves her, and to be sure she loves you as dearly as her own soul; it is a matter in vain to deny it; because as why, everybody, that is in the least acquainted with my lady, must see it; for, poor dear lady, she can't dissemble: and if two people who loves one another a'n't happy, why who should be so? Happiness don't always depend upon what people has; besides, my lady has enough for both. To be sure, therefore, as one may say it, it would be all the pity in the world to keep two such lovers asunder; nay, I am convinced, for my part, you will meet together at last; for, if it is to be, there is no preventing it.'

Whether Jones gave strict attention to all the foregoing harangue I cannot determine; but he never once attempted to answer, nor did she once stop till Partridge came running into the room, and informed him that the great lady was upon the stairs.

Nothing could equal the dilemma to which Jones was now reduced. Honour knew nothing of any acquaintance that subsisted between him and Lady Bellaston, and she was almost the last person in the world to whom he would have communicated it. In this hurry and distress, he took (as is common enough) the worst course, and, instead of exposing her to the lady, which would have been of little consequence, he chose to expose the lady to her; he therefore resolved to hide Honour, whom he had but just time to convey behind the bed, and to draw the curtains.

The hurry in which Jones had been all day engaged on account of his poor landlady and her family, the terrors occasioned by Mrs Honour, and the confusion into which he was thrown by the sudden arrival of Lady Bellaston, had altogether driven former thoughts out of his head; so that it never once occurred to his memory to act the part of a sick man; which, indeed, neither the gaiety of his dress, nor the freshness of his countenance, would have at all supported.

He received her ladyship, therefore, rather agreeably to her desires than to her expectations, with all the good humour he could muster in his countenance, and without any real or affected appearance of the least disorder.

Lady Bellaston no sooner entered the room, than she squatted herself down on the bed: 'So, my dear Jones,' said she, 'you find nothing can detain me long from you. Perhaps I ought to be angry with you, that I have neither seen nor heard from you all day; for I perceive your distemper would have suffered you to come abroad: nay, I suppose you have not sat in your chamber all drest up like a fine lady to see company after a lying-in; but, however, don't think I intend to scold you.'

'Nay, Lady Bellaston,' said Jones, 'I am sure your ladyship will not upbraid me with neglect of duty, when I only waited for orders. Who, my dear creature, hath reason to complain? Who missed an appointment, last night, and left an unhappy man to expect, and wish, and sigh, and languish?'

'Do not mention it, my dear Mr Jones,' cried she. 'If you knew the occasion, you would pity me. In short, it is impossible to conceive what women of condition are obliged to suffer from the impertinence of fools, in order to keep up the farce of the world. I am glad, however, all your languishing and wishing have done you no harm; for you never looked better in your life. Upon my faith! Jones, you might at this instant sit for the picture of Adonis.'

There are certain words of provocation which men of honour hold can properly be answered only by a blow. Among lovers possibly there may be some expression which can be answered only by a kiss. Now the compliment which Lady Bellaston now made Jones seems to be of this kind, especially as it was attended with a look, in which the lady conveyed more soft ideas than it was possible to express with her tongue.

Jones was certainly at this instant in one of the most disagreeable and distressed situations imaginable; for, though the provocation was given by the lady, Jones could not receive satisfaction, nor so much as offer to ask it, in the presence of a third person; seconds in this kind of duels not being according to the law of arms. As this objection did not occur to Lady Bellaston, who was ignorant of any other woman being there but herself, she waited some time in great astonishment for an answer from Jones, who, conscious of the ridiculous figure he made, stood at a distance, and, not daring to give the proper answer, gave none at all. The lady had already changed colour two or three times; had got up from the bed and sat down again, while Jones was wishing the ground to sink under him, or the house to fall on his head, when an odd accident freed him from an embarrassment.

This was no other than the arrival of young Nightingale, dead drunk; or rather in that state of drunkenness which deprives men of the use of their reason, without depriving them of the use of their limbs.

Mrs Miller and her daughters were in bed, and Partridge was smoking his pipe by the kitchen fire; so that he arrived at Mr Jones's chamber door without any interruption. This he burst open, and was entering without any ceremony, when Jones started from his seat and ran to oppose him, which he did so effectually, that Nightingale never came far enough within the door to see who was sitting on the bed.

Nightingale had in reality mistaken Jones's apartment for that in which himself had lodged; he therefore strongly insisted on coming in, often swearing that he would not be kept from his own bed. Jones, however, prevailed over him, and delivered him into the hands of Partridge, whom the noise on the stairs soon summoned to his master's assistance.

And now Jones was unwillingly obliged to return to his own apartment, where at the very instant of his entrance he heard Lady Bellaston venting an exclamation, though not a very loud one; and at the same time saw her flinging herself into a chair in a vast agitation, which in a lady of tender constitution would have been an hysteric fit.

In reality the lady, frightened with the struggle between the two men, of which she did not know what would be the issue, as she heard Nightingale swear many oaths he would come to his own bed, attempted to retire to her known place of hiding, which to her great confusion she found already occupied by another.

'Is this usage to be borne, Mr Jones?' cries the lady. 'Basest of men!——What wretch is this to whom you have exposed me?' —'Wretch!' cries Honour, bursting in a violent rage from her place of concealment——'Marry come up!——Wretch forsooth? ——as poor a wretch as I am, I am honest; this is more than some folks who are richer can say.'

Jones, instead of applying himself directly to take off the edge of Mrs Honour's resentment, as a more experienced gallant would have done, fell to cursing his stars, and lamenting himself as the most unfortunate man in the world; and presently after, addressing himself to Lady Bellaston, he fell to some very absurd protestations of innocence. By this time the lady, having recovered the use of her reason, which she had as ready as any woman in the world, especially on such occasions, calmly replied: 'Sir, you need make no apologies, I see now who the person is; I did not at first know Mrs Honour: but now I do, I can suspect nothing wrong between her and you; and I am sure she is a woman of too good sense to put any wrong constructions upon my visit to you; I have been always her friend, and it may be in my power to be much more hereafter.'

Mrs Honour was altogether as placable as she was passionate. Hearing, therefore, Lady Bellaston assume the soft tone, she likewise softened hers.——'I'm sure, madam,' says she, 'I have been always ready to acknowledge your ladyship's friendships to me; sure I never had so good a friend as your ladyship——and to be sure, to be sure it doth not become a servant as I am to think about such a great lady—I mean I was a servant: for indeed I am nobody's servant now, the more miserable wretch is me.—I have lost the best mistress——' Here Honour thought fit to produce a shower of tears. 'Don't cry, child,' says the good lady; 'ways perhaps may be found to make you amends. Come to me to-morrow morning.' She then took up her fan which lay on the ground, and without even looking at Jones, walked very majestically out of the room; there being a kind of dignity in the impudence of women of quality, which their inferiors vainly aspire to attain to in circumstances of this nature.

Jones followed her downstairs, often offering her his hand, which she absolutely refused him, and got into her chair without taking any notice of him, as he stood bowing before her.

At his return upstairs, a long dialogue past between him and Mrs Honour, while she was adjusting herself after the discomposure she had undergone. The subject of this was his infidelity to her young lady; on which she enlarged with great bitterness; but Jones at last found means to reconcile her, and not only so, but to obtain a promise of most inviolable secrecy, and that she would the next morning endeavour to find out Sophia, and bring him a further account of the proceedings of the squire.

Notwithstanding all the obligations she had received from Jones, Mrs Miller could not forbear in the morning some gentle remonstrance for the hurricane which had happened the preceding night in his chamber. These were, however, so gentle and so friendly, professing, and indeed truly, to aim at nothing more than the real good of Mr Jones himself, that he, far from being offended, thankfully received the admonition of the good woman.

But though Mrs Miller did not refrain from a short expostulation, yet the occasion of his being summoned downstairs that morning was of a much agreeable kind, being indeed to perform the office of a father to Miss Nancy, and to give her in wedlock to Mr Nightingale, who was now ready drest, and full as sober as many of my readers will think a man ought to be who receives a wife in so imprudent a manner.

And here perhaps it may be proper to account for his appearance in the condition in which we have seen him the night before.

Now when the uncle had arrived at his lodgings with his nephew,

171

partly to indulge his own inclinations (for he dearly loved his bottle), and partly to disqualify his nephew from the immediate execution of his purpose, he ordered wine to be set on the table; with which he so briskly plyed the young gentleman, that this latter, who, though not much used to drinking, did not detest it so as to be guilty of disobedience or want of complacence by refusing, was soon completely finished.

Just as the uncle had obtained this victory, and was preparing a bed for his nephew, a messenger arrived with a piece of news, which so entirely disconcerted and shocked him, that he in a moment lost all consideration for his nephew, and his whole mind became entirely taken up with his own concerns.

This sudden and afflicting news was no less than that his daughter had taken the opportunity of almost the first moment of his absence, and had gone off with a neighbouring young clergyman; against whom, though her father could have had but one objection, namely, that he was worth nothing, yet she had never thought proper to communicate her amour even to that father; and so artfully had she managed, that it had never been once suspected by any, till now that it was consummated.

Old Mr Nightingale no sooner received this account, than in the utmost confusion he ordered a post-chaise to be instantly got ready, and, having recommended his nephew to the care of a servant, he directly left the house, scarce knowing what he did, nor whither he went.

The uncle thus departed, when the servant came to attend the nephew to bed, had waked him for that purpose, and had at last made him sensible that his uncle was gone, he, instead of accepting the kind offices tendered him, insisted on a chair being called; with this the servant, who had received no strict orders to the contrary, readily complied; and, thus being conducted back to the house of Mrs Miller, he had staggered up to Mr Jones's chamber, as hath been before recounted.

This bar of the uncle being now removed (though young Nightingale knew not as yet in what manner), and all parties being quickly ready, the mother, Mr Jones, Mr Nightingale, and his love, stept into a hackney-coach, which conveyed them to Doctors' Commons; where Miss Nancy was, in vulgar language, soon made an honest woman, and the poor mother became, in the purest sense of the word, one of the happiest of all human beings.

CHAPTER THIRTY-FIVE

CONTAINING LOVE-LETTERS OF SEVERAL SORTS

MR JONES, at his return home, found the following letters lying on his table, which he luckily opened in the order they were sent.

· LETTER I

'Surely I am under some strange infatuation; I cannot keep my resolutions a moment, however strongly made or justly founded. Last night I resolved never to see you more; this morning I am willing to hear if you can, as you say, clear up this affair. If you can forge an excuse, I almost promise you to believe it.——Come to me directly.'

LETTER II

'If you ever expect to be forgiven, or even suffered within my doors, come to me this instant.'

LETTER III

'I now find you was not at home when my notes came to your lodgings. The moment you receive this let me see you;—I shall not stir out; nor shall anybody be let in but yourself. Sure nothing can detain you long.'

Jones had just read over these three billets, when Mr Nightingale came into the room. 'Well, Tom,' said he, 'any news from Lady Bellaston, after last night's adventure?' (for it was now no secret to any one in that house who the lady was). 'The Lady Bellaston?' answered Jones very gravely.——'Nay, dear Tom,' cries Nightingale, 'don't be so reserved to your friends. Though I was too drunk to see her last night, I saw her at the masquerade. Do you think I am ignorant who the queen of the fairies is?'—— 'And did you really then know the lady at the masquerade?' said Jones. 'Yes, upon my soul, did I,' said Nightingale, 'and have given you twenty hints of it since, though you seemed always so tender on that point, that I would not speak plainly. I fancy, my friend, by your extreme nicety in this matter, you are not so well acquainted with the character of the lady as with her person. Don't be angry, Tom, but upon my honour, you are not the first young fellow she hath debauched. Her reputation is in no danger, believe me.'

Though Jones had no reason to imagine the lady to have been of the vestal kind when his amour began; yet, as he was thoroughly ignorant of the town, and had very little acquaintance in it, he had no knowledge of that character which is vulgarly called a demirep; that is to say, a woman who intrigues with every man she likes, under the name and appearance of virtue; and who, though some over-nice ladies will not be seen with her, is visited (as they term it) by the whole town, in short, whom everybody knows to be what nobody calls her.

Jones, having very attentively heard all that Nightingale had to say, fetched a deep sigh; which the other, observing, cried, 'Heyday! why, thou art not in love, I hope! Had I imagined my stories would have affected you, I promise you should never have heard them.'—'O my dear friend!' cries Jones, 'I am so entangled with this woman, that I know not how to extricate myself. In love, indeed! no, my friend, but I am under obligations to her, and very great ones. Since you know so much, I will be very explicit with you. It is owing, perhaps, solely to her, that I have not, before this, wanted a bit of bread. How can I possibly desert such a woman?—and yet I must desert her, or be guilty of the blackest treachery to one who deserves infinitely better of me than she can; a woman, my Nightingale, for whom I have a passion which few can have an idea of. I am half distracted with doubts how to act.'—'And is this other, pray, a honourable mistress?' cries Nightingale. 'Honourable!' answered Jones; 'no breath ever yet durst sully her reputation. The sweetest air is not purer, the limpid stream not clearer, than her honour.'—'And can you, my good friend,' cries Nightingale, 'with such an engagement as this upon your hands, hesitate a moment about quitting such a——'—'Hold,' said Jones, 'no more abuse of her: I detest the thought of ingratitude.'—'Pooh!' answered the other, 'you are not the first upon whom she hath conferred obligations of this kind. She is remarkably liberal where she likes; though, let me tell you, her favours are so prudently bestowed, that they should rather raise a man's vanity than his gratitude.' In short, Nightingale proceeded so far on his head, and told his friend so many stories of the lady, which he swore to the truth of, that he entirely removed all esteem for her from the breast of Jones; and he began to look on all the favours he had received rather as wages than benefits. The result of all was, that, though his turning himself out of her service, would be the loss of his bread; yet he determined to quit her, if he could but find a handsome pretence: which being communicated to his friend, Nightingale considered a little, and then said, 'I have it, my boy! I have found out a sure method; propose marriage to her, and I would venture hanging upon the success.'—'Marriage?' cries Jones. 'Ay, propose marriage,' answered Nightingale, 'and she will declare off in a moment. I knew a young fellow whom she kept formerly, who made the offer to her in earnest, and was presently turned off for his pains.'

Jones declared he could not venture the experiment. 'Perhaps,' said he, 'she may be less shocked at this proposal from one man than from another. And if she should take me at my word, where am I then? caught in my own trap, and undone for ever.'—'No,' answered Nightingale, 'not if I can give you an expedient by which you may at any time get out of the trap.'——'What expedient can that be?' replied Jones. 'This,' answered Nightingale. 'The young fellow I mentioned, who is one of the most intimate acquaintances I have in the world, is so angry with her for some ill offices she hath since done him, that I am sure he would, without any difficulty, give you a sight of her letters; upon which you may decently break with her; and declare off.'

After some hesitation, Jones, upon the strength of this assurance, consented; but, as he swore he wanted the confidence to propose the matter to her face, he wrote the following letter, which Nightingale dictated:

'MADAM,

'I am extremely concerned, that, by an unfortunate engagement, I should have missed receiving the honour of your ladyship's commands the moment they came; and the delay which I must now suffer of vindicating myself to your ladyship greatly adds to this misfortune. O, Lady Bellaston! what a terror have I been in, for fear your reputation should be exposed by these perverse accidents! There is one only way to secure it. I need not name what that is. Only permit me to say, that as your honour is as dear to me as my own, so my sole ambition is to have the glory of laying my liberty at your feet; and believe me when I assure you, I can never be made completely happy, without you generously bestow on me a legal right of calling you mine for ever.—I am,

madam,
with most profound respect,
your ladyship's most obliged,
obedient, humble servant,
THOMAS JONES.'

To this she presently returned the following answer:

'SIR,

'When I read over your serious epistle, I could, from its coldness and formality, have sworn that you already had the legal right you mention; nay, that we had for many years composed that monstrous animal a husband and wife. Do you really then imagine me a fool? or do you fancy yourself capable of so entirely persuading me out of my senses, that I should deliver my whole fortune into your power, in order to enable you to support your pleasures at my expense?'

Jones, by the advice of his privy-council, replied:

'MADAM,
 'It is impossible to express how much I am shocked at the suspicion you entertain of me. Can Lady Bellaston have conferred favours on a man whom she could believe capable of so base a design? or can she treat the most solemn tie of love with contempt? If such be your opinion of me, I must pray for a sudden opportunity of returning those pecuniary obligations, which I have been so unfortunate to receive at your hands; and for those of a more tender kind, I shall ever remain, &c.' And so concluded in the very words with which he had concluded the former letter.

The lady answered as follows:

'I see you are a villain! and I despise you from my soul. If you come here I shall not be at home.'

Though Jones was well satisfied with his deliverance from a thraldom which those who have ever experienced it will, I apprehend, allow to be none of the lightest, he was not, however, perfectly easy in his mind. There was in this scheme too much of fallacy to satisfy one who utterly detested every species of falsehood or dishonesty.

Nightingale highly exulted in the success of his stratagem, upon which he received many thanks and much applause from his friend. He answered 'Dear Tom, we have conferred very different obligations on each other. To me you owe the regaining your liberty; to you I owe the loss of mine. But if you are as happy in the one instance as I am in the other, I promise you we are the two happiest fellows in England.'

The two gentlemen were now summoned down to dinner, where Mrs Miller, who performed herself the office of a cook, had exerted her best talents to celebrate the wedding of her daughter. This joyful circumstance she ascribed principally to the friendly behaviour of Jones; her whole soul was fired with gratitude towards him, and all her looks, words, and actions, were so busied in expressing it, that her daughter, and even her new son-in-law, were very little objects of her consideration.

Dinner was just ended when Mrs Miller received a letter from Mr Allworthy, and the purport of it was, his intention to come immediately to town, with his nephew Blifil, and a desire to be accommodated with his usual lodgings, which were the first floor for himself, and the second for his nephew.

The cheerfulness which had before displayed itself in the countenance of the poor woman was a little clouded on this occasion. This news did indeed a good deal disconcert her. To repay so disinterested a match with her daughter, by presently turning her new son-in-law out of doors, appeared to her very unjustifiable on the one hand; and on the other, she could scarce bear the thoughts of making any excuse to Mr Allworthy. When he settled the annuity of £50 a year on Mrs Miller, he told her, 'it was in consideration of always having her first floor when he was in town (which he scarce ever intended to be), but that she might let it at any other time, for that he would always send her a month's warning.' He was now, however, hurried to town so suddenly, that he had no opportunity of giving such notice. Mrs Miller could not conceal her uneasiness at this letter; with the contents of which she had no sooner acquainted the company, and given some hints of her distress, than Jones, her good angel, presently relieved her anxiety. 'As for myself, madam,' said he, 'my lodging is at your service at a moment's warning; and Mr Nightingale, I am sure, as he cannot yet prepare a house fit to receive his lady, will consent to return to his new lodging, whither Mrs Nightingale will certainly consent to go.' With which proposal both husband and wife agreed.

The cheeks of Mrs Miller began again to glow with additional gratitude to Jones; but, perhaps, Mr Jones having in his last speech called her daughter Mrs Nightingale (it being the first time that agreeable sound had ever reached her ears), gave the fond mother more satisfaction, and warmed her heart more towards Jones, than his having dissipated her present anxiety.

The next day was then appointed for the removal of the new-married couple, and of Mr. Jones, who was likewise to be provided for in the same house with his friend. And now the serenity of the company was again restored, all except Jones, who, though he outwardly accompanied the rest in their mirth, felt many a bitter pang on the account of his Sophia, which were not a little heightened by the news of Mr Blifil's coming to town (for he clearly saw the intention of his journey); and what greatly aggravated his concern was, that Mrs Honour, who had promised to inquire after Sophia, and to make her report to him early the next evening, had disappointed him.

'SIR,

'I shud sartenly haf kaled on you a cordin too mi prommiss haddunt itt bin that hur laschipp prevent mee; for to bee sur, Sir, you nose very well that evere persun must luk furst at ome, and sartenly such anuther offar mite not have ever hapned, so as I

shud ave bin justly to blam, had I not excepted of it when her
lashipp was so veri kind as to offar to mak mee hur one uman
without mi ever askin any such thing, to be sur shee is won of
thee best ladis in thee wurld, and pepil who sase to the kontrari
must bee veri wiket pepil in thare harts. To bee sur if ever I
ave sad any thing of that kine it as bin thru ignorens, and I am
hartili sorri for it. I wish ure Onur all thee gud luk in the wurld;
and I don't cuestion but thatt u will haf Madam Sofia in the end;
butt ass to miself ure onur nose I kant bee of ani farder sarvis
to u in that matar, nou bein under thee cumand off anuther
parson, and nott mi one mistress, I begg ure Onur to say nothing
of what past, and belive me to be, sir, ure Onur's umble servant
to cumand till deth,

'HONOUR BLACKMORE.'

Various were the conjectures which Jones entertained on this
step of Lady Bellaston; who, in reality, had little farther design
than to secure within her own house the repository of a secret,
which she chose should make no farther progress than it had made
already; but mostly, she desired to keep it from the ears of
Sophia.

While Jones was terrifying himself with the apprehension of a
thousand dreadful machinations, which he imagined to be at the
bottom of the promotion of Honour. Partridge came capering into
the room, as was his custom when he brought, or fancied he
brought, any good tidings. He had been dispatched that morning
by his master, with orders to endeavour, by the servants of Lady
Bellaston, or by any other means, to discover whither Sophia
had been conveyed; and he now returned, and with a joyful
countenance told our hero that he had found the lost bird.
'I have seen, sir,' says he, 'Black George, the gamekeeper, who is
one of the servants whom the squire hath brought with him to
town. I knew him presently, though I have not seen him these
several years. Well, sir, we no sooner knew each other, than, after
many hearty shakes by the hand, we agreed to go to an ale-house and
take a pot, and by good luck the beer was some of the best I have
met with since I have been in town. Now, sir, I am coming to the
point; for no sooner did I name you, and told him that you and I
came to town together, and had lived together ever since, than
he called for another pot, and swore he would drink to your health,
and then I made haste home to tell you the news.'
'What news?' cries Jones, 'you have not mentioned a word of
my Sophia!'—'Bless me! I had like to have forgot that. Indeed,
we mentioned a great deal about your Madam Western and
George told me all; that Mr Blifil is coming to town in order to be
married to her. He had best make haste then, says I, or somebody will have her before he comes; and, indeed, says I, Mr Sea-

grim, he certainly loves her above all the women in the world. I would have both you and she know, that it is not for her fortune he follows her; for I can assure you, there is another lady, one of much greater quality and fortune than she can pretend to, who is so fond of somebody that she comes after him day and night.'

Here Jones fell into a passion with Partridge, for having, as he said, betrayed him; but the poor fellow answered, he had mentioned no name: 'Besides, sir,' said he, 'I can assure you, George is sincerely your friend, and wished Mr Blifil at the devil more than once; nay, he said he would do anything in his power upon earth to serve you.'

'Well,' says Jones, a little pacified, 'you say this fellow, who, I believe, indeed, is enough inclined to be my friend, lives in the same house with Sophia?'

'In the same house!' answered Partridge; 'why, sir, he is one of the servants of the family, and very well drest I promise you he is; if it was not for his black beard you would hardly know him.'

'One service then at least he may do me,' says Jones; 'sure he can convey a letter to my Sophia.'

'You have hit the nail *ad unguem*,' cries Partridge, 'how came I not to think of it? I will engage he shall do it upon the very first mentioning.'

'Well, then,' said Jones, 'do you leave me at present, and I will write a letter, which you shall deliver to him to-morrow morning; for I suppose you know where to find him.'

'O yes, sir,' answered Partridge, 'I shall certainly find him again; there is no fear of that. The liquor is too good for him to stay away long. I make no doubt but he will be there every day he stays in town.'

'So you don't know the street then where my Sophia is lodged?' cries Jones.

'Indeed, sir, I do,' says Partridge.

'What is the name of the street?' cries Jones.

'The name, sir? why, here, sir, just by,' answered Partridge, 'not above a street or two off. I don't, indeed, know the very name; for, as he never told me, if I had asked, you know, it might have put some suspicion into his head. No, no, sir, let me alone for that. I am too cunning for that, I promise you.'

'Thou art most wonderfully cunning, indeed,' replied Jones; 'however, I will write to my charmer, since I believe you will be cunning enough to find him to-morrow at the ale-house.'

And now, having dismissed the sagacious Partridge, Mr Jones sat himself down to write, in which employment we shall leave him for a time.

CHAPTER THIRTY-SIX

THE DISTRESSED SITUATION OF SOPHIA

WE must now convey the reader to Mr Western's lodgings, which were in Piccadilly.

Here, when Sophia alighted from the hackney-coach, which brought her from the house of Lady Bellaston, she desired to retire to the apartment provided for her; to which her father very readily agreed, and whither he attended her himself. A short dialogue then passed between them, in which he pressed her vehemently to give her consent to the marriage with Blifil, who, as he acquainted her, was to be in town in a few days; but, instead of complying, she gave a more peremptory and resolute refusal than she had ever done before. This so incensed her father, that after many bitter vows, that he would force her to have him whether she would or no, he departed from her with many hard words and curses, locked the door, and put the key into his pocket.

While Sophia was left with no other company than what attend the closest state prisoner, namely, fire and candle, the squire sat down to regale himself over a bottle of wine, with his landlord. In this agreeable society Mr Western past that evening and great part of the succeeding day. All this time Sophia past by herself; for her father swore she should never come out of her chamber alive, unless she first consented to marry Blifil; nor did he ever suffer the door to be unlocked, unless to convey her food, on which occasions he always attended himself.

The landlady of the house where the squire lodged had begun very early to entertain a strange opinion of her guests. However, she was informed that the squire was a man of vast fortune, and as she had taken care to exact a very extraordinary price for her rooms, she did not think proper to give any offence; for, though she was not without some concern for the confinement of poor Sophia, of whose great sweetness of temper and affability the maid of the house had made so favourable a report, which was confirmed by all the squire's servants, yet she had much more concern for her own interest, than to provoke one, whom, as she said, she perceived to be a very hastish kind of gentleman.

Though Sophia eat but little, yet she was regularly served with her meals; indeed, I believe, if she had liked any one rarity, that the squire, however angry, would have spared neither pains nor cost to have procured it for her.

The dinner-hour being arrived, Black George carried her up a pullet, the squire himself (for he had sworn not to part with the key) attending the door. As George deposited the dish, Sophia would have had him take the pullet back, saying, she could not eat; but George begged her to try, and particularly recommended to her the eggs, of which he said it was full.

The eggs of pullets, partridges, pheasants, &c., were, as George well knew, the most favourite dainties of Sophia. It was therefore no wonder that he, who was a very good-natured fellow, should take care to supply her with this kind of delicacy, at a time when all the servants in the house were afraid she would be starved; for she had scarce swallowed a single morsel in the last forty hours.

And Sophia, herself, after some little consideration, began to dissect the fowl, which she found to be as full of eggs as George had reported it.

But, if she was pleased with these, it contained something which would have delighted the Royal Society much more; for if a fowl with three legs be so invaluable a curiosity, at what price shall we esteem a bird which so totally contradicts all the laws of animal economy, as to contain a letter in its belly?

Sophia, not withstanding her long fast, and notwithstanding her favourite dish was there before her, no sooner saw the letter than she immediately snatched it up, tore it open, and read as follows:

'MADAM,

'Was I not sensible to whom I have the honour of writing, I should endeavour, however difficult, to paint the horrors of my mind at the account brought me by Mrs Honour; but as tenderness alone can have any true idea of the pangs which tenderness is capable of feeling, so can this most amiable quality, which my Sophia possesses in the most eminent degree, sufficiently inform her what her Jones must have suffered on this melancholy occasion. Is there a circumstance in the world which can heighten my agonies, when I hear of any misfortune which hath befallen you? Surely there is one only, and with that I am accursed. It is, my Sophia, the dreadful consideration that I am myself the wretched cause. Pardon me if I ask you, whether my advice, my assistance, my presence, my absence, my death, or my tortures can bring you any relief? Believe me, madam, I so sincerely love you better than myself, that my great and principal end is your happiness. My first wish (why would not fortune indulge me in it?) was, and pardon me if I say, still is, to see you every moment the happiest of women; my second wish is, to hear you are so; but no misery on earth can equal mine, while I think you owe an uneasy moment to him who is,

Madam,

in every sense, and to every purpose,

your devoted,

Thomas Jones.'

In the evening, while Sophia was meditating on the letter she had received, or on something else, a violent noise from below disturbed her meditations. This noise was no other than a round bout at altercation between two persons. One of the combatants, by his voice, she immediately distinguished to be her father; but she did not so soon discover the shriller pipes to belong to the organ of her aunt Western, who was just arrived in town, where having, by means of one of her servants, learned where her brother lodged, she drove directly to his lodgings.

The squire and the landlord were smoking their pipes together, when the arrival of the lady was first signified. The squire no sooner heard her name, than he immediately ran down to usher her upstairs; for he was a great observer of such ceremonials, especially to his sister, of whom he stood more in awe than of any other human creature, though he never would own this, nor did he perhaps know it himself.

Mrs Western, on her arrival in the dining-room, having flung herself into a chair, began thus to harangue: 'Well, surely, no one ever had such an intolerable journey. I think the roads, since so many turnpike acts, are grown worse than ever. La, brother, how could you get into this odious place? Well, and where's my niece? Have you been to wait upon Lady Bellaston yet?—'Ay, ay,' cries the squire, 'your niece is safe enough; she is upstairs in chamber.'—'How!' answered the lady, 'is my niece in this house, and does she not know of my being here?'—'No, nobody can well get to her,' says the squire, 'for she is under lock and key. I have her safe; I vetched her from my lady cousin the first night I came to town, and I have taken care o' her ever since; she is as secure as a fox in a bag, I promise you.'—'Good heaven!' returned Mrs Western, 'what do I hear? I thought what a fine piece of work would be the consequence of my consent to your coming to town yourself! nay, it was indeed your own headstrong will, nor can I charge myself with having ever consented to it. Did not you promise me, brother, that you would take none of these headstrong measures? Was it not by these headstrong measures that you forced my niece to run away from you in the country? Have you a mind to oblige her to take such another step?' If you expect I should stay a moment longer in this wretched house, or that I should ever own you again as my relation, or that I should ever trouble myself again with the affairs of your family,

I insist upon it that my niece be set at liberty this instant.' This she spoke with so commanding an air, standing with her back to the fire, with one hand behind her, and a pinch of snuff in the other, that I question whether Thalestris, at the head of her Amazons, ever made a more tremendous figure. It is no wonder, therefore, that the poor squire was not proof against the awe which she inspired. 'There,' he cried, throwing down the key, 'there it is, do whatever you please. I intended only to have kept her up till Blifil came to town, which can't be long; and now if any harm happens in the meantime, remember who is to be blamed for it.'

'I will answer it with my life,' cries Mrs Western, 'but I shall not intermeddle at all, unless upon one condition, and that is, that you will commit the whole entirely to my care, without taking any one measure yourself, unless I shall eventually appoint you to act. If you ratify these preliminaries, brother, I yet will endeavour to preserve the honour of your family; if not, I shall continue in a neutral state.'

And now having summoned a servant to show her to Sophia, she departed, bearing the key with her.

She was no sooner gone, than the squire (having first shut the door) ejaculated twenty bitches, and as many hearty curses against her, not sparing himself for having ever thought of her estate; but added, 'Now one hath been a slave so long, it would be pity to lose it at last, for want of holding out a little longer. The bitch can't live for ever, and I know I am down for it upon the will.'

And now the squire having ordered in another bottle, which was his usual method when anything either pleased or vexed him, did, by drinking plentifully of this medicinal julap, so totally wash away his choler, that his temper was become perfectly placid and serene, when Mrs Western returned with Sophia into the room. The young lady had on her hat and capuchin, and the aunt acquainted Mr Western, 'that she intended to take her niece with her to her own lodgings; for, indeed, brother,' says she, 'these rooms are not fit to receive a Christian soul in.'

'Very well, madam,' quoth Western, 'whatever you please. The girl can never be in better hands than yours; I have said fifty times that you was one of the most sensible women in the world.'

'Nay, brother,' says Mrs Western, 'I have always, I'm sure, given you as favourable a character. You must own you have a little too much hastiness in your temper; but when you will allow yourself time to reflect, I never knew a man more reasonable.'

'Why then, sister, if you think so,' said the squire, 'here's your good health with all my heart. I am a little passionate sometimes, but I scorn to bear any malice. Sophy, do you be a good girl, and do everything your aunt orders you.'

'I have not the least doubt of her,' answered Mrs Western.

'She hath had already an example before her eyes in the behaviour of that wretch her cousin Harriet, who ruined herself by neglecting my advice. O brother, what think you? You was hardly gone out of hearing, when you set out for London, when who should arrive but that impudent fellow with the odious Irish name—that Fitzpatrick. He broke in abruptly upon me without notice, or I would not have seen him. He ran on a long, unintelligible story about his wife, to which he forced me to give him a hearing; but I made him very little answer. I suppose the wretch will endeavour to find us out, but I beg you will not see her, for I am determined I will not.'

'I zee her!' answered the squire; 'you need not fear me. I'll ge no encouragement to such undutiful wenches. It is well for the fellow, her husband, I was not at huome. Od rabbit it, he should have taken a dance thru the horse-pond, I promise un. You zee, Sophy, what undutifulness brings volks to. You have an example in your own family.'

'Brother,' cries the aunt, 'you need not shock my niece by such odious repetitions. Why will you not leave everything entirely to me?'—'Well, well, I wull, I wull,' said the squire.

And now Mrs Western, luckily for Sophia, put an end to the conversation by ordering chairs to be called. I say luckily, for had it continued much longer, fresh matter of dissension would, most probably, have arisen between the brother and sister; between whom education and sex made the only difference; for both were equally violent and equally positive: they had both a vast affection for Sophia, and both a sovereign contempt for each other.

CHAPTER THIRTY-SEVEN

IN WHICH JONES GOES TO A PLAY

THE arrival of Black George in town, and the good offices which that grateful fellow had promised to do for his old benefactor, greatly comforted Jones in the midst of all the anxiety and uneasiness which he had suffered on the account of Sophia; from whom, by the means of the said George, he received the following answer to his letter, which Sophia, to whom the use of pen, ink, and paper was restored with her liberty, wrote the very evening when she departed from her confinement:

'SIR,

'As I do not doubt your sincerity in what you write, you will be pleased to hear that some of my afflictions are at an end, by the arrival of my aunt Western, with whom I am at present, and with whom I enjoy all the liberty I can desire. One promise my aunt hath insisted on my making, which is, that I will not see or converse with any person without her knowledge and consent. This promise I have most solemnly given, and shall most inviolably keep: and though she hath not expressly forbidden me writing, yet that must be an omission from forgetfulness; or this, perhaps, is included in the word conversing. However, as I cannot but consider this as a breach of her generous confidence in my honour, you cannot expect that I shall, after this, continue to write myself or to receive letters, without her knowledge. Though there is one thing in which I can never comply with the best of fathers, yet am I firmly resolved never to act in defiance of him, or to take any step of consequence without his consent. A firm persuasion of this must teach you to divert your thoughts from what fortune hath (perhaps) made impossible. This your own interest persuades you. This may reconcile, I hope, Mr Allworthy to you; and if it will, you have my injunctions to pursue it. Fortune may, perhaps, be some time kinder to us both than at present. Believe this, that I shall always think of you as I think you deserve, and am,

Sir,
your obliged humble servant,
SOPHIA WESTERN.

Mr Jones having spent three hours in reading and kissing the aforesaid letter, and being, at last, in a state of good spirits, he agreed to carry an appointment, which he had before made, into execution. This was, to attend Mrs Miller, and her younger daughter, into the gallery at the playhouse, and to admit Mr Partridge as one of the company.

In the first row then of the first gallery did Mr Jones, Mrs Miller, her youngest daughter, and Partridge, take their places. Partridge immediately declared it was the finest place he had ever been in.

As soon as the play, which was *Hamlet, Prince of Denmark*, began, Partridge was all attention, nor did he break silence till the entrance of the ghost; upon which he asked Jones, 'What man that was in the strange dress; something,' said he, 'like what I have seen in a picture. Sure it is not armour, is it?' Jones answered, 'That is the ghost.' To which Partridge replied with a smile, 'Persuade me to that, sir, if you can. Though I can't say I ever actually saw a ghost in my life, yet I am certain I should know one, if I saw him, better than that comes to. No, no, sir, ghosts don't appear in such dresses as that, neither.' In this mistake, which caused much laughter in the neighbourhood of Partridge, he was suffered to continue, till the scene between the ghost and Hamlet, when Partridge gave that credit to Mr Garrick, which he had denied to Jones, and fell into so violent a trembling, that his knees knocked against each other. Jones asked him what was the matter, and whether he was afraid of the warrior upon the stage? 'O la! sir,' said he, 'I perceive now it is what you told me. I am not afraid of anything; for I know it is but a play. And if it was really a ghost, it could do one no harm at such a distance, and in so much company.'

The grave-digging scene next engaged the attention of Partridge, who expressed much surprize at the number of skulls thrown upon the stage. To which Jones answered, 'That it was one of the most famous burial-places about town.'—'No wonder then,' cries Partridge, 'that the place is haunted. But I never saw in my life a worse grave-digger. I had a sexton, when I was a clerk, that should have dug three graves while he is digging one. The fellow handles a spade as if it was the first time he had ever had one in his hand.' Upon Hamlet's taking up the skull, he cried out, 'Well! it is strange to see how fearless some men are: I never could bring myself to touch anything belonging to a dead man, on any account.—He seemed frightened enough too at the ghost, I thought.'

Little more worth remembering occurred during the play, at the end of which Jones asked him, 'Which of the players he had liked best?' To this he answered, with some appearance of indignation at the question, 'The king, without doubt.'—'Indeed, Mr Partridge,' says Mrs Miller, 'you are not of the same opinion with the town; for they are all agreed, that Hamlet is acted by the best player who ever was on the stage.'—'He the best player!' cries Partridge, with a contemptuous sneer, 'why, I could act as well as he myself. I am sure, if I had seen a ghost, I should have looked in the very same manner, and done just as he did. And then, to be sure, in that scene, as you called it, between him and his mother, where you told me he acted so fine, why, Lord help me, any man, that is, any good man, that had such a mother, would have done exactly the same. I know you are only joking with me; but indeed, madam, though I was never at a play in London, yet I have seen acting before in the country; and the king for my money; he speaks all his words distinctly, half as loud again as the other.—Anybody may see he is an actor.'

While Mrs Miller was thus engaged in conversation with Partridge, a lady came up to Mr Jones, whom he immediately knew to be Mrs Fitzpatrick. She said, she had seen him from the other part of the gallery, and had taken that opportunity of speaking to him, as she had something to say, which might be of great service to himself. She then acquainted him with her lodgings, and made him an appointment the next day in the afternoon; at which time Jones promised to attend her.

Thus ended the adventure at the playhouse; where Partridge had afforded great mirth, not only to Jones and Mrs Miller, but to all who sat within hearing, who were more attentive to what he said, than to anything that passed on the stage.

He durst not go to bed at all that night, for fear of the ghost; and for many nights after sweated two or three hours before he went to sleep, with the same apprehensions, and waked several times in great horrors, crying out, 'Lord have mercy upon us! there it is.'

Mr Jones, at the appointed hour, attended on Mrs Fitzpatrick; but before we relate the conversation which now past, it may be proper, according to our method, to return a little back, and to account for so great an alteration of behaviour in this lady. The preceding day, when, hearing from Lady Bellaston that Mr Western was arrived in town, she went to pay her duty to him, at his lodgings at Piccadilly, where she was received with many scurvy compellations too coarse to be repeated, and was even threatened to be kicked out of doors. From hence, an old servant of her aunt Western, with whom she was well acquainted, conducted her to the lodgings of that lady, who treated her not more kindly, but more politely; or, to say the truth, with rudeness in another way. In short, she returned from both, plainly convinced, not only that her scheme of reconciliation had proved abortive, but that she must for ever give over all thoughts of bringing it about by any means whatever. From this moment desire of revenge only filled her mind; and in this temper meeting Jones at the play, an opportunity seemed to her to occur of effecting this purpose.

The reader must remember that he was acquainted by Mrs. Fitzpatrick, in the account she gave of her own story, with the fondness Mrs Western had formerly shewn for Mr Fitzpatrick at Bath, from the disappointment of which Mrs Fitzpatrick derived the great bitterness her aunt had expressed toward her. She had, therefore, no doubt but that the good lady would as easily listen to the addresses of Mr Jones as she had before done to the other; for the superiority of charms was clearly on the side of Mr Jones; and the advance which her aunt had since made in age, she concluded (how justly I will not say), was an argument rather in favour of her project than against it.

Therefore, when Jones attended, after a previous declaration of her desire of serving him, she very explicitly mentioned her scheme to him, and advised him to make sham addresses to the older lady, in order to procure an easy access to the younger, informing him at the same time of the success which Mr Fitzpatrick had formerly owed to the very same stratagem.

187

Mr Jones expressed great gratitude to the lady for the kind intentions towards him which she had expressed, and indeed testified, by this proposal; but, he said, he was afraid Miss Western would never agree to an imposition of this kind, as well from her utter detestation of all fallacy, as from her avowed duty to her aunt.

Mrs Fitzpatrick was a little nettled at this.

'Indeed, sir,' answered the lady, with some warmth, 'I cannot think there is anything easier than to cheat an old woman with a profession of love, when her complexion is amorous; and, though she is my aunt, I must say there never was a more liquorish one than her ladyship. Can't you pretend that the despair of possessing her niece, from her being promised to Blifil, has made you turn your thoughts towards her? To my aunt, indeed, I pretend no duty, nor doth she deserve any. However, sir, I have given you my advice; and if you decline pursuing it, I shall have the less opinion of your understanding—that's all.'

Jones, however, persisted in declining the undertaking, which had not, indeed, the least probability of success. He easily perceived the motives which induced Mrs Fitzpatrick to be so eager in pressing her advice. He said he would not deny the tender and passionate regard he had for Sophia; but was so conscious of the inequality of their situations, that he could never flatter himself so far as to hope that so divine a young lady would condescend to think on so unworthy a man; nay, he protested, he could scarce bring himself to wish she should.

When Jones had finished his exclamations, Mrs Fitzpatrick heaved a deep sigh, and, taking her eyes off from Jones, on whom they had been some time fixed, and dropping them on the ground, she cried, 'Indeed, Mr Jones, I pity you; but it is the curse of such tenderness to be thrown away on those who are insensible of it. I know my cousin better than you, Mr Jones, and I must say, any woman who makes no return to such a passion, and such a person, is unworthy of both.'

'Sure, madam,' said Jones, 'you can't mean——'—'Mean!' cries Mrs Fitzpatrick, 'I know not what I mean; there is something, I think, in true tenderness bewitching; few women ever meet it in men, and fewer still know how to value it when they do. Sure she must be the most contemptible of women who can overlook such merit.'

The manner and look with which all this was spoke, infused a suspicion into Jones, which we don't care to convey in direct words to the reader. Instead of making any answer, he said, 'I am afraid, madam, I have made too tiresome a visit'; and offered to take his leave.

'Not at all, sir,' answered Mrs Fitzpatrick.——'Indeed I pity you, Mr Jones; indeed I do: but if you are going, consider of the scheme I have mentioned—I am convinced you will approve it —and let me see you again as soon as you can.—To-morrow morning if you will, or at least some time to-morrow. I shall be at home all day.'

Jones, then, after many expressions of thanks, very respectfully retired; nor could Mrs Fitzpatrick forbear making him a present of a look at parting, by which if he had understood nothing, he must have had no understanding in the language of the eyes. In reality, it confirmed his resolution of returning to her no more.

Fortune, however, who was not his friend, resolved, as he intended to give her no second opportunity, to make the best of this; and accordingly produced the tragical incident which we are now in sorrowful notes to record.

Mr Fitzpatrick being acquainted by Mrs Western with the place to which his wife was retired, set forward to London.

The reader hath been already often informed of the jealous temper of this gentleman. He may likewise be pleased to remember the suspicion which he had conceived of Jones at Upton, upon his finding him in the room with Mrs Waters.

And now, as he was inquiring in the street after his wife and had just received directions to the door, unfortunately Mr Jones was issuing from it.

Fitzpatrick did not yet recollect the face of Jones; however, seeing a young well-dressed fellow coming from his wife, he made directly up to him, and asked him what he had been doing in that house? 'for I am sure,' said he, 'you must have been in it, as I saw you come out of it.'

Jones answered very modestly, 'That he had been visiting a lady there.' To which Fitzpatrick replied, 'What business have you with the lady?' Upon which Jones, who now perfectly remembered the voice, features, and indeed coat, of the gentleman, cried out—'Ha, my good friend! give me your hand; I hope there is no ill blood remaining between us, upon a small mistake which happened so long ago.'

'Upon my soul, sir,' said Fitzpatrick, 'I don't know your name nor your face.'—'Indeed, sir,' said Jones, 'neither have I the pleasure of knowing your name, but your face I very well remember to have seen before at Upton, where a foolish quarrel happened between us, which, if it is not made up yet, we will now make up over a bottle.'

'At Upton!' cried the other;——'Ha! upon my soul, I believe your name is Jones?'—'Indeed,' answered he, 'it is.'—'O! upon my soul,' cries Fitzpatrick, 'you are the very man I wanted to meet.—Upon my soul I will drink a bottle with you presently; but first I will give you a great knock over the pate. There is for you, you rascal. Upon my soul, if you do not give me satisfaction for that blow, I will give you another.' And then, drawing his sword, put himself in a posture of defence, which was the only science he understood.

Jones was a little staggered by the blow, which came somewhat unexpectedly; but presently recovering himself, he also drew, and though he understood nothing of fencing, prest on so boldly upon Fitzpatrick, that he beat down his guard, and sheathed one half of his sword in the body of the said gentleman, who had no sooner received it, than he stept backwards, dropped the point of his sword, and leaning upon it, cried, 'I have satisfaction enough: I am a dead man.'

'I hope not,' cries Jones, 'but whatever be the consequence, you must be sensible you have drawn it upon yourself.' At this instant a number of fellows rushed in and seized Jones, who told them he should make no resistance, and begged some of them at least would take care of the wounded gentleman.

'Ay,' cries one of the fellows, 'the wounded gentleman will be taken care enough of; for I suppose he hath not many hours to live. As for you, sir, you have a month at least good yet.'— 'D—n me, Jack,' said another, 'he hath prevented his voyage; he's bound to another port now'; and many other such jests was our poor Jones made the subject of by these fellows, who were indeed a gang employed by Lord Fellamar, and had dogged him into the house of Mrs Fitzpatrick, waiting for him at the corner of the street when this unfortunate accident happened.

The officer who commanded this gang very wisely concluded, that his business was now to deliver his prisoner into the hands of the civil magistrate.

Jones was now conducted before the justice, where the surgeon who dressed Mr Fitzpatrick appeared, and deposed that he believed the wound to be mortal; upon which the prisoner was committed to the Gatehouse. It was very late at night, so that Jones would not send for Partridge till the next morning; and, as he never shut his eyes till seven, so it was near twelve before the poor fellow, who was greatly frightened at not hearing from his master so long, received a message which almost deprived him of his being when he heard it.

He went to the Gatehouse with trembling knees and a beating heart, and was no sooner arrived in the presence of Jones, than he lamented the misfortune that had befallen him with many tears, looking all the while frequently about him in great terror; for as the news now arrived that Mr Fitzpatrick was dead, the poor fellow apprehended every minute that his ghost would enter the room. At last he delivered him a letter, which he had like to have forgot, and which came from Sophia by the hands of Black George.

Jones presently dispatched every one out of the room, and, having eagerly broke open the letter, read as follows:

'You owe the hearing from me again to an accident which I own surprizes me. My aunt hath just now shown me a letter from you to Lady Bellaston, which contains a proposal of marriage. I am convinced it is your own hand; and what more surprizes me is, that it is dated at the very time when you would have me imagine you was under such concern on my account.—I leave you to comment on this fact. All I desire is, that your name may never more be mentioned to

'S. W.'

Of the present situation of Mr Jones's mind, and of the pangs with which he was now tormented, we cannot give the reader a better idea than by saying, his misery was such that even Thwackum would almost have pitied him. But, bad as it is, we shall at present leave him in it.

CHAPTER THIRTY-EIGHT

IN WHICH MR WESTERN PAYS A VISIT TO HIS SISTER, IN COMPANY
WITH MR BLIFIL

THE morning after his arrival in London, Mr Blifil waited on Mr Western, by whom he was most kindly and graciously received, and from whom he had every possible assurance (perhaps more than was possible) that he should very shortly be as happy as Sophia could make him; nor would the squire suffer the young gentleman to return to his uncle till he had, almost against his will, carried him to his sister.

Mrs Western was reading a letter on prudence, and matrimonial politics, to her niece, when her brother and Blifil broke in with less ceremony than the laws of visiting require. Sophia no sooner saw Blifil than she turned pale, and almost lost the use of all her faculties; but her aunt, on the contrary, waxed red, and, having all her faculties at command, began to exert her tongue on the squire.

'Brother,' said she, 'I am astonished at your behaviour; will you never learn any regard to decorum? Do you think yourself at liberty to invade the privacies of women of condition, without the least decency or notice?'——'Why, what a pox is the matter now?' quoth the squire; 'one would think I had caught you at ——'—'None of your brutality, sir, I beseech you,' answered she.——'You have surprized my poor niece so, that she can hardly, I see, support herself.——Go, my dear, retire, and endeavour to recruit your spirits; for I see you have occasion.' At which words Sophia, who never received a more welcome command, hastily withdrew.

'To be sure, sister,' cries the squire, 'you are mad, when I have brought Mr Blifil here to court her, to force her away.'

'Sure, brother,' says she, 'you are worse than mad, when you know in what situation affairs are, to——I am sure I ask Mr Blifil's pardon, but he knows very well, to whom to impute so disagreeable a reception. For my own part, I am sure I shall always be very glad to see Mr Blifil; but his own good sense would not have suffered him to proceed so abruptly, had you not compelled him to it.'

Blifil bowed and stammered, and looked like a fool; but Western, without giving him time to form a speech for the purpose, answered, 'Well, well, I am to blame, if you will, I always am, certainly; but come, let the girl be fetched back again, or let Mr Blifil go to her.——He's come up on purpose, and there is no time to be lost.'

'Brother,' said she, 'whatever message Mr Blifil thinks proper to send to my niece, shall be delivered to her; and I suppose she will want no instructions to make a proper answer. I am convinced she will not refuse to see Mr Blifil at a proper time.'—'The devil she won't!' answered the squire. 'Odsbud!—Don't we know—I say nothing, but some volk are wiser than all the world.——If I might have had my will, she had not run away before: and now I expect to hear every moment she is guone again. For as great a fool as some volk think me, I know very well she hates——'— 'No matter, brother,' replied Mrs Western, 'I will not hear my niece abused. It is a reflection on my family. She is an honour to it; and she will be an honour to it, I promise you. I will pawn my whole reputation in the world on her conduct.——I shall be glad to see you, brother, in the afternoon; for I have somewhat of importance to mention to you.—At present, Mr Blifil, as well as you, must excuse me; for I am in haste to dress.' Blifil then took a ceremonious leave of Mrs Western, who was altogether as ceremonious on her part; and then they departed, the squire muttering to himself with an oath, that Blifil should see his daughter in the afternoon.

We must now return a few days. The moment Mrs Western had arrived at her lodgings, a card was dispatched with her compliments to Lady Bellaston; who no sooner received it than, with the impatience of a lover, she flew to her cousin, rejoiced at this fair opportunity of making Lord Fellamar's proposals to a woman of sense, and who knew the world, than to a gentleman whom she honoured with the appellation of Hottentot; though, indeed, from him she apprehended no danger of a refusal.

The two ladies being met after very short previous ceremonials, fell to business, which was indeed almost as soon concluded as begun; for Mrs Western no sooner heard the name of Lord Fellamar than her cheeks glowed with pleasure; but when she was acquainted with the eagerness of his passion, the earnestness of his proposals, and the generosity of his offer, she declared her full satisfaction in the most explicit terms.

In the progress of their conversation their discourse turned to Jones, and both cousins very pathetically lamented the unfortunate attachment which both agreed Sophia had to that young fellow; and Mrs Western entirely attributed it to the folly of her brother's management. She concluded, however, at last, with declaring her confidence in the good understanding of her niece, who, though she would not give up her affection in favour of Blifil, will, I doubt not, says she, soon be prevailed upon to sacrifice a simple inclination to the addresses of a fine gentleman, who brings her both a title and a large estate: 'For, indeed,' added she, 'I must do Sophy the justice to confess this Blifil is but a hideous kind of fellow, as you know, Bellaston, all country gentlemen are, and hath nothing but his fortune to recommend him.'

'Nay,' said Lady Bellaston, 'I don't then so much wonder at my cousin; for I promise you this Jones is a very agreeable fellow, and hath one virtue, which the men say is a great recommendation to us. What do you think, Mrs Western—I shall certainly make you laugh; nay, I can hardly tell you myself for laughing—will you believe that the fellow hath had the assurance to make love to me? But if you should be inclined to disbelieve it, here is evidence enough, his own handwriting, I assure you.' She then delivered her cousin the letter with the proposals of marriage, which, if the reader hath a desire to see, he will find already on record.

'Upon my word, I am astonished,' said Mrs Western; 'this is, indeed, a masterpiece of assurance. With your leave, I may possibly make some use of this letter.'—'You have my full liberty,' cries Lady Bellaston, 'to apply it to what purpose you please. However, I would not have it shewn to any but Miss Western, nor to her unless you find occasion.'—'Well, and how did you use the fellow?' returned Mrs Western. 'Not as a husband,' said the lady; 'I am not married, I promise you, my dear. You know, Bell, I have tried the comforts once already; and once, I think, is enough for any reasonable woman.'

This letter Lady Bellaston thought would certainly turn the

balance against Jones in the mind of Sophia, and she was emboldened to give it up, partly by her hopes of having him instantly dispatched out of the way, and partly by having secured the evidence of Honour, who, upon sounding her, she saw sufficient reason to imagine was prepared to testify whatever she pleased.

Mr Allworthy and Mrs Miller were just sat down to breakfast, when Blifil, who had gone out very early that morning, returned to make one of the company.

He had not been long seated before he began as follows: 'Good Lord! my dear uncle, what do you think hath happened? I vow I am afraid of telling it you, for fear of shocking you with the remembrance of ever having shewn any kindness to such a villain.'—'What is the matter, child?' said the uncle. 'I fear I have shewn kindness in my life to the unworthy more than once. But charity doth not adopt the vices of its objects.'—'O, sir!' returned Blifil, 'it is not without the secret direction of Providence that you mention the word adoption. Your adopted son, sir, that Jones, that wretch whom you nourished in your bosom, hath proved one of the greatest villains upon earth.'—'By all that's sacred, 'tis false,' cries Mrs Miller. 'Mr Jones is no villain. He is one of the worthiest creatures breathing; and if any other person had called him villain, I would have thrown all this boiling water in his face.' Mr Allworthy looked very much amazed at this behaviour. But she did not give him leave to speak, before, turning to him, she cried, 'I hope you will not be angry with me; I would not offend you, sir, for the world; but, indeed, I could not bear to hear him called so.'—'I must own, madam,' said Allworthy, very gravely, 'I am a little surprized to hear you so warmly defend a fellow you do not know.'—'O! I do know him, Mr Allworthy,' said she, 'indeed I do; I should be the most ungrateful of all wretches if I denied it. O! he hath preserved me and my little family; we have all reason to bless him while we live.—And I pray Heaven to bless him, and turn the hearts of his malicious enemies. I know, I find, I see, he hath such.'—'You surprize me, madam, still more,' said Allworthy; 'sure you must mean some other. It is impossible you should have any such obligations to the man my nephew mentions.'—'Too surely,' answered she, 'I have obligations to him of the greatest and tenderest kind. Believe me, sir, when you have heard the story which I shall tell you (for I will tell you all), you will be so far from being offended, that you will own (I know your justice so well), that I must have been the most despicable and most ungrateful of wretches if I had acted any other part than I have.'

'Well, madam,' said Allworthy, 'I shall be very glad to hear any good excuse for a behaviour which, I must confess, I think wants an excuse. And now, madam, will you be pleased to let my nephew proceed in his story without interruption. What is this new instance? What hath he done of late?'—'What,' cries Blifil, 'notwithstanding all Mrs Miller hath said, I am very sorry to relate, and what you should never have heard from me, had it not been a matter impossible to conceal from the whole world. In short, he hath killed a man; I will not say murdered—for perhaps it may not be so construed in law, and I hope the best for his sake.'

Allworthy looked shocked, and blessed himself; and then, turning to Mrs Miller, he cried, 'Well, madam, what say you now?'

'Why, I say, sir,' answered she, 'that I never was more concerned at anything in my life; but, if the fact be true, I am convinced the man, whoever he is, was in fault. Heaven knows there are many villains in this town who make it their business to provoke young gentlemen. Nothing but the greatest provocation could have tempted him; for of all the gentlemen I ever had in my house, I never saw one so gentle or so sweet-tempered. He was beloved by every one in the house, and every one who came near it.'

While she was thus running on, a violent knocking at the door interrupted their conversation, for, as she concluded this was a visitor to Mr Allworthy, she hastily retired.

Mrs Miller had not long left the room when Mr Western entered.

'There,' says he, 'there is fine business forwards now. The hounds have changed at last; and when we imagined we had a fox to deal with, od-rat it, it turns out to be a badger at last!'

'Pray, my good neighbour,' said Allworthy, 'drop your metaphors, and speak a little plainer.'—'Why, then,' says the squire, 'to tell you plainly, we have been all this time afraid of a son of a whore of a bastard of somebody's, I don't know whose, not I. And now here's a confounded son of a whore of a lord, who may be a bastard too for what I know or care, for he shall never have a daughter of mine by my consent. They have beggared the nation, but they shall never beggar me.'

'You surprize me much, my good friend,' said Allworthy. 'Why, zounds! I am surprized myself,' answered the squire. 'I went to zee sister Western last night, according to her own appointment, and there I was had into a whole room full of women. There was my lady cousin Bellaston, and my Lady Betty, and my Lady Catherine, and my lady I don't know who; d—n me, if ever you catch me among such a kennel of hoop-petticoat b—s! "O! certainly one of the greatest matches in England," says one cousin' (here he attempted to mimic them); '"A very advantageous offer indeed," cries another cousin (for you must know they be all my cousins, though I never zeed half o' um before). "Surely," says my Lady Bellaston, "cousin, you must be out of your wits to think of refusing such an offer." '

'Now I begin to understand,' says Allworthy; 'some person hath made proposals to Miss Western, which the ladies of the family approve, but is not to your liking.'

'My liking!' said Western, 'how the devil should it? I tell you it is a lord, and those are always volks whom you know I always resolved to have nothing to do with. Besides, ben't I engaged to you, and did I ever go off any bargain when I had promised?'

'As to that point, neighbour,' said Allworthy, 'I entirely release you from any engagement. No contract can be binding between parties who have not a full power to make it at the time, nor ever afterwards acquire the power of fulfilling it.'

'Slud! then,' answered Western, 'I tell you I have power, and I will fulfill it. Come along with me directly to Doctors' Commons, I will get a licence; and I will go to sister and take away the wench by force, and she shall ha un, or I will lock her up, and keep her upon bread and water as long as she lives.'

'Mr Western,' said Allworthy, 'shall I beg you will hear my full sentiments on this matter?'—'Hear thee; ay, to be sure I will,' answered he. 'Why, then, sir,' cries Allworthy, 'I can truly say, without a compliment either to you or the young lady, that when this match was proposed, I embraced it very readily and heartily, from my regard to you both. An alliance between two families so nearly neighbours, and between whom there had always existed good harmony, I thought a most desirable event; and with regard to the young lady, not only the concurrent opinion of all who knew her, but my own observation assured me that she would be an inestimable treasure to a good husband. I shall say nothing of her personal qualifications, which certainly are admirable; her good nature, her charitable disposition, her modesty, are too well known to need any panegyric.

'Indeed, I heartily wished to receive so great a jewel into my family; but though I may wish for many good things, I would not, therefore, steal them, or be guilty of any violence or injustice to possess myself of them. Now to force a woman into a marriage contrary to her consent or approbation, is an act of such injustice and oppression, that I wish the laws of our country could restrain it; for, is it not cruel, nay, impious, to force a woman into that state against her will; for her behaviour in which she is to be accountable to the highest and most dreadful court of judicature, and to answer at the peril of her soul? To dischage the matrimonial duties in an adequate manner is no easy task; Shall we tear her very heart from her, while we enjoin her duties to which a whole heart is scarce equal?

'For these reasons, my best neighbour, as I see the inclinations of this young lady are most unhappily averse to my nephew, I must decline any further thoughts of the honour you intended him, though I assure you I shall always retain the most grateful sense of it.'

'Well, sir,' said Western (the froth bursting forth from his lips the moment they were uncorked), 'you cannot say but I have heard you out, and now I expect you'll hear me. First then, I desire you to answer me one question—Did not I beget her? did not I beget her? answer me that. But I believe you will allow me to be her father, and if I be, am I not to govern my own child? I ask you that, am I not to govern my own child? and if I am to govern her in other matters, surely I am to govern her in this, which concerns her most. What the devil in hell can I do more? Zounds! I'd zee all the world d—n'd bevore her little vinger should be hurt. Indeed, Mr Allworthy, I must say, take it how you will, that I thought you had more sense.'

Allworthy resented this reflection only with a smile; nor could he, if he would have endeavoured it, have conveyed into that smile any mixture of malice or contempt.

Blifil now desired to be permitted to speak a few words. 'As to using any violence on the young lady, I am sure I shall never consent to it. My conscience will not permit me to use violence on any one, much less on a lady for whom, however cruel she is to me, I shall always preserve the purest and sincerest affection; but yet I have read that women are seldom proof against perseverance. As for this lord, Mr Western is so kind to prefer me to him; and sure, sir, you will not deny but that a parent hath at least a negative voice in these matters; nay, I do not find the lady herself is inclined to give him any countenance; alas! I am too well assured she is not; I am too sensible that wickedest of men remains uppermost in her heart.'

'Ay, ay, so he does,' cries Western.

'But surely,' says Blifil, 'when she hears of this murder which he hath committed, if the law should spare his life——'

'What's that?' cries Western. 'Murder! hath he committed a murder, and is there any hopes of seeing him hanged?—Tol de rol, tol lol de rol.' Here he fell a singing and capering about the room.

'Well, well,' cries the squire, Tol lol de rol! 'I never heard better news in my life—Do, prithee, dear Allworthy, come and dine with me: I have bespoke a shoulder of mutton roasted, and a spare-rib of pork, and a fowl and egg-sauce.'

Mr Allworthy at last agreed to this invitation, and soon after the squire went off, singing and capering at the hopes of seeing the speedy tragical end of poor Jones.

When he was gone, Mr Allworthy resumed the aforesaid subject with much gravity. He told his nephew, 'He wished with all his heart he would endeavour to conquer a passion, in which I cannot,' says he, 'flatter you with any hopes of succeeding. It is certainly a vulgar error, that aversion in a woman may be conquered by perseverance. Indifference may, perhaps, sometimes yield to it. But a fixed dislike, as I am afraid this is, will rather gather strength than be conquered by time. Besides, my dear, I have another apprehension which you must excuse. I am afraid this passion which you have for this fine young creature hath her beautiful person too much for its object, and is unworthy of the name of that love which is the only foundation of matrimonial felicity. Examine your heart, therefore, thoroughly, my good boy, and if, upon examination, you have but the least suspicion of this kind, I am sure your own virtue and religion will impel you to drive so vicious a passion from your heart, and your good sense will soon enable you to do it without pain.'

The reader may pretty well guess Blifil's answer; but, if he should be at a loss, we are not at present at leisure to satisfy him, as our history now hastens on to matters of higher importance, and we can no longer bear to be absent from Sophia.

CHAPTER THIRTY-NINE

AN EXTRAORDINARY SCENE BETWEEN SOPHIA AND HER AUNT

THE lowing heifer and the bleating ewe, in herds and flocks, may ramble safe and unregarded through the pastures. But if a plump doe be discovered to have escaped from the forest, and to repose herself in some field or grove, the whole parish is presently alarmed, every man is ready to set dogs after her; and, if she is preserved from the rest by the good squire, it is only that he may secure her for his own eating.

None ever tasted more of this persecution than poor Sophia. Her ill stars were not contented with all that she had suffered on account of Blifil, they now raised her another pursuer, who seemed likely to torment her no less than the other had done.

The servants were no sooner departed after dinner, than Mrs Western, who had opened the matter to Sophia, informed her, 'That she expected his lordship that very afternoon, and intended to take the first opportunity of leaving her alone with him.' —'If you do, madam,' answered Sophia, with some spirit, 'I shall take the first opportunity of leaving him by himself.'— 'How! madam!' cries the aunt; 'is this the return you make me for my kindness in relieving you from your confinement at your father's?'—'You know, madam,' said Sophia, 'the cause of that confinement was a refusal to comply with my father in accepting a man I detested; and will my dear aunt, who hath relieved me from that distress, involve me in another equally bad?'—'And do you think then, madam,' answered Mrs Western, 'that there is no difference between my Lord Fellamar and Mr Blifil?'—'Very little, in my opinion,' cries Sophia; 'and, if I must be condemned to one, I would certainly have the merit of sacrificing myself to my father's pleasure.'—'Then my pleasure, I find,' said the aunt, 'hath very little weight with you; but that consideration shall not move me. I act from nobler motives. The view of aggrandizing my family, of ennobling yourself, is what I proceed upon. Have you no sense of ambition? Are there no charms in the thoughts of having a coronet on your coach?'—'None, upon my honour,' said Sophia. 'A pincushion upon my coach would please me just as well.'

'But, child, dear child,' said the aunt, 'be reasonable; can you invent a single objection?'—'I have already, I think, told you a sufficient objection,' answered Sophia. 'What?' cries the aunt; 'I remember none.'—'Sure, madam,' said Sophia, 'I told you he had used me in the rudest and vilest manner.'—'Indeed, child,' answered she, 'I never heard you, or did not understand you:— but what do you mean by this rude, vile manner?'—'Indeed, madm,' said Sophia, 'I am almost ashamed to tell you. He caught me in his arms, and pulled me down upon the settee, and thrust his hand into my bosom, and kissed it with such violence that I have the mark upon my left breast at this moment.'—'Indeed!' said Mrs Western. 'Yes, indeed, madam,' answered Sophia; 'my father luckily came in at that instant, or Heaven knows what rudeness he intended to have proceeded to.'—'I am astonished and confounded,' cries the aunt. 'No woman of the name of Western hath been ever treated so since we were a family. I would have torn the eyes of a prince out, if he had attempted such freedoms with me. It is impossible! sure, Sophia, you must invent this to raise my indignation against him.'—'I hope, madam,' said Sophia, 'you have too good an opinion of me to imagine me capable of telling an untruth. Upon my soul it is true.'—'I should have stabbed him to the heart, had I been present,' returned the aunt. 'Yet surely he could have no dishonourable design; it is impossible! he durst not: besides, his proposals shew he hath not; for they are not only honourable, but generous. I have had lovers formerly, not so long ago neither; several lovers, though I never would consent to marriage, and I never encouraged the least freedom. It is a foolish custom, and what I never would agree to. No man kissed more of me than my cheek.'—'You will pardon me, dear madam,' said Sophia, 'if I make one observation: you own you have had many lovers, and the world knows it, even if you should deny it. You refused them all, and, I am convinced, one coronet at least among them.'—'You say true, dear Sophy,' answered she; 'I had once the offer of a title.'— 'Why, then,' said Sophia, 'will you not suffer me to refuse this once?'—'It is true, child,' said she, 'I have refused the offer of a title; but it was not so good an offer; that is, not so very, very good an offer.'—'Yes, madam,' said Sophia; 'but you have had very great proposals from men of vast fortunes. It was not the first nor the second, nor the third advantageous match that offered itself.'—'I own it was not,' said she. 'Well, madam,' continued Sophia, 'and why may not I expect to have a second, perhaps, better than this? You are now but a young woman, and I am convinced would not promise to yield to the first lover of fortune, nay, or of title too. I am a very young woman, and sure I need not despair.'—'Well, my dear, dear Sophy,' cries the aunt, 'what would you have me say?'—'Why, I only beg that I may not be left alone, at least this evening; grant me that, and I will submit, if you think, after what is past, I ought to see him in your company.'—'Well, I will grant it,' cries the aunt. 'Sophy, you know I love you, and can deny you nothing. You know the easiness of my nature; I have not always been so easy. I have been formerly thought cruel; by the men, I mean. Sophy, I was never so handsome as you, and yet I had something of you formerly. I am a little altered. Kingdoms and states, undergo alterations, and so must the human form.' Thus run she on for near half an hour upon herself, and her conquests, and her cruelty, till the arrival of my lord, who, after a most tedious visit, during which Mrs Western never once offered to leave the room, retired, not much more satisfied with the aunt than with the niece; for Sophia had brought her aunt into so excellent a temper, that she consented to almost everything her niece said; and agreed that a little distant behaviour might not be improper to so forward a lover.

Thus Sophia, by a little well-directed flattery, for which surely none will blame her, obtained a little ease for herself, and, at least, put off the evil day. And now we have seen our heroine in a better situation than she hath been for a long time before, we will look a little after Mr Jones, whom we left in the most deplorable situation that can be well imagined.

When Mr Allworthy and his nephew went to meet Mr Western, Mrs Miller set forwards to her son-in-law's lodgings, in order to acquaint him with the accident which had befallen his friend Jones; but he had known it long before from Partridge (for Jones, when he left Mrs Miller, had been furnished with a room in the same house with Mr Nightingale). The good woman found her daughter under great affliction on account of Mr Jones, whom having comforted as well as she could, she set forwards to the Gatehouse, where she heard he was, and where Mr Nightingale was arrived before her.

The firmness and constancy of a true friend is a circumstance so extremely delightful to persons in any kind of distress, that the distress itself is more than compensated by bringing this comfort with it.

Whether it was that Fortune was apprehensive lest Jones should sink under the weight of his adversity, or whether she really abated somewhat of her severity towards him, she seemed a little to relax her persecution, by sending him the company of two such faithful friends, and what is perhaps more rare, a faithful servant. For Partridge, though he had many imperfections, wanted not fidelity; and though fear would not suffer him to be hanged for his master, yet the world, I believe, could not have bribed him to desert his cause.

While Jones was expressing great satisfaction in the presence of his friends, Partridge brought an account that Mr Fitzpatrick was still alive, though the surgeon declared that he had very little hopes. Upon which, Jones fetching a deep sigh, Nighingale said to him, 'My dear Tom, why should you afflict yourself so upon an accident, which, whatever be the consequence, can be attended with no danger to you, and in which your conscience cannot accuse you of having been the least to blame? If the fellow should die, what have you done more than taken away the life of a ruffian in your own defence? So will the coroner's inquest certainly find it; and then you will be easily admitted to bail; and, though you must undergo the form of a trial, yet it is a trial which many men would stand for you for a shilling.'—'Come, come, Mr Jones,' says Mrs Miller, 'chear yourself up. I knew you could not be the aggressor, and so I told Mr Allworthy, and so he shall acknowledge too, before I have done with him.'

Jones gravely answered, 'That whatever might be his fate, he should always lament the having shed the blood of one of his fellow-creatures, as one of the highest misfortunes which could have befallen him. But I have another misfortune of the tenderest kind——O! Mrs Miller, I have lost what I held most dear upon earth.'—'That must be a mistress,' said Mrs Miller; 'but come, come: I know more than you imagine' (for indeed Partridge had blabbed all); 'and I have heard more than you know. Matters go better, I promise you, than you think; and I would not give Blifil sixpence for all the chance which he hath of the lady.'

'Indeed, my dear friend, indeed,' answered Jones, 'you are an entire stranger to the cause of my grief. If you was acquainted with the story, you would allow my case admitted of no comfort. I apprehend no danger from Blifil.

'I see you are acquainted with the lady (how you came by our information I know not), who sits, indeed, very near my heart If you could contrive to deliver this (giving her a paper from his pocket,) I shall for ever acknowledge your goodness.'

'Give it me,' said Mrs Miller. 'If I see it not in her own possession before I sleep, may my next sleep be my last! Comfort yourself, my good young man! be wise enough to take warning from past follies, and I warrant all shall be well, and I shall yet see you happy with the most charming young lady in the world; for I so hear from every one she is.'

'Believe me, madam,' said he, 'I do not speak the common cant of one in my unhappy situation. Before this dreadful accident happened, I had resolved to quit a life of which I was become sensible of the wickedness as well as folly. Though I have been hurried into vices, I do not approve a vicious character, nor will I ever, from this moment, deserve it.'

Mrs Miller expressed great satisfaction in these declarations, in the sincerity of which she averred she had an entire faith; and now the remainder of the conversation past in the joint attempts of that good woman and Mr Nightingale to cheer the dejected spirits of Mr Jones, in which they so far succeeded as to leave him much better comforted and satisfied than they found him: to which happy alteration nothing so much contributed as the kind undertaking of Mrs Miller to deliver his letter to Sophia, which he despaired of finding any means to accomplish; for when Black George produced the last from Sophia, he informed Partridge that she had strictly charged him, on pain of having it communicated to her father, not to bring her any answer. He was, moreover, not a little pleased to find he had so warm an advocate to Mr Allworthy himself in this good woman, who was, in reality, one of the worthiest creatures in the world.

Sophia was dressing, when she was acquainted that there was a gentlewoman below to wait on her. As she was neither afraid nor ashamed, to see any of her own sex, Mrs Miller was immediately admitted.

Curtsies and the usual ceremonials between women who are strangers to each other, being past, Sophia said, 'I have not the pleasure to know you, madam.'—'No, madam,' answered Mrs Miller, 'and I must beg pardon for intruding upon you. But I was desired, madam, by a very unhappy young gentleman, to deliver you this letter.' Sophia changed colour when she saw the direction, well knowing the hand, and after some hesitation, said: 'I could not conceive, madam, from your appearance, that your business had been of such a nature.—Whomever you brought this letter from, I shall not open it. I should be sorry to entertain an unjust suspicion of any one; but you are an utter stranger to me.'

'If you will have patience, madam,' answered Mrs Miller, 'I will acquaint you who I am, and how I came by that letter.'—

'I have no curiosity, madam, to know anything,' cries Sophia; 'but I must insist on your delivering that letter back to the person who gave it you.'

Mrs Miller then fell upon her knees, and in the most passionate terms implored her compassion; to which Sophia answered: 'Sure, madam, it is surprizing you should be so very strongly interested in the behalf of this person. I would not think, madam——'—'No, madam,' says Mrs Miller, 'you shall not think anything but the truth. I will tell you all, and you will not wonder that I am interested. He is the best-natured creature that ever was born.'——She then began and related the story.——After this she cried, 'This, madam, this is his goodness; I have tender obligations to him. He hath preserved my child.'——Here, after shedding some tears, she concluded with saying, 'Now, madam, you shall judge whether I can ever do enough for so kind, so good, so generous a young man; and sure he is the best and worthiest of all human beings.'

The alterations in the countenance of Sophia had hitherto been chiefly to her disadvantage, and had inclined her complexion to too great paleness; but she now waxed redder, if possible, than vermilion, and cried, 'I know not what to say; certainly what arises from gratitude cannot be blamed——But what service can my reading this letter do your friend, since I am resolved never——' Mrs Miller fell again to her entreaties, and begged to be forgiven, but she could not, she said, carry it back. 'Well, madam,' says Sophia, 'I cannot help it, if you will force it upon me.—Certainly you may leave it, whether I will or no.' What Sophia meant, or whether she meant anything, I will not presume to determine; but Mrs Miller actually understood this as a hint, and presently laying the letter down on the table, took her leave, having first begged permission to wait again on Sophia; which request had neither assent nor denial.

The letter lay upon the table no longer than till Mrs Miller was out of sight; for then Sophia opened and read it.

This letter did very little service to his cause; for it consisted of little more than confessions of his own unworthiness, and bitter lamentations of despair, together with the most solemn protestations of his unalterable fidelity to Sophia, of which, he said he hoped to convince her, if he had ever more the honour of being admitted to her presence; and that he could account for the letter to Lady Bellaston in such a manner, that, though it would not entitle him to her forgiveness, he hoped at least to obtain it from her mercy. And concluded with vowing that nothing was ever less in his thoughts than to marry Lady Bellaston.

Though Sophia read the letter twice over with great attention, his meaning still remained a riddle to her; nor could her invention suggest to her any means to excuse Jones. She certainly remained very angry with him, though indeed Lady Bellaston took up so much of her resentment, that her gentle mind had but little left to bestow on any other person.

That lady was most unluckily to dine this very day with her aunt Western, and in the afternoon they were all three, by appointment, to go together to the opera, and thence to Lady Thomas Hatchet's drum. Sophia would have gladly been excused from all, but would not disoblige her aunt; and as to the arts of counterfeiting illness, she was so entirely a stranger to them, that it never once entered into her head.

Another misfortune which befell poor Sophia, was the company of Lord Fellamar, whom she met at the opera, and who attended her to the drum.

Having in this chapter twice mentioned a drum, a word which our posterity, it is hoped, will not understand in the sense it is here applied, we shall, in a moment describe it.

A drum, then, is an assembly of well-dressed persons of both sexes, most of whom play at cards, and the rest do nothing at all; while the mistress of the house performs the part of the land-lady at an inn, and like the landlady of an inn prides herself in the number of her guests, though she doth not always, like her, get anything by it.

No wonder then, as so much spirits must be required to support any vivacity in these scenes of dulness, that we hear persons of fashion eternally complaining of the want of them; a complaint confined entirely to upper life. How insupportable must we imagine this round of impertinence to have been to Sophia at this time; how difficult must she have found it to force the appearance of gaiety into her looks, when her mind dictated nothing but the tenderest sorrow, and when every thought was charged with tormenting ideas!

CHAPTER FORTY

A PATHETIC SCENE BETWEEN MR ALLWORTHY AND MRS MILLER

MRS MILLER had a long discourse with Mr Allworthy, at his return from dinner, in which she acquainted him with Jones's having unfortunately lost all which was pleased to bestow on him at their separation; and with the distresses to which that loss had subjected him; of all which she had received a full account from the faithful retailer Partridge. She then explained the obligations she had to Jones; not that she was entirely explicit with regard to her daughter; for though she had the utmost confidence in Mr Allworthy, and though there could be no hopes of keeping an affair secret which was unhappily known to more than half a dozen, yet she could not prevail with herself to mention those circumstances which reflected most on the chastity of poor Nancy, but smothered that part of her evidence as cautiously as if she had been before a judge, and the girl was now on her trial for the murder of a bastard.

Allworthy said, there were few characters so absolutely vicious as not to have the least mixture of good in them. 'However,' says he, 'I cannot deny but that you have some obligations to the fellow, bad as he is, and I shall therefore excuse what hath past already, but must insist you never mention his name to me more; for, I promise you, it was upon the fullest and plainest evidence that I resolved to take the measures I have taken.'—'Well, sir,' says she, 'I make not the least doubt but time will shew all matters in their true and natural colours, and that you will be convinced this poor young man deserves better of you than some other folks that shall be nameless.'

'Madam,' cries Allworthy, a little ruffled, 'I will not hear any reflections on my nephew; and if ever you say a word more of that kind, I will depart from your house that instant. He is the worthiest and best of men; and I once more repeat it to you, he hath carried his friendship to this man to a blameable length, by too long concealing facts of the blackest die. The ingratitude of the wretch to this good young man is what I most resent; for, madam, I have the greatest reason to imagine he had laid a plot to supplant my nephew in my favour, and to have disinherited him.'

'I am sure, sir,' answered Mrs Miller, a little frightened (for, though Mr Allworthy had the utmost sweetness and benevolence in his smiles, he had great terror in his frowns), 'I shall never speak against any gentleman you are pleased to think well of. I am sure, sir, such behaviour would very little become me, especially when the gentleman is your nearest relation; but, sir, you must not be angry with me, you must not indeed, for my good wishes to this poor wretch. How often have I heard you call him your son? How often have you prattled to me of him with all the fondness of a parent? Nay, sir, I cannot forget the many tender expressions, the many good things you have told me of his beauty, and his virtues; of his good nature and generosity. I am sure, sir, I cannot forget them, for I find them all true. I have experienced them in my own cause. When I consider the cruel reverse of fortune which this poor youth, to whom I am so much obliged, hath suffered; when I consider the loss of your favour, which I know he valued more than his life, I must, I must lament the misery of one whom you have loved, and I shall ever love.'

Allworthy was pretty much moved with this speech, but it seemed not to be with anger; for, after a short silence, taking Mrs Miller by the hand, he said very affectionately to her, 'Come, madam, let us consider a little about your daughter. I cannot blame you for rejoicing in a match which promises to be advantageous to her, but you know this advantage, in a great measure, depends on the father's reconciliation. I know Mr Nightingale very well, and have formerly had concerns with him; I will make him a visit, and endeavour to serve you in this matter. I believe he is a worldly man; but as this is an only son, and the thing is now irretrievable, perhaps he may in time be brought to reason. I promise you I will do all I can for you.'

Many were the acknowledgments which the poor woman made to Allworthy for this kind and generous offer, nor could she refrain from taking this occasion again to express her gratitude towards Jones, 'to whom,' said she, 'I owe the opportunity of giving you, sir, this present trouble.' Allworthy gently stopped her; but he was too good a man to be really offended with the effects of so noble a principle as now actuated Mrs Miller; and indeed, had not this new affair inflamed his former anger against Jones, it is possible he might have been a little softened towards him, by the report of an action which malice itself could not have derived from an evil motive.

Mr Allworthy and Mrs Miller had been above an hour together, when their conversation was put an end to by the arrival of Blifil and Mr Dowling, the attorney, a great favourite with Mr Blifil, and whom Mr Allworthy, at the desire of his nephew, had made his steward; and had likewise recommended him to Mr Western, from whom the attorney received a promise of being promoted to the same office upon the first vacancy; and, in the meantime, was employed in transacting some affairs which the squire then had in London in relation to a mortgage.

This was the principal affair which then brought Mr Dowling to town; therefore he took the same opportunity to charge himself with some money for Mr Allworthy, and to make a report to him of some other business; in all which, as it was of much too dull a nature to find any place in this history, we will leave the uncle, nephew, and their lawyer concerned, and resort to Sophia.

Though that young lady had brought her aunt into great good humour by those soothing methods which we have before related, she had not brought her in the least to abate of her zeal for the match with Lord Fellamar. This zeal was now inflamed by Lady Bellaston, who had told her the preceding evening, that she was well satisfied from the conduct of Sophia, and from her carriage to his lordship, that all delays would be dangerous, and that the only way to succeed was to press the match forward with such rapidity that the young lady should have no time to reflect, and be obliged to consent while she scarce knew what she did; in which manner, she said, one-half of the marriages among people of condition were brought about.

A hint of the same kind was given by the same lady to Lord Fellamar; and both these so readily embraced the advice, that the very next day was, at his lordship's request, appointed by Mrs Western for a private interview between the young parties. This was communicated to Sophia by her aunt, and insisted upon in such high terms, that, after having urged everything she possibly could invent against it without the least effect, she at last agreed to give the highest instance of complacence which any young lady can give, and consented to see his lordship.

After his lordship had made many declarations of the most pure and ardent passion to the silent blushing Sophia, she at last collected all the spirits she could raise, and with a trembling low voice said, 'My lord, you must be yourself conscious whether your former behaviour to me hath been consistent with the professions you now make.'—'Is there,' answered he, 'no way by which I can atone for madness? what I did, I am afraid, must have too plainly convinced you, that the violence of love had deprived me of my senses.'—'Indeed, my lord,' said she, 'it is in your power to give me a proof of an affection which I much rather wish to encourage, and to which I should think myself more beholden.'—'Name it, madam,' said my lord, very warmly. 'My lord,' says she, looking down upon her fan, 'you may obtain my gratitude, my good opinion, every kind thought and wish which it is in my power to bestow; nay, you may obtain them with ease, for sure to a generous mind it must be easy to grant my request. Let me beseech you, then, to cease a pursuit in which you can never have any success. For your own sake as well as mine, I entreat this favour; for sure you are too noble to have any pleasure in tormenting an unhappy creature. What can your lordship propose but uneasiness to yourself by a perseverance, which, upon my honour, upon my soul, cannot, shall not prevail with me, whatever distresses you may drive me to.' Here my lord fetched a deep sigh, and then said: 'Is it then, madam, that I am so unhappy to be the object of your dislike and scorn; or will you pardon me if I suspect there is some other?' Here he hesitated, but he concluded his speech with saying, 'That if she had pre-engaged herself to any gentleman, however unhappy it would make him, he should think himself bound in honour to desist.' Perhaps my lord laid too much emphasis on the word gentleman; for we cannot else well account for the indignation with which he inspired Sophia, who, in her answer, seemed greatly to resent some affront he had given her.

While she was speaking, with her voice more raised than usual, Mrs Western came into the room, the fire glaring in her cheeks, and the flames bursting from her eyes. 'I am ashamed,' says she, 'my lord, of the reception which you have met with. I assure your lordship, we are all sensible of the honour done us; and I must tell you, Miss Western, the family expect a different behaviour from you.' Here my lord interfered on behalf of the young lady, but to no purpose; the aunt proceeded till Sophia pulled out her handkerchief, threw herself into a chair, and burst into a violent fit of tears.

The remainder of the conversation between Mrs Western and his lordship, till the latter withdrew, consisted of bitter lamentations on his side, and on hers of the strongest assurances that her niece should and would consent to all he wished. 'Indeed, my lord,' says she, 'the girl hath had a foolish education, neither adapted to her fortune nor her family. Her father, I am sorry to say it, is to blame for everything. The girl hath silly country notions of bashfulness. Nothing else, my lord, upon my honour; I am convinced she hath a good understanding at the bottom, and will be brought to reason.'

This last speech was made in the absence of Sophia; for she had some time before left the room, with more appearance of passion than she had ever shown on any occasion; and now his lordship, after many expressions of thanks to Mrs Western, many ardent professions of passion which nothing could conquer, and many assurances of perseverance, which Mrs Western highly encouraged, took his leave for this time.

Before we relate what now passed between Mrs Western and Sophia, it may be proper to mention an unfortunate accident which had happened, and which had occasioned the return of Mrs Western with so much fury, as we have seen.

The maid who at present attended on Sophia was recommended by Lady Bellaston, she was a very sensible girl, and had received the strictest instructions to watch her young lady very carefully. These instructions were communicated to her by Mrs Honour, into whose favour Lady Bellaston had now so ingratiated herself, that the violent affection which the good waiting-woman had formerly borne to Sophia was entirely obliterated by that great attachment which she had to her new mistress.

Now, when Mrs Miller was departed, Betty (for that was the name of the girl), returning to her young lady, found her very attentively engaged in reading a long letter, and the visible emotions which she betrayed on that occasion might have well accounted for some suspicions which the girl entertained; but indeed they had yet a stronger foundation, for she had overheard the whole scene which passed between Sophia and Mrs Miller.

Mrs Western was acquainted with all this matter by Betty, who, after receiving many commendations and some rewards for her fidelity, was ordered, that, if the woman who brought the letter came again, she should introduce her to Mrs Western herself.

Unluckily, Mrs Miller returned at the very time when Sophia was engaged with his lordship. Betty, according to order, sent her directly to the aunt; who, being mistress of so many circumstances relating to what had past the day before, easily imposed upon the poor woman to believe that Sophia had communicated the whole affair; and so pumped everything out of her which she knew relating to the letter and relating to Jones.

Mrs Western, having drained Mrs Miller of all she knew, which, indeed, was but little, but which was sufficient to make the aunt suspect a great deal, dismissed her with assurances that Sophia would not see her, that she would send no answer to the letter, nor ever receive another; nor did she suffer her to depart without a handsome lecture on the merits of an office to which she could afford no better name than that of procuress.—This discovery had greatly discomposed her temper, when, coming into the apartment next to that in which the lovers were, she overheard Sophia very warmly protesting against his lordship's addresses. At which the rage already kindled burst forth, and she rushed in upon her niece in a most furious manner, as we have already described, together with what past at that time till his lordship's departure.

No sooner was Lord Fellamar gone, than Mrs Western returned to Sophia, whom she upbraided in the most bitter terms for the ill use she had made of the confidence reposed in her; and for her treachery in conversing with a man with whom she had offered but the day before to bind herself in the most solemn oath never more to have any conversation. Sophia protested she had maintained no such conversation. 'How, how! Miss Western,' said the aunt; 'will you deny your receiving a letter from him yesterday?'—'A letter, madam!' answered Sophia, somewhat surprized. 'It is not very well bred, miss,' replies the aunt, 'to repeat my words. I say a letter, and I insist upon your showing it me immediately.'—'I scorn a lie, madam,' said Sophia; 'I did receive a letter, but it was without my desire, and, indeed, I may say, against my consent.'—'Indeed, indeed, miss,' cries the aunt, 'you ought to be ashamed of owning you had received it at all; but where is the letter? for I will see it.'

To this peremptory demand, Sophia paused some time before she returned an answer; and at last only excused herself by declaring she had not the letter in her pocket, which was, indeed, true; upon which her aunt, losing all manner of patience, asked her niece this short question, whether she would resolve to marry Lord Fellamar, or no? to which she received the strongest negative. Mrs Western then replied with an oath, or something very like one, that she would early the next morning deliver her back into her father's hand.

Sophia then began to reason with her aunt in the following manner: 'Why, madam, must I of necessity be forced to marry at all? Consider how cruel you would have thought it in your own case, and how much kinder your parents were in leaving you to your liberty. What have I done to forfeit this liberty? I will never marry contrary to my father's consent, nor without asking yours ——And when I ask the consent of either improperly, it will be then time enough to force some other marriage upon me.'—'Can I bear to hear this,' cries Mrs Western, 'from a girl who hath now a letter from a murderer in her pocket?'—'I have no such letter, I promise you,' answered Sophia; 'and, if he be a murderer, he will soon be in no condition to give you any further disturbance.'—'How, Miss Western!' said the aunt, 'have you the assurance to speak of him in this manner; to own your affection for such a villain to my face?'—'Sure, madam,' said Sophia, 'you put a very strange construction on my words.'—'Indeed, Miss Western,' cries the lady, 'I shall not bear this usage; you have learnt of your father this manner of treating me; he hath taught you to give me the lie. He hath totally ruined you by this false system of education; and, please heaven, he shall have the comfort of its fruits; for once more I declare to you, that to-morrow morning I will carry you back.'

Sophia remonstrated all she could; but her aunt was deaf to all she said. In this resolution therefore we must at present leave her, as there seems to be no hopes of bringing her to change it.

CHAPTER FORTY-ONE

WHAT HAPPENED TO MR JONES IN THE PRISON

Mr Jones passed about twenty-four melancholy hours by himself, unless when relieved by the company of Partridge, before Mr Nightingale returned; not that this worthy young man had deserted or forgot his friend; for, indeed, he had been much the greatest part of the time employed in his service.

He had heard, upon inquiry, that the only persons who had seen the beginning of the unfortunate encounter were a crew belonging to a man-of-war which then lay at Deptford. To Deptford therefore he went in search of this crew, where he was informed that the men he sought after were all gone ashore. He then traced them from place to place, till at last he found two of them drinking together, with a third person, at a hedge-tavern near Aldersgate.

Nightingale desired to speak with Jones by himself (for Partridge was in the room when he came in). As soon as they were alone, Nightingale, taking Jones by the hand, cried, 'Come, my brave friend, be not too much dejected at what I am going to tell you——I am sorry I am the messenger of bad news; but I think it is my duty to tell you.'—'I guess already what that bad news is,' cries Jones. 'The poor gentleman then is dead.'——'I hope not,' answered Nightingale. 'He was alive this morning; though I will not flatter you; I fear, from the accounts I could get, that his wound is mortal. But if the affair be exactly as you told it, your own remorse would be all you would have reason to apprehend, let what would happen; but forgive me, my dear Tom, if I entreat you to make the worst of your story to your friends. If you disguise anything to us, you will only be an enemy to yourself.'

'What reason, my dear Jack, have I ever given you,' said Jones, 'to stab me with so cruel a suspicion?'—'Have patience,' cries Nightingale, 'and I will tell you all. After the most diligent inquiry I could make, I at last met with two of the fellows who were present at this unhappy accident, and I am sorry to say, they do not relate the story so much in your favour as you yourself have told it.'—'Why, what do they say?' cries Jones. 'Indeed what I am sorry to repeat, as I am afraid of the consequence of it to you. They say that they were at too great a distance to overhear any words that passed between you: but they both agree that the first blow was given by you.'—'Then, upon my soul,' answered Jones, 'they injure me. He not only struck me first, but struck me without the least provocation. What should induce those villains to accuse me falsely?'—'Nay, that I cannot guess,' said Nightingale, 'and if you yourself, and I, who am so heartily your friend, cannot conceive a reason why they should belie you, what reason will an indifferent court of justice be able to assign why they should not believe them? For heaven's sake, my dear friend, recollect yourself; for, if this should appear to be the fact, it will be your business to think in time of making the best of your interest. I would not shock you; but you know, I believe, the severity of the law, whatever verbal provocations may have been given you.'—'Alas! my friend,' cries Jones, 'what interest hath such a wretch as I? Besides, do you think I would even wish

211

to live with the reputation of a murderer? If I had any friends could I have the confidence to solicit them to speak in the behalf of a man condemned for the blackest crime in human nature? Believe me, I have no such hope; but I have some reliance on a throne still greatly superior; which will, I am certain, afford me all the protection I merit.'

He then concluded with many solemn and vehement protestations of the truth of what he had at first asserted.

The faith of Nightingale was now again staggered, and began to incline to credit his friend, when Mrs Miller appeared, and made a sorrowful report of the success of her embassy; which when Jones had heard, he cried out most heroically, 'Well, my friend, I am now indifferent as to what shall happen, at least with regard to my life; and if it be the will of Heaven that I shall make an atonement with that for the blood I have spilt, I hope the Divine Goodness will one day suffer my honour to be cleared, and that the words of a dying man, at least, will be believed, so far as to justify his character.'

A very mournful scene now past between the prisoner and his friends, until the entrance of the turnkey, who acquainted Jones that there was a lady without who desired to speak with him when he was at leisure.

Jones declared his surprize at this message. He said, 'He knew no lady in the world whom he could possibly expect to see there.' However, as he saw no reason to decline seeing any person, Mrs Miller and Mr Nightingale presently took their leave, and he gave orders to have the lady admitted.

If Jones was surprized at the news of a visit from a lady, how greatly was he astonished when he discovered this lady to be no other than Mrs Waters!

Who this Mrs Waters was, the reader pretty well knows; he will therefore be pleased to remember that this lady departed from Upton in the same coach with Mr Fitzpatrick and the other Irish gentleman, and in their company travelled to Bath.

Now there was a certain office in the gift of Mr Fitzpatrick at that time vacant, namely that of a wife: for the lady who had lately filled that office had resigned, or at least deserted her duty. Mr Fitzpatrick therefore, having thoroughly examined Mrs Waters on the road, found her extremely fit for the place, which, on their arrival at Bath, he presently conferred upon her, and she without any scruple accepted. As husband and wife this gentleman and lady continued together all the time they stayed at Bath, and as husband and wife they arrived together in town.

Whether Mr Fitzpatrick was so wise a man as not to part with one good thing till he had secured another, which he had at present only a prospect of regaining; or whether Mrs Waters had so well discharged her office, that he intended still to retain her as principal, and to make his wife (as is often the case) only her deputy, I will not say; but certain it is, he never mentioned his wife to her, nor ever once hinted his purpose of repossessing his wife; much less did he ever mention the name of Jones.

As Mr Fitzpatrick, however, had not the clearest way of telling a story at any time, and was now, perhaps, a little more confused than usual, it was some time before she discovered that the gentleman who had given him this wound was the very same person from whom her heart had received a wound, which, though not of a mortal kind, was yet so deep that it had left a considerable scar behind it. But no sooner was she acquainted that Mr Jones himself was the man who had been committed to the Gatehouse for this supposed murder, than she took the first opportunity of committing Mr Fitzpatrick to the care of his nurse, and hastened away to visit the conqueror.

She now entered the room with an air of gaiety, which received an immediate check from the melancholy aspect of poor Jones, who started and blessed himself when he saw her. Upon which he said, 'Nay, I do not wonder at your surprize; I believe you did not expect to see me; for few gentlemen are troubled here with visits from any lady, unless a wife. Indeed, I little thought, when we parted at Upton, that our next meeting would have been in such a place.'—'Indeed, madam,' says Jones, 'I must look upon this visit as kind; few will follow the melancholy, especially to such dismal habitations.'—'I protest, Mr Jones,' says she, 'I can hardly persuade myself you are the same agreeable fellow I saw at Upton. Why, your face is more miserable than any dungeon in the universe. What can be the matter with you?'—'I thought, madam,' said Jones, 'as you knew of my being here, you knew the unhappy reason.'—'Pugh!' says she, 'you have pinked a man in a duel, that's all.' Jones exprest some indignation at this levity, and spoke with the utmost contrition for what had happened. To which she answered, 'Well, then, sir, if you take it so much to heart, I will relieve you; the gentleman is not dead, and, I am pretty confident, is in no danger of dying. The surgeon, indeed, says, unless from a fever, of which there are at present no symptoms, he apprehends not the least danger of life.' Jones shewed great satisfaction at this report; upon which she affirmed the truth of it, adding, 'By the most extraordinary accident in the world I lodge at the same house; and have seen the gentleman, and I promise you he doth you justice, and says, whatever be the consequence, that he was entirely the aggressor, and that you was not in the least to blame.'

Jones expressed the utmost satisfaction at the account which Mrs Waters brought him. He told her several facts of which she was ignorant, as the adventure of the muff, and other particulars, concealing only the name of Sophia. He then lamented the follies and vices of which he had been guilty; every one of which, he said, had been attended with such ill consequences, that he should be unpardonable if he did not take warning, and quit those vicious courses for the future. He lastly concluded with assuring her of his resolution to sin no more, lest a worse thing should happen to him.

Mrs Waters with great pleasantry ridiculed all this, as the effects of low spirits and confinement. She repeated some witticisms about the devil when he was sick, and told him, 'She doubted not but shortly to see him at liberty, and as lively a fellow as ever; and then,' says she, 'I don't question but your conscience will be safely delivered of all these qualms that it is now so sick in breeding.'

Many more things of this kind she uttered, some of which it would do her no great honour, and it ended at last with perfect innocence, and much more to the satisfaction of Jones than of the lady; for the former was greatly transported with the news she had brought him; but the latter was not altogether so pleased with the penitential behaviour of a man whom she had, at her first interview, conceived a very different opinion of from what she now entertained of him.

Thus the melancholy occasioned by the report of Mr Nightingale was pretty well effaced; but the dejection into which Mrs Miller had thrown him still continued. The account she gave so well tallied with the words of Sophia herself in her letter, that he made not the least doubt but that she had disclosed his letter to her aunt, and had taken a fixed resolution to abandon him.

While Jones was employed in those unpleasant meditations, Partridge came stumbling into the room with his face paler than ashes, his eyes fixed in his head, his hair standing on end, and every limb trembling. In short, he looked as he would have done had he seen a spectre, or had he, indeed, been a spectre himself.

Jones, who was little subject to fear, could not avoid being somewhat shocked at this sudden appearance. He did, indeed, himself change colour, and his voice a little faltered while he asked him, What was the matter?

'I hope, sir,' said Partridge, 'you will not be angry with me. Indeed I did not listen, but I was obliged to stay in the outward room. I am sure I wish I had been a hundred miles off, rather than have heard what I have heard.'—'Why, what is the matter?' said Jones. 'The matter, sir? O good Heaven!' answered Partridge, 'was that woman who is just gone out the woman who was with you at Upton?'—'She was, Partridge,' cried Jones. 'And did you really, sir, go to bed with that woman?' said he, trembling. 'I am afraid what past between us is no secret,' said Jones. 'Nay, but pray, sir, for Heaven's sake, sir, answer me,' cries Partridge. 'You know I did,' cries Jones. 'Why then, the Lord have mercy

214

upon your soul, and forgive you,' cries Partridge; 'but as sure as I stand here alive, you have been a-bed with your own mother.'

Upon these words Jones became in a moment a greater picture of horror than Partridge himself. He was, indeed, for some time struck dumb with amazement, and both stood staring wildly at each other. At last his words found way, and in an interrupted voice he said, 'How! how! what's this you tell me?'—'Nay, sir,' cries Partridge, 'I have not breath enough left to tell you now, but what I have said is most certainly true.—That woman who now went out is your own mother. How unlucky was it for you, sir, that I did not happen to see her at that time, to have prevented it! Sure the devil himself must have contrived to bring about this wickedness.'

'Sure,' cries Jones, 'what thou hast told me, Partridge, hath almost deprived me of my senses! And was Mrs Waters, then— but why do I ask? for thou must certainly know her——If thou hast any affection for me, nay, if thou hast any pity, let me beseech thee to fetch this miserable woman back again to me. O good Heavens! incest——with a mother! To what am I reserved!' He then fell into the most violent and frantic agonies of grief and despair, in which Partridge declared he would not leave him; but at last, having vented the first torrent of passion, he came a little to himself; and then, having acquainted Partridge that he would find this wretched woman in the same house where the wounded gentleman was lodged, he dispatched him in quest of her.

After a fruitless search of two or three hours, Partridge returned back to his master, without having seen Mrs Waters. Jones, who was in a state of desperation at his delay, was almost raving mad when he brought him his account. He was not long, however, in this condition before he received the following letter:

'SIR,

'Since I left you I have seen a gentleman, from whom I have learned something concerning you which greatly surprizes and affects me; but as I have not at present leisure to communicate a matter of such high importance, you must suspend your curiosity till our next meeting, which shall be the first moment I am able to see you. O, Mr Jones, little did I think, when I past that happy day at Upton, the reflection upon which is like to embitter all my future life, who it was to whom I owed such perfect happiness. Believe me to be ever sincerely your unfortunate.

'J. WATERS.

'P.S.—I would have you comfort yourself as much as possible, for Mr Fitzpatrick is in no manner of danger; so that whatever other grievous crimes you may have to repent of, the guilt of blood is not among the number.'

Jones having read the letter, let it drop (for he was unable to hold it, and indeed had scarce the use of any one of his faculties). Partridge took it up, and having received consent by silence, read it likewise; nor had it upon him a less sensible effect. While they both remained speechless, the turnkey entered the room, and, without taking any notice of what sufficiently discovered itself in the faces of them both, acquainted Jones that a man without desired to speak with him. This person was presently introduced, and was no other than Black George.

As sights of horror were not so usual to George as they were to the turnkey, he instantly saw the great disorder which appeared in the face of Jones. This he imputed to the accident that had happened, which was reported in the very worst light in Mr Western's family; he concluded, therefore, that the gentleman was dead, and that Mr Jones was in a fair way of coming to a shameful end.

The poor fellow, therefore, scarce refrained from a tear at the present sight. He told Jones he was heartily sorry for his misfortunes, and begged him to consider if he could be of any manner of service. 'Perhaps, sir,' said he, 'you may want a little matter of money upon this occasion; if you do, sir, what little I have is heartily at your service.'

Jones shook him very heartily by the hand, and gave him many thanks for the kind offer he had made; but answered, 'He had not the least want of that kind.' Upon which George began to press his services more eagerly than before. Jones again thanked him, with assurances that he wanted nothing which was in the power of any living man to give. 'Come, come, my good master,' answered George, 'do not take the matter so much to heart. Things may end better than you imagine; to be sure you an't the first gentleman who hath killed a man, and yet come off.'—'You are wide of the matter, George,' said Partridge, 'the gentleman is not dead, nor like to die. Don't disturb my master, at present, for he is troubled about a matter in which it is not in your power to do him any good.'—'You don't know what I may be able to do, Mr Partridge,' answered George; 'if his concern is about my young lady, I have some news to tell my master.'—'What do you say, Mr George?' cried Jones. 'Hath anything lately happened in which my Sophia is concerned? My Sophia! how dare such a wretch as I mention her so profanely!'—'I hope she will be yours yet,' answered George. 'Why yes, sir, I have something to tell you about her. Madam Western hath just brought Madam Sophia home, and there hath been a terrible to do. I could not possibly learn the very right of it; but my master he hath been in a vast big passion, and so was Madam Western, and I heard her say as she went out of doors into her chair, that she would never set foot in master's house again. I don't know what's the matter, not

216

I, but everything was very quiet when I came out; but Robin, who waited at supper, said he had never seen the squire for a long while in such good humour with young madam; that he kissed her several times, and swore she should be her own mistress, and he never would think of confining her any more. I thought this news would please you, and so I slipped out, though it was so late, to inform you of it.' Mr Jones assured George that it did greatly please him; for though he should never more presume to lift his eyes towards that incomparable creature, nothing could so much relieve his misery as the satisfaction he should always have in hearing of her welfare.

The reader will be pleased to hear how this great goodwill of the squire towards his daughter was brought about.

Mrs Western, on her first arrival at her brother's lodging, began to set forth the great honours and advantages which would accrue to the family by the match with Lord Fellamar, which her niece had absolutely refused; in which refusal, when the squire took the part of his daughter, she fell immediately into the most violent passion, and so irritated and provoked the squire, that neither his patience nor his prudence could bear it any longer; upon which there ensued between them both so warm a bout at altercation, that perhaps the regions of Billingsgate never equalled it.

When Mrs Western was gone, Sophia, who had been hitherto silent, as well indeed from necessity as inclination, began to return the compliment which her father had made her, in taking her part against her aunt, by taking his likewise against the lady. This was the first time of her so doing, and it was in the highest degree acceptable to the squire. Again, he remembered that Mr Allworthy had insisted on an entire relinquishment of all violent means; and, indeed, as he made no doubt but that Jones would be hanged, he did not in the least question succeeding with his daughter by fair means; he now, therefore, once more gave a loose to his natural fondness for her, which had such an effect on the dutiful, grateful, tender, and affectionate heart of Sophia, that had her honour, given to Jones, and something else, perhaps, in which he was concerned, been removed, I much doubt whether she would not have sacrificed herself to a man she did not like, to have obliged her father. She promised him she would make it the whole business of her life to oblige him, and would never marry any man against his consent; which brought the old man so near to his highest happiness, that he was resolved to take the other step, and went to bed completely drunk.

CHAPTER FORTY-TWO

ALLWORTHY VISITS OLD NIGHTINGALE

THE morning after these things had happened, Mr Allworthy went, according to his promise, to visit old Nightingale, with whom his authority was so great, that, after having sat with him three hours, he at last prevailed with him to consent to see his son.

Here an accident happened of a very extraordinary kind; Mr Allworthy, at his entrance into Mr Nightingale's, saw Black George; he took no notice of him, nor did Black George imagine he had perceived him.

However, when their conversation on the principal point was over, Allworthy asked Nightingale, 'Whether he knew one George Seagrim, and upon what business he came to his house? 'Yes,' answered Nightingale, 'I know him very well, and a most extraordinary fellow he is, who, in these days, hath been able to hoard up £500 from renting a very small estate of £30 a-year.'—'And this is the story which he hath told you?' cries Allworthy. 'Nay, it is true, I promise you,' said Nightingale, 'for I have the money now in my own hands, in five bank-bills, which I am to lay out either in a mortgage, or in some purchase in the north of England.' The bank-bills were no sooner produced at Allworthy's desire, than he blessed himself at the strangeness of the discovery. He presently told Nightingale that these bank-bills were formerly his, and then acquainted him with the whole affair. Nightingale no sooner heard the story than he exclaimed against the fellow in terms much severer than the justice and honesty of Allworthy had bestowed on him.

Allworthy desired Nightingale to retain both the money and the secret till he should hear farther from him; and, if he should in the meantime see the fellow, that he would not take the least notice to him of the discovery which he had made. He then returned to his lodgings, where he found Mrs Miller in a very dejected condition, on account of the information she had received from her son-in-law. Mr Allworthy, with great cheerfulness, told her that he had much good news to communicate; and, with little further preface, acquainted her that he had brought Mr Nightingale to consent to see his son, and did not in the least doubt to effect a perfect reconciliation between them.

Mrs Miller received this account with great thankfulness, and no less pleasure; but so uncommon was her friendship to Jones, that I am not certain whether the uneasiness she suffered for his sake did not overbalance her satisfaction at hearing a piece of news tending so much to the happiness of her own family; nor whether even this very news, as it reminded her of the obligations she had to Jones, did not hurt as well as please her; when her grateful heart said to her, 'While my own family is happy, how miserable is the poor creature to whose generosity we owe the beginning of all this happiness!'

Allworthy told her he had still something more to impart, which he believed would give her pleasure. 'I think,' said he, 'I have discovered a pretty considerable treasure belonging to the young gentleman, your friend; but perhaps, indeed, his present situation may be such that it will be of no service to him.' The latter part of the speech gave Mrs Miller to understand who was meant, and she answered with a sigh, 'I hope not, sir.'—'I hope so too,' cries Allworthy, 'with all my heart; but my nephew told me this morning he had heard a very bad account of the affair.'—— 'Good Heaven! sir,' said she—'Well, I must not speak, and yet it is certainly very hard to be obliged to hold one's tongue when one hears.'——'Madam,' said Allworthy, 'you may say whatever you please, you know me too well to think I have a prejudice against any one; and as for that young man, I assure you I should be heartily pleased to find he could acquit himself of everything, and particularly of this sad affair. You can testify the affection I have formerly borne him. The world, I know, censured me for loving him so much. I did not withdraw that affection from him without thinking I had the justest cause. Believe me, Mrs Miller, I should be glad to find I have been mistaken.' Mrs Miller was going eagerly to reply, when a servant acquainted her that a gentleman without desired to speak with her immediately. Allworthy then inquired for his nephew, and was told that he had been for some time in his room with the gentleman who used to come to him, and whom Mr Allworthy guessing rightly to be Mr Dowling, he desired presently to speak with him.

When Dowling attended, Allworthy put the case of the banknotes to him, without mentioning any name, and asked in what manner such a person might be punished. To which Dowling answered, 'He thought he might be indicted on the Black Act; but said, as it was a matter of some nicety, it would be proper to go to counsel. He said he was to attend counsel presently upon an affair of Mr Western's, and if Mr Allworthy pleased he would lay the case before them.' This was agreed to; and then Mrs Miller, opening the door, cried, 'I ask pardon, I did not know you had company'; but Allworthy desired her to come in, saying he had finished his business. Upon which Mr Dowling withdrew, and Mrs Miller introduced Mr Nightingale the younger, to return thanks for the great kindness done him by Allworthy: but she had scarce patience to let the young gentleman finish his speech before she interrupted him, saying, 'O sir! Mr Nightingale brings great news about poor Mr Jones: he hath been to see the wounded gentleman, who is out of all danger of death, and, what is more, declares he fell upon poor Mr Jones himself, and beat him. I am sure, sir, you would not have Mr Jones be a coward. If I was a man myself, I am sure, if any man was to strike me, I should draw my sword. Do pray, my dear, tell Mr Allworthy, tell him all yourself.' Nightingale then confirmed what Mrs Miller had said; and concluded with many handsome things of Jones, who was, he said, one of the best-natured fellows in the world, and not in the least inclined to be quarrelsome. Here Nightingale was going to cease, when Mrs Miller again begged him to relate all the many dutiful expressions he had heard him make use of towards Mr Allworthy. 'To say the utmost good of Mr Allworthy,' cries Nightingale, 'is doing no more than strict justice, and can have no merit in it: but indeed, I must say, no man can be more sensible of the obligations he hath to so good a man than is poor Jones. Indeed, sir, I am convinced the weight of your displeasure is the heaviest burthen he lies under. But I ask pardon, sir, I am afraid I presume to intermeddle too far in so tender a point.' 'Indeed, Mr Nightingale,' answered Allworthy, 'I applaud your generous friendship, and I wish he may merit it of you. I confess I am glad to hear the report you bring from this unfortunate gentleman; and, I may, perhaps, in time, be brought to think better than lately I have of this young man; for this good gentlewoman here, nay, all who know me, can witness that I loved him as dearly as if he had been my own son. Indeed, I have considered him as a child sent by fortune to my care. I still remember the innocent, the helpless situation in which I found him. I feel the tender pressure of his little hands at this moment. He was my darling, indeed he was.' At which words he ceased, and the tears stood in his eyes.

As the answer which Mrs Miller made may lead us into fresh matters, we will here stop to account for the visible alteration in Mr Allworthy's mind, and the abatement of his anger to Jones.

This alteration was occasioned by a letter he had just received from Mr Square.

'MY WORTHY FRIEND,—I informed you in my last that I was forbidden the use of the waters, as they were found by experience rather to increase than lessen the symptoms of my distemper. I must now acquaint you with a piece of news, which, I believe, will afflict my friends more than it hath afflicted me. Dr Harrington and Dr Brewster have informed me that there is no hopes of my recovery.

'I have somewhere read, that the great use of philosophy is to learn to die. I will not therefore so far disgrace mine, as to show any surprize at receiving a lesson which I must be thought to have so long studied.

'When I reflect on the actions of my past life, I know of nothing which sits heavier upon my conscience than the injustice I have been guilty of to that poor wretch, your adopted son. I have, indeed, not only connived at the villany of others, but been myself active in injustice towards him. Believe me my dear friend, when I tell you, on the word of a dying man, he hath been basely injured. As to the principal fact, upon the misrepresentation of which you discarded him, I solemnly assure you he is innocent. When you lay upon your supposed death-bed, he was the only person in the house who testified any real concern; and what happened afterwards arose from the wildness of his joy on your recovery; and, I am sorry to say it, from the baseness of another person (but it is my desire to justify the innocent, and to accuse none). Believe me, my friend, this young man hath the noblest generosity of heart, the most perfect capacity for friendship, the highest integrity, and indeed every virtue which can ennoble a man. He hath some faults, but among them is not to be numbered the least want of duty or gratitude towards you. On the contrary, I am satisfied, when you dismissed him from your house, his heart bled for you more than for himself.

'Worldly motives were the wicked and base reasons of my concealing this from you so long: to reveal it now I can have no inducement but the desire of serving the cause of truth, of doing right to the innocent, and of making all the amends in my power for a past offence. I hope this declaration, therefore, will have the effect desired, and will restore this deserving young man to your favour; the hearing of which, while I am yet alive, will afford the utmost consolation to,

Sir,

Your most obliged,

obedient humble servant,

THOMAS SQUARE.'

The reader will, after this, scarce wonder at the revolution so visibly appearing in Mr Allworthy, notwithstanding he received from Thwackum, by the same post, another letter of a very different kind, which we shall here add, as it may possibly be the last time we shall have occasion to mention the name of that gentleman.

'SIR,
'I am not at all surprized at hearing from your worthy nephew a fresh instance of the villany of Mr Square's young pupil. I shall not wonder at any murders he may commit; and I

heartily pray that your own blood may not seal up his final com
mitment to the place of wailing and gnashing of teeth.

'Had not my hand been withheld from due correction, I ha
scourged much of this diabolical spirit out of a boy, of whom
from his infancy, I discovered the devil had taken such entir
possession. But reflections of this kind now come too late.

'I am sorry you have given away the living of Western s
hastily. I should have applied on that occasion earlier, had
thought you would not have acquainted me previous to the dis
position.——Your objection to pluralities is being righteous over
much. If there were any crime in the practice, so many godl
men would not agree to it. If the vicar of Aldergrove should di
(as we hear he is in a declining way), I hope you will think of me
since I am certain you must be convinced of my most sincer
attachment to your highest welfare—a welfare to which al
worldly considerations are as trifling as the small tithes mentione
in Scripture are, when compared to the weighty matters of th
law.

> I am, sir,
> Your faithful humble servant,
> ROGER THWACKUM.'

This was the first time Thwackum ever wrote in this authorita
tive stile to Allworthy, and of this he had afterwards sufficien
reason to repent, as in the case of those who mistake the highes
degree of goodness for the lowest degree of weakness. Allworth
had indeed never liked this man. He knew him to be proud an
ill-natured; but he was at the same time an excellent scholar, an
most indefatigable in teaching the two lads. So that, upon th
whole, though Allworthy did not esteem nor love the man, yet h
could never bring himself to part with a tutor to the boys, wh
was, both by learning and industry, extremely well qualified fc
his office; and he hoped, that as they were bred up in his ow
house, and under his own eye, he should be able to correct what
ever was wrong in Thwackum's instructions.

CHAPTER FORTY-THREE

MR ALLWORTHY, in his last speech, had recollected some tender ideas concerning Jones, which had brought tears into the good man's eyes. This Mrs Miller observing, said, 'Yes, yes, sir, your goodness to this poor young man is known, notwithstanding all your care to conceal it; but there is not a single syllable of truth in what those villains said. Mr Nightingale hath now discovered the whole matter. It seems these fellows were employed by a lord, who is a rival of poor Mr Jones, to have pressed him on board a ship.——I assure them I don't know who they will press next. Mr Nightingale here hath seen the officer himself, who is a very pretty gentleman, and hath told him all, and is very sorry for what he undertook, which he would never have done, had he known Mr Jones to have been a gentleman; but he was told that he was a common strolling vagabond.'

Allworthy stared at all this, and declared he was a stranger to every word she said. 'Yes, sir,' answered she, 'I believe you are.—— It is a very different story, I believe, from what those fellows told the lawyer.'

'What lawyer, madam? what is it you mean?' said Allworthy. 'Nay, nay,' said she, 'this is so like you to deny your own goodness: but Mr Nightingale here saw him.'—'Saw whom, madam?' answered he. 'Why, your lawyer, sir,' said she, 'that you so kindly sent to inquire into the affair.'—'I am still in the dark, upon my honour,' said Allworthy. 'Why then do you tell him, my dear sir,' cries she. 'Indeed, sir,' said Nightingale, 'I did see that very lawyer who went from you when I came into the room, at an ale-house in Aldersgate, in company with two of the fellows who were employed by Lord Fellamar to press Mr Jones, and who were by that means present at the unhappy encounter between him and Mr Fitzpatrick.'—'I own, sir,' said Mrs Miller, 'when I saw this gentleman come into the room to you, I told Mr Nightingale that I apprehended you had sent him thither to inquire into the affair.' Allworthy showed marks of astonishment in his countenance at this news, and was indeed for two or three minutes struck dumb by it. At last, addressing himself to Mr Nightingale, he said, 'I must confess myself, sir, more surprized at what you tell me than I have ever been before at anything in my whole life. Are you certain this was the gentleman?'—'I am most certain,' answered Nightingale. 'At Aldersgate?' cries Allworthy. 'And was you in company with this lawyer and the two fellows?'—'I was, sir,' said the other, 'very near half an hour.'—'Well, sir,' said Allworthy, 'and in what manner did the lawyer behave? did you hear all that past between him and the fellows?'—'No, sir,' answered Nightingale, 'they had been together before I came. —In my presence the lawyer said little; but, after I had several times examined the fellows, who persisted in a story directly contrary to what I had heard from Mr Jones, and which I find by Mr Fitzpatrick was a rank falshood, the lawyer then desired the fellows to say nothing but what was the truth, and seemed to speak so much in favour of Mr Jones, that, when I saw the same person with you, I concluded your goodness had prompted you to send him thither.'—'And did you not send him thither?' says Mrs Miller. 'Indeed I did not,' answered Allworthy; 'nor did I know he had gone on such an errand till this moment.'—'I see it all!' said Mrs Miller, 'upon my soul, I see it all! No wonder they have been closeted so close lately. Son Nightingale, let me beg you run for these fellows immediately——find them out if they are above-ground. I will go myself.'——'Dear madam,' said Allworthy, 'be patient, and do me the favour to send a servant up-stairs to call Mr Dowling hither, if he be in the house, or, if not, Mr Blifil.' Mrs Miller went out muttering something to herself, and presently returned with an answer, 'That Mr Dowling was gone; but that the t'other,' as she called him, 'was coming.'

Allworthy was of a cooler disposition than the good woman, whose spirits were all up in arms in the cause of her friend. He was not, however, without some suspicions which were near akin to hers. When Blifil came into the room, he asked him with a very serious countenance, and with a less friendly look than he had ever before given him, 'Whether he knew anything of Mr Dowling's having seen any of the persons who were present at the duel between Jones and another gentleman?'

There is nothing so dangerous as a question which comes by surprize on a man whose business it is to conceal truth, or to defend falshood. Besides, the sudden and violent impulse on the blood, occasioned by these surprizes, causes frequently such an alteration in the countenance, that the man is obliged to give evidence against himself. And such indeed were the alterations which the countenance of Blifil underwent from this sudden question, that we can scarce blame the eagerness of Mrs Miller, who immediately cryed out, 'Guilty, upon my honour! guilty, upon my soul!'

Mr Allworthy sharply rebuked her for this impetuosity; and then turning to Blifil, who seemed sinking into the earth, he said, 'Why do you hesitate, sir, at giving me an answer? You certainly must have employed him; for he would not, of his own accord, I believe, have undertaken such an errand, and especially without acquainting me.'

Blifil then answered, 'I own, sir, I have been guilty of an offence, yet may I hope your pardon?'——'My pardon,' said Allworthy, very angrily.——'Nay, sir,' answered Blifil, 'I knew you would be offended; yet surely my dear uncle will forgive the effects of the most amiable of human weaknesses. Compassion for those who do not deserve it, I own is a crime; and I will own I did send Mr Dowling, not on a vain and fruitless inquiry, but to discover the witnesses, and to endeavour to soften their evidence. This, sir, is the truth; which, though I intended to conceal from you, I will not deny.'

'I confess,' said Nightingale, 'this is the light in which it appeared to me from the gentleman's behaviour.'

'Now, madam,' said Allworthy, 'I believe you will once in your life own you have entertained a wrong suspicion, and are not so angry with my nephew as you was.'

Mrs Miller was silent; for, though she could not so hastily be pleased with Blifil, whom she looked upon to have been the ruin of Jones, yet in this particular instance he had imposed upon her as well as upon the rest; so entirely had the devil stood his friend.

As health is more perfectly established by recovery from some diseases; so anger, when removed, often gives new life to affection. This was the case of Mr Allworthy; for Blifil having wiped off the greater suspicion, the lesser, which had been raised by Square's letter, sunk of course, and was forgotten; and Thwackum, with whom he was greatly offended, bore alone all the reflections which Square had cast on the enemies of Jones.

As for that young man, the resentment of Mr Allworthy began more and more to abate towards him. He told Blifil, 'He did not only forgive the extraordinary efforts of his good nature, but would give him the pleasure of following his example.' Then, turning to Mrs Miller with a smile which would have become an angel, he cryed, 'What say you, madam? shall we take a hackney-coach, and all of us together pay a visit to your friend? I promise you it is not the first visit I have made in a prison.'

Few, I hope, are capable of feeling what now passed in the mind of Blifil; but those who are, will acknowledge, that it was impossible for him to raise any objection to this visit. Fortune, however, stood his friend, and prevented his undergoing so great a shock; for at the very instant when the coach was sent for, Partridge arrived, and, having called Mrs Miller from the company, acquainted her with the dreadful accident lately come to light; and hearing Mr Allworthy's intention, begged her to find some means of stopping him: 'For,' says he, 'the matter must at all hazards be kept a secret from him; and if she should now go, he will find Mr Jones and his mother, who arrived just as I left him, lamenting over one another the horrid crime thay have ignorantly committed.'

The poor woman, who was almost deprived of her senses at his dreadful news, was never less capable of invention than at present. However, as women are much readier at this than men, she bethought herself of an excuse, and, returning to Allworthy, said, 'I am sure, sir, you will be surprized at hearing any objection from me to the kind proposal you just now made; and yet I am afraid of the consequence of it, if carried immediately into execution. You must imagine, sir, that all the calamities which have lately befallen this poor young fellow must have thrown him into the lowest dejection of spirits; and now, sir, should we all on a sudden fling him into such a violent fit of joy, as I know your presence will occasion, it may, I am afraid, produce some fatal mischief, especially as his servant, who is without, tells me he is very far from being well.'

'Is his servant without?' cries Allworthy; 'pray call him hither. I will ask him some questions concerning his master.'

Partridge was at first afraid to appear before Mr Allworthy; but was at length persuaded, after Mrs Miller, who had often heard his whole story from his own mouth, had promised to introduce him.

Allworthy recollected Partridge the moment he came into the room, though many years had passed since he had seen him.

'And are you,' said Allworthy to Partridge, 'the servant of Mr Jones?'—'I can't say, sir,' answered he, 'that I am regularly a servant, but I live with him, an't please your honour, at present *Non sum qualis eram,* as your honour very well knows.'

Mr Allworthy then asked him many questions concerning Jones, as to his health, and other matters; to all which Partridge answered, without having the least regard to what was, but considered only what he would have things appear; for a strict adherence to truth was not among the articles of this honest fellow's morality, or his religion.

During this dialogue Mr Nightingale took his leave, and presently after Mrs Miller left the room, when Allworthy likewise dispatched Blifil; for he imagined that Partridge, when alone with him, would be more explicit than before company.

'Sure, friend,' said the good man, 'you are the strangest of all human beings. Not only to have suffered as you have formerly for obstinate persisting in a falshood, but to persist in it thus to the last, and to pass thus upon the world for a servant of your own son! What interest can you have in all this? What can be your motive?'

'I see, sir,' said Partridge, 'that your honour is prepossessed against me, and resolved not to believe anything I say, and, therefore, what signifies my protestations? but yet there is one above who knows that I am not the father of this young man.'

'How!' said Allworthy, 'will you yet deny what you was formerly convicted of upon such unanswerable, such manifest evidence? Nay, what a confirmation is your being now found with this very man, of all which twenty years ago appeared against you! I thought you had left the country! nay, I thought you had been long since dead.—In what manner did you know anything of this young man?'

'If your honour will have patience to hear me,' said Partridge, 'I will tell you all.' Being bid go on, he proceeded thus: 'When your honour conceived that displeasure against me, it ended in my ruin soon after; for I lost my little school; and the minister, thinking, I suppose, it would be agreeable to your honour, turned me out from the office of clerk; so that I had nothing to trust to but the barber's shop, which, in a country place like that, is a poor livelihood; and when my wife died (for till that time I received a pension of £12 a-year from an unknown hand, which indeed I believe was your honour's own, for nobody that ever I heard of doth these things besides)—but, as I was saying, when she died, this pension forsook me; so that now, as I owed two or three small debts, which began to be troublesome to me, and as I found all my usual means of living had forsook me, I packed up my little all as well as I could, and went off.

'The first place I came to was Salisbury, where I got into the service of a gentleman belonging to the law, and one of the best gentlemen that ever I knew, for he was not only good to me, but I know a thousand good and charitable acts which he did and I have known him often refuse business because it was paltry and oppressive.'—'You need not be so particular,' said Allworthy; 'I know this gentleman, and a very worthy man he is, and an honour to his profession.'——'Well, sir,' continued Partridge, 'From hence I removed to Lymington, where I was above three years in the service of another lawyer, who was likewise a very good sort of a man, and to be sure one of the merriest gentlemen in England. Well——'—'Pray,' said Allworthy, 'do not be so particular, I have heard nothing of your son yet.'—'O it was a great many years,' answered Partridge, 'before I saw my son, as you are pleased to call him. Then, sir, it was about half a year ago that hearing of a place at Gloucester where the barber was just dead, I went thither, and there I had been about two months when Mr Jones came thither.' He then gave Allworthy a very particular account of their first meeting, and of everything, as well as he could remember, which had happened from that day to this; frequently interlarding his story with panegyrics on Jones, and not forgetting to insinuate the great love and respect which he had for Allworthy. He concluded with saying, 'Now, sir, I have told your honour the whole truth.' And then repeated a most solemn protestation, 'That he was no more the father of Jones

227

than of the Pope of Rome'; and imprecated the most bitter curses on his head, if he did not speak truth.

'What am I to think of this matter?' cries Allworthy. 'For what purpose should you so strongly deny a fact which I think it would be rather your interest to own?'—'Nay, sir,' answered Partridge (for he could hold no longer), 'if your honour will not believe me, you are like soon to have satisfaction enough. I wish you had mistaken the mother of this young man, as well as you have his father.' And now being asked what he meant, with all the symptoms of horror, both in his voice and countenance, he told Allworthy the whole story, which he had a little before expressed such desire to Mrs Miller to conceal from him.

Allworthy was almost as much shocked at this discovery as Partridge himself had been while he related it. 'Good heavens!' says he, 'in what miserable distresses do vices and imprudence involve men! How much beyond our designs are the effects of wickedness sometimes carried!' He had scarce uttered these words, when Mrs Waters came hastily and abruptly into the room. Partridge no sooner saw her than he cried, 'Here, sir, here is the very woman herself. This is the unfortunate mother of Mr Jones. I am sure she will acquit me before your honour. Pray, madam——'

Mrs Waters, without paying any regard to what Partridge said, and almost without taking any notice of him, advanced to Mr Allworthy. 'I believe, sir, it is so long since I had the honour of seeing you, that you do not recollect me.'—'Indeed,' answered Allworthy, 'you are so very much altered, on many accounts, that had not this man already acquainted me who you are, I should not have immediately called you to my remembrance. Have you, madam, any particular business which brings you to me?' Allworthy spoke this with great reserve; for the reader may easily believe he was not well pleased with the conduct of this lady; neither with what he had formerly heard, nor with what Partridge had now delivered.

Mrs Waters answered: 'Indeed, sir, I have very particular business with you; and it is such as I can impart only to yourself. I must desire, therefore, the favour of a word with you alone: for I assure you what I have to tell you is of the utmost importance.'

Partridge was then ordered to withdraw, but before he went, he begged the lady to satisfy Mr Allworthy that he was perfectly innocent. To which she answered, 'You need be under no apprehension, sir; I shall satisfy Mr Allworthy very perfectly of that matter.'

Mrs Waters remaining a few moments silent, Mr Allworthy could not refrain from saying, 'I am sorry, madam, to perceive by what I have since heard, that you have made so very ill a use

———'—'Mr Allworthy,' says she, interrupting him, 'I know I have faults, but ingratitude to you is not one of them. I never can nor shall forget your goodness, which I own I have very little deserved; but be pleased to waive all upbraiding me at present, as I have so important an affair to communicate to you concerning this young man, to whom you have given my maiden name of Jones.'

'Have I then,' said Allworthy, 'ignorantly punished an innocent man, in the person of him who hath just left us? Was he not the father of the child?'—'Indeed he was not,' said Mrs Waters. 'You may be pleased to remember, sir, I formerly told you, you should one day know; and I acknowledge myself to have been guilty of a cruel neglect, in not having discovered it to you before. Indeed, I little knew how necessary it was.'—'Well, madam,' said Allworthy, 'be pleased to proceed.'—'You must remember, sir,' said she, 'a young fellow, whose name was Summer.'—'Very well,' cries Allworthy, 'he was the son of a clergyman of great learning and virtue, for whom I had the highest friendship.'—'So it appeared, sir,' answered she; 'for I believe you bred the young man up, and maintained him at the university; where, I think, he had finished his studies, when he came to reside at your house; a finer man, I must say, the sun never shone upon; for, besides the handsomest person I ever saw, he was so genteel, and had so much wit, and good breeding.'—'Poor gentleman,' said Allworthy, 'he was indeed untimely snatched away; and little did I think he had any sins of this kind to answer for; for I plainly perceive you are going to tell me he was the father of your child.'

'Indeed, sir,' answered she, 'he was not.'—'How!' said Allworthy, 'to what then tends all this preface?'—'To a story,' said she, 'which I am concerned falls to my lot to unfold to you. O, sir! prepare to hear something which will surprize you, will grieve you.'—'Speak,' said Allworthy, 'I am conscious of no crime, and cannot be afraid to hear.'—'Sir,' said she, 'that Mr Summer, the son of your friend, educated at your expense, who, after living a year in the house as if he had been your own son, died there of the small-pox, was tenderly lamented by you, and buried as if he had been your own; that Summer, sir, was the father of this child.'—'How!' said Allworthy; 'you contradict yourself.'—'That I do not,' answered she; 'he was indeed the father of this child, but not by me.'—'Take care, madam,' said Allworthy, 'do not, to shun the imputation of any crime, be guilty of falshood.'—'Indeed, sir,' says she, 'I am not his mother; nor would I now think myself so for the world.'—'I know your reason,' said Allworthy, 'and shall rejoice as much as you to find it otherwise; yet you must remember, you yourself confest it before me.'—'So far what I confest,' said she, 'was true, that these hands conveyed the infant to your bed; conveyed it thither at the command of its mother; at her commands I afterwards owned it, and thought myself, by her generosity, nobly rewarded, both for my secrecy and my shame.'—'Who could this woman be?' said Allworthy. 'Indeed, I tremble to name her,' answered Mrs Waters. 'By all this preparation I am to guess that she was a relation of mine,' cried he. 'Indeed she was a near one.' At which words Allworthy started, and she continued: 'You had a sister, sir.'— 'A sister!' repeated he, looking aghast. 'As there is truth in heaven,' cries she, 'your sister was the mother of that child you found between your sheets.'—'Can it be possible?' cries he. 'Good heavens!'—'Have patience, sir,' said Mrs Waters, 'and I will unfold to you the whole story. Just after your departure for London, Miss Bridget came one day to the house of my mother. She was pleased to say, she had heard an extraordinary character of me, for my learning and superior understanding to all the young women there. She then bid me come to her to the great house; where, when I attended, she employed me to read to her. She expressed great satisfaction in my reading, shewed great kindness to me, and made me many presents. At last she began to catechize me on the subject of secrecy, to which I gave her such satisfactory answers, that, at last, having locked the door of her room, she took me into her closet, and then locking that door likewise, she said "she should convince me of the vast reliance she had on my integrity, by communicating a secret in which her honour, and consequently her life, was concerned." She then inquired of me if I thought my mother might safely be confided in. I answered, I would stake my life on her fidelity. She then imparted to me the great secret which laboured in her breast, and which, I believe, was delivered with more pains than she afterwards suffered in childbirth. It was then contrived that my mother and myself only should attend at the time, and that Mrs Wilkins should be sent out of the way, as she accordingly was, to the very furthest part of Dorsetshire, to inquire the character of a servant; for the lady had turned away her own maid near three months before; during all which time I officiated about her person upon trial, as she said, though, as she afterwards declared, I was not sufficiently handy for the place. This, and many other such things which she used to say of me, were all thrown out to prevent any suspicion which Wilkins might hereafter have, when I was to own the child; for she thought it could never be believed she would venture to hurt a young woman with whom she had entrusted such a secret. You may be assured, sir, I was well paid for all these affronts, which, together with being informed with the occasion of them, very well contented me. Indeed, the lady had a greater suspicion of Mrs Wilkins than of any other person not that she had the least aversion to the gentlewoman, but she thought her incapable of keeping a secret, especially from you sir; for I have often heard Miss Bridget say, that, if Mrs Wilkins had committed a murder, she believed she would acquaint you with it. At last the expected day came, and Mrs Wilkins, who had been kept a week in readiness, and put off from time to time, upon some pretence or other, that she might not return too soon, was dispatched. Then the child was born, in the presence only of myself and my mother, and was by my mother conveyed to her own house, where it was privately kept by her till the evening of your return, when I, by the command of Miss Bridget, conveyed it into the bed where you found it. And all suspicions were afterwards laid asleep by the artful conduct of your sister, in pretending ill-will to the boy, and that any regard she showed him was out of mere complacence to you.'

Mrs Waters then made many protestations of the truth of this story, and concluded by saying, 'Thus, sir, you have at last discovered your nephew; for so I am sure you will hereafter think him, and I question not but he will be both an honour and a comfort to you.'

'I need not, madam,' said Allworthy, 'express my astonishment at what you have told me; and yet surely you would not, and could not, have put together so many circumstances to evidence an untruth. I confess I recollect some passages relating to that Summer, which formerly gave me a conceit that my sister had some liking to him. I mentioned it to her; for I had such a regard to the young man, as well on his own account as on his father's, that I should willingly have consented to a match between them; but she exprest the highest disdain of my unkind suspicion, as she called it; so that I never spoke more on the subject. Good heavens! Well! the Lord disposeth all things.—— Yet sure it was a most unjustifiable conduct in my sister to carry this secret with her out of the world.'—'I promise you, sir,' said Mrs Waters, 'she always profest a contrary intention, and frequently told me she intended one day to communicate it to you. She said, indeed, she was highly rejoiced that her plot had succeeded so well, and that you had of your own accord taken such a fancy to the child, that it was yet unnecessary to make any express declaration. Oh! sir, had that lady lived to have seen this poor young man turned like a vagabond from your house: nay, sir, could she have lived to hear that you had yourself employed a lawyer to prosecute him for murder of which he was not guilty——Forgive me, Mr Allworthy, I must say it was unkind.—Indeed, you have been abused, he never deserved it of you.'—'Indeed, madam,' said Allworthy, 'I have been abused by the person, whoever he was, that told you so.'—'Nay, sir.' said she, 'I would not be mistaken, I did not presume to say you were guilty of any wrong. The gentleman who came to me proposed no such matter; he only said, taking me for Mr Fitzpatrick's wife, that, if Mr Jones had murdered my husband, I should be assisted with any money I wanted to carry on the prosecution, by a very worthy gentleman, who, he said, was well apprized what a villain I had to deal with. It was by this man I found out who Mr Jones was; and this man, whose name is Dowling, Mr Jones tells me is your steward. I discovered his name by a very odd accident; for he himself refused to tell it me; but Partridge, who met him at my lodgings the second time he came, knew him formerly at Salisbury.'

'And did this Mr Dowling,' says Allworthy, with great astonishment in his countenance, 'tell you that I would assist in the prosecution?'——'No, sir,' answered she, 'I will not charge him wrongfully. He said I should be assisted, but he mentioned no name. Yet you must pardon me, sir, if from circumstances I thought it could be no other.'——'Indeed, madam,' says Allworthy, 'from circumstances I am too well convinced it was another. Good Heaven! by what wonderful means is the blackest and deepest villany sometimes discovered!—Shall I beg you, madam, to stay till the person you have mentioned comes, for I expect him every minute? nay, he may be, perhaps, already in the house.'

Allworthy then stept to the door, in order to call a servant, when in came, not Mr Dowling, but Mr Western. He no sooner saw Allworthy, than, without considering in the least the presence of Mrs Waters, he began to vociferate in the following manner: 'Fine doings at my house! A rare kettle of fish I have discovered at last! who the devil would be plagued with a daughter?'—'What's the matter, neighbour?' said Allworthy. 'Matter enough,' answered Western; 'when I thought she was just a coming to; what do you think I have found out? that the little b— hath bin playing tricks with me all the while, and carrying on a correspondence with that bastard of yours. Sister Western, whom I have quarrelled with upon her account, sent me word o't, and I ordered her pockets to be searched when she was asleep, and here I have got un signed with the son of a whore's own name. I have not had patience to read half o't, but I find plainly it is all about love; and indeed what should it be else? I have packed her up in her chamber again, and to-morrow morning down she goes into the country, unless she consents to be married directly, and there she shall live in a garret upon bread and water all her days; and the sooner such a b— breaks her heart the better, though, d—n her, that I believe is too tough. She will live long enough to plague me.'—'Well, neighbour,' answered Allworthy, 'if you will give me leave, I will undertake to argue with the young lady.'—'Will you?' said Western; 'why that is kind now, and neighbourly, and mayhap you will do more than I have been able to do with her; for I promise you she hath a very good opinion of you.'—'Well, sir,' said Allworthy, 'if you will go home, and release the young lady from her captivity, I will wait upon her within this half-hour.'—'But suppose,' said Western, 'she should run away with un in the meantime? For lawyer Dowling tells me there is no hopes of hanging the fellow at last; for that the man is alive, and like to do well, and that he thinks Jones will be out of prison again presently.'—'How!' said Allworthy; 'what, did you employ him then to inquire or to do anything in that matter?'—'Not I,' answered Western, 'he mentioned it to me just now of his own accord.'—'Just now!' cries Allworthy, 'why, where did you see him then? I want much to see Mr Dowling.'—'Why, you may see un an you will presently at my lodgings; for there is to be a meeting of lawyers there this morning about a mortgage. And do for once take a fool's advice; never think of dealing with her by gentle methods, take my word for it, those will never do. I have tried 'um long enough. She must be frightened into it, there is no other way.'—'I will do all I can,' said Allworthy; 'for I promise you there is nothing I wish for more than an alliance with this amiable creature.'—'Nay, the girl is well enough for matter o' that,' cries the squire; 'a man may go farther and meet with worse meat; that I may declare o' her, though she be my own daughter. And if she will but be obedient to me, there is never a father within a hundred miles o' the place, that loves a daughter better than I do; but I see you are busy with the lady here, so I will go home and expect you; and so your humble servant.'

As soon as Mr Western was gone, Mrs Waters said, 'I see, sir, the squire hath not the least remembrance of my face. I believe, Mr Allworthy, you would not have known me either. I am very considerably altered since that day when you so kindly gave me that advice, which I had been happy had I followed.'—'Indeed, madam,' cries Allworthy, 'it gave me great concern when I first heard the contrary.'—'Indeed, sir,' says she, 'I was ruined by a very deep scheme of villany, which if you knew, though I pretend not to think it would justify me in your opinion, it would at least mitigate my offence, and induce you to pity me: you are not now at leisure to hear my whole story; but this I assure you, I was betrayed by the most solemn promises of marriage; nay, in the eye of heaven I was married to him.'—'I am sorry, madam,' said Allworthy, 'you made so ill a use of your learning. Indeed, it would have been well that you had been possessed of much more, or had remained in a state of ignorance. And yet, madam, I am afraid you have more than this sin to answer for.'—'During his life,' answered she, 'which was above a dozen years, I most solemnly assure you I had not. And consider, sir, on my behalf, what is in the power of a woman stript of her reputation and left destitute; whether the good-natured world will suffer such a stray sheep to return to the road of virtue, even if she was never so desirous. I protest, then, I would have chose it had it been in my power; but necessity drove me into the arms of Captain

233

Waters, with whom, though still unmarried, I lived as a wife for many years, and went by his name. I parted with this gentleman at Worcester, on his march against the rebels, and it was then I accidentally met with Mr Jones, who rescued me from the hands of a villain. Indeed, he is the worthiest of men. No young gentleman of his age is, I believe, freer from vice, and few have the twentieth part of his virtues; nay, whatever vices he hath had, I am firmly persuaded he hath now taken a resolution to abandon them.'—'I hope he hath,' cries Allworthy, 'and I hope he will preserve that resolution. I must say, I have still the same hopes with regard to yourself. This you may be assured of, Mrs Waters, that whenever I find you are sincere in good intentions, you shall want no assistance in my power to make them effectual.'

Mrs Waters fell now upon her knees before him, and, in a flood of tears, made him many most passionate acknowledgments of his goodness, which, as she truly said, savoured more of the divine than human nature.

Allworthy raised her up, and spoke in the most tender manner, making use of every expression which his invention could suggest to comfort her, when he was interrupted by the arrival of Mr Dowling, who, upon his first entrance, seeing Mrs Waters, started, and appeared in some confusion; from which he soon recovered himself as well as he could, and then said he was in the utmost haste to attend counsel at Mr Western's lodgings.

Allworthy, without making any answer to this, bolted the door, and then, advancing with a stern look to Dowling, he said, 'Whatever be your haste, sir, I must first receive an answer to some questions. Do you know this lady?'——'That lady, sir!' answered Dowling, with great hesitation. Allworthy then, with the most solemn voice, said, 'Look you, Mr Dowling, as you value my favour, or your continuance a moment longer in my service, do not hesitate nor prevaricate; but answer faithfully and truly to every question I ask.——Do you know this lady?'——'Yes, sir,' said Dowling, 'I have seen the lady.'—'Where, sir?'—'At her own lodgings.'—'Upon what business did you go thither, sir; and who sent you?'—'I went, sir, to inquire, sir, about Mr Jones.'—'And who sent you to inquire about him?'—'Who, sir? why, sir, Mr Blifil sent me.'—'And what did you say to the lady concerning that matter?'—'Nay, sir, it is impossible to recollect every word.'— 'Will you please, madam, to assist the gentleman's memory?'—'He told me, sir,' said Mrs Waters, 'that if Mr Jones had murdered my husband, I should be assisted by any money I wanted to carry on the prosecution, by a very worthy gentleman, who was well apprized what a villain I had to deal with. These, I can safely swear, were the very words he spoke.'—'Were these the words, sir?' said Allworthy. 'I cannot charge my memory exactly,' cries Dowling, 'but I believe I did speak to that purpose.'—'And did

234

Mr Blifil order you to say so?'—'I am sure, sir, I should not have gone on my own accord, nor have willingly exceeded my authority in matters of this kind. If I said so, I must have so understood Mr Blifil's instructions.'—'Look you, Mr Dowling,' said Allworthy; 'I promise you before this lady, that whatever you have done in this affair by Mr Blifil's order, I will forgive, provided you now tell me strictly the truth; for I believe what you say, that you would not have acted of your own accord, and without authority in this matter.——Mr Blifil then likewise sent you to examine the two fellows at Aldersgate?'—'He did, sir.'—'Well, and what instructions did he then give you? Recollect as well as you can, and tell me, as near as possible, the very words he used.'——'Why, sir, Mr Blifil sent me out to find out the persons who were eye-witnesses of this fight. He said, he feared they might be tampered with by Mr Jones, or some of his friends. He said, blood required blood; and that not only all who concealed a murderer, but those who omitted anything in their power to bring him to justice, were sharers in his guilt. He said, he found you was very desirous of having the villain brought to justice, though it was not proper you should appear in it.'—'He did so?' says Allworthy. 'Yes, sir,' cries Dowling; 'I should not, I am sure, have proceeded such lengths for the sake of any other person living but your worship.'—'What lengths, sir?' said Allworthy. 'Nay, sir,' cries Dowling, 'I would not have your worship think I would, on any account, be guilty of subornation of perjury; but there are two ways of delivering evidence. I told them, therefore, that if any offers should be made them on the other side, they should refuse them, and that they might be assured they should lose nothing by being honest men, and telling the truth. I said, we were told that Mr Jones had assaulted the gentleman first, and that, if that was the truth, they should declare it; and I did give them some hints that they should be no losers.'—'I think you went lengths indeed,' cries Allworthy. 'Nay, sir,' answered Dowling, 'I am sure I did not desire them to tell an untruth;——nor should I have said what I did, unless it had been to oblige you.'—— 'You would not have thought, I believe,' says Allworthy, 'to have obliged me, had you known that this Mr Jones was my own nephew.'——'I am sure, sir,' answered he, 'it did not become me to take any notice of what I thought you desired to conceal.'— 'How!' cries Allworthy, 'and did you know it then?'—'Nay, sir,' answered Dowling, 'if your worship bids me speak the truth, I am sure I shall do it.—Indeed, sir, I did know it; for they were almost the last words which Madam Blifil ever spoke, which she mentioned to me as I stood alone by her bedside, when she delivered me the letter I brought your worship from her.'—'What letter?' cries Allworthy. 'The letter, sir,' answered Dowling, 'which I brought from Salisbury, and which I delivered into the

235

hands of Mr Blifil.'——'O heavens!' cries Allworthy. 'Well, and what were the words? What did my sister say to you?'—'She took me by the hand,' answered he, 'and, as she delivered me the letter, said, "I scarce know what I have written. Tell my brother, Mr Jones is his nephew—He is my son.—Bless him," says she, and then fell backward, as if dying away. I presently called in the people, and she never spoke more to me, and died within a few minutes afterwards.' Allworthy stood a minute silent, lifting up his eyes; and then, turning to Dowling, said, 'How came you, sir, not to deliver me this message?'—'Your worship,' answered he, 'must remember that you was at that time ill in bed; and, being in a violent hurry, as indeed I always am, I delivered the letter and message to Mr Blifil, who told me he would carry them both to you, which he hath since told me he did, and that your worship, partly out of friendship to Mr Jones, and partly out of regard to your sister, would never have it mentioned, and did intend to conceal it from the world; and therefore, sir, if you had not mentioned it to me first, I am certain I should never have thought it belonged to me to say anything of the matter, either to your worship or any other person.'

Allworthy appeared well satisfied with this relation, and, having enjoined on Dowling strict silence as to what had past, conducted that gentleman himself to the door, lest he should see Blifil, who was returned to his chamber, where he exulted in the thoughts of his last deceit on his uncle, and little suspected what had since passed below-stairs.

As Allworthy was returning to his room, he met Mrs Miller in the entry, who, with a face all pale and full of terror, said to him, 'O! sir, I find this wicked woman hath been with you, and you know all; yet do not on this account abandon the poor young man. Consider, sir, he was ignorant it was his own mother; and the discovery itself will most probably break his heart, without your unkindness.'

'Madam,' says Allworthy, 'I am under such an astonishment at what I have heard, that I am really unable to satisfy you; but come with me into my room. Indeed, Mrs Miller, I have made surprizing discoveries, and you shall soon know them.'

The poor woman followed him trembling; and now Allworthy, going up to Mrs Waters, took her by the hand, and then, turning to Mrs Miller, said, 'What reward shall I bestow upon this gentlewoman, for the services she hath done me?—O! Mrs Miller, you have a thousand times heard me call the young man to whom you are so faithful a friend, my son. Little did I think he was indeed related to me at all.—Your friend, madam, is my nephew; he is the brother of that wicked viper which I have so long nourished in my bosom.——She will herself tell you the whole story, and how the youth came to pass for her son. Indeed, Mrs Miller, I

236

am convinced that he hath been wronged, and that I have been abused; abused by one whom you too justly suspected of being a villain. He is, in truth, the worst of villains.'

The joy which Mrs Miller now felt, bereft her of the power of speech, and might perhaps have deprived her of her senses, if not of life, had not a friendly shower of tears come seasonably to her relief. At length, recovering so far as to be able to speak, she cried, 'And is my dear Mr Jones then your nephew, sir, and not the son of this lady? And are your eyes opened to him at last? And shall I live to see him as happy as he deserves?'—'He certainly is my nephew,' says Allworthy, 'and I hope all the rest.'— 'And is this the dear good woman, the person,' cries she, 'to whom all this discovery is owing?'—'She is indeed,' says Allworthy. 'Why, then,' cried Mrs Miller, 'may Heaven shower down its choicest blessings upon her head, and for this one good action forgive her all her sins, be they never so many!'

Mrs Waters then informed them that she believed Jones would very shortly be released; for that the surgeon was gone, in company with a nobleman, to the justice who committed him, in order to certify that Mr Fitzpatrick was out of all manner of danger, and to procure his prisoner his liberty.

Allworthy said he should be glad to find his nephew there at his return home; but that he was then obliged to go on some business of consequence. He then called to a servant to fetch him a chair, and presently left the two ladies together.

Mr Blifil, hearing the chair ordered, came downstairs to attend upon his uncle; for he never was deficient in such acts of duty. He asked his uncle if he was going out, which is a civil way of asking a man whither he is going: to which the other making no answer, he again desired to know when he would be pleased to return?—Allworthy made no answer to this neither, till he was just going into his chair, and then, turning about, he said: 'Harkee, sir, do you find out, before my return, the letter which your mother sent me on her deathbed.' Allworthy then departed, and left Blifil in a situation to be envied only by a man who is just going to be hanged.

CHAPTER FORTY-FOUR

A FURTHER CONTINUATION

ALLWORTHY took an opportunity, whilst he was in the chair, of reading the letter from Jones to Sophia, which Western delivered him; and there were some expressions in it concerning himself which drew tears from his eyes. At length he arrived at Mr Western's, and was introduced to Sophia.

When the first ceremonies were past, and the gentleman and lady had taken their chairs, a silence of some minutes ensued; during which the latter, who had been prepared for the visit by her father, sat playing with her fan, and had every mark of confusion both in her countenance and behaviour. At length Allworthy, who was himself a little disconcerted, began thus: 'I am afraid, Miss Western, my family hath been the occasion of giving you some uneasiness; to which, I fear, I have innocently become more instrumental than I intended. Be assured, madam, had I at first known how disagreeable the proposals had been, I should not have suffered you to have been so long persecuted.

'Sir,' said Sophia, with a little modest hesitation, 'this behaviour is most kind and generous, and such as I could expect only from Mr Allworthy; but as you have been so kind to mention this matter, you will pardon me for saying, I am convinced, sir, you are too good and generous to resent my refusal of your nephew. Our inclinations are not in our own power; and whatever may be his merit, I cannot force them in his favour.'—'I sincerely believe you, madam,' replied Allworthy, 'and I heartily congratulate you on your prudent foresight, since by so justifiable a resistance you have avoided misery indeed!—'You speak now, Mr Allworthy,' cries she, 'with a delicacy which few men are capable of feeling! If I had married Mr Blifil——'—'Pardon my interrupting you, madam,' answered Allworthy, 'but I cannot bear the supposition. —Believe me, Miss Western, I rejoice from my heart, I rejoice in your escape.——I have discovered the wretch for whom you have suffered all this cruel violence from your father to be a villain.'— 'How, sir!' cries Sophia; 'you must believe this surprizes me.'—— 'It hath surprized me, madam,' answered Allworthy, 'and so it will the world. At present let us not mention so detested a name. I have another matter of a very serious nature to propose.— 'O! Miss Western, I know your vast worth, nor can I so easily part with the ambition of being allied to it.—I have a near relation, madam, a young man whose character is, I am convinced, the very opposite to that of this wretch, and whose fortune I will make equal to what his was to have been. Could I, madam, hope you would admit a visit from him?' Sophia, after a minute's silence, answered, 'I will deal with the utmost sincerity with Mr Allworthy. I have determined at present to listen to no such proposals from any person. My only desire is to be restored to the affection of my father, and to be again the mistress of his family. This, sir, I hope to owe to your good offices. Let me beseech you, do not, the very moment when you have released me from one persecution, do not engage me in another as miserable and as fruitless.'—'Indeed, Miss Western,' replied Allworthy, 'I am capable of no such conduct; and if this be your resolution, he must submit to the disappointment, whatever torments he may suffer under it.'—'I must smile now, Mr Allworthy,' answered Sophia, 'when you mention the torments of a man whom I do not know, and who can consequently have so little acquaintance with me.'— 'Pardon me, dear young lady,' cries Allworthy, 'I begin now to be afraid he hath had too much acquaintance for the repose of his future days; since, if ever man was capable of a sincere, violent, and noble passion, such, I am convinced, is my unhappy nephew's for Miss Western.'—'A nephew of yours, Mr Allworthy!' answered Sophia. 'It is surely strange. I never heard of him before.'—'Indeed, madam,' cries Allworthy, 'it is only the circumstance of his being my nephew to which you are a stranger, and which, till this day, was a secret to me.—Mr Jones, who has long loved you, he! he is my nephew!'—'Mr Jones your nephew, sir!' cries Sophia; 'can it be possible?'—'He is, indeed, madam,' answered Allworthy; 'he is my own sister's son—as such I shall always own him; nor am I ashamed of owning him. I am much more ashamed of my past behaviour to him; but I was as ignorant of his merit as of his birth. Indeed, Miss Western, I have used him cruelly——Indeed I have.'——Here the good man wiped his eyes, and after a short pause proceeded: 'I never shall be able to reward him for his sufferings without your assistance.—— Believe me, most amiable young lady, I must have a great esteem of that offering which I make to your worth. I know he hath been guilty of faults; but there is great goodness of heart at the bottom. Believe me, madam, there is.' Here he stopped, seeming to expect an answer, which he presently received from Sophia, after she had a little recovered herself from the hurry of spirits into which so strange and sudden information had thrown her— 'You must pardon me, Mr Allworthy,' answered Sophia; 'I cannot listen to a proposal of this kind. Mr Jones, I am convinced, hath much merit; but I shall never receive Mr Jones as one who is to be my husband—Upon my honour I never will.'—'Pardon me, madam,' cries Allworthy, 'if I am a little surprized, after what I have heard from Mr Western——I hope the unhappy young man hath done nothing to forfeit your good opinion, if he had ever the honour to enjoy it.—Perhaps he may have been misrepresented to you, as he was to me. The same villany may have injured him everywhere.—He is no murderer, I assure you; as he hath been called.'—'Mr Allworthy,' answered Sophia, 'I have told you my resolution. I wonder not at what my father hath told you; but, whatever his apprehensions or fears have been, if I know my heart, I have given no occasion for them; since it hath always been a fixed principle with me, never to have married without his consent. This is, I think, the duty of a child to a parent; and this, I hope, nothing could ever have prevailed with me to swerve from. I do not indeed conceive that the authority of any parent can oblige us to marry in direct opposition to our inclinations. To avoid a force of this kind, which I had reason to suspect, I left my father's house, and sought protection elsewhere. This is the truth of my story; and if the world, or my father, carry my intentions any farther, my own conscience will acquit me.'—'I hear you, Miss Western,' cries Allworthy, 'with admiration. I admire the justness of your sentiments; but surely there is more in this. I am cautious of offending you, young lady; but am I to look on all which I have hitherto heard or seen as a dream only? And have you suffered so much cruelty from your father on the account of a man to whom you have been always absolutely indifferent?'—'I beg, Mr Allworthy,' answered Sophia, 'you will not insist on my reasons;—yes, I have suffered indeed; I will not, Mr Allworthy, conceal——I will be very sincere with you—I own I had a great opinion of Mr Jones—I believe—I know I have suffered for my opinion—I have been treated cruelly by my aunt, as well as by my father; but that is now past—I beg I may not be farther pressed; for, whatever hath been, my resolution is now fixed. Your nephew, sir, hath many virtues—he hath great virtues, Mr Allworthy. I wish Mr Jones very well. I sincerely wish him well; and I repeat it again to you, whatever demerit he may have to me, I am certain he hath many good qualities. At present there is not a man upon earth whom I would more resolutely reject than Mr Jones; nor would the addresses of Mr Blifil himself be less agreeable to me.'

Western had been long impatient for the event of this conference, and was just now arrived at the door to listen; when, having heard the last sentiments of his daughter's heart, he lost all temper, and, busting open the door in a rage, cried out: 'It is a lie! It is a d—n'd lie! It is all owing to that d—n'd rascal Jones; and if she could get at un, she'd ha un any hour of the day.' Here Allworthy interposed, and addressing himself to the squire with some anger in his look, he said, 'Mr Western, you have not kept your word with me. You promised to abstain from all violence.'—'Why, so I did,' cries Western, 'as long as it was possible; but to hear a wench telling such confounded lies—

Zounds! doth she think, if she can make vools of other volk, she can make one of me?——No, no, I know her better than thee dost.'—'I am sorry to tell you, sir,' answered Allworthy, 'it doth not appear, by your behaviour to this young lady, that you know her at all. Place that confidence in the young lady which she so well deserves, and I am certain you will be the happiest father on earth.'——'I confidence in her?' cries the squire. ' 'Sblood! what confidence can I place in her, when she won't do as I would ha' her? Let her gi' but her consent to marry as I would ha' her, and I'll place as much confidence in her as wouldst ha' me.'——'You have no right, neighbour,' answered Allworthy, 'to insist on any such consent. A negative voice your daughter allows you, and God and nature have thought proper to allow you no more.'—'A negative voice!' cries the squire. 'Ay! ay! I'll show you what a negative voice I ha.—Go along, go into your chamber, go, you stubborn——'—'Indeed, Mr Western,' said Allworthy, 'indeed you use her cruelly—I cannot bear to see this—you shall, you must behave to her in a kinder manner. She deserves the best of treatment.'—'Yes, yes,' said the squire, 'I know what she deserves: now she's gone, I'll shew you what she deserves. See here, sir, here is a letter from my cousin, my Lady Bellaston, in which she is so kind to gi' me it understand that the fellow is got out of prison again; and here she advises me to take all the care I can o' the wench. Odzookers! neighbour Allworthy, you don't know what it is to govern a daughter.'

The squire ended his speech with some compliments to his own sagacity; and then Allworthy acquainted him with the whole discovery which he had made concerning Jones, with his anger to Blifil, and with every particular which hath been disclosed to the reader in the preceding chapters.

Men over-violent in their dispositions are, for the most part, as changeable in them. No sooner then was Western informed of Mr Allworthy's intention to make Jones his heir, than he joined heartily with the uncle in every commendation of the nephew, and became as eager for her marriage with Jones, as he had before been to couple her to Blifil.

Here Mr Allworthy was again forced to interpose, and to relate what had passed between him and Sophia, at which he testified great surprize.

The squire was silent a moment, and looked wild with astonishment at this account. At last he cried out, 'Why, what can be the meaning of this, neighbour Allworthy? Vond o' un she was, that I'll be sworn to.——Odzookers! I have hit o't. As sure as a gun I have hit o' the very right o't. It's all along o' zister. The girl hath got a hankering after this son of a whore of a lord. I vound 'em together at my cousin, my Lady Bellaston's. He hath turned the head o' her, that's certain—but d—n me if he shall ha her—I'll ha no lords nor courtiers in my vamily.'

Allworthy now made a long speech, in which he very earnestly recommended gentle methods to Mr Western, as those by which he might be assured of succeeding best with his daughter. He then took his leave, and returned back to Mrs Miller, but was forced to comply with the earnest entreaties of the squire, in promising to bring Mr Jones to visit him that afternoon, that he might, as he said, 'make all matters up with the young gentleman.' At Mr Allworthy's departure, Western promised to follow his advice in his behaviour to Sophia, saying, 'I don't know how 'tis, but d—n me, Allworthy, if you don't make me always do just as you please; and yet I have as good an estate as you, and am in the commission of the peace as well as yourself.'

CHAPTER FORTY-FIVE

WHEREIN THE HISTORY BEGINS TO DRAW TOWARDS A CONCLUSION

WHEN Allworthy returned to his lodgings, he heard Mr Jones was just arrived before him. He hurried therefore instantly into an empty chamber, whither he ordered Mr Jones to be brought to him alone.

It is impossible to conceive a more tender or moving scene than the meeting between the uncle and nephew (for Mrs Waters, as the reader may well suppose, had at her last visit discovered to him the secret of his birth). After Allworthy had raised Jones from his feet, where he had prostrated himself and received him into his arms, 'O my child!' he cried, 'how have I been to blame! how have I injured you! What amends can I ever make you for those unkind, those unjust suspicions which I have entertained, and for all the sufferings they have occasioned to you?'— 'Am I not now made amends?' cries Jones. 'Would not my sufferings, if they had been ten times greater, have been now richly repaid? To be again restored to your presence, to your favour; to be once more thus kindly received by my great, my noble, my generous benefactor.'

'Indeed, child,' cries Allworthy, 'I have used you cruelly.' He then explained to him all the treachery of Blifil, and again repeated expressions of the utmost concern, for having been induced by that treachery to use him so ill. 'O, talk not so!' answered Jones; 'Indeed, sir, you have used me nobly. The wisest man might be deceived as you were; and, under such a deception, the best must have acted just as you did. Your goodness displayed itself in the midst of your anger, just as it then seemed. I owe everything to that goodness, of which I have been most unworthy. I am not a hardened sinner; I thank Heaven, I have had time to reflect on my past life, where, though I cannot charge myself with any gross villainy, yet I can discern follies and vices more than enough to repent and to be ashamed of; follies which have been attended with dreadful consequences to myself, and have brought me to the brink of destruction.'—'I am rejoiced, my dear child,' answered Allworthy, 'to hear you talk thus sensibly. You now see, Tom, to what dangers imprudence alone may subject virtue (for virtue, I am now convinced, you love in a great degree). You say, however, you have seen your errors, and will reform them. I firmly believe you, my dear child; and therefore, from this moment, you shall never be reminded of them by me. Remember them only yourself so far as for the future to teach you the better to avoid them. At these words Jones fetched a deep sigh; upon which, when Allworthy remonstrated, he said, 'Sir, I will conceal nothing from you: I fear there is one consequence of my vices I shall never be able to retrieve. O, my dear uncle! I have lost a treasure.'—'You need say no more,' answered Allworthy; 'I will be explicit with you; I know what you lament; I have seen the young lady, and have discoursed with her concerning you. This I must insist on, as an earnest of your sincerity in all you have said, that you obey me in one instance, to abide intirely by the determination of the young lady, whether it shall be in your favour or no. She hath already suffered enough from solicitations which I hate to think of; she shall owe no further constraint to my family: I know her father will be as ready to torment her now on your account as he hath formerly been on another's; but I am determined she shall suffer no more confinement, no more violence, no more uneasy hours.'—'O, my dear uncle!' answered Jones, 'lay, I beseech you, some command on me, in which I shall have some merit in obedience. Believe me, sir, the only instance in which I could disobey you would be to give an uneasy moment to my Sophia. I have sinned against her beyond all hope of pardon; and guilty as I am, my guilt unfortunately appears to her in ten times blacker than the real colours. O, my dear uncle! I find my follies are irretrievable; and all your goodness cannot save me from perdition.'

A servant now acquainted them that Mr Western was below-stairs; for his eagerness to see Jones could not wait till the afternoon. Upon which Jones, whose eyes were full of tears, begged his uncle to entertain Western a few minutes, till he a little recovered himself; to which the good man consented, and, having ordered Mr Western to be shewn into a parlour, went down to him.

Mrs Miller no sooner heard that Jones was alone than she came eagerly into the room, and, advancing towards Jones, wished him heartily joy of his new-found uncle and his happy reconciliation; adding, 'I wish I could give you joy on another account, my dear child; but anything so inexorable I never saw.'

Jones, with some appearance of surprize, asked her what she meant. 'Why then,' says she, 'I have been with the young lady, and have explained all matters to her, as they were told to me by my son Nightingale. She can have no longer any doubt about the letter; of that I am certain; for I told her my son Nightingale was ready to take his oath, if she pleased, that it was all his own invention, and the letter of his inditing. I told her the very reason of sending the letter ought to recommend you to her the more, as it was all upon her account, and a plain proof that you was resolved to quit all your profligacy for the future. I am sure I have said all I can; but all to no purpose. She remains inflexible. She says, she had forgiven many faults on account of youth; but expressed such detestation of the character of a libertine, that she absolutely silenced me. I often attempted to excuse you; but the justness of her accusation flew in my face. Upon my honour, she is a lovely woman, and one of the sweetest and most sensible creatures I ever saw. I could have almost kissed her for one expression she made use of. "I once fancied, madam," said she, "I had discovered great goodness of heart in Mr Jones; and for that I own I had a sincere esteem; but an entirely profligacy of manners will corrupt the best heart in the world; and all which a good-natured libertine can expect is, that we should mix some grains of pity with our contempt and abhorrence." She is an angelic creature, that is the truth on't.' —'O, Mrs Miller!' answered Jones, 'can I bear to think I have lost such an angel?'—'Lost! no,' cries Mrs Miller; 'I hope you have not lost her yet. Resolve to leave such vicious courses, and you may yet have hopes.'

Here the conversation was interrupted by the arrival of Western, who could no longer be kept out of the room even by the authority of Allworthy himself; though this, as we have often seen, had a wonderful power over him.

Western immediately went up to Jones, crying out, 'My old friend Tom, I am glad to see thee with all my heart! all past must be forgotten; I could not intend any affront to thee, because, as Allworthy here knows, nay, dost know it thyself, I took thee for another person; and where a body means no harm, what signifies a hasty word or two? One Christian must forget and forgive another.'—'I hope, sir,' said Jones, 'I shall never forget the many obligations I have had to you; but as for any offence towards me, I declare I am an utter stranger.'—'A't,' says Western, 'then give me thy fist; a't as hearty an honest cock as any in the kingdom. Come along with me; I'll carry thee to thy mistress this moment.' Here Allworthy interposed; and the squire being unable to prevail either with the uncle or nephew, was, after some l'tigation, obliged to consent to delay introducing Jones to Sophia till the afternoon; at which time Allworthy, as well in compassion to Jones as in compliance with the eager desires of Western, was prevailed upon to promise to attend at the tea-table.

When Mr Western was departed, Jones began to inform Mr Allworthy and Mrs Miller that his liberty had been procured by two noble lords, who, together with a friend of Mr Nightingale's, had attended the magistrate by whom he had been committed, and by whom, on the surgeon's oaths, that the wounded person was out of all manner of danger from his wound, he was discharged.

One only of these lords, he said, he had ever seen before, and that no more than once; but the other had greatly surprized him, by asking his pardon for an offence he had been guilty of towards him, occasioned, he said, entirely by his ignorance who he was.

Now the reality of the case, with which Jones was not acquainted till afterwards, was this: The lieutenant whom Lord Fellamar had employed, according to the advice of Lady Bellaston, to press Jones as a vagabond into the sea-service, when he came to report to his lordship the event which we have before seen, spoke very favourably of the behaviour of Mr Jones on all accounts, and strongly assured that lord that he must have mistaken the person, for that Jones was certainly a gentleman; insomuch that his lordship, who was strictly a man of honour, and would by no means have been guilty of an action which the world in general would have condemned, began to be much concerned for the advice which he had taken.

Within a day or two after this, Lord Fellamar happened to dine with the Irish peer, who, in a conversation upon the duel, acquainted his company with the character of Fitzpatrick; to which, indeed, he did not do strict justice, especially in what related to his lady. He said she was the most innocent, the most injured woman alive, and that from compassion alone he had undertaken her cause. He then declared an intention of going the next morning to Fitzpatrick's lodgings, in order to prevail with him, if possible, to consent to a separation from his wife, who, the peer said, was in apprehensions for her life, if she should ever return to be under the power of her husband. Lord Fellamar agreed to go with him, that he might satisfy himself more concerning Jones and the circumstances of the duel; for he was by no means easy concerning the part he had acted. The moment his lordship gave a hint of his readiness to assist in the delivery of the lady, it was eagerly embraced by the other nobleman, who depended much on the authority of Lord Fellamar, as he thought it would greatly contribute to awe Fitzpatrick into a compliance; and perhaps he was in the right; for the poor Irishman no sooner saw these noble peers had undertaken the cause of his wife, than he submitted, and articles of separation were soon drawn up and signed between the parties.

Fitzpatrick was now become so indifferent to that matter, that he spoke highly in favour of Jones to Lord Fellamar, took all the blame upon himself, and said the other had behaved very much like a gentleman and a man of honour; and upon that lord's further inquiry concerning Mr Jones, Fitzpatrick told him he was nephew to a gentleman of very great fashion and fortune, which was the account he had just received from Mrs Waters after her interview with Dowling.

Lord Fellamar now thought it behoved him to do everything in his power to make satisfaction to a gentleman whom he had so grossly injured, and without any consideration of rivalship (for he had now given over all thoughts of Sophia), determined to procure Mr Jones's liberty, being satisfied, as well from Fitzpatrick as his surgeon, that the wound was not mortal. He therefore prevailed with the Irish peer to accompany him to the place where Jones was confined, to whom he behaved as we have already related.

When Allworthy returned to his lodgings, he immediately carried Jones into his room, and then acquainted him with the whole matter, as well what he had heard from Mrs Waters as what he had discovered from Mr Dowling.

Jones expressed great astonishment and no less concern at this account, but without making any comment or observation upon it. And now a message was brought from Mr Blifil, desiring to know if his uncle was at leisure, that he might wait upon him. Allworthy started and turned pale, and then in a more passionate tone than I believe he had ever used before, bid the servant tell Blifil he knew him not.—'Pardon me, dear sir,' said Jones; 'a moment's reflection will, I am sure, convince you. My own brother and your nephew! Let me beseech you, sir, to do nothing by him in the present height of your anger. Consider, my dear uncle, I was not myself condemned unheard.' Allworthy stood silent a moment, and then, embracing Jones, he said, with tears gushing from his eyes, 'O my child! to what goodness have I been so long blind! I am equally astonished at the goodness of your heart, and the quickness of your understanding. Go to him, therefore, and use your own discretion; yet do not flatter him with any hopes of my forgiveness; for

I shall never forgive villany farther than my religion obliges me, and that extends not either to our bounty or our conversation.'

Jones went up to Blifil's room, whom he found in a situation which moved his pity, though it would have raised a less amiable passion in many beholders. He had cast himself on his bed, where he lay abandoning himself to despair, and drowned in tears; not in such tears as flow from contrition; no, these tears were such as the frighted thief sheds in his cart, and are indeed the effects of that concern which the most savage natures are seldom deficient in feeling for themselves.

It would be unpleasant and tedious to paint this scene in full length. Let it suffice to say, that the behaviour of Jones was kind to excess. He omitted nothing which his invention could supply, to raise and comfort the drooping spirits of Blifil, before he communicated to him the resolution of his uncle that he must quit the house that evening. He offered to furnish him with any money he wanted, assured him of his hearty forgiveness of all he had done against him, that he would leave nothing unattempted to effectuate a reconciliation with his uncle.

Blifil was at first sullen and silent, balancing in his mind whether he should yet deny all; but, finding at last the evidence too strong against him, he betook himself at last to confession. He then asked pardon of his brother in the most vehement manner, prostrated himself on the ground, and kissed his feet.

Jones could not so far check his disdain, but that it a little discovered itself in his countenance at this extreme servility. He raised his brother the moment he could from the ground, and advised him to bear his afflictions more like a man; repeating, at the same time, his promises, that he would do all in his power to lessen them; for which Blifil, making many professions of his unworthiness, poured forth a profusion of thanks; and then, he having declared he would immediately depart to another lodging, Jones returned to his uncle.

Among other matters, Allworthy now acquainted Jones with the discovery which he had made concerning the £500 bank-notes. 'I have,' said he, 'already consulted a lawyer, who tells me, to my great astonishment, that there is no punishment for a fraud of this kind. Indeed, when I consider the black ingratitude of this fellow toward you, I think a highwayman, compared to him, is an innocent person.'

'Good Heaven!' says Jones, 'is it possible?—I am shocked beyond measure at this news. I thought there was not an honester fellow in the world.——The temptation of such a sum was too great for him to withstand; for smaller matters have come safe to me through his hand. Indeed, my dear uncle, you must suffer me to call it weakness rather than ingratitude; for I am convinced the poor fellow loves me; for it is not above a day or two ago, that he visited me in my confinement, and offered me any money I wanted. Consider, sir, what a temptation to a man who hath tasted such bitter distress, it must be, to have a sum in his possession which must put him and his family beyond any future possibility of suffering the like.'

'Child,' cries Allworthy, 'you carry this forgiving temper too far. Such mistaken mercy is not only weakness, but borders on injustice, and is very pernicious to society, as it encourages vice. I am convinced the fellow is a villain, and he shall be punished; at least as far as I can punish him.'

This was spoken with so stern a voice, that Jones did not think proper to make any reply; besides, the hour appointed by Mr Western now drew so near, that he had barely time left to dress himself.

Partridge had scarce seen his master since the happy discovery. The poor fellow was unable to contain or express his transports. He behaved like one frantic, and made almost as many mistakes while he was dressing Jones as I have seen made by Harlequin in dressing himself on the stage.

His memory, however, was not in the least deficient. He recollected now many omens and presages of this happy event, some of which he had remarked at the time, but many more he now remembered; and concluded with saying, 'I always told your honour something boded in my mind that you would one time or other have it in your power to make my fortune.'

CHAPTER FORTY-SIX

APPROACHING STILL NEARER TO THE END

JONES, being now completely dressed, attended his uncle to Mr Western's. He was, indeed, one of the finest figures ever beheld, and his person alone would have charmed the greater part of womankind.

Sophia, who, angry as she was, appeared so extremely beautiful, that even Allworthy, when he saw her, could not forbear whispering to Western, that he believed she was the finest creature in the world. To which Western answered, in a whisper, overheard by all present, 'So much the better for Tom;—for d—n me if he shan't ha the tousling her. Sophia was all over scarlet at these words, while Tom's countenance was altogether as pale, and he was almost ready to sink from his chair.

The tea-table was scarce removed before Western lugged Allworthy out of the room, telling him he had business of consequence to impart, and must speak to him that instant in private before he forgot it.

The lovers were now alone, and it will, I question not, appear strange to many readers, now that with safety they were at liberty to say or do whatever they pleased, they should both remain for some time silent and motionless; both sat with their eyes cast downwards on the ground, and for some minutes continued in perfect silence.

Mr Jones during this interval attempted once or twice to speak, but was absolutely incapable, muttering only, or rather sighing out, some broken words; when Sophia at length, partly out of pity to him, and partly to turn the discourse from the subject which she knew well enough he was endeavouring to open, said:

'Sure, sir, you are the most fortunate man in the world in this discovery.'—'And can you really, madam, think me so fortunate,' said Jones, sighing, 'while I have incurred your displeasure?'—Nay, sir,' says she, 'as to that, you know best whether you have deserved it.'—'Indeed, madam,' answered he, 'you yourself are as well apprized of all my demerits. Justice, I know, must condemn me.—Yet not for the letter I sent to Lady Bellaston. Of that I most solemnly declare you have had a true acount.' He then insisted much on the security given him by Nightingale of a fair pretence for breaking off, if, contrary to their expectations, her ladyship should have accepted his offer; but confest that he had been guilty of a great indiscretion to put such a letter as that into her power, 'which,' said he, 'I have dearly paid for, in the effect it has upon you.'—'I do not, I cannot,' says she, 'believe otherwise of that letter than you would have me. My conduct, I think, shows you clearly I do not believe there is much in that. And yet, Mr Jones, have I not enough to resent? After what past at Upton, so soon to engage in a new amour with another woman, while I fancied, and you pretended, your heart was bleeding for me? Indeed, you have acted strangely. Can I believe the passion you have profest to me to be sincere? Or, if I can, what happiness can I assure myself of with a man capable of so much inconstancy?'—'O! my Sophia,' cries he, 'do not doubt the sincerity of the purest passion that ever inflamed a human breast. Inconstancy to you! O Sophia! if you can have goodness enough to pardon what is past, do not let any cruel future apprehensions shut your mercy against me. No repentance was ever more sincere. O! let it reconcile me to my heaven in this dear bosom.'—'Sincere repentance, Mr Jones,' answered she, 'will obtain the pardon of a sinner, but it is from one who is a perfect judge of that sincerity. A human mind may be imposed on; time alone, Mr Jones, can convince me that you are a true penitent, and have resolved to abandon these vicious courses, which I should detest you for, if I imagined you capable of persevering in them.' —'Do not imagine it,' cries Jones. 'Don't believe me upon my word; I have a better security, a pledge for my constancy, which it is impossible to see and to doubt.'—'What is that?' said Sophia, a little surprized. 'I will show you, my charming angel,' cried Jones, seizing her hand and carrying her to the glass. 'There, behold it there in that lovely figure, in that face, that shape, those eyes, that mind which shines through these eyes; can the man who shall be in possession of these be inconstant? Impossible! my Sophia.' Sophia blushed and half smiled; but, forcing again her brow into a frown: 'If I am to judge,' said she, 'of the future by the past, my image will no more remain in your heart when I am out of your sight, than it will in this glass when I am out of the room.'—'By heaven, by all that is sacred!' said Jones, 'it never was out of my heart. The first moment of hope that my Sophia might be my wife, taught it me at once; and all the rest of her sex from that moment became as little the objects of desire to my sense as of passion to my heart.'—'Well,' says Sophia, 'the proof of this must be from time. Your situation, Mr Jones, is now altered, and I assure you I have great satisfaction in the alteration. You will now want no opportunity of being near me, and convincing me that your mind is altered too.'—'O! my angel,' cries Jones, 'how shall I thank thy goodness! O! am I not assured that the blessed day will come, when I shall call you mine; when fears shall be no more; when I shall have that dear, that vast, that exquisite, ecstatic delight of making my Sophia happy?'—— 'Indeed, sir,' said she, 'that day is in your own power.'——'O! my dear, my divine angel,' cried he, 'these words have made me mad with joy.——But I must, I will thank those dear lips which have so sweetly pronounced my bliss.' He then caught her in his arms, and kissed her with an ardour he had never ventured before.

At this instant Western, who had stood some time listening, burst into the room, and, with his hunting voice and phrase, cried out, 'To her, boy, to her, go to her.——That's it, little honeys, O that's it! Well, what, is it all over? Hath she appointed the day, boy? What, shall it be to-morrow or next day? And dost consent then?'—'No, indeed, sir,' says Sophia, 'I have given no such consent.'——'And wunt not ha un then to-morrow, nor next day?' says Western.——'Indeed, sir,' says she, 'I have no such intention.' —'But I can tell thee,' replied he, 'why hast nut; only because thou dost love to be disobedient, and to plague and vex thy father.' —'Pray, sir,' said Jones, interfering——'I tell thee thou art a puppy,' cries he. 'When I vorbid her, then it was all nothing but sighing and whining, and languishing and writing; now I am vor thee, she is against thee. All the spirit of contrary, that's all. She is above being guided and governed by her father, that is the whole truth on't. It is only to disoblige and contradict me.'—'What would my papa have me do?' cries Sophia. 'What would I ha thee do?' says he; 'Why, gi' un thy hand this moment.'——'Well, sir,' says Sophia, 'I will obey you.—There is my hand, Mr Jones.'—'Well, and will you consent to ha un to-morrow morning?' says Western.——'I will be obedient to you, sir,' cries she.——'Why then to-morrow morning be the day,' cries he. 'Why then to-morrow morning shall be the day, papa, since you will have it so,' says Sophia. Jones then kissed her hand in an agony of joy, while Western began to caper and dance about the room, presently crying out: 'Where the devil is Allworthy? He is without now, a talking with that d——d lawyer Dowling, when he should be minding other matters.' He then sallied out in quest of him, and very opportunely left the lovers to enjoy a few tender minutes alone.

But he soon returned with Allworthy, saying, 'If you won't believe me, you may ask her yourself. Hast not gin thy consent, Sophy, to be married to-morrow?'—'Such are your commands, sir,' cries Sophia, 'and I dare not be guilty of disobedience.'—'I hope, madam,' cries Allworthy, 'my nephew will merit so much goodness, and will be always as sensible as myself of the great honour you have done my family. I am convinced you have bestowed yourself on one who will be sensible of your great merit, and who will at least use his best endeavours to deserve it.'—'His best endeavours!' cries Western, 'that he will, I warrant un.—— Harkee, Allworthy, I'll bet thee five pounds to a crown we have a boy to-morrow nine months; but prithee tell me what wut ha! Wut ha Burgundy, Champaigne, or what? for, please Jupiter, we'll make a night on't.'—'Indeed, sir,' said Allworthy, 'you must excuse me; both my nephew and I were engaged before I suspected this near approach of his happiness.'—'Why, prithee, who art engaged to?' cries the squire.——Allworthy then informed him, as likewise of the company.——'Odzookers!' answered the squire, 'I will go with thee, and so shall Sophy! for I won't part with thee to-night; and it would be barbarous to part Tom and the girl.' This offer was presently embraced by Allworthy, and Sophia consented, having first obtained a private promise from her father that he would not mention a syllable concerning her marriage.

Young Nightingale had been that afternoon, by appointment, to wait on his father, who received him much more kindly than he expected. There likewise he met his uncle, who was returned to town in quest of his new-married daughter.

He was no sooner informed by his nephew where his daughter and her husband were, than he declared he would go instantly to her. And when he arrived there, he scarce suffered her to fall upon her knees before he took her up, and embraced her with a tenderness which affected all who saw him; and in less than a quarter of an hour was as well reconciled to both her and her husband as if he had himself joined their hands.

In this situation were affairs when Mr Allworthy and his company arrived to complete the happiness of Mrs Miller, who no sooner saw Sophia than she guessed everything that had happened; and so great was her friendship to Jones, that it added not a few transports to those she felt on the happiness of her own daughter.

There have not, I believe, been many instances of a number of people met together, where every one was so perfectly happy as in this company.

The evening was spent in much true mirth. All were happy, but those the most who had been most unhappy before. Their former sufferings and fears gave such a relish to their felicity, as even love and fortune, in their fullest flow, could not have given without the advantage of such a comparison.

Thus, dear reader, we have at length brought our history to a conclusion, in which, to our great pleasure, though contrary, perhaps, to thy expectation, Mr Jones appears to be the happiest of all humankind; for what happiness this world affords equal to the possession of such a woman as Sophia, I sincerely own I have never yet discovered.

As to the other persons who have made any considerable figure in this history, as some may desire to know a little more concerning them, we will proceed, in as few words as possible, to satisfy their curiosity.

Allworthy hath never yet been prevailed upon to see Blifil, but he hath yielded to the importunity of Jones, backed by Sophia, to settle £200 a-year upon him; to which Jones hath privately added a third. Upon this income he lives in one of the northern counties, about 200 miles distant from London, and lays up £200 a-year out of it, in order to purchase a seat in the next parliament from a neighbouring borough, which he had bargained for with an attorney there. He is also lately turned Methodist, in hopes of marrying a very rich widow of that sect, whose estate lies in that part of the kingdom.

Square died soon after he writ the before-mentioned letter; and as to Thwackum, he continues at his vicarage. He hath made many fruitless attempts to regain the confidence of Allworthy, or to ingratiate himself with Jones, both of whom he flatters to their faces, and abuses behind their backs. But in his stead, Mr Allworthy hath lately taken Mr Abraham Adams into his house, of whom Sophia is grown immoderately fond, and declares he shall have the tuition of her children.

Mrs Fitzpatrick is separated from her husband, and retains the little remains of her fortune. She lives in reputation at the polite end of the town, and is so good an economist, that she spends three times the income of her fortune, without running in debt. She maintains a perfect intimacy with the lady of the Irish peer; and in acts of friendship to her repays all the obligations she owes to her husband.

Mrs Western was soon reconciled to her niece Sophia, and hath spent two months together with her in the country. Lady Bellaston made the latter a formal visit at her return to town, where she behaved to Jones as to a perfect stranger, and, with great civility, wished him joy on his marriage.

Mr Nightingale hath purchased an estate for his son in the neighbourhood of Jones, where the young gentleman, his lady, Mrs Miller, and her little daughter reside, and the most agreeable intercourse subsists between the two families.

As to those of lower account, Mrs Waters returned into the country, had a pension of £60 a-year settled upon her by Mr Allworthy, and is married to Parson Supple, on whom, at the instance of Sophia, Western hath bestowed a considerable living.

Black George, hearing the discovery that had been made, ran away, and was never since heard of; and Jones bestowed the money on his family, but not in equal proportions, for Molly had much the greater share.

As for Partridge, Jones hath settled £50 a-year on him; and he hath again set up a school, in which he meets with much better encouragement than formerly, and there is now a treaty of marriage on foot between him and Miss Molly Seagrim, which through the mediation of Sophia, is likely to take effect.

We now return to take leave of Mr Jones and Sophia. Western hath resigned his family seat, and the greater part of his estate, to his son-in-law, and hath retired to a lesser house of his in another part of the country, which is better for hunting.

Sophia hath already produced two fine children, a boy and a girl, of whom the old gentleman is so fond, that he spends much of his time in the nursery, where he declares the tattling of his little grand-daughter, who is above a year and a half old, is sweeter music than the finest cry of dogs in England.

Allworthy was likewise greatly liberal to Jones on the marriage, and hath omitted no instance of shewing his affection to him and his lady, who love him as a father. Whatever in the nature of Jones had a tendency to vice, has been corrected by continual conversation with this good man, and by his union with the lovely and virtuous Sophia. As there are not to be found a worthier man and woman, than this fond couple, so neither can any be imagined more happy. They preserve the purest and tenderest affection for each other, an affection daily encreased and confirmed by mutual endearments and mutual esteem. Nor is their conduct towards their relations and friends less amiable than towards one another. And such is their indulgence, and their beneficence to those below them, that there is not a neighbour, a tenant, or a servant, who doth not most gratefully bless the day when Mr Jones was married to his Sophia.

THE END